Julius Matthias

MICHELLE MAZEL

JULIUS MATTHIAS
— A PACT WITH THE DEVIL —

LIBRARY OF CONGRESS CATALOGING-IN-PUBLICATION DATA
Julius Matthias
Authored by Michelle Mazel
ISBN: 978-0-997603842
LCCN: 2016917432

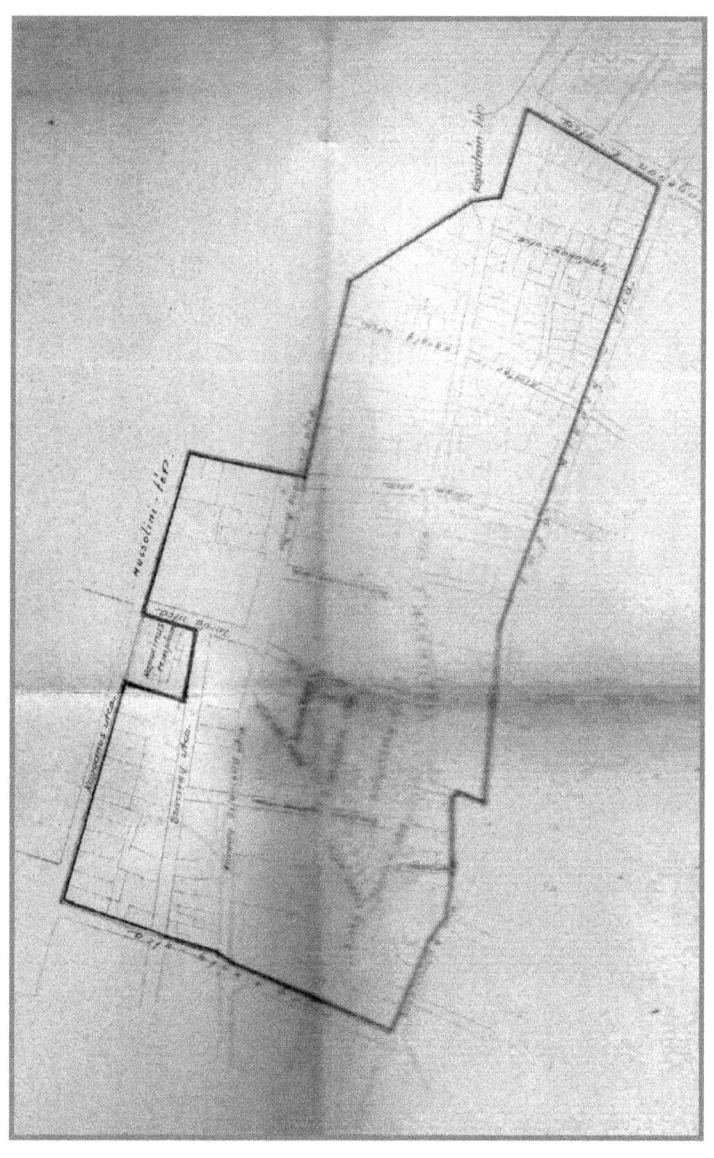

Proposed map for the ghetto in Nagyvarad (Oradea) – 1944

PROLOGUE

IT IS KNOWN AS THE GATEWAY to Transylvania, that narrow passage between the Carpathian Mountains and the endless Hungarian plain through which invading armies have to pass. Nearly two thousand years ago, Roman soldiers built a fortified camp on the left bank of the Cris River and called it Varadinum, a name that successive invaders—from Ottoman Turks to members of the Austro-Hungarian Empire—adapted to their own languages. By the middle of the nineteenth century, the Austro-Hungarian Empire was in its death throes. Budapest and Bucharest were fighting for control of Transylvania and the city on the Cris that the former call Nagyvarad ("greater Varad") and the latter Oradea Mare ("great Oradea"). The town's inhabitants watched helplessly as the tide ebbed and flowed, taking them from one ruler to another, from one official language to another and then back again. Tension ran high between ethnic Hungarians and ethnic Rumanians vying for supremacy, even though both united at times against the Jews who had been living for centuries at the foot of the medieval fortress guarding the river.

Today Romania has won the battle and is at peace with Hungary. The River Cris still runs turbulently toward the Danube, but Oradea, deprived of its strategic value, is a somnolent provincial town where few are willing to talk about the day their city lost part of its soul.

On the afternoon of the day it happened—May 3, 1944—a man walked hurriedly away from the city, his doctor's bag in his hand. The city lay behind him; the woods were in sight. Years of war had turned the once asphalted road into churned earth. As rain began falling, the man walked faster, to take shelter in the forest. Under the leafing trees, nature was running riot after the long and harsh winter; red and yellow spring flowers mixed with new green shoots. The path led downward, and he could hear water running. One of the myriad small streams crisscrossing the woods must have been nearby. The man realized he was thirsty. That was no surprise; he had neither eaten nor drunk since his early breakfast at home, in a world that had since ceased to exist.

He could not think of food, but he knew he had to drink. He made his way to a brook swollen by melting snow and the heavy spring rains, and he knelt down. The face he saw reflected in the eddying water shocked him, and he closed his eyes. When he opened them again, he saw other images: two little faces dancing on the waves of a small stream—perhaps that very stream? A blond head and a darker one, Sandor and Julius, tanned to the same golden hue by that year's endless summer. They had managed to evade the supervision of Julius's big sister, Anni, and to escape into the forest. Having gorged themselves on berries, they were busy trying to catch fish with their bare hands. How old could they have been? Five? Not much more.

The much older Julius, staring at the reflection, was surprised to find himself smiling. This sunny image from half a century ago gave him the strength to stand up and take the first hesitant steps on the hazardous road that might lead him to freedom.

1

A PACT WITH THE DEVIL

THE STORY OF JULIUS BEGINS toward the end of the nineteenth century in the little city by the river Cris, then under Hungarian rule. A girl from a poor Jewish family ran away to marry a Protestant farmer. Her parents, having observed the ritual seven days of mourning for one who was henceforth dead to them, never uttered her name again. Five years later an epidemic sweeping through the Jewish quarter carried them both off, leaving their younger daughter a penniless orphan at fifteen. The elders of the community decided to find a husband for her right away, since rumor had it that her disowned sister was offering to give her a home. But how to find a match for a girl with no dowry and such shameful relatives?

Fortuitously, there was a young man in search of a bride to run his household; his widowed mother had also died in the epidemic. A learned scholar who had to forgo further studies for lack of money, he held a modest position as a teacher in a Talmud Torah, the community school where poor children received their education. The pay was not much, but an upstairs apartment went with the job. Someone had the happy notion of joining the two in matrimony. The bride would get a small dowry from the community, which would also pay for the wedding. Nobody asked her what she thought of the match. The groom let himself be persuaded to wed the girl, who was very pretty. Thus were the parents of Julius united in matrimony in 1875.

Julius had no memories of the first years of his life, a period he knew only through the stories told by family members and from a few yellowing photographs. In one of them, a tall, gaunt young man—Aaron, his father, barely eighteen at the time, his eyes hidden behind thick glasses—stood very straight near a slip of a girl with frightened gray-blue eyes in a round childish face—Gitte, the mother he never knew because she died giving birth to him. In the next faded photo, a too thin young woman with haunted eyes held a baby girl. After four miscarriages Gitte was a mother at last.

Donna, her sister, helped her deliver the child safely. Life had not been kind to the outcast. Her husband and her two children had died when a fire swept through their wooden house; she had not been home that night, having gone to help her sister-in-law who was in labor. Still, she had not been left penniless. Thrifty by nature, she had some savings. She found a home with Klara, the sister-in-law she had been treating that fateful night. Besides, she kept working as a midwife and a healer, a talent she had discovered she possessed.

The two sisters reunited with Aaron's reluctant consent, though he adamantly refused to meet his sister-in-law. The child was so tiny; it was feared at first that she would not survive. That she did was thanks to Donna. Little Anna, soon nicknamed Anni, thrived. Finally, Gitte was happy.

She would have been happier still to stop at that one child, but Aaron had set his heart on a boy. Six years and four miscarriages later, she was brought to bed prematurely. The birth was difficult. There was no money for a doctor, and the worried father left the house to pray for a son at the newly erected Orthodox synagogue nearby. When he came back much later, a tall woman dressed all in black confronted him. Someone—he never knew who—had summoned Donna, who had arrived too late to save her sister. Gitte had died without knowing she had given birth to a healthy baby boy. She was thirty years old.

"You have the son you wanted, but you no longer have a wife," Donna told the brother-in-law she was meeting for the first time. "I shall stay to take care of the children. It was her last wish, and you must respect it."

Wordlessly, Aaron left the room. Without seeking permission that would surely have been denied, Donna wrapped the baby in a blanket and brought him to Klara, who had just had another son and who agreed to nurse the motherless child together with her own little Sandor. A week later she brought the baby home for the circumcision ceremony, the *brith mila*. Aaron named the boy Julius, after his grandfather. Then she took him back to the farm, where he was to live until he was weaned.

During that lengthy period, she would come early to Aaron's house to take care of Anna and leave at dusk to go back to the farm. This was not enough to stop busy tongues from wagging. How could a man tasked with educating young children consort, if only in the daytime, with a woman who had been cast out by the community—even if she was his late wife's sister?

In yet another faded photograph, a somber bridegroom held the hand of his small son, and a beaming Anna stood next to the bride. Aaron was marrying Donna, who had publicly repented and cleansed herself by plunging three times into the mikveh, the ritual bath. Rabbi Zussman, who had officiated at the groom's first wedding, blessed the new union.

Many years later a grown-up Julius asked the woman he loved like a mother why she had married his father, a man she did not love and with whom she had nothing in common.

"I did it for you," she replied. "Anni looked at me with my sister's eyes, and you were a helpless baby. I must admit too that I was over forty and could no longer hope to marry again and have another child. I was a widow living with my husband's family, where everything reminded me of him and our children, and it was getting harder and harder. I longed for my earlier life, the bread I used to make for Shabbat as a child, the festivals…I wanted to grow old among my people. It has not always been easy, but I have never regretted my decision. Your father and I, it is true we had nothing in common at first except our love for you both, but we grew fond of one another. Anni became the daughter I never had, and you—you are my whole life."

Against all odds the marriage was a success. Donna knew how to run a household and keep a tight budget, which was a good thing, since money was always scarce. She gave the children the loving care they needed. At the same time, she refused to sever her ties to her former in-laws and was a frequent visitor to the farm. Early on Anni and Julius understood that they must not tell their father about their forays into a world of plenty and forbidden food. With Sandor as his willing partner, the boy would happily pursue hens and ducks, making them run away squawking before sidling into the kitchen and filching a thick slab of bread covered in jam or butter. This period would have a decisive influence on his life. While other little Jewish boys played only with members of the community and accepted without question the dietary laws and constraints of a traditional way of life, Julius was acquainting himself with a parallel universe in which he felt equally at home.

His first real memories dated to the year 1896 when he turned six. It was not the norm in those days to celebrate a girl's bat mitzvah, the landmark twelfth birthday, which signifies that she will henceforth be considered a responsible adult. Yet a photograph commemorated that occasion. A smiling Donna held the hand of Julius, who had also inherited his mother's eyes and blond curls. Anna was radiantly beautiful in a simple dress with a white collar, her golden locks framing a face hauntingly like her mother's.

What Julius remembered most about the event was that immediately after it, his sister stopped going to the farm. "There are no girls there, only boys," explained Donna when he asked her why—an answer he found puzzling, for this was nothing new. Sandor had a brother older than Anni and another a little younger. Julius had known them forever and played with them often.

Comprehension came later. They were at an age when boys and girls turn to less innocent games, especially living on a farm; it was time to separate them. That was not all. Anna would have no dowry. Finding a good match for her would not be easy. She was so beautiful that the mothers of other girls already looked at her askance. There could be no breath of scandal attached to her name.

Donna, who knew firsthand what it was like to be ostracized, had worked out a long-term plan. First she managed to convince Aaron to give his daughter some schooling as soon as she was of an age to understand. Later she used her own savings to pay for piano lessons twice a week with a respectable widow—an opportunity for Anna to meet other girls her age. As fate would have it, among the little group of pupils thus formed, there were three named Magda. There was little Magda, the shy, dark-haired daughter of the piano teacher; a saucy redhead whose mother was a seamstress; and the one they called Magda the Great. Soon suitable nicknames were found for the first two: the teacher's daughter, who had a Russian grandmother, became Lena; the redhead Madi.

The third, the eldest of the three, remained in sole possession of the name. She was not very pretty, with her pasty complexion, cold black eyes, and rather stout figure. However, she was by far the richest, being the only child of the Szamuely family, who owned the town's biggest pharmacy. She had neither talent nor patience for the piano and attended the lessons only to please her father who made no secret of his intention to turn her into an accomplished young lady and marry her off quickly in order to have grandchildren who would take over the pharmacy in the fullness of time. It was not what she wanted. Her own dream, as she kept telling the other girls, was to study pharmacy herself and to be the one to succeed her father.

Anni never went to the lessons alone. When Donna was busy, Anni's little brother accompanied her to the piano teacher's house and waited for her. She did not always go straight home afterward, sometimes visiting her friends Lena and Madi, who were always nice to the boy. Only once did he enter the portals of the grand Szamuely house. Magda's mother gave him a big slice of pie and a sweet orange drink; the pharmacist pinched his cheek and asked jovially if he was a good student. The child answered truthfully that he was.

When school was out, he looked for his best friend, Sandor, who attended a secular school a mile away. Their friendship was not without problems. Aaron wouldn't let the Christian boy into his house, but the two met whenever they could. As dark as his friend was blond, the farmer's son did not care for school and often acted without thinking. They ran wild in the town or, more often, in the countryside There Klara, Sandor's mother, made Julius wear a woolen hat to hide the side curls that the Jewish boy wore according to tradition. "No need to draw attention," she would say. He did not understand but put on the hat and changed into her older boy's cast-off pants and shirt "to save his own good clothes." She knew these were the only clothes he had. She also knew the black trousers and vest were distinctly Jewish.

The year 1889 brought momentous change to the family. To better affirm its control over the mosaic of peoples making up the kingdom, Hungary ordered all its subjects to take Hungarian names. The measure was essentially directed against ethnic Rumanians, who longed to be back under the rule of Bucharest, but it applied as well to the Jewish community, who greeted it with deep mistrust. Aaron, who never read the secular press, wouldn't have done anything about it had Donna not insisted, warning him of dire consequences if he did not obey the edict. They discussed names with the children who showed little interest in the matter—Anna because she knew she would take her husband's name when she married and Julius because he was too young to care.

When Donna suggested Matthias, a Hungarian name with biblical connotations, they all agreed. None of them was aware of the fact that it was the first name of her beloved first husband, and she was not about to tell.

When the new school year started, Julius, who had cut off his curls and put his skullcap in his pocket on Donna's advice, joined his friend, Sandor, in the town's public school. Aaron worked himself into a rare display of temper, which did not sway his son, and warned him that his Christian schoolmates would make his life a misery. He was wrong; Sandor's two older brothers were still at school and let it be known that the boy was under their protection. He proved himself a gifted student and often helped his friend, who was not doing so well.

It was a difficult time for the Matthias family. Aaron was deeply wounded by what he saw as Donna's attempt to turn his son away from religion. He was also worried about his daughter. Anna was almost sixteen; she had fulfilled her earlier promise of great beauty. He was anxious to marry her off quickly and looked for a good man who would take her without a dowry—a pious widower perhaps. Her friend, Lena, a year older, was already married and had moved to the neighboring town of Cluj with her husband, a respectable businessman. Redheaded Madi had left very suddenly to live with relatives in Budapest and unkind things were being whispered about the reason for her departure. The Szamuelys were negotiating a very advantageous match for Magda the Great: the son of a rich Budapest banker, a relative of her mother. Menachem "Manny" Nagy was rumored to be good looking and smart and already had a law degree. Anni, dreading the fate her father was planning for her, cried herself to sleep every night, and Donna desperately searched for a way out for the girl she loved as her own child.

At that point a miracle happened. The story of the events of that fateful summer was told so often to the child, Julius, that he grew to know it by heart. For some reason the pharmacist's daughter had become close to Donna; she often went with her to search for the medicinal herbs the older woman used in her healing. Having sworn her to secrecy, Magda told her she wasn't ready to give up her dream of taking over the family pharmacy one day. Therefore, she did not want to marry Manny and follow him to Budapest. She would run away instead with Jozef, her father's young assistant, convinced that her parents would have no choice but to agree to the match for fear of scandal.

The older woman was appalled. "Don't even think of doing it!" she warned her. "Your father may adore you, but he is proud and quick to take offense. He might disown you altogether. There must be another way."

The two women agreed on a different course of action. When the young man arrived from Budapest with his family, Magda asked him to walk with her by the river in order to get acquainted. The river walk was a very public place and no chaperone was needed; both sets of parents approved. By a carefully planned piece of luck, the young couple encountered Anna and her little brother. The two girls embraced; introductions were made. Magda, wearing a costly dress of brown brocade that did nothing for her figure and gave her face a sallow tint, invited Anna, lovelier than ever in her simple blue frock, to join them. She then went on ahead with a surprised Julius.

Manny made polite conversation with Anna and soon fell under her spell. When his bride-to-be told him regretfully that she had to be getting home, he came to his senses and begged her pardon. She immediately put him at ease by confessing that she loved another man, asking him not to say anything to her parents or his.

Left in the dark, the two families decided on another visit and another. The young people again went for a walk. A month later Manny announced to his stunned parents that, far from marrying the heiress to the Szamuely fortune, he had fallen in love with the penniless daughter of a poor teacher. They refused to give their permission at first, but he held his own.

In another photograph, of much better quality than the previous ones, Manny smiled at his bride, a vision in white. Soon afterward, Magda wedded her Jozef in a sumptuous ceremony. Emil Szamuely had had to agree to the match in order not to become the laughingstock of the community. He never forgave Anna for having betrayed her friend and stolen the man his daughter was to marry. Magda took great care not to set him straight.

A year after the wedding, for the first time in their lives, the Matthias family left the town where they were born and took the train to Budapest to attend the circumcision ceremony of Anna's firstborn. The banker and his wife had been discreetly helping Anna's family, and life had become easier. Aaron was moved to tears when he held his first grandchild in his arms. It was the start of a new beginning for the ill-matched couple, united in their delight at their daughter's happiness. Aaron was still upset with his son for going to a secular school but came to terms with the fact that he was no match for his wife.

Months went by. Julius would soon be thirteen, and his father, preparing him for the bar mitzvah ceremony, delighted in his quick mind and ready understanding. No photograph commemorated the actual event, but Julius behaved quite creditably. Aaron Matthias received the congratulations of his fellow worshippers in the synagogue where he had been praying since the boy was born. Anna, expecting again, did not come, but Manny made the trip and presented his young brother-in-law with a gold coin bearing the effigy of Empress Maria Theresa. Julius dutifully handed it to his father, who refused it with one of his rare smiles.

Aaron, whose health was failing, did not know that the boy was leading a double life. Julius excelled at school, but when he was not studying, he was with Sandor. The farmer's son was forever getting into fights, and Julius learned early on to defend himself. Among their friends, very few knew that the tall blond boy with the steady blue eyes was Jewish, and those who did know did not care. He was always ready to help at the farm or to assist a friend having trouble with his homework.

Julius Matthias, slowly emerging from childhood, did not quite know where he belonged. He fit in wherever he was, feasting at Christmas with the Toths on the farm and fasting on Yom Kippur with his family. He observed Jewish dietary laws only at home or with members of the community and ate with relish whatever Klara put on the table when he came visiting. On Shabbat, he dutifully accompanied his father to the synagogue but felt no religious spark whatsoever.

If truth be told, Julius was quite satisfied with his lot. He had no money but enjoyed life to the fullest. He experienced his first sexual encounter very early when, together with Sandor, he came upon some lively Gypsy girls camping with their tribe on their way to the south. To his surprise Donna severely called him to task. He never knew who had told her, though he suspected it was Sandor's mother, since the two women had remained very close.

"Julius, my boy," Donna told him. "I am not going to say that what you did was wrong. But you must know two things. The first is that easy girls easily get nasty ailments that can ruin a young man's life. The second is that sooner or later, someone is going to be offended by the fact that a Jew is sleeping with a Christian girl, no matter how lax her morals. That could be a major problem for you. Believe me, you are still very young. Leave the girls alone, and stick to your studies."

He took her words to heart, perhaps because the Gypsies had moved on, and devoted all his energies to school, graduating with distinction at barely eighteen. He spoke Hungarian and German effortlessly and won first prize in mathematics and physics. Taking home the ornate tomes he had received together with his diploma, he reflected bitterly on the unfairness of life. While some of his classmates, whose achievements were far below his but who came from moneyed families, were getting ready to pursue their studies at the universities of their choice, he, the best student of all, would not be able to afford to. He had no wish to be a schoolteacher like his father or go to a rabbinical seminary, the only two options open to him. And yet he had a dream— to be a doctor. He could not have put into words why he so passionately desired to embrace what he believed to be the greatest vocation on earth but was painfully aware that his was an impossible dream.

What was left? He toyed with the idea of joining the Hungarian army. Sandor's big brother, Attila, a sergeant by now, had promised to take care of him. He decided to discuss it with his aunt who reacted violently.

"Julius, you don't know what you are talking about. A soldier's life is not for you. You would be utterly miserable."

To which he replied with some bitterness: "Utterly miserable? And you think it will be better if I stay here while my classmates depart happily for the universities they have chosen? Dear aunt, I have made up my mind. Who knows? One day I may save enough money to go back to my studies."

She looked at him long and hard before answering. "Julius, listen carefully. Before making a hasty decision, let me think about this. I have an idea, but it might take some doing. Promise?"

He promised but with no real hope. What could she do? Appeal to Anna's rich in-laws? They were delighted with the two healthy boys she had given them and had grown fond of the girl but not to the point of financing the long and expensive years of studies her brother would need to become a doctor.

A few days later, Donna knocked on his door, looking unusually grave. "Listen, Julius, I may have found a solution, but I am not sure it would be such a good thing for you."

"A solution? A way for me to go to medical school? Who cares about a good thing? For that I would make a pact with the devil!"

She winced and closed the door very carefully behind her. "A pact with the devil? You may not be so far wrong. First you have to swear that if you do not want to go ahead with the proposal, you will never speak of it again. Swear!"

He swore with a smile. The memory of that whispered conversation in his narrow room with an iron bed, a rickety cupboard, and a table with a few books, and nothing on the blank walls since Aaron did not allow what he called pagan images in the house, would remain with him forever. A gray light filtered through the narrow window. Donna was whispering, and he had to move closer to hear what she was telling him. To hear but not to believe.

Magda—Magda the Great, the Szamuely daughter—had been widowed a year before, her husband having been killed in an accident. She wanted to have the children her husband had been unable to give her. In spite of the age difference, she had fallen in love with Julius. If he agreed to marry her, she would convince her parents to pay for his medical studies.

"Magda wants to marry me? Aunt Donna, are you out of your mind?"

"So you don't agree?"

"I don't agree? If it were possible, I would marry her today. But there is not a hope in hell. Her parents will never agree, whatever you may think. You yourself have told me many times that they've hated us since Anni's wedding. I can't believe that Magda is still talking to you."

"That's my business. Just wait, and say nothing. But remember: she is seven years older than you are and has quite a temper. Living with her may not be pleasant."

"You don't understand. If I can't study medicine, I am joining the army. Do you think life there will be pleasant? Besides, you are seven years older than Father. You made a marriage of convenience, and it has not turned out so badly. Why can't I do the same?"

Donna shook her head. "Very well. Say nothing, do nothing, and be patient for a little while."

Less than a week later, Aaron Matthias was summoned to the pharmacy. He came back torn between disbelief and hope. Szamuely wanted Julius for his daughter and was ready to pay for his son-in-law to study to be a pharmacist and to become a partner in the family business. The young couple would, of course, live in the big house with her parents.

A deeply disappointed Julius would have none of it. That was not what he wanted. He was not about to give up his dream, work for a man he did not know, and live under his roof. If he could not study medicine, he would enlist.

His father looked at him wonderingly but said simply, "Do what you think best."

Julius wondered why. Donna explained the situation to him. "Your father isn't going to say no, because he is aware of the fact that he can't give you anything. He worries a lot about you. He doesn't show it, but that's his way. He loves you dearly but can't bring himself to accept you as you are— as someone who does not care about religion. In his heart he wishes you would meet a pious young girl who would bring you back into the fold. Not someone like Magda, whose parents are barely observant and who might not raise your future children properly. In a way he is relieved now that you have turned down that proposal."

"What about you?"

"Me? I don't really care for the match but thought it might be the only way for you to fulfill your dream. If that's not the case, you are better off not going through with it."

But that was not the end of it. Emil Szamuely was not ready to take no for an answer and dispatched a servant to fetch Julius. It was not a pleasant meeting. Magda's father had married late and was nearing fifty. He was well aware of the fact that he was one of the richest and most influential members of the community. Not being very tall, he held himself erect to make the most of his portly stature. On that fateful day, he was not the jovial man who had pinched Julius's cheek ten years earlier. There was no offer of a drink, and Julius was not asked to take a seat.

Emil looked sneeringly at the young man who had dared to defy him and, moreover, was a good ten inches taller. He told Julius his behavior was beyond the pale. "I believe you forget who you are, where you live, and who your parents are. I would never have tolerated the thought of giving you my daughter's hand in marriage had I not been persuaded that you would be grateful for the great honor being bestowed upon you. Instead you have the gall to demur, to set down conditions. Being a pharmacist is not good enough for you; you will settle for nothing less than being a doctor."

He shook his head sorrowfully and went on. "But you are young and may not have understood the situation. My daughter has asked me to give you another chance. Take it. Show you are aware of the exceptional opportunity being offered to you, not only to study and acquire a respectable trade but also to be accepted into one of the most prominent families in this city."

Julius, who had listened with increasing indignation to that tirade, was hard put not to retort angrily but managed to keep his temper. "I do thank you for your kindness and for the honor you are offering me. However, my heart is set on becoming a doctor and nothing else. I shall therefore bid you good day."

His father and his aunt were anxiously awaiting his return. He faithfully reported the conversation he had had. Aaron sighed, but Donna made him repeat his answer.

"That's all you said?" she wanted to know. "You were polite to him? You did not get angry? You did not yell?"

"No, though I wanted to, because he talked to me as if I were one of his employees who had misbehaved. In a way I can understand. He does not like the match at all and probably thinks his daughter must be out of her mind to choose such an insignificant spouse. What does it matter now?"

"What does it matter! If you did manage to keep your temper and not to offend him, all is not lost. Say nothing, and be patient for a few more days."

He said nothing, not even to Sandor, with whom he was spending most of his days now that school was out and his future so uncertain. Every day Donna told him that things were moving in the right direction, but he was hard put to believe her. What he did not know was that Magda, who still dreamed of taking over after her father's death and did not want her future husband to supplant her behind the imposing counter of the family pharmacy, was waging an all-out war on his behalf. It took two whole weeks, but in the end Emil Szamuely capitulated—on his own terms. In another difficult confrontation with Julius, he set down his conditions. The wedding would take place without delay; Magda would accompany her husband to the university. The young couple would spend all their vacations under the pharmacist's roof. Julius was to swear on the Bible that he would never leave his wife.

He agreed to all these demands with a smile. Not only was his dream about to come true, but he was going to study medicine—not at the nearest medical school in Budapest but in Vienna, former capital of the Austro-Hungarian empire and seat of the most prestigious medical school of the time.

2

THE MEDICAL STUDENT

THE WEDDING WAS a quiet affair held in the Szamuely home. Magda was barely out of her widow's weeds, explained her father. Anna and her husband were not invited. On the traditional picture taken on the happy day—August 1, 1908—the groom looked absurdly young and ill at ease in his first made-to-measure costume, and the bride wore a strained smile. The newlyweds left immediately for Vienna. After a brief stay in a boardinghouse recommended by a friend of the pharmacist, they moved into a small but well-appointed apartment.

A twenty-minute walk brought Julius to the venerable buildings of the university where some six thousand students came and went daily, the best scholars of the fading Austro-Hungarian empire and its future leaders. In between lessons he could stroll to the spacious garden of the town hall nearby or sit down at one of the many coffeehouses for which the city was justly famous. In the evening Magda waited for him in the great double poster. At eighteen, could one ask for more?

It turned out that one could. Julius found it increasingly difficult to cope with his wife's indifference. She hardly talked to him, showed no interest whatsoever in what he did, and made it clear that his friends would not be welcome in *her* house. He often caught her looking at him with a weary resignation he found hard to fathom. He could not understand her. She had married him because she was fond of him; had he disappointed her so quickly?

And yet there were the nights…In the beginning he had found her tense, fearful almost, which was absurd: hadn't she been married for six years? It soon got better, and she was the one to draw him to the conjugal bed, surprising him with the intensity of her passion and her very vocal responses. Not that he complained. But come morning the ardors of the night were as if they had never been. When she joined him for breakfast, which was not often, she never had a smile or a kind word for him.

Her indifference hurt him deeply. He had felt flattered at the thought that this woman, who could have had her pick of eligible husbands, had not only chosen him but had fought her parents to get them to accept the match. If she did not care for him, why had she wanted to marry him? On the other hand, he could see that she was lonely and bored; she missed her mother, her friends, and the pharmacy while he had a whole new world to explore and discover. He told himself not to worry. Things were bound to get better.

And they did in a not wholly unexpected way. Magda started feeling sick in the morning and faint in the afternoon. At first she opposed his efforts to get her to see a doctor and yielded only reluctantly at his insistence. When the man told them with a broad smile that they were about to be parents, she had a strange reaction: she flatly refused to believe him. Then, when he convinced her, she started sobbing helplessly.

"You see, Doctor," she said, "before my first husband died, we had tried for six years to have a child and failed, so I had begun to fear I could not conceive."

"Are you happy?" asked Julius as they were making their way home.

"Very. I need that child," she answered coldly.

"What do you mean?"

There was no answer, and that night, for the first time, she turned away from him, pleading tiredness. But sleep did not come easily to the very puzzled young man. Hadn't Donna told him that Magda wanted a young husband so she could have the children Jozef had been unable to give her?

The young couple returned home for the end-of-the-year vacation. It was a difficult time for Julius. The Szamuelys were over the moon with the news and fussed over their daughter—while remaining coldly hostile toward their son-in-law, as if he had nothing to do with this long-awaited pregnancy. Emil barely addressed him; Golda ignored him completely. Worse, he was banished from his wife's room because she said she needed her rest.

There were nevertheless a few good moments. He spent many hours with his father and aunt, who seemed never to hear enough details about his new life and were happily wondering whether the new grandchild would be a boy or a girl. He also managed to escape twice to go hunting and fishing in the forest with Sandor.

January 1909 saw Julius embark alone on a train back to Vienna, Magda having decided to stay with her mother until the baby was born. Julius, who had had no say in her decision, had not protested; it would have made no difference anyway since he was totally dependent upon his in-laws. He studied harder than ever and ended that first year with outstanding results. Then he headed home, arriving just in time for the birth of his son.

Magda was mellower than he had ever seen her; Emil was incoherent with joy, and Golda went as far as to hug the son-in-law who had brought such happiness to the family. As the young man held his firstborn in his arms, tears welled in his eyes.

"See?" he told himself. "Things are getting better. All will be well."

Nevertheless, the news that his wife did not intend to go back with him at the end of the summer did not quite take him by surprise. Emil, who spent hours over little Georgy's cot, had declared that only in Nagyvarad could the baby and his mother get the care they needed; Magda agreed whole-heartedly; basking in her father's approval and cosseted by her mother, she had no wish to leave. At the start of his second year of medical school, Julius, convinced his wife would never come back to Vienna, decided to leave the flat and rented a room conveniently situated near the university. Because of his name, his landlady, an elderly widow, thought he was a Protestant from Hungary; he did not set her straight on that point. It was agreed that her maid would clean the room and do his laundry for a small fee.

There followed four years he would always remember as the best of his life. He was being initiated into the mysteries of medical science; he was part of a modern and liberated society. Forget Nagyvarad and its provincial and bigoted people! In the evenings he would meet fellow students in one of the many coffeehouses in the former capital of the

Austro-Hungarian Empire for passionate discussions about the fate of the world. Surprisingly there were quite a number of women who, braving the taboos of the time, had come to study in this prestigious place. Sometimes he ended up in one of their beds because the enforced abstinence caused by his wife's absence was hard to bear.

Nobody knew that the handsome, blue-eyed blond student who ate whatever was put on his plate was Jewish. Many believed, like his landlady, that Julius Matthias was indeed a Protestant from Hungary. Such was the case with Marie Christine, one of the handful of women studying medicine. Wife of an Austrian nobleman, she was French. Julius walked her home one evening after a lesson that had ended later than usual.

"Come up and have a drink," she suggested when they reached their destination. Once in her opulent apartment, she mentioned artlessly that the count had remained in the family castle to manage his vast estates and the maid would not be back until noon the following day. She then took his hand and led him into her bedchamber, where a fire was burning in the grate. She displayed a great deal of enthusiasm and ingenuity but soon stopped, surprised.

"Don't tell me you are Jewish!"

"I thought you knew. Do you want me to go?"

"Certainly not. It was just so unexpected. But tell me, how come you are so blond, and where did you get eyes the color of the sea?"

"I see that you have a poetic turn of mind," said Julius, much relieved. "No one has ever told me my eyes are the color of the sea. I believe I owe them to my mother, whose grandparents came from Odessa in Russia."

"And I see you haven't studied the classics. Athena, daughter of Zeus, had eyes the color of the sea."

"I must admit that part of my education has been neglected...But tell me, why did you choose to study in Vienna and not in Paris, where there is also a reputed school of medicine?"

"I would not have been accepted there. You are not the only one who has secrets, my dear Julius."

"Don't tell me you are Jewish too!"

"No, and that would not have been a bar to my being accepted. The French have other ways to demonstrate their anti-Semitism. The fact is the school prides itself on being elitist, and my father, who never studied anything, made his fortune selling foundation garments in the marketplace."

"The count must have been very much in love."

"The count came to France looking for a rich wife. His father had just died, leaving him debts and a mortgaged estate. Eventually he had to choose between a banker's daughter or that of a rich businessman."

"Let me guess. The banker was Jewish."

"Correct. Mind you, he was far more presentable than my father, but since the count had no intention of presenting either of them to his highborn family, he chose the best-looking girl. Me, obviously."

"Why did you accept? You wanted to be a countess?"

"No, I wanted to be a doctor. He swore that through his relations, he would get me accepted here in Vienna, and he kept his word. Enough said. By tomorrow you and I will have forgotten this conversation. Right now I want to see whether your cowl-less monk is ready to resume his devotions..."

This was to be the first of many encounters. Julius, who was not yet twenty, found in the lovely countess an accomplished lover who taught him many things, among them how to practice contraception, an art still in its infancy at the time. Though there were condoms available, they were unpleasant and far too thick. Marie Christine used a small sponge drenched in vinegar, which, strategically placed, stopped unwanted sperm with a great deal of reliability—a lesson he would not forget and would recommend later.

Julius did not let dalliance get in the way of his studies and worked hard to maintain his consistently perfect grades. Having discovered that many medical terms were in Latin, he decided to learn that ancient language and was fortunate enough to find a French nobleman supplementing his meager revenues by taking students. The man had an impressive collection of tin soldiers retracing the campaigns of Emperor Napoleon, during which, he used to say proudly, no less than four ancestors of his had perished on the battlefield.

There were dozens and dozens of the colored figurines, not all in pristine condition, and he was constantly trying to repair them, painting and gluing with great care while declaiming verses written by a Frenchman named Victor Hugo, whom he called the greatest poet of the time. He had a special fondness for a set of heroic verses called the "Legend of the Ages," where his pupil was greatly surprised to encounter characters made familiar by the reading of the Bible. The two men—one at the end of his life, the other just beginning—came from vastly different backgrounds but somehow became friends. The lonely young man spent entire evenings in his tutor's company; by the time he graduated, he had not only mastered Latin but spoke passable French and could quote whole chunks of Victor Hugo.

Twice a year—for the winter and summer vacations—Julius took a train to Nagyvarad. He did not look forward to these enforced stays at the pharmacist's house. Only his little son welcomed him. Now that she had a child, Magda had lost all interest in sex. She shared her bed with him but often feigned sleep when he joined her. His mother-in-law still made snide remarks about the alleged treachery of his sister; Emil Szamuely expected him to lend a hand in the pharmacy during his vacation "to help defray the cost of his lengthy studies." Whenever Julius could, he escaped to meet Sandor and go hunting or fishing in the forest. He brought whatever he caught to Donna. His father was not well and depended more and more on his wife, his senior by seven years.

During his third year in Vienna, Julius was so busy studying he could not go home in December; in the summer he stayed for only a month. The fourth year—the one before the last—he did not go at all, writing that he had to work more than ever to be sure to take the demanding final exams successfully and not risk having to stay another year. Magda did not answer his letter, but that was nothing new; she was a very indifferent correspondent. He was therefore struck dumb when, early in August 1912, he was woken up by the entrance of his wife and his father-in-law. He blinked, wondering whether he was dreaming.

"Has something happened to father? To Donna?" he asked fearfully.

"Everything is fine," answered the pharmacist testily. "You haven't been home in a long time, and your wife was naturally anxious to see you. I have some business to settle here, so I took her along." While he talked he opened the door of the small bathroom, then that of the wall cupboard. "I never imagined I would see you in such dismal lodgings," he added.

Julius checked the time. Barely seven, and on a Saturday too! "I need a few minutes to get dressed. Go to the Excelsior Hotel. It's on your right when you walk out. I will meet you there in half an hour," he said in a tone that brooked no argument.

His unexpected visitors walked out without a word. While he was dressing he gave a hard look at the room he had called home for the past three years. A narrow bed along one wall; opposite, a desk topped by a few shelves filled with books. Two chairs and a tall cupboard running the entire length of the third wall completed the furnishings. But the window opened on a well-tended garden where the sun often shone, and the small bathroom boasted a shower—an almost unheard of luxury at the time.

"My landlady's maid cleans the room twice a week. She washes and irons my clothes. And the rent is very reasonable," he explained a little later, sitting in the plush salon of the Excelsior, drinking the excellent coffee that gave the place its well-deserved reputation. "Furthermore it is very well situated. I can walk to my classes in a matter of minutes."

"But how do you receive your friends?" Asked his wife.

He burst out laughing. "Receive my friends? Magda, I do not receive them. I meet them in a coffeehouse or restaurant, but mostly at the university. You have to remember I am studying most of the time. But let's talk about you. Where are you staying? How long are you going to be here?"

"Father has a number of engagements in Vienna, and he thought it would make a pleasant change for you to spend a few days with me at an inn he knows some ten miles out of the city. After all, you are on vacation. No, don't thank him. You deserve the rest. How soon can you be ready?"

In next to no time they were on their way to what turned out to be a quite extraordinary week. The inn was comfortable but not fussy; the food was good. They would go for long walks in the forest, and at night his wife welcomed him in a way he had not known since their early days in Vienna. He would have better enjoyed the very first vacation of his life had Magda not remained so strangely silent, except when talking about their son, who had recently turned three.

"The time has come to give him a brother or a sister," she eventually said in one of their last walks, shedding some light on her nocturnal ardors. On the morning of their departure, she dropped her bombshell. "Father is getting an office ready for you at the pharmacy. You will be able to receive your patients there."

"Magda, I am not going to work in the pharmacy."

"I don't think you understand the situation," she replied in the tone of voice she used to reprimand her maid. "Father promised to pay for your studies—this he has done. You and I shall of course go on living under his roof, since you will not be able to keep us in the style to which I am accustomed. You can't possibly receive patients at home, nor is Father willing to assume the cost of offices in town."

"I am sorry, but there is no way I shall ever work at the pharmacy, and even less, work for your father. I shall find a solution when the time comes."

"Listen, I do understand," she replied in a more conciliatory tone. "I even tried to change Father's mind. He would not budge. I am convinced that when you come home for good, you will see that this is the only solution. In the meantime, try not to talk about it with him."

Nothing was said when the pharmacist came to pick up his daughter and her husband, but the mood was frosty. He did not even embrace Julius, who was in for another surprise when he returned to his lodgings, and not a pleasant one. His landlady was waiting in the hall, a scowl on her usually pleasant face.

"Young man, I find myself obliged to ask you to vacate the premises immediately. Here is the money you have already paid for the half month and for September. My new lodger moves in the day after tomorrow, and the room has to be thoroughly cleaned. No, I have no wish to explain. You have to make other arrangements. If you have not left by the morning, I shall complain to the dean of the school of medicine." She then walked into her own apartment, leaving him rooted in his spot.

It was Frieda, the maid, coming to bring him his laundry and get her wages, who explained what had happened. "The other gentleman, the one who said he was your father-in-law, had made her very angry. He came when you were away and demanded to see your room, and when she refused he hinted she knew you were receiving ladies of doubtful morality here. I thought Madam would have a spasm. She had the coachman thrown him out. Her son came to see her soon after, and he told her to look for another lodger. She did say you had always behaved with great propriety, but he reminded her that she had to think of her reputation, and of his."

Julius made other arrangements, the first being to accept the flattering offer he had received from Professor Ludwig Steiner, one of the directors of the new general hospital recently opened not far from the school of medicine.

"My dear young man," the great man had said, familiarly, taking Julius's arm as they were leaving class. "You are an excellent student, and there is not much more for you to learn. What you need is hands-on experience. We need an intern at the hospital; the post is yours. You can start as soon as you want."

"I can't thank you enough for your kind words and your generous offer," Julius replied, "but as you know, I am not yet free. There are courses I have to take, practical work— ."

"Pshaw! Don't let that worry you. If you are ready to be on duty at night and during the weekends, you will have sufficient free time to fulfill all your obligations at the medical school, which, by the way, is less than five minutes away on foot. Did I tell you our interns are lodged in an annex behind the hospital?"

Thus began a new life. No more long evenings and fiery discussions with friends in smoked-filled coffeehouses. No more passionate nights with the countess, who forgave him readily and still had a warm smile for him when they met in class. Julius did not mind. He was discovering a far more exacting mistress—medicine—and went from learned medical treatises to real illnesses. At night he was often the first to meet patients, to decide when to wait for the morning and when to wake up the doctor on call. With still a year to go before he obtained his diploma, he was already becoming a doctor.

At the same time, his bank account was pleasantly growing. He no longer had to pay rent and was saving the funds the pharmacist was sending him regularly every month and part of his salary as well, since he lived in the hospital, where he often had his meals. He knew how important money would be when he returned home; faced with the hostility of his in-laws, it would give him a measure of independence and hopefully enable him to hold on until he started earning his own wages, which might take time.

Magda's visit had another consequence: she was expecting again.

A few days before Christmas, Professor Steiner made another surprise offer. Julius encountered him by chance as he was leaving the school, and Steiner invited him to join him for a drink at his favorite haunt, the Demel coffeehouse. Julius wasn't one for drinking; there had been no liquor in his father's house, and soon after his arrival in Vienna he had discovered that alcohol held no special attraction for him. That evening he ordered a cup of hot chocolate smothered in whipped cream along with a generous slice of cake.

He had not gone out in months and realized how much he had missed the crowds and the mood. Though it was late, every table was taken. A poet easily identified by his long hair and his flowing tie was holding court in front of a tableful of admiring students; small groups were talking animatedly while in a corner three young men hunched together were conversing in whispers, throwing uneasy glances toward the entrance as if fearing the police would come bursting in at any moment. There was a small patient queue of people waiting for one of the tables to be free.

"My dear Julius, I have asked you to come here with me tonight for a very special reason," said the professor, who had lighted his pipe and was puffing contentedly. "When I offered you the position of intern a few months ago, some of my colleagues at the hospital expressed their doubts because of your youth and lack of experience. The steadiness of your character and your dedication soon put these doubts to rest. I am happy to say we are all very pleased with you. Even the nurses, usually so merciless when judging new doctors, are singing your praises. Therefore, it is with great satisfaction that I extend to you an invitation to join our staff at the end of the year when you graduate. Needless to say, you will be awarded a salary and other benefits far superior to what you earn today." And he sat back, beaming.

Julius was struck dumb. For a minute he allowed himself to hope. Not to have to go back to Nagyvarad, to live under his father-in-law's roof, to have to battle to practice medicine the way he wanted; to start his career in a prestigious hospital instead, to keep living in this marvelous city—this was a dream beyond his wildest hopes. But soon reality took over. This was not to be. He had given his word. He tried to explain to the professor, who was shaking his head incredulously.

"My dear young man, I must say this is beyond belief. Are you saying you are honor bound to go back? This is all very well, but have you given a thought to your future, to the future of your family? I do not know the town of Nagyvarad, but I know many similar towns. Forgive me if I am brutally frank: no hospital will welcome you. To be precise, even if one was to do so, you would never progress. There would always be another doctor, perhaps not as qualified as you are but a good Christian, to be promoted over you. Yes, I know you are Jewish. I have known it from the beginning through a chance encounter with someone from your hometown. Your wife, your father-in-law, cannot be unaware of the situation. To turn your back on what would surely be a brilliant career, to cut yourself off from hospitals, and to content yourself with tending to the poor in a second-rate office—and for what? For an oath given when you were not yet eighteen? My boy, in less than two years here you will be able to repay the cost of your studies, with interest, to your father in law!"

"I can't." Julius could barely get the words out. "Of course I could do it, present them with my decision, tell them I am not coming back. I would give anything to be able to do so, but I can't. It would be a tragedy for my family. My wife would not follow me. She would remain at home with her parents and with my children, whom she would never let me see again. There would be a terrible scandal. But I thank you from the bottom of my heart. I shall never forget your generosity and your help."

They parted wordlessly, and the young man walked back to the hospital without feeling the light snow that had started falling on that winter night and now mingled with his tears. For the first time, he had been made to feel the full weight of the shackles he had assumed so blithely. And yet, as he was falling asleep in his room in the hospital annex, he told himself he had no one to blame but himself. He might have made a pact with the devil, but to give the devil his due, he had kept his part of the bargain. The desperate boy ready to enlist had seen his dream come true and was about to become a doctor. Now it was his turn to keep his part of the contract.

3

DR. JULIUS MATTHIAS

WEDNESDAY, JUNE 18, 1913. A little tense in his formal dress but with sheer happiness shining through, a tall young man with blond curls cropped short reverently held a rolled-up vellum. The poor little boy from the Talmud Torah had just been handed his doctor's diploma, summa cum laude. The elegant audience seated on the red and gold seats of the reception hall of the school of medicine applauded politely. The day was doubly auspicious: Julius was also celebrating his twenty-third birthday, which made him one of the youngest graduates. Additionally, he was the only one not to have any member of his family present on this festive occasion. Magda, who had had her second child, a boy, two months earlier, could not undertake such a long journey. His father was unwell, and the faithful Donna remained at his side. Julius did not really mind. They did not belong to his Viennese life.

The night before there had been a final meeting at a famed beer house. It had been a bittersweet reunion; the little group of close friends who had come from the four corners of the old Austro-Hungarian Empire knew they would not meet again. Addresses and promises to keep in touch had been duly exchanged, but they all knew that distance would bring oblivion. The Countess, who was also graduating and would be leaving Vienna immediately after the ceremony, had been there and asked Julius to walk her home. He accepted gladly and spent his last Viennese night in her bed. After months of enforced celibacy, he allowed himself to be carried away one last time.

"I have missed you, handsome Julius," she whispered while they were resting.

"Nice of you to say so, though I had the impression you weren't often alone…"

"Jealous? No, don't answer. You are right, and it is just as well. You see, my dear, we have much in common, and I might have grown too fond of you."

"Much in common, Madame la Countesse?"

"Don't laugh. Do you know that when we started our medical studies here, we were, you and I, the only two married students? I hazard to say you were probably no more in love with your wife than I was with my husband and that we were both very lonely. No, I don't want you to answer. Let us make the most of the few hours left to us."

That night the young man felt there was something desperate in the way she clung to him. Like him, but for different reasons, she was afraid of what the future held.

"You see," she told him bleakly when they had gravitated to the kitchen where she warmed up some leftover soup in a big earthen pot, "Franz-Jozef, my husband, has kept his part of the bargain and has let me finish my medical studies. Not that he believed I would succeed; like all men of his type and class, he has no great opinion of women and their abilities. While not exactly unhappy about my achievements—after all, a woman doctor has a certain *je ne sais quoi*—he finds himself in a quandary. Studying was one thing; actually practicing is a very different proposition. I shall have to negotiate, and I am afraid I know his price. Not money; no, my father gave him plenty when we got married, and I must admit he has used it wisely and well. His estate now brings in enough to keep him and his family in the style he has always dreamed of being able to afford. No, what he wants now is an heir, if not two. Even if I manage to have a boy straightaway and another one a year or two later, I shall be cooped up in the castle for at least three years. And that is the best possible case. I may have several daughters before the hoped-for heir appears…It does not bear thinking about."

She stood up in one fluid movement to open her last bottle of French champagne.

Julius left her at four in the morning and walked back to the hospital unhurriedly, savoring those last carefree moments. Later in the day, after the graduation ceremony, he would take the train to Nagyvarad, where the pharmacist was waiting for him. The streets were still empty at such an early hour, though a faint pink hue on the horizon told of the approaching dawn. He realized with surprise that he had never seen the sun rising over the city. He had spent sleepless nights trying to save patients or, less critically, preparing for exams. However, walking alone in the great metropolis whose heart seemed to be beating at a slower rate, was a unique experience for him.

A scant few hours later, he was seated on the stage not far from the Countess; she was a picture of decorum in her elegant black outfit, imported at great cost, from the leading Parisian fashion house of Charles Worth, she had told him earlier when she'd seen him admiring it draped on a dummy in her living room. Marie Christine did not throw a single glance in his direction that morning. She was focusing all her attention on her husband who had driven from his estate for the occasion. From his choice seat in the first row, the Count applauded with aristocratic reserve when his wife was handed the diploma attesting that she was now qualified to practice medicine.

The lengthy ceremony over, the young Dr. Matthias was making his way toward the exit when he felt a hand on his shoulder.

"Julius, we are proud of you," someone said heartily.

He turned round and found himself facing his sister's husband, a man he had not seen in years.

"Manny! What are you doing here?"

"What am I doing here? I came to enjoy my brother-in-law's triumph. I was going to take you out yesterday evening to celebrate, but I couldn't find you. Your former landlady told me that she did not know where you were, and your postal address care of general delivery was not much help. Never mind. You are leaving Vienna this morning, right? And you never thought to make a stop in Budapest to see your sister and your nephews? Where is your baggage?"

"I left my suitcase at the porter's lodge. I intend to change there and take a cab to the railway station."

"You have been here for five years and you have only one suitcase?"

"I went back two months ago for the birth of my son, Andreas, and I took that opportunity to bring home my things—mostly books. Regarding your first question, I have less than thirty minutes to change trains in Budapest, and

I arrive there in the middle of the night anyway. I am not sure I would be all that welcome at three in the morning. More questions?"

"None. Just follow me. All will be explained."

He led a bemused Julius outside. A uniformed chauffeur was standing guard next to a gleaming yellow automobile.

"Here we are," said Manny. "Hand your ticket to Istvan. He will take your seat on the train. Go change, and bring your suitcase. You are going to Budapest with me. You may admire the car. It is the latest Daimler. Fifty miles an hour is nothing for it when the roads are good, which, unfortunately, doesn't happen often. We shall stop for lunch and still be home in time for dinner. Don't worry, I shall have you taken to the station in time for your train to Nagyvarad and see to it that your wife is informed of your exact time of arrival. Go!"

Julius soon returned. Manny secured his case in the trunk, all the while extolling the many outstanding points of the car, praising the double ignition system while his hapless brother-in-law, who did not understand a single thing, looked on. Some of Julius's friends stopped to admire the car, and an appreciative little group formed around it, soon joined by the Countess and her husband. He was not exactly handsome but tall and well built, with an open countenance and none of the supercilious attitude so often seen in members of his caste.

Marie Christine put a hand on his arm. "Darling," she said, "this is Dr...." She paused as if looking for a name. "Dr. Matthias, right? But I don't know the name of his friend with the car."

Julius, ill at ease, completed the introduction.

"Nagy?" repeated the Count. "Banker in Budapest? I congratulate you on your choice of car."

The two men exchanged visiting cards and got into an animated but perfectly incomprehensible (to Julius) discussion on the relative merits of Daimler and Mercedes. Before leaving, the Count took Julius aside and whispered: "Be careful with that Jew. He will run rings around a naive young doctor like you."

Julius found himself blushing and wordlessly went to take his seat in the car where he received another unwelcome piece of advice.

"Careful, my boy. The Count is the kind of man to send some faithful retainers to thoroughly thrash the presumptuous individual daring to look a little too warmly at his Countess." Manny then set the car in motion without waiting for a reply from his brother-in-law who was blushing again.

Thus did Dr. Julius Matthias depart in style from the hallowed grounds of the university which had been the focus of his existence for five long years. He stole a look at his brother-in-law who was expertly piloting his Daimler between the many horse-drawn carriages and the flow of passersby thronging the narrow winding streets. Slim and fit in his made-to-measure motoring outfit, the banker looked much younger than his thirty-four years, and his abundant black hair showed no sign of receding.

Judging by the expensive new car, the family bank was doing well. What was unclear was why he had bothered to come today. He and Julius had not met that often; whenever they did they got on well despite the age difference, but that was not reason enough to come all the way from Budapest, two hundred miles away, on bumpy roads not always suitable for motorized travel. Manny, thought Julius, would probably explain during their lunch break. In the meanwhile, he was fully enjoying this sunny escapade, which was in such stark contrast to the dubious comfort of the second-class seat he had been planning to take.

Manny had booked a table in a majestic establishment surrounded by a well-tended garden. A uniformed mechanic immediately came to drive the car into a hangar where the oil level would be checked and the tank filled. A deferential maître d'hôtel led them to a secluded table, and a waiter hastened to bring then a mouthwatering array of dishes.

"Since we don't have much time, I took the liberty of ordering ahead when I booked," said Manny. "I hope you don't mind."

"Just as well. I have a feeling this will make a pleasant change from my usual fare. But tell me, you didn't come all the way from Budapest just to see me, did you?"

"Hardly. I was visiting some of our business correspondents in Switzerland, and since the dates meshed, I thought it might be a good idea to renew our acquaintance. To tell you the truth, if you didn't have your sister's unruly curls and her eyes, I am not sure I would have recognized you. The last time we met, you were still a gangly youth—no offense—and today I find a man. Anyway I thought we might take this opportunity to discuss a few issues."

"Nothing serious I hope? Anna and the children are well?"

"Yes, everything is fine. In fact, a year from now Karol, our eldest, will be thirteen, and I hope you will join us for the bar mitzvah celebration even though Magda won't come."

"Why?"

"Let's not get into that right now. The food here is superb and deserves our undivided attention. We shall resume this talk over our coffee."

Puzzled but not overly worried, Julius ate with relish what was undoubtedly the best meal he had had in his life. When coffee was served, Manny lit a fat cigar and leaned back in his chair.

"Anni and I went to see Aaron and Aunt Donna a few weeks ago. We hadn't seen them in quite a while."

"Yes, they were very disappointed that you didn't come for Andreas' circumcision ceremony two months ago."

"We didn't come because we were not invited, but that is another story. The point is, we found your father very tired, and Anni told him how worried she was. He replied with a smile that he was going to retire at the end of the school year and that you intended to rent a small apartment for him. Is that true?"

"Yes indeed. Father may be a few years short of his sixtieth birthday, but he is in poor health. He has trouble breathing at times, his heart is tired, and he should stop working. Which means he has to leave the apartment that goes with the job. You don't think it is the right thing to do?"

"Probably, but being a banker, I ask myself a number of questions. Your father won't have much money, and Donna's savings won't go far. Anni and I are more than ready to help with the upkeep of Aaron's new lodgings, but we don't quite see how you will be able to do the same. According to Donna, your in-laws have set up an office for you in the pharmacy, and I don't believe they will pay you enough to be able to help your father. Don't be offended, but your sister and I thought it would be better to have this discussion before Aaron leaves a steady job with an apartment."

"I understand, and I am not offended in the slightest. I am well aware of the fact that you have been quietly sending money to Donna these many years. No, don't interrupt, I know it's true, and I am very grateful to you both. Regarding my plans—my dear Manny, I have known for quite some time that Szamuely and his wife are not going to assist me in opening offices downtown. So I have been busy setting aside as much money as I could. I have been working in a Viennese hospital, which put a room at my disposal, and I took most of my meals there. I may not have been earning a banker's salary, but I was also saving the monthly remittance I received from my father-in-law. Altogether I have a tidy sum set aside, enough to pay the rent for a modest apartment for my parents and help them now and then."

"Bravo. That was very well done, and it changes the situation, especially since we shall be contributing our share. However, what will happen when your money runs out? What are you going to do?"

"Forget about my setting up my shingle behind the counter of the pharmacy. That was not part of the deal when I married Magda. I have been lucky. When I came to see the new baby, I found the time to present myself to the director of the Jewish hospital and hand him a letter of recommendation from the head of the hospital where I was working in Vienna. If truth be told, I was not hopeful. I was wrong. First because the Jewish hospital underwent extensive renovations not so long ago and is now reasonably well equipped, if not in the same class as my former hospital. Second and most important because I was immediately offered a full-time position, with the right to have my own private patients. I can't tell you how relieved I was. Not only is my future secure, but I will not have to cut myself off from the world of hospitals and will be able to keep on learning and keep abreast of the latest discoveries in the field of medicine. I shall start immediately."

"Now, this is what I call very good news," said the banker heartily. "Congratulations again. Your sister will be much relieved; she was worried about you. But are you going to be able to support your wife and children?"

"At first certainly not, but that is, unfortunately, not a problem. You see, during that same visit, my father in-law informed me that he was putting the finishing touches on what he called the family home. A house on Teleky Street along the Cris River, not too far from the town hall, the theater, and the great synagogue. Magda and I will have our own apartments. As far as my wife is concerned, she will not leave until I earn enough money to set her up in a similar style."

"Won't Szamuely be angry with you?"

"Let him be. If he kicks me out, I shall move in with my father or take a room at the hospital. But he won't do it. He is far too afraid of scandal. Tell me, what makes you think Magda won't come to your son's bar mitzvah?"

"The same old story. She still accuses your sister of stealing her fiancé—that's me."

"Well, she probably feels sorry she let such a splendid match go and finds me a poor substitute."

"Believe me, she has only herself to blame. I don't know what you have been told, and in any case it's an old story now, but I assure you that your sister's conduct was above reproach—and so was mine. And I would not say you make a poor substitute. Doctors are people of consequence in our community."

"Then why does Magda, who must know the truth, accuse Anni?"

"Because her parents do not know what really happened, and she does not want them to know. From her point of view, the less they see of Anni and me, the better."

"So why marry me? If she had not done so, she would have had no occasion whatsoever to meet with you!"

"Frankly, this is a question that puzzles your sister, and it puzzles me as well. Donna said Magda was afraid her father would leave the pharmacy to a distant cousin; she wanted children of her own to inherit it. For that she needed a husband. You were not bad looking, and she thought you would do her bidding. Now she has two sons and does not quite know what to do with you. She certainly does not wish to see you at the pharmacy, possibly undermining her position. In that sense she will secretly be happy to learn that the danger is past, but don't expect her to defend you. For what it's worth, you can count on us. Enough said; we have to be on our way. Let me make a quick call home to tell Anni when to expect us."

Julius, remembering how surprised his wife had been to discover she was pregnant, was not quite convinced but saw no point in arguing.

They made another stop because Manny wanted his brother-in-law to try his hand at driving. Julius demurred but let himself be persuaded and, after a few minutes at the wheel, was almost sorry to have to relinquish his seat. They reached Budapest as the last golden rays of the setting sun brushed the spires and palaces of the city.

The Nagys lived in a pleasant house hidden behind high walls. A gardener opened the gate to let the car in, and Anni rushed to embrace the brother she had not seen in years and drew him inside. There he met her three children: Karol, the eldest; Tibor, the second; and little Myriam, a year older than his own Georgy. Later in the evening, after a sumptuous dinner that Julius barely tasted, as he was not accustomed to having two big meals in one day, the two men retreated to the library with a bottle of choice French cognac. Manny appeared preoccupied.

"Listen," he said, "I want to talk to you about something else, but not a word to your sister. I wonder if you know how bad the situation is on the political front today. We are just emerging from a war that engulfed the Balkans. The Ottoman Empire can no longer defend its far-flung European territories. Germany is trying to draw Austria into a new Germanic empire; in the Balkans the Slavs would like to get rid of both the Turks and the Austro-Hungarians, perhaps to become part of greater Russia. Serbia is not ready to accept the annexing of Bosnia-Herzegovina by Austria five years ago, and Russia, having opposed the move, is still angry. Turkey, enfeebled though it is, had to be pacified with the payment of a huge sum of money.

"You may remember how Hungary tried to keep all its minorities together by forcing them to take Hungarian family names. On the other side of Europe, France is desperate to get back the provinces lost to Germany. The whole continent is unsettled, and this, of course, is not good for the financial system. What is worse for us here is that it has led to a surge of anti-Semitism fueled by the rising influence of Germany. I have to tell you that I am worried. Deeply worried. There is nothing we can do at the moment, but I would advise you to keep your money safe. Avoid local banks and, if you can, buy gold coins; they will keep their value even in times of crisis."

"I am happy to say I followed your advice ahead of time," answered Julius, smiling. "I had the good fortune to meet one of the young Rothschilds, who was studying law in Vienna, and he talked me into opening an account with a Swiss bank, which accepted me upon his recommendation. To quote him, drafts drawn on that bank are accepted throughout Europe and even in America. Mind you, I shall still need to have an account with a local bank, both for my salary from the hospital and for the eventual transfer of my savings to Geneva."

"One of the younger Rothschilds! You certainly did not waste your time in Vienna. He was certainly right on both counts. Julius, my boy, I am beginning to think your sister and I were wrong to worry about you. You have a head on your shoulders…I wonder where you got it from. If you wish I shall be happy to give you a letter for our Nagyvarad agent. He will take care of you personally and with the greatest discretion."

"I won't say no, and I thank you. Getting back to the political situation, how does it concern us? What exactly are you afraid of?"

"I take it you did not exactly keep abreast of what was going on outside your little world?"

"Not so little, but you are right. I have to admit I rarely read the papers."

"All right. Let's name but a few burning issues. Our dual monarchy system—having a single ruler both for Austria, of which he is the emperor, and for Hungary, where he is king—is fraught with problems. Many here believe Hungary is forced to shoulder more than its share of the union's expenditures and must provide far too many soldiers for the army. Then there are some who think every man should have a vote, but I for one don't think it would be a good thing. Regarding our community, a number of Jews recently arrived from Poland have amassed great riches in a short time and display them a little too openly. On the other hand, a number of Jewish revolutionaries are making irresponsible declarations and drawing a lot of negative attention. Not surprisingly anti-Semitism is on the rise, and there have been a few unpleasant incidents. Our family is behaving with the utmost caution. We have only Jewish employees. I leave my car at home here and go about my business with our carriage and our old coachman. We don't go out much, and I enjoy expensive restaurants only when I am abroad. I assume the situation is a little better in a backwater like Nagyvarad—no offense meant—but you will have to tread carefully."

"You don't think it will get better in the long term?"

"Unfortunately not. It will only get worse." He drank a mouthful of what Julius had to admit was very good cognac before declaring bleakly, "I have to tell you that sooner or later, the Jews will have no choice but to leave this country. And that includes people like us, who are barely observant."

"Leave Hungary! To go where? Don't tell me you have let yourself be convinced by the crazy theories of Theodor Herzl and that you intend to settle in his Utopia—a Jewish state he imagined rising from the sands of the Middle East!"

"I am not so sure *Utopia* is the right word. You know, I heard him speak some ten years ago—his father was a banker too, by the way—and I was impressed. But don't worry; I certainly do not intend to go back to the land of our biblical ancestors. I am seriously considering emigrating to America. Not now, not right away, not as long as my father is alive. He is too old, too rooted in the life, the house he was born in and where he lives still. I have, however, set things in motion. Our bank has made a few investments there. You may remember Esther, my elder sister. She was at our wedding. She married an engineer, and they went to live in the north of the United States, in a town called Chicago. They have three children. They are all coming next year for the bar mitzvah, and afterward Karol will go back with them."

"You are sending your thirteen-year-old son away? What has Anni to say about that?"

"Anni—of course she would not hear of it at first. Then… Let me tell you what happened a few weeks ago, and you will understand. Anni needed a new hat—have you noticed that women are never happy with the hats they have? No? Anyway, she went with Myriam to her favorite boutique, *Chic de Paris* it's called, though I venture no one there has ever gotten close to the French border. It's just across the street from our favorite tea shop, *Swarts and Sons*. The little girl saw the place and immediately started demanding a chocolate éclair. Anni told her she wanted to try on a few hats first, and the child started crying. She is our youngest, so she is a little spoilt. By me, mainly.

"By chance Rabbi Goldwasser and his wife, who are old friends of my parents', walked by and offered to buy Myriam her cake while Anni tried on hats. As she walked out, she heard the child's terrified cries. Passersby, seeing this sweet blue-eyed, blond little girl with Jews in traditional garb, immediately assumed they were kidnapping a Christian child to cut her throat and use her blood to make unleavened bread for Passover. It was awful. When Anni yelled that this was her daughter, who was Jewish as well, and that she had entrusted her to the old couple, the crowd started jeering and spitting at her. Fortunately, very fortunately, our coachman arrived at the scene and started cracking his whip in a threatening manner."

He shook his head and drank another mouthful of cognac. "You will tell me that similar things have happened in the past. You may remember that in 1882, accusations of ritual murder against the Jews of a small town got out of control. Believe me, when it happens to you it is a completely different story. Old Mrs. Goldwasser took to her bed for a whole week; Myriam had nightmares for far longer and no longer wants to visit *Swarts*—or even to eat chocolate éclairs. As for Anni, now she is the one wanting to send Karol to the States. She is unhappy at having to part with her firstborn, but she wants to do what's best for him. She is also pushing me to take concrete steps to prepare for our own departure. Julius, have you never thought of leaving?"

"I can't say I have. Nagyvarad is quiet enough these days. After all we—I mean the Jewish community—make up a third of the population of the town, more if you do not count the suburbs and the surrounding farms. There are some thirty synagogues and many prosperous businesses. As far as I know, there haven't been any problems, just nasty remarks from time to time. I am afraid that as far as Jews are concerned, they face the same situation the world over, even in your New World. I have heard there are clubs and even hotels that do not accept Jews. If I ever decided to leave, it would be for Vienna, where I have had some gratifying proposals. But Magda will never abandon her pharmacy."

"You are the head of the family!"

"I wish it were that simple. I have obligations, and not only in the financial sense."

"To the end of your days? It is ridiculous."

"Maybe in your eyes. Believe me, I have thought long and hard about the problem in the last few months. Marrying Magda was, for me, a miraculous way out of a hopeless situation. Yes, I had to agree to terms I now have to honor. It won't be easy, but in all fairness, I must say I would make the same decision today."

Anna's entrance put an end to the discussion. With rare tact Manny stood up, saying he had to see to something, and left brother and sister alone. His wife sat down in the armchair he had just vacated. She was wearing a very becoming dress of soft blue silk and a delicate gold necklace drew attention to her lovely neck. Married for thirteen years and the mother of three children, she was still as slim and graceful as she had been on her wedding day. Julius could not but contrast her appearance with that of his own wife who was barely a year older. Undoubtedly another reason for Magda's reluctance to meet her...

He met his sister's troubled glance. "Is there anything wrong?"

She smiled her wonderful smile. "Playing big brother, Yuli?"

"Why not? I have at least ten inches on you!"

They burst out laughing at the same time, but she turned somber again. "I do worry about you, little brother. Here you are, twenty-three years old, not bad looking, already a doctor, and instead of having fun, meeting girls, enjoying life, you are on your way to a wife who does not love you and in-laws who can't stand you... What a mess! And it's all my fault. If I had not married Manny..."

Suddenly she was crying. He took her hand. "Your fault! Where did you get that crazy notion? If you had not married him, you would have married some pious member of the community or the widower Father was so fond of. Today you would have half a dozen children or more pulling at your skirts, and you would not smile very often. As for myself, had I not wed Magda, I would be a soldier in the Hungarian army, with no great hope of ever becoming an officer. We would both be very unhappy. So don't say 'what a mess.' Dry your tears, and stop worrying about me. Come on, Anni, give me a smile!"

She smiled tremulously. "You are right. I shan't mention it again. But I want you to know that you will always be welcome in our home. There will always be a room for you. Don't you forget it."

That night Julius did not sleep well. He left Budapest at dawn, but it was noon by the time he reached his destination, the train having made dozens of stops on the way. At one point it stopped for a whole hour in the middle of nowhere, its engine gently chugging, for a mysterious reason no one had seen fit to tell the weary passengers.

Hundreds of people were waiting on the Nagyvarad platform. Peasants in traditional garb and shopkeepers jostled army officers in full regalia; there were also small clusters of black-garbed Jews. Some were there to welcome friends or relatives. Most were on their way to the Transylvanian capital city—Klauzenburg, Kolozvar, or Cluj for the German, Hungarian, and Romanian speakers, respectively. It did not take long for Julius to see there was no one waiting for him, not even the Szamuely coachman. He walked out with dragging feet, a bitter smile on his face. He tried to tell himself that train schedules were so erratic, it was difficult to ascertain exact arrival times; that today, being Thursday, was a working day; that less than two months had elapsed since his last visit. But he could not help coming to the conclusion that this was a deliberate slight to show him how little he meant to his wife and her family.

Nagyvarad aspired to be a little Paris. Julius had no knowledge of France beyond what his Latin teacher had told him, but compared to Vienna and its nearly one million inhabitants, and to Budapest, with only slightly less, the reality was less flattering. Under the merciless light of the sun at its zenith, the city of his birth and its fewer than one hundred thousand inhabitants could not hide the fact that it was no more than a provincial backwater with delusions of grandeur. There was little beyond the impressive main square with its theater and a handful of public buildings (including the white synagogue—the biggest in Europe, recently built by the Neolog branch of Judaism, the closest it had to a reform movement) and the Tramway lines crisscrossing the town center, which were a source of great pride for the locals.

This was nothing new, but the young doctor was suddenly having to come to terms with the fact that he was back for good. Henceforth, home would be the river Cris and the ochre-tinted houses reflected in its turbulent waters, a handful of coffeehouses in the main square fighting for a motley clientele of civil servants, army officers, painters and poets, grain traders, and Jewish merchants—the last group studiously ignored by the others. One could feel something of what Manny was talking about—not hatred so much as deep distrust and undisguised contempt.

Julius shivered in spite of the heat but immediately squared his shoulders. He was not going to give in so easily. Hailing a cab, he directed it to the Jewish hospital. The reception there was everything he could have hoped for; two hours later, after an excellent lunch with the director, he left and took another cab to the Talmud Torah. His father was still recovering from his cold but got out of bed to give his blessing to the son he was so proud of; he wanted to know every little detail about the graduation ceremony and the praise heaped on the young man and listened with rapt attention. A beaming Donna made him eat a slice of his favorite cake, baked that very day for his return. Before leaving, Julius promised to spend his first Shabbat at his father's house.

By the time he reached the imposing Szamuely mansion, it was almost six in the evening and the pharmacist had worked himself into a towering rage. "Here you are at last! Where have you been? I waited for you at the pharmacy the whole afternoon. I intended to explain your duties, so you could start work in the morning. Because of your thoughtlessness, precious time has been lost. I am warning you that this attitude will not be tolerated. If you believe that you deserve special treatment because you are my son-in-law, you are very much mistaken."

Julius forced himself to stay calm and took a long look at his father-in-law. The man was losing his fight against stoutness; excess fat was blurring his authoritarian features. Julius told himself he was lucky not to have to work for him.

"Let me tell you, I am a doctor, and that's what I shall do, and nothing else," he said quietly but firmly. "I have had the honor of being offered a full-time position at the Jewish hospital, and I shall take up my duties Sunday morning."

Emil Szamuely stood stock still but only for a moment and replied that he was going to have a word with the director of the hospital.

"I am convinced," he declared pompously, "that when he understands you accepted this position in spite of your prior commitments, he will cancel his offer."

"I am warning you," said Julius, incandescent with rage but doing his best not to show it. "Should I be prevented from working at the hospital through your intervention, I shall consider myself free of all my commitments and return forthwith to Vienna, where an even better position awaits me. I shall, of course, expect my wife and my children to come with me." He thought Szamuely would have a stroke on the spot. Breathing heavily, the man turned around and left.

Thus began a long purgatory. Julius was relegated to a small bedroom since his wife, who was breastfeeding, claimed she needed her rest. His father-in-law did not speak to him. They met only at dinner, a largely silent meal. Georgy was now shying away from this stranger his beloved grandfather detested. Surprisingly Golda treated him civilly enough. This was a good thing, since the tall thin woman who never said much ruled the household with an iron hand; the servants, taking their cue from her, took good care of his room and his effects.

The young doctor left early and returned late; sometimes he stayed overnight at the hospital. Silent for the most part at home—if the Szamuely mansion could be called home—he opened up with his patients. He listened to them and found words to comfort them. Infants and children smiled at his entrance, and old people held out their hands to him. Julius had not forgotten one of the first pieces of advice he had received when he had begun working at his Vienna hospital and never went alone to see a woman patient. It was a good thing since many smiled at him invitingly.

"Only my wife does not find me attractive," he often thought bitterly when the memory of Marie Christine troubled his solitary nights. Enforced celibacy was hard to bear, but there was not much he could do. Here the smallest indiscretion would have ruined his career. He might have thought he was too young to live only for his work, but he knew only too well he had no choice. But what was he to do with his free time?

Magda spent her days at the pharmacy where a room—perhaps the one intended for him—had been turned into a nursery for the baby; Emil had a high chair installed for Georgy behind the tall wooden counter and delighted in the presence of the grandson he intended to groom as his successor. The lonely young man took to spending one night a week at his father's house, where he was sure to receive a warm welcome. By an extraordinary piece of luck for his parents, he had found a ground-floor flat with a tiny garden less than five minutes' walk from the hospital. Aaron enjoyed sitting in the sunshine and was feeling better than he had in years. He was giving private lessons and preparing young boys for their bar mitzvahs, earning more money than he had done as a teacher.

Donna smiled a lot and had gained weight, which suited her. She had, of course, immediately planted her favorite herbs in the garden, and her faithful patients had followed her to the new house. This woman, who had never studied, had a natural knack for treating a number of minor ailments and knew when to keep her hands off and recommend a visit to the doctor. Julius, who valued her opinion, always took her with him when making house calls at a woman's home.

Though his indifference to things religious had not abated, he tried to go to Friday services at least once a month with his father who was touchingly proud of him. "At least I have made these two people happy," Julius told himself when loneliness threatened to overcome him. A few colleagues invited him to their homes, but he had to decline regretfully. Magda refused to go with him, and he could not return the invitations in any case. What was left? Going out in the evening? Alone? He did have Sandor, his childhood friend, now happily married to Martha, a plump peasant woman who was expecting their first child. Sandor had been left sole owner of the family farm on his parents' deaths, after buying out Zoltan and Attila, his two brothers, who had chosen army careers. Apprehensive at first with her husband's friend—a doctor and a Jew!—Martha had quickly grown to like him. She now treated him like a member of the family, and Julius had his own room in the attic where he stored clothes suitable for his jaunts in the forest. Farm workers and neighbors alike were now coming for advice to the Jewish doctor who was never too busy to listen to them and never charged them for his advice.

In September Sandor came to fetch him and his aunt in his new carriage, and they got home in time to deliver Martha of a healthy baby boy, immediately called Julius in his honor. Weeks and months went by. Dr. Matthias was making a name for himself at the hospital for the soundness of his diagnoses and for his overall kindness; word was spreading, and he made more and more house calls. The year 1913 came to an end, and the denizens of Nagyvarad celebrated the advent of the New Year. Julius heard the clock strike twelve at the farm after a festive dinner. A little later the door of his attic room opened, and a distant relative of Martha's, who was also a guest that evening, entered. She was pleasant looking, more than attractive, and he did not send her away.

4

THE DAY THAT CHANGED EVERYTHING

ON SUNDAY, JUNE 14, 1914, almost a year to the day after his homecoming, Dr. Matthias took the train to Budapest with his father and his aunt to attend the bar mitzvah of Karol Nagy. To nobody's surprise Magda did not accompany them; furthermore, she had also adamantly refused to let Georgy go, deeming him too young at five to be separated from his mother.

Anna met Julius, Aaron, and Donna at the station and brought them home. Manny's sister, Esther, was already there, with her husband; their three children merrily and noisily ran around the house and garden. Aaron and Donna could not get enough of Anna's children and delighted in their beloved daughter's happiness. However, for the young doctor it was not an easy time. He could not help but contrast that happy household with the wasteland that was his own. Yet there was something bracing in the cosmopolitan atmosphere of the Hungarian capital, something that brought back memories of his Vienna years.

In the evening the men of the family and some close friends of the banker would gather in the library and far into the night discuss the latest news about the volatile international situation and the storm that all saw coming but did not believe could be averted. The growing influence of Jewish revolutionaries was another source of concern. As soon as the festivities were over, Manny intended to send his wife and the two younger children to Geneva, where the family had a comfortable house by a lake. Karoly, of course, would be leaving for America with his aunt. Secretly Julius wondered whether his brother-in-law was not being overly pessimistic. He was soon to find out he wasn't.

Manny, who had not forgotten Julius's birthday, had secured a box at the opera for his guests on Thursday, June 18—not an easy feat, since everyone wanted to see *The Merry Widow*, the new success by Hungarian composer Franz Lehar. Aaron Matthias was not of the party; his principles did not let him attend what he was sure was a spectacle both frivolous and lacking in morality, and he declared himself perfectly happy to stay with the children. His son's evening dress might not have been made to measure like that of the banker, but he cut a fine figure nevertheless, as attested to by the covert glances from female members of the audience.

As chance would have it, during the intermission he saw one of his former professors and walked over to say hello. The man introduced him to the couple he was with, a count whose name he did not catch, still handsome though he must have been over sixty, and his countess, who was wearing a deceptively simple dress over her ample curves but sported a splendid diamond necklace. While Julius bent to kiss her hand, she gave him a playful snap of her fan.

"Tell me, Doctor, what is a man of your class doing with this parvenu Jewish banker and his hook-nosed kin?" she asked chidingly.

He let go the fat little hand laden with rings and straightened abruptly. "Mr. Nagy is my sister's husband, and I am therefore part of his kin," he replied and turned his back on the little group.

The professor ran after him. "My dear Matthias, please don't take this incident personally," he said paternally. "Count Von Thuringen has a Jewish mistress, very beautiful by the way, and that unpleasant remark was aimed at him. You can be sure she had no intention of offending you."

"I thank you for this explanation, even if I do not share your conclusion. Let us hope the next time you and I meet, it will be under happier circumstances." Still fuming, Julius wanted to tell Manny what had happened, but his brother-in-law raised his hand to stop him.

"Not now. Let's talk about it tomorrow—and not a word to your sister."

Slightly surprised, Julius returned to his seat without a word.

Early the next morning, after a restless night he left the house where all still slept and went for a walk along the Danube River, pausing to admire the many palaces and churches gleaming under the already brilliant sun; there was not a cloud to be seen. He would have lingered more but felt it was time to turn back. On his way he found a boutique painted with the colors of the Hungarian flag and boasting the patriotic name Budapest Fashions. Smaller letters declared that the owner was Maria Corvin. It was not open yet—the time was barely eight thirty—but he stopped to admire the lacy confections displayed with charming artistry. He was trying to guess his wife's reaction should he bring her a rather revealing night robe when rapid steps came closer.

"We open at ten," said a warm, sultry voice that sounded vaguely familiar. Turning around he faced an elegant lady wearing a close-fitting dark-green dress that emphasized her charms as well as the unusual color of her hair, the shade of strawberry blond so prized by Venetians painters. She had the tiniest of hats, but it was delightful. Again there was something familiar about the heart-shaped face, the green eyes artfully made up, the sensual mouth a tad too large but incredibly alluring.

She smiled. "Have we met?" she asked in that throaty voice.

"Madi?" he replied uncertainly.

She took a backward step, the better to look at him, and said wonderingly, "Yuli? Julius?"

They both burst out laughing. It was indeed the third Magda, the redheaded daughter of the Nagyvarad seamstress, who had left the town so suddenly fifteen years ago.

"You came to see me?" she asked provocatively.

"I would certainly have done so had I known you were here, but since I did not, I just happened upon this elegant establishment as I was on my way back to my sister and her husband."

"If you are not in a hurry, have breakfast with me. I just came back with fresh croissants, and the coffee must be about ready."

He accepted. Afterward he wondered why. Because he was glad to see her? Because he had not had breakfast yet? Whatever the reason, he followed her as she unlocked the door and walked in. The place was in semidarkness; she led him toward a staircase half hidden behind a recessed alcove.

"I live above the boutique. It is very convenient," she threw over her shoulder, answering the question he had not asked. He found himself in a sunny room opening onto a wide balcony, sheltered from curious glances by a green trellis. A low sofa ran along one side. On a wicker table, everything was in place for a solitary meal, but that was soon remedied. He watched her as she bustled around, setting coffee, croissants, butter, and jam on the embroidered tablecloth. She was exactly the same age as Anni but looked somewhat older while still being extremely attractive. The dress displayed her curves to her advantage, and the tiny scrap of creamy lace tucked into her cleavage was not really intended to hide the proud bosom he saw at close quarters when she leaned toward him to pour the coffee. He rather thought she noticed and enjoyed his admiration.

The coffee was just the way he liked it and the croissants still warm. He ate more than his share while she looked on smiling, telling him about the boutique, of which she was inordinately proud, and about the hats she designed herself.

"Who is Maria Corvin? The owner?" he asked.

"No, it's me," was the startling answer. "Don't be so surprised. I changed my name legally." And she added bitterly, "These days a Hungarian name is an asset, even for a fashion shop. You must have noticed my patriotic sign."

"Come on. You haven't done too badly," he said admiringly. "A smart boutique in the best part of town, an apartment… and in a relatively short time too!"

Madi sighed. "You mean your brother-in-law didn't tell you anything?"

"What about? Did his bank lend you the money?"

"His bank lent me money! You must be joking. When he sees me, he crosses the road or turns his back on me. Your sister too."

"You had a quarrel?"

"Julius, we never exchanged a word. I am not respectable enough for him and even less for your sister. What I have I owe to the generosity of a Hungarian nobleman. Need I say more?"

This time he understood. "Don't tell me you are the friend of that Von Thuringen!"

"So he did tell you about it!"

"No. I met the man and his wife at the opera yesterday."

"They couldn't have mentioned me."

"Let me explain," said Julius before recounting exactly what had happened the night before. She stood up and went to sit on the low sofa and began speaking, her eyes lost in the distance.

"You probably remember my sudden departure which set tongues wagging. It was said that I had let myself be seduced by the son of a rich family and that I was pregnant. It was not true. What had happened was far worse. I had gone to deliver a dress to one of my mother's best customers, and I was to wait and see if it needed any alterations. She was not at home, so the servants led me to a utility room with just an ironing board and a daybed. I was there for ages, and I must have fallen asleep. That's how her husband found me. He was drunk, and he thought I was one of the housemaids. It was his weight on me that woke me up."

She dabbed at her eyes with a fine lace handkerchief. "I barely had time to understand what was happening. I was sixteen; he was big and strong. There was nothing I could do. Then...then I ran home sobbing. My mother was devastated. We didn't know what to do. Go and complain? Think of the scandal, what it would have done to my reputation...And then my mother would lose all her customers, and we would starve. We were in utter despair. That very evening the woman came—I mean the wife. It was a dreadful meeting; I don't know which of us felt worse. It was weird. Nothing was said in so many words. Much later, when I thought of that evening, I came to the conclusion that it was not the first time her husband had behaved like that, but usually he chose his victims from among the household help. One thing was sure: she knew what she wanted—to avoid a scandal—and was ready to pay for it. A lot. By the time she left, she had come to an agreement with my mother. All our debts would be paid, Mother would become the owner of the apartment we rented, and money had been set aside to send me to Budapest where I would be apprenticed to a milliner. At no time did they discuss what had happened to me. When I dared ask what I should do if I found myself pregnant, the woman looked daggers at me and said with finality that she would see that my mother got the money to take care of it."

"My poor Madi! Your mother agreed to let you go just like that?'

"My mother lived in fear of falling sick, of not being able to work, of being kicked out of the apartment. She also knew that a word from that woman could ruin her. Mind you, I understood that too much later. Too late. I left and never came back, not even for her funeral. To make a long story short, I was indeed apprenticed to a milliner, a very good one, and some three years later I went to deliver a hat to a countess at the end of the day. The husband was there. He was going to his club and offered to see me home. He behaved with the utmost propriety. The following day he was waiting for me when I left work. What more is there to say? We are still together. He set me up in this place that he put in my name—a name he encouraged me to change. He loves me in his own way. And he is generous. Generous but demanding."

At that point she broke down and burst into a flood of tears. Julius went to sit by her side and took her in his arms to comfort her. Her perfume was an enticing mix of violet and some heavier scent. Their eyes met. She turned into his embrace and kissed him feverishly and then leaned back into the sofa, taking him with her. He barely had time to tell himself it was madness before succumbing to temptation.

Since that long-ago New Year's night at Sandor's, he had not held a woman in his arms. Madi stopped kissing him only to help him take off her dress and tell him not to worry about precautions. It was as intense as it was brief. She pushed him away with a small satisfied smile and disappeared inside the apartment. When she came back, perfectly coiffed and dressed, it was his turn to go and put his clothes in order. Upon his return he found her seated at the table. She poured herself a cup of coffee and offered him the last remaining croissant.

Stretching like a cat, she looked at him with a sunny smile. "Yuli, dear, you really needed that! What's the matter? Is your wife neglecting you? By the way, whom did you marry? Anyone I know?"

"I married Magda," he replied neutrally.

"Lena? Little Magda? What am I saying? I saw her husband a month ago in town. Besides, she is too old for you."

"You're right. I didn't marry little Magda. I married the third one."

"Magda Szamuely from the pharmacy? You can't be serious. She is Jozef Fried's wife."

"He died some years ago."

She was not convinced. "Magda Szamuely is at least seven years older than you, has a nasty temper, and is far from pretty. Why would you marry her?"

He shrugged. "Her father paid for my medical studies in Vienna. Five years." And with a mirthless smile, he added, "You see, men sell themselves too…"

She shook her head. "How can you say that? Don't even think it. There is no shame in an arranged marriage. You are respectable. A doctor. From the Vienna School of Medicine. Do you have children?"

"Two boys."

"Lucky you. I shall never have children—a botched abortion nearly killed me."

"I am sorry."

"Don't be. That's the way of the world, and I am not complaining. Neither the count nor his children would have tolerated a Jewish bastard in the family. The fact is I have been lucky. Many girls like me end up in the gutter. But enough with this. This morning, thanks to you, I have known a few minutes of happiness. It seems that, in one respect at least, our situations are similar; we have to find elsewhere what we can't get from our partners, and we have to be discreet about it. Though I fail to see why your wife—"

"She has had her own bedroom since our second child was born a year ago."

"She is out of her mind!" commented Madi with conviction. "But why don't you follow your father-in-law's example?"

"Isn't it what I am doing? He and Golda have been sleeping apart for years."

"Yes, but he has a mistress."

"Emil, a mistress?" Julius burst out laughing.

"You really don't know? It's been going on for a long time, but maybe it has changed now. When I left, it was Paula Rapaport, a twenty-year-old penniless widow. He set her up in an apartment not too far from the pharmacy and used to visit her every afternoon, saying he was going to check on his suppliers. Suppliers!" She started laughing at Julius's stupefaction. "Don't be so surprised. Men are all the same. They want the same thing, and if they can't get it at home, they look elsewhere. You, a doctor, should know that better than I." She stood up. "I have to go back to my hats. Forget this charming interlude, and don't come back: the count is very possessive and very jealous, and I can't afford to offend him."

He left by another staircase leading directly to the street, feeling elated and perplexed at the same time. Was the story about Emil true? He had no way of checking, and in any case now was not the time.

In order to respect the sanctity of the Sabbath, the traditional family picture was taken early on Friday afternoon. Karol, slightly ill at ease in his first grown-up suit, stood very straight between his father, more elegant than ever with a carnation in his lapel, and his mother, lovely in a demure dress of soft gray. Behind them the grandparents, and then

Julius, Esther, and her husband. The young children of the two couples were sitting on the floor. A poignant image of a happy family.

The following day the ceremony went without a hitch. Karol, called to the Torah for the first time, read his text well. Barely thirteen, he was already a handsome teenager, nearly five foot six, with his mother's blue eyes. Letting the family and guests make their way to the banker's house less than half a mile away, Julius walked more slowly with his father, who appeared inordinately tired. Halfway there Julius made him sit down on a street bench for a few minutes. Listening to his father's labored breathing, Julius reflected once again that, though not yet sixty, his father was an old man, and there was no cure to reverse a deterioration that was, to him, inexplicable. They stayed there without speaking for nearly a quarter of an hour. The weather was still fine despite a few clouds in the sky, and a tree shaded the bench from the midday sun.

"I was against the match," said Aaron Matthias suddenly. "I did not like Manny. His family is good enough, but I could see he was not observant, and I was afraid he would lead Anni astray. I had found a good match for her, older perhaps but respectful of our religious tradition. He was a widower with two small children, an excellent situation, and a large apartment. He had noticed Anni at the synagogue and had spoken to me a year after his wife's death. Your sister was fifteen at the time, and I said she was too young, that he should wait another year. He was impatient and talked to me about her nearly every week."

He stopped to catch his breath. "I knew she did not want him and that Donna supported her, but I intended to have my way. I thought she would get used to the idea and understand how lucky she was. She would have her own home, servants; she would never be cold or hungry; she would have a husband to take care of her. And then Manny came with his father to ask for her hand. I was about to refuse, but I saw that Donna knew about it and was in favor. So I said I wanted to discuss this with my daughter and would give my answer in the morning."

He stopped again, closed his eyes for a moment, and went on. "That evening I faced Donna and told her I would not budge; Anna would marry the widower. We had a terrible quarrel—the first and the last of our married life. We hurled insults at each other, taking care to keep our voices down so as not to wake you up, you and your sister, and I was perilously close to striking her. I caught myself in time and went down to my office on the ground floor to cool down. I don't know how, but I fell asleep almost immediately."

He stopped again, looking into the distance, seemingly lost in memories. "Suddenly your mother appeared before me. She was pale, as white as she had been on her deathbed, and she was crying. 'Aaron,' she told me, 'I will not let you destroy my daughter as you destroyed me. What little happiness I had was due to my little Anna. Her sweet smile lightened my burden. Now you must repay the heavy debt you incurred. Let the child marry the man she loves. If you refuse, if you condemn her to a joyless union she does not want, I shall come back to torment you, night after night to the end of your days.'

"I woke up in a cold sweat and frozen with fright and could not go back to sleep. In the morning I gave my consent to the match. I must say I have never regretted it. She is happy, she has handsome and well-mannered children, and she raises them with respect for our religion and its traditions. It is to her mother that she owes all this, but I have never told her. Come on, it's time to go. They must be waiting for us."

Julius helped him to his feet and, as they resumed their walk, asked him whether his mother had appeared again when he was about to marry Magda. The old man shook his head. "It is a good question. I knew it was an advantageous union for you, and I knew Magda was not a pleasant person and would not make you happy. So I thought I would leave the decision to Gitte. If she did not show herself again, it would mean she had no objection. She did not come that night, and I gave you my blessing. Later, much later, I realized the poor woman never even knew you. It takes a powerful emotion to get the departed to show themselves to the living. I blame myself, my boy, I blame myself…"

"Don't blame yourself, Father. I am quite satisfied with my lot."

"Don't lie to me, son. You never smile and you are not happy."

"Do you know many happy people, Father? Have you been happy? When you were young, didn't you have other dreams? Don't you often tell me that man must make do with whatever heaven has in store for him? I regret nothing, and you must not blame yourself. Enough said. Let us rejoice with your eldest grandson and with his parents. Tomorrow Karol leaves for America. Who knows when we shall all meet again."

The banker's house was full. Family and guests mingled in the spacious drawing room or in the garden where a marquee had been set up. The food was superb without being ostentatious; the bar was well stocked, and there was even French champagne, imported at great cost for the occasion. The Nagy family was well known and respected, and their bank was doing well. Members of the Budapest business community, not all of them Jewish, mingled with the town's Jewish elite, scions of families who had moved to the Hungarian capital centuries ago and had little in common with the parvenus who had so recently left their Polish ghettos.

Half hidden behind the open French windows leading into the garden, Dr. Julius Matthias, glass in hand, contemplated the scene. This demonstration of harmonious coexistence appeared to belie the fears of his brother-in-law. There were problems—witness the outburst of the countess at the opera—but they were nowhere as serious as Manny and his close friends imagined, and there was no reason to think they would get worse, at least in the foreseeable future. Julius would gladly have discussed the subject with him, but it would have to wait since the banker was dutifully circulating among his other guests.

Julius turned his mind to his own situation. When the time came for Georgy to have his bar mitzvah, he thought ruefully, the celebrations would be nowhere as fancy. After a moment's reflection, he started to laugh quietly. The child was barely five years old; the event was still eight years away! It did not stop him from feeling restless. He knew no one and did not feel like striking up a conversation with a stranger. Donna had shepherded the children to the playroom on the second floor. His father was lying down after the morning's exertions.

Anni, charming in the demure dress she had worn the day before, a single row of pearls for ornament—the Nagys were careful not to show off their riches—was smiling as she greeted her guests while keeping an eye on the servants to make sure they promptly removed discarded plates and replenished the chafing dishes as soon as they were empty. Julius could not take his eyes off her. Like him, she had come a long way since leaving the poor apartment where she had been born and where she had lived until her wedding day. Unlike him, she had found happiness. He thought of his wife, but it was another Magda who came to mind: redheaded Magda, her subtle violet-scented perfume, her supple body arching under his...

He shook his head. Now was not the time! He made his way to the bar to get another glass of champagne but the second Nagy boy, Tibor, stopped him.

"What happened?" asked Julius, smiling. "You managed to escape Auntie Donna? Is it too boring for you upstairs?"

The boy took the question seriously. "No, Uncle Julius. Father sent me. He wants you to join him in the library. He says it's urgent, but you must come discreetly so as not to alarm the guests." Mission accomplished, the child noiselessly went away but still took the time to snatch a few sweets from the table.

Julius looked around. Manny was nowhere to be seen. Had he felt unwell or...was it Julius's father? He hastened to the library where he found his host alone by the telephone, looking worried.

"Yuli! Here you are at last. I have here someone called Sandor on the phone. He apologizes for calling on the Shabbat but says it is urgent."

In two quick steps, Julius was at the table and picked up the phone. "Sandor? Something wrong at the farm? What?" He heard his friend talking, but the words did not make sense.

He felt faint and had to hold on to the table to stop himself from falling. Manny held a chair for him, and he sat down heavily. Sandor was still talking, and Julius shook his head as if his friend could see him. "I understand," he said. "Thank you, Sandy. Listen, I don't know how yet, but I am coming. If you can, go to my father's synagogue, I believe you know it, and ask for Rabbi Zussman. Tell him what happened, and ask him to come to the house immediately after Shabbat. Thank you." He put down the telephone and turned his ashen face to his host. "It's Georgy. My little Georgy. He is dead. He drowned in the river this morning."

"How is it possible? There must be a mistake. The river is not that close to the house. He could not have gone there alone. Besides, who is this Sandor, and why is he the one to tell you? Surely your wife, your father-in-law—"

"That's just the point," replied Julius wearily. "He was with my father-in-law. That is, he was supposed to be with him. Szamuely usually takes the child with him on Shabbat, and I was dumb enough never to ask questions. You see, in fact he was going to see his mistress. Apparently he has one. Of course I knew nothing about that. What he did was he paid a servant to take care of the boy. Sandor says half the town knew. This morning the girl let herself be distracted by a passing young man. Georgy saw his chance and went to the river. He adores the water. I mean, he adored…"

He put his head in his hands. Manny, who had come closer, put a hand on his shoulder. Without looking up the young doctor went on. "The Szamuelys have no intention of telling me. They are going to bury the child as soon as Shabbat is over and hope I don't ask too many questions when I come back. They don't know that the brother of one of their maids works for Sandor. You see, Sandor is the nephew of Donna's first husband. You know the story. We grew up together, and he is the only one I can really depend on. But here I am talking, talking instead of rushing to the station. There must be a train; even if I have to change, I should arrive in time to see my little one for the last time, to kiss him good-bye and to accompany him—"

"You can do better," said Manny crisply. "Istvan is here. He will take the Daimler and drive you home. No, don't argue. That's the best way. I would go with you, but—"

"I don't know how to thank you. No, no, you mustn't leave your family and your guests. But won't you need your car tomorrow?"

"Don't worry about that. If I need a car, I will rent one. Do you want your father to go with you?"

"On no account. Let him have this day of happiness. Karol is the eldest of his grandchildren, and he doesn't know if he will ever see him again. Georgy's death will break his heart. No, say nothing, not even to my sister. If anyone asks where I am, say something about an emergency at the hospital. No one will care. Manny, thanks again. I won't forget this."

Less than fifteen minutes later, Julius, who had stopped only to change clothes and pick up the medical bag he was never without, walked out through the servants' entrance and joined Istvan who was waiting a short way off in the yellow Daimler. They left immediately. The driver, a solidly built man in his thirties, was going fast, too fast perhaps, but there was no time to lose. They had some two hundred miles to cover on roads not always suitable for automobiles.

It was fortunate that this Saturday, June 20, on the eve of summer, was practically the longest day of the year. Departing shortly before three in the afternoon, they had a little over six hours before the end of the Shabbat when preparations for the funeral would get underway. The funeral...Lost in thought, Julius gazed upon the pleasant countryside going by without really seeing it. He felt an overwhelming fury. He kept thinking about his merry little boy not long out of babyhood. Georgy, his firstborn son, flesh of his flesh, and yet a child he had not known well enough because Georgy had been totally taken over by a grandfather who intended to groom him to be his heir. Julius had wanted to take the boy with him to Budapest, explaining that Donna would be there to take care of him, that Anni had small children of her own. To no avail. Magda had been adamant. And when he had raised his voice, the frightened little boy had burst into sobs and wailed that he wanted to stay with his mother. Julius had given in. He too was therefore guilty—guilty of having abdicated his parental authority because he had not been ready to fight.

He realized he was crying. Istvan did not say a word, keeping his attention firmly on the road. They were going so fast that the wind was drying Julius's tears almost immediately. As the car raced through the endless Hungarian plain, the young doctor swore he would care better for baby Andreas. He would remain under the Szamuely roof until the end of the shiva, the ritual week of mourning, but not an instant more. Afterward he would leave with the child. Should Magda refuse to go with them, he would consider himself free of his vows.

Unfortunately, this resolve did nothing to assuage his pain and his despair. As a doctor he knew that the child had probably died in a matter of minutes, without even understanding what was happening. This did not stop the dreadful images that rose to mind: Georgy, who did not know how to swim, vainly fighting the river's strong current, the terror of the little boy trying to breathe and choking on the eddying waters. Whom did he call to for help before his mouth was forever closed? Who had he extended his chubby arms to in vain?

Twice the driver stopped for refueling. He must have known the way since he knew exactly where he could find the petrol he needed. In a matter of minutes, they were on the road again. Happily, they encountered very few people. Farmers and peasants who had risen early were already back at home. Istvan barely slowed when going through the many villages, as if he was feeling the same urgency as his passenger. Later Julius learned that Manny had promised the man an extraordinary bonus should he manage the journey in less than five hours. He earned it.

Julius directed him through the narrow streets of Nagyvarad and made him stop on the other side of the river, some three hundred yards from the house. There was no point in offending the neighbors by arriving in a showy automobile half an hour before the end of Shabbat. It had been agreed that the driver would check in to a small hotel and wait for the arrival of his master. Trying not to look at the river Cris flowing lazily under the bridge, the young doctor crossed quickly. He found the Szamuely house strangely silent, though he heard a faint sobbing coming from the basement. He went down quickly. The place was in darkness, but a tall candle threw a pale light on the body of his son lying on a white trestle table. It was the boy's nurse who was crying. Julius took a deep breath and turned to the woman who stood up at his approach.

"Go heat some water and bring him clean garments," Julius said.

"But it is Shabbat!"

"The hell with Shabbat!" he replied. Startled, she scuttled away. He closed the child's eyes which showed surprise more than panic and waited. When she came back, they washed and prepared the little body together. The nurse, a stout young brunette who wore an ugly black dress, had chosen, without thinking, Georgy's favorite costume: a sailor's outfit. A few minutes later, clean and combed, the child rested on an embroidered white cloth flanked by two candles. Then and only then did Julius Matthias sit down to look at his dead son. The smooth little face; the rounded little body. Georgy loved sweets, and his grandfather never refused him. Once again Julius felt tears welling up, but then he heard heavy steps coming down. The pharmacist arrived with an old crone he had retained to prepare the body. The two men exchanged hostile glances.

"It was not necessary to violate the sanctity of the Shabbat to do by yourself a task better left to more qualified persons," said the older man savagely.

"The sanctity of Shabbat? You should have thought about it before abandoning my child to a slut in order to visit your mistress!" He thought the man would have a stroke.

"How dare you talk to me like that under my own roof!" bellowed the pharmacist.

"Don't worry. I shall not remain under this roof a minute longer than necessary. As soon as the shiva is over, I shall leave this accursed house forever, taking my son, Andreas, with me."

"I shall not allow it!"

"I don't need your permission. Now shut up and show some respect for the child lying here, the innocent victim of your despicable behavior!"

There was a dry cough and they both turned toward the entrance. Szamuely's wife had just come in with Magda. How much had they heard? Enough, probably. Golda's anguish was there for all to see as she gazed upon her beloved grandson. Julius looked at his wife. Her eyes were dry and her face expressionless. No one said anything. And then Rabbi Zussman arrived. The first thing he did was to gather the young doctor in his arms, who let the tears flow at this first manifestation of sympathy he had received since his arrival.

Not much later, a sad little group departed for the cemetery in the darkening night. In his arms, Julius was carrying the small body wrapped in a white shroud. After a while he realized that more and more people were joining the slow procession; members of the congregation to which Aaron had belonged for so long had come to accompany his grandson to his last resting place and were joined by some of Julius's colleagues from the hospital who had somehow heard of the tragedy.

In the vast cemetery, a flickering light guided them to where the gravediggers were finishing their task. Then the young father was forced to relinquish his burden and lay it down on the ground. The sad ritual got underway. But when it was Julius's turn to speak, he did not extol the goodness of the dead child and his many virtues, as was the custom. In a broken voice, he asked the child's forgiveness for not having taken better care of him, which was his solemn duty as a father. Then, in a strong and confident voice, he recited Kaddish, the prayer traditionally recited by a son at his father's grave.

It was all over soon. One by one friends and acquaintances laid small stones on the pitiful little mound and came to shake Julius' hand before fading into the night. Only then did Sandor, who had waited patiently until the end, walk out of the shadows. Wordlessly he drew his friend to him. The two men then turned their backs toward the house of the pharmacist who had already left with his wife and his daughter.

At some point the young doctor made two discoveries. The first, not so strange after all, was that he was hungry, having eaten nothing since noon. The second, barely more startling, was that from the moment he had arrived in Nagyvarad he had not exchanged a single word with his wife, the mother of the little boy that she had buried almost five years to the day after bringing him into the world.

5

BETWEEN PAST AND PRESENT

THE ANCIENT RITUAL OF SHIVA, a strict mourning period of seven days—hence its name, derived from the Hebrew word for seven—is intended to ease the living through the first days of sorrow and help them come to terms with the stark finality of death. In the morning the bereaved family went to the seldom-used drawing room to receive the callers who came throughout the week bringing sympathy and comfort. The wooden shutters had been partially opened to let in some light but keep out the June sun, and the place was in semidarkness.

Emil Szamuely, flanked by his wife and daughter, sat on a long upholstered seat. Julius, unshaven and with his shirt torn as tradition demanded, chose a chair opposite them but slightly to the right, in order not to have to face his father-in-law. A pitcher of iced water and some fruit had been placed on a table for the visitors. They started coming early. The friends of the pharmacist would shake his hand and sit down nearby after saluting the young doctor who was surrounded by his hospital colleagues. A little later, patients started trickling in surprising everyone. Julius was deeply moved. He had been back barely a year but had made his presence felt. For these men and women, he was not the poor boy who had married the rich pharmacist's daughter. To them he was the good doctor Matthias, their doctor. Their eyes shone when he remembered their names and asked about their health. He in turn drew a measure of comfort from their warmth. It did not assuage the terrible pain that tore at his heart but somehow let in a sliver of hope; perhaps with time it would lessen.

After three in the afternoon, his father arrived. The flood of visitors had temporarily stopped; the town was dozing in the heat of the first day of summer. The house was quiet. Emil and his wife were resting upstairs; so was Magda. Julius was alone in the gloom of the drawing room. Though he had not had any sleep the previous night, he was beyond tired, a sensation not altogether foreign to him; more than once he had gone to the university in the morning after a sleepless night spent at a patient's bedside. However, he knew he would have to rest soon.

Indeed, he must have nodded off for a few moments, because he opened his eyes to see his father. Julius had not heard him come in. Haggard, unshaven, his shirt torn, Aaron could barely stand. Without Sandor and Donna holding him upright, he surely would have fallen. The old man stumbled into his son's welcoming arms, tears flowing freely. Julius led him gently to an armchair and felt his pulse. It was far too fast.

"When did you leave Budapest?" Julius asked.

It was Donna who answered. "There was a train at seven in the morning, but we had to change twice. I told your father he should wait for a direct train, but he would not listen. He did not sleep at all last night and made us leave at five, even though no one was up yet. He ate absolutely nothing on the way, but I made him drink a glass of sweet tea at each stop, and he managed to rest a little. But it was very hot, and you know how stubborn he is: he absolutely refused to take off his jacket. I wrote a note to Anni asking her to tell Sandor to wait for us at the station if he could. He was there when we arrived which was a blessing because your father could not have walked another step alone. I wanted to go home first so he could eat something and change, but he would have none of it."

Under Julius's hand his father's pulse was getting steadier; Aaron breathed more easily. The old man smiled at his son and fell asleep. Donna gazed at him with anxious fondness and left, murmuring that she needed to refresh herself. Sandor wanted to take his leave but let himself be persuaded to sit for a minute, as long as the pharmacist did not come down.

The two friends exchanged glances. They were exactly the same age, and if the one had been marked by long hours spent in the sun, the other had been aged by his studies and daily contact with his patients. They did not have to speak to understand one another. Indeed, Sandor said, very quietly so as not to disturb Aaron, that he thought his wife was expecting again.

Julius tried to smile. "I suppose it had to happen. How old is the first one, nine months? I will come after the shiva, and we shall see."

"If it's a boy, we'll call him Georgy," added the farmer diffidently. His friend closed his eyes, fighting tears. Fortunately Donna walked in. Sandor got up, mumbling that he could not stay any longer, and hugged Julius before leaving. Aaron was still asleep.

"Do you think he will be all right?" asked his wife.

"I hope so," Julius replied. "He is tired—the shock, the heat, the lengthy train ride. You must make him rest."

"If only I could." She sighed. "He feels responsible, you know."

"Responsible? How? He was not even there!"

"I see you still don't know your father. He can—and does—feel responsible for anything that goes wrong in the family, especially if it concerns you. He wanted a son more than anything else, and he got one, but his wife had to die, and the guilt is tearing him apart to this day. Listen, Yuli, I have had a few words with the maids in the kitchen, and they told me everything. This is terrible! How could he…"

She stopped as heavy treads announced that the pharmacist was coming back with his wife and daughter. Aaron Matthias opened his eyes and straightened up. It was a fraught moment. There was open enmity in the glances they exchanged. Szamuely chose not to speak and sat on the couch. The maids brought in two pitchers of water and a plate of freshly baked biscuits. The afternoon visitors trickled in. At dusk Rabbi Zussman arrived with some of his congregants to pray Minha—the afternoon service. When night fell the visitors started leaving.

"Time to go home and get some rest," said Donna, and her husband stood up willingly.

"I am coming with you to help Father," said Julius in a tone that brooked no argument.

At that point Golda Szamuely surprised everyone by stating she was going as well, to get some fresh air. The night was balmy, a true summer night; the moon was high in a cloudless sky. Leaning on his son's arm, the old man set a slow pace for the little group; the trip, which normally lasted ten minutes, took half an hour.

When they reached the house, Golda surprised them again. "Donna, there is something I have to tell you. May I come in?"

"Well, of course, but you will have to wait a little. I must help Aaron into bed."

"Thank you. Julius, don't go. This concerns you as well."

The apartment the young doctor had found for his parents had only one bedroom and a large room doing duty as living room and dining room, with French windows leading to the garden. The windows were open that night and let in the scent of the flowers Donna had planted.

Golda, who had never been there before, could not hide her surprise. "Was it Manny who rented the apartment for your parents?"

"No, that was me," replied Julius, "but of course my sister helps with the upkeep."

"And do you think you will be able to keep on helping when you have your own apartment? Or have you forgotten your decision to move out of our home?"

"I certainly haven't, and I hope I shall be able to do both."

Golda shook her head without replying and sat down by the dining table. She was clearly impatient to get whatever she had to say off her chest and kept looking at the closed bedroom door, waiting for Donna to come back. Julius observed her with a measure of sympathy. She had lost a beloved grandson, and the whole town now knew that her husband was unfaithful. No doubt she had been aware of the situation, but still…He wondered what she so urgently needed to ask Donna. He did not have to wait long to find out. The minute his aunt came back, Golda went on the offensive.

"It is high time we had a frank discussion."

"What about?" Donna, who had sat down, was nonplussed.

"I want to know why you destroyed my daughter, not once but twice. I have never done you any harm; on the contrary, when you married, Aaron I defended you against those who would have ostracized you. I never said a word when Anna was included in the little group taking piano lessons with Ada Finkelstein. Yet it would have taken only one word from me—one—and Ada would have turned you down. When Magda decided to befriend your daughter, I said nothing and even welcomed her into our home. I wasn't expecting thanks, but I never thought she would slyly manipulate to steal my daughter's fiancé!"

"You know that Magda did not want the match—"

"Oh, please!" said Golda sharply. "Not that ridiculous argument again. Magda only pretended to want the pharmacy; she went there only to please her father. That union with our Budapest relative had been arranged for a long time. We were waiting for the young man to graduate from law school and for Magda to turn seventeen. She had never raised the slightest objection to the match."

"But—"

"Listen to me. Let us admit that for whatever reason, she had doubts. Maybe she did not want to leave Nagyvarad and move so far from her family. Maybe she was intimidated by Manny, who was older and far more sophisticated than the men or boys she knew. Young girls often feel insecure at that stage. She would have gotten over it. Manny would have known how to bring her round. She would have had a splendid wedding, would have wanted for nothing, and would have had a man of her own milieu for a husband—good looking, intelligent, and rich instead of that miserable Jozef she married to save face. But that would not have suited you, would it? When my poor child came to you with her fears, when she asked for your advice, instead of calming her, reassuring her, you hatched your dirty plot. The so-called fortuitous meeting between Anna, wearing her best dress and only too happy to steal the man intended for the girl who saw her as her friend. And you let her carry out her plan until it was too late to stop it. It is monstrous, you hear me? Monstrous!"

Julius, aghast, kept switching his glance from his aunt who, hunched in her chair, listened with no outward reaction to the damning words, to his mother-in-law, who was working herself into a frenzy. Could this be true? Could Donna be guilty of such duplicity and cause the ruin of a girl who had done her no harm in order to secure the happiness of one she saw as her daughter?

Golda was still talking. "Yes, you planned well. Your Anna is happy. And you ruined my daughter. She married that good-for-nothing Jozef. He should have been grateful, but instead he made her life a misery, was disrespectful to her, and told all and sundry it was her fault they didn't have children. Under our own roof! For six long years, Magda was in hell. Providence freed her. I hope I shall be forgiven for rejoicing at his death. My child was free. At twenty-four she was still young enough to start her life anew. Marry a man worthy of her. Leave the house where she was under her father's thumb. I didn't even wait until the shiva was over to start looking for a suitable match.

"In a matter of days, we had seven worthy candidates lined up. Magda is our only child, our sole heir. She had lost a lot of weight; she was a handsome, self-assured young woman. We had narrowed the choice down to two upstanding men from good families, with means of their own. She would have led the life she was meant to live. But you, Donna, would have none of it. I can't begin to fathom the arguments you used to make her agree to this preposterous match. This has nothing to do with you, Julius. You wanted to be a doctor and were ready to marry Magda—though, I wager, not without misgivings—to achieve your dream. You were better looking than the others, and my daughter told us she was fond of you. Still, she knew she would have to remain under our roof and be dependent on us for years to come. I opposed the match, but there was nothing I could do when Emil gave his blessing. I tried to believe I had been wrong, that things would work out for the best.

"Magda got pregnant, and we were overjoyed. The birth of Georgy was nothing short of a miracle. I dared to hope. I was wrong. When I see my daughter, I feel my heart breaking. She never smiles, and I can't remember when I last heard her joyful laugh—Magda, who was such a merry child. All she thinks about is the pharmacy. She neglects her own children. Yesterday, when our beloved little boy died, she did not shed a single tear. Julius, you are unhappy too, through no fault of your own. There is only one person here who is responsible for all this misery. Donna, I want answers."

"Golda, you are wrong," said the older woman soberly, "but I am not sure I can tell you things that touch upon your daughter that she told me in confidence."

"You must. I am sure Julius is as anxious as I am to know the truth."

Once again the young doctor's gaze went from one woman to the other. He wanted to understand but was afraid to discover what his aunt was hiding. He chose to shake his head without saying a word.

His mother-in-law stood up and put her fists on the table. "Donna, I rather thought you would refuse to answer and looked for a way to force you to. I believe I have found it. Yesterday Julius announced he would leave our house and take Andreas with him. My husband will do anything to stop him. That includes convincing Magda to refuse to go or to let the child go on the grounds that her husband is in no position to support her and the boy who is barely a year old. Julius can divorce her, but he is not going to get custody of his son."

She stopped to watch her son-in-law, who had gone pale at the reality of the threat, and went on. "Now, if you tell me what really happened, if you can convince me that I am wrong and that you acted in good faith, I can make Julius's wish happen. What you probably don't know is that I have far more money than Emil, and my family saw to it that I could use it freely. I own a house on the road to Cluj, a matter of minutes from the hospital. It is well appointed, and there is even a garden—not very large but big enough, surrounded by a stout fence. Andreas will be able to play safely there. It so happens that the place is vacant at this moment. Julius, if your aunt can persuade me, I shall turn the house over to you personally. Magda will not be able to refuse to follow you." She sat down and looked expectantly at Donna, who appeared shaken.

"What if you don't believe me?" asked Donna.

"All you have to do is convince Julius. I know him for an honest man. If he accepts your explanations, I shall make good on my promise, whatever my own reservations."

"Very well. This is indeed a generous offer. And maybe the time has come for him to know the truth. But you will have to let me tell you what happened in my own way—the way I lived through the events, the way I heard about them through Magda. Yes, your daughter and I got on rather well, and she knew she could confide in me and ask for my advice—the way I heard about them through Anna and even through you, Julius, though you probably don't remember,

"First let us go back to that summer morning in 1900. Manny and Magda, strolling along the river, met Anna. Anna was wearing her best dress, as you said. Golda, do you know how many dresses she had? No, don't try to guess. She had two dresses. A gray one she wore every day and a blue dress for Shabbat—that is the one she had on that day, a Shabbat, while she was walking with her little brother, as she did every Shabbat. Aaron left early for morning prayer, and Anna and Julius waited for him, and then they all came home for lunch. Magda often went to meet them, and she knew that around eleven in the morning she could find her friend sitting on a bench, always the same one, while the boy threw pebbles into the water. No need to arrange a meeting; Magda knew she would probably see her at the usual time and place. On one point you are right: even in her simple blue dress, already well worn, Anna is lovely. Now, let us turn to your daughter. How many dresses did she have then, do you remember?"

"What does it matter?"

"I shall tell you. In spite of the many dresses she already owned, you had six new outfits made for her for the first and subsequent meetings with her future husband and his family. She showed them off to Anna who could not stop talking about them. Now, which of these elegant outfits was she wearing on that all-important day? A brown dress, not cheap perhaps but one that made her look matronly. How could you possibly let her wear that? Why didn't you, as her mother, insist on something a little more flattering?"

"You know very well that..." Golda looked uneasily at her son-in-law.

"Julius is a doctor. You may talk freely."

"If you know the answer, why ask? Yes, it was the wrong time of the month and none of the new dresses would fit."

"Why not ask the seamstress to let out the seams?"

"Magda did not want to. She said that for a day or two, it was not worth it."

"Not worth it!" Donna shook her head. "For that first meeting with a young man who had never seen her! But never mind. The following week Magda and Anna met again at the same place. Anna wore her blue dress. But Magda? Magda had on an old dress that did not suit her at all."

"She still felt bloated. It didn't matter anyway; she had already told Manny she wasn't going to marry him, and he came back to see Anni, because he had fallen in love with her the first time."

"You believe this?"

"What do you mean?"

"Think about it. After months of negotiations about the dowry and the wedding, Manny came with his parents to meet the young lady who would be his wife. Now you are saying that on the very first day, she told him she didn't want to marry him. If this was true, don't you think he would have explained the situation to his parents and they would have returned to Budapest immediately?"

"He came back for your daughter!"

"Come on! He saw her for only a few minutes, with her little brother. Anna was young and shy; she probably didn't utter more than a few words. He may have found her charming, but that's a long way from considering marriage to a penniless girl, from deliberately deceiving his parents, letting them go ahead with the details of the marriage contract and coming back the following week."

"But that's precisely what happened!"

"Well, that is not what Anni said. She told me that Magda and Manny sat on the bench and had a long conversation. Magda appeared to know so much about banks and banking that the young man was impressed. Later she told Anni she had gone several times to see your banker friend, Baumholz, to ask him about his work. You probably remember. Anyway, my daughter just listened. Everything thus led Manny to understand that his attention was welcome. He therefore came back. There was another encounter on the bench with Anna and her blue dress. This time the talk was not about banks but about honeymoon plans."

"Impossible! You are lying."

Donna sighed. "Julius, you were still a child, barely ten years old, but do you remember that when you came home, you asked me why we could not go to Venice as well?"

"I think you're right," Julius replied. "Now that you mention it, it's all coming back. I didn't know where Venice was, and I asked. Anna shushed me, but Manny laughed and told me all about it. He mentioned gondolas, and when we came back, I asked you to draw me one. Funny, I had completely forgotten."

"What about you, Golda? Are you sure you didn't hear about Venice?"

"Yes, but it was all part of their plan! Magda explained everything later."

"Plan? What plan? Deceiving you, her mother, her father, Manny's parents? You don't find that strange?"

"What are you insinuating?"

"Let me get to the third and last meeting, two weeks after that second encounter. Manny came again, with his parents, to finalize everything. And what was the Szamuely heiress wearing then? The dowdy brown dress from the first meeting. Anna could not believe her eyes. Magda's hair was badly done and she looked awful. And you, her mother, did nothing. You let her receive her guests like that; you didn't insist on having the hairdresser come in, on putting some rouge on her cheeks, on making her wear something a little more flattering."

"She had been unwell, some stomach flu. She had been sick a few times. I wanted to postpone the visit, but she insisted—probably in order not to disappoint Anna. So what?"

"Golda, I am sorry, but you asked for it. Here was a young girl about to meet her intended. All of a sudden, she did not want him anymore. She put on weight, she wore ample clothes, she felt nauseous…"

"How dare you? You should be ashamed of yourself! Magda was an innocent young girl who knew nothing about men and didn't show any interest in them. She was forever reading books and never went out alone at night."

"Yes, she was innocent. Too innocent, and she knew nothing about the realities of life. What had you taught her—you, her mother? That the purpose of marriage was to have children; that only married people had children; that it was the woman's duty to submit to her husband for that purpose and only for that purpose. That this duty could be painful but had to be accepted without demur, for such was a woman's destiny. A duty that you, her mother, no longer had to endure, since you could no longer have children."

"I see that she hid nothing from you!" Two red spots were burning on the pharmacist's wife's cheeks. "And of course you told her the opposite?"

"I am sorry to say I did not. She was not my daughter, and I did not feel I had the right to do so. I assumed—wrongly, as it turned out—that she was better protected than I had been."

"What do you mean?"

"You see Golda, I was raised in complete ignorance, just like your daughter, maybe even worse. My parents were very strict. I never went out alone, and I wore long skirts and petticoats over thick woolen stockings. Once a week I would go with my uncle Herman to a farm in the countryside to buy eggs and live chickens, later to be ritually slaughtered in our yard. One morning Herman felt unwell. My mother was in poor health and never left her room; that's why at seventeen I wasn't married yet. Father needed me to keep house for him and take care of my little sister.

"Anyway, on that day Father reluctantly decided to send me to the farm alone—a matter of six or seven miles. The two baskets were ready, but they were heavy. The farmer's younger son bashfully suggested that I go in his cart; he had to go to town to buy supplies. I had seen him many times. He was a tall, silent young man, more at ease with animals than with human beings. I gratefully accepted, glad not to have to walk back with such a heavy burden.

"We didn't exchange a single word on the way. As we drew near, I asked him to set me down at the edge of the wood less than a mile from home because I didn't want people to see me with this Christian boy. He understood very well. When he stopped, I was afraid he would try to help me down, so I jumped quickly, and I stumbled. The pain was so intense, I thought my leg was broken. He knelt by my side and tried to feel my ankle. The stocking was too thick, so he took it off gently. Golda, I told you, I was an innocent young girl, but when he touched me…Nothing my parents had told me had prepared me for what I felt. Had I understood what was happening, I would have stopped him immediately. He was a good man, and he would not have forced me. But I didn't understand, and I let myself be carried away."

She sighed. "It happened nearly fifty years ago, but I have never forgotten that instance of pleasure in the forest. You know the rest. I found myself pregnant, and he did the decent thing and married me. Don't look so horrified. If I am telling you all this, it is because the same thing happened to your daughter. She didn't realize what was happening and did not try to stop it. And found herself pregnant."

"I don't believe you. She would have come to me for help, not to you."

"She knew I was a midwife. She hoped I could help her. There are, however, things I am not prepared to do."

"This can't be true. You are lying. She married Jozef three months later, and she had lost all the weight she had put on."

"After spending a month in Bucharest, ostensibly to get over the shock of Manny's wedding to Anna; in reality to get rid of the child."

"I don't believe it."

"Suit yourself. But on that fateful third encounter, Manny took one look at your daughter and understood immediately. He had some harsh words for her. Julius, Anna was in shock. She didn't want to leave her friend, so she sent you home to look for a glove she told you she had lost, and you complained bitterly about it. In any case Magda faced ruin. That was when she took off for home and made up that preposterous story about Manny falling in love with Anna in order to preempt him. When he arrived both sets of parents condemned him roundly. I must say he behaved extremely well under the circumstances."

"Because he married Anna?"

"Your daughter had not left him much choice. He could have told the truth and ruined her for good, since she could not have hidden her condition much longer. He could have gone back to Budapest, leaving my poor Anna with her reputation in tatters. He did neither. He kept silent and asked for my child's hand in marriage. I am convinced he eventually told part of the story—if not to his mother at least to his father. In any case you can see why Magda cannot bear to be in Anna's company."

Golda still refused to believe. "Weren't the young couple supposed to wed in September? If Magda was already showing in June—"

"She believed to the last minute that she would get rid of the child in time. She drank smelly concoctions; she stole medicine from the pharmacy. To no avail."

"I won't believe my daughter let herself be seduced by that Jozef. Besides, he would not have dared. And in their six years of marriage, he could not get her pregnant, while Julius did it almost immediately."

"Golda, who mentioned Jozef?"

That was too much. Golda hid her head in her hands. "Then who? No, it's not true. It can't be true. Why didn't she marry the man who had gotten her in that situation? Why Jozef?"

"Regarding the man responsible—forgive me, but I swore a solemn oath to your daughter. Suffice to say he could not have married her then. Now, why Jozef? She thought either he would not notice or he would keep his mouth shut and be happy to enter into a union with the heiress to a pharmacy. How wrong she was! He had noticed her comings and goings, had seen her silhouette and had understood. After the wedding he never let her forget. Never for a minute. Why do you think she let him treat her the way he did? She lived in dread that he would tell the world that the reason she could not have children was because of what had been done in Bucharest."

"My poor child, my poor little Magda. How dreadful. Donna, could you please make me a cup of hot tea with plenty of sugar? I need it."

All of a sudden, some of the tension had gone out of the room. "Dare I ask, then, why she married Julius?" asked the pharmacist's wife with a twisted smile.

"Even after the death of her husband, Magda didn't feel safe. She was afraid he had told her secret to one of his cronies, afraid that one day after she remarried, someone would come and threaten her with exposure. You have to understand that she still came to see me secretly, because she felt she could safely confide in me. I was aware of her fears. We talked a lot, and she knew how worried I was about the boy. I even told her if he could not be a doctor, he would enlist in the army. That's how she came to decide to marry him. She knew I would say nothing; neither would Manny or Anna. Regarding Yuli—she was convinced that even if he should learn the truth, he would do nothing about it. It was cold-blooded calculation on her part. What she did not take into consideration was that she would lose her freedom and remain her father's dependent forever."

"And yet…it doesn't make sense. I admit I noticed nothing, suspected nothing, perhaps because I so wanted that match with Manny. I had been planning it for years, selfishly perhaps. With my only child living in Budapest, I would have gone there frequently, perhaps settling down there to be near my grandchildren. You know how things stand between me and my husband. He wouldn't have opposed a separation, provided it was done discreetly. At the time he was not so bitter; he was a different man. But I digress. Emil is a difficult man, but he knows his job and is good at it. He studied hard, and after many years of answering his customers' queries, he has a fair understanding of medicine—which is why he is so jealous of you, Julius. So how is it that he saw nothing?"

"And who says he saw nothing? Who says he didn't understand, too late, what was happening? How else would that seventeen-year-old girl who had never left home have known where to go in Bucharest? How did she get the money? Why did he agree to that union with Jozef? Golda, you saw how that young man treated your daughter. Didn't you ever ask yourself why your husband let him get away with that? Emil too was terrified of a scandal. That's why Magda was so sure she could talk him into accepting Julius. What she didn't realize was there was a price to pay. Your husband has never forgiven her for putting him into this position. He tolerates her because of the grandchildren she has given him. He was going to leave the pharmacy to Georgy, and he let her know it. I once heard him saying it."

"If only she had come to me, trusted me...Yet something is still unclear. Why is Emil so set against you, Donna? And why does Magda, who knows the truth, not defend you?"

"That's easy. According to him I should have told him what was happening right at the beginning, when there was still time to do something about it—though what he meant by that I am not sure. Whatever it was, he couldn't have thought she would still be able to marry Manny. The young man would have known on their wedding night that his bride was no longer...Magda might have deluded herself into thinking that once the union was consummated, the groom would have said nothing, especially in view of her considerable dowry. But Emil knew better."

"Why didn't you tell him?"

"I did think about it. This was the very first thing that came to mind when I heard the story. The problem is... Golda, you know your husband. You know his temper. What would have been the outcome if he had learned about it, and from me? He would have been so furious, there would have been no reasoning with him. Today he sees things differently, but then? Magda was terrified at the very idea of having to confront him, and she swore she would throw herself into the river rather than face his wrath. She had me swear on Julius' head that I would keep silent. What could I do?"

She sighed. "Now, for her, I am part of a past she desperately wants to forget. She has also come to understand that she should have approached her father. Being what she is, she finds it easier to blame someone else, to accuse me of having deceived her, of having helped my daughter steal her fiancé, as she puts it, and live the life she wanted for herself."

"To think I saw nothing, heard nothing, understood nothing," said Golda. "My daughter had to go to a stranger for help. I let hell into my home. What to do now? Donna, I beg your forgiveness. You have been faithful and kept your word, and I have wronged you. Julius, tomorrow the house will be in your name. You can move in at the end of the week. I shall also make an allowance for my daughter so she will no longer be dependent on her father for everything. Perhaps all is not lost. She has a good husband, a man who is respected, who gave her two beautiful children." She stopped to wipe her eyes and went on. "And who, I hope, will give her many more. Now, son, I would be grateful if you walked me home. This has been an exhausting day."

6

TORMENTS

THE MOON WAS HIGH in the night sky, but under the leafy trees of the silent cemetery it was dark. Stirred by the wind blowing intermittently, the myriad leaves made a hushed sound, as if thousands of sighs were rising from the ancient graves. Here, near his mother and his infant son, the young doctor had found refuge. Having walked Golda Szamuely home, he had felt he could not possibly go in with her and somehow found himself on the road to the cemetery. Now, lying on a derelict tomb, his hands behind his head, he felt a pain almost physical, which rose and fell in waves while he contemplated a world that had just been smashed into smithereens.

False. It was all false. They had all lied to him from the first; they had all kept on lying to him year after year. He had let himself be led by the nose like the village idiot. The fairy tale he had been fed, of a starry-eyed Magda in love with him, was nothing but a sinister joke concocted to hide the truth. After the first bitter experience with Jozef, the pharmacist had been looking to forever bury a shameful secret and thought that in Julius he would find a naïve and compliant son-in-law. Far from being an act of generosity, sending him to pursue costly studies in Vienna had been a well-thought-out decision. Attending the more modest and less costly Budapest school of medicine had been out of the question; Julius would have been expected to live with his sister and her husband. Magda would certainly not have gone with him; there would also have been a very real risk of Anna telling her brother the truth.

There was more. The union of the Szamuely heiress to a mere stripling seven years her junior was bound to set tongues wagging. Better send the young man away for five years; he would come back more mature and with a doctor's diploma. Meanwhile busy tongues would have found other targets. The plan had been successful beyond the pharmacist's wildest dreams. The young man he had reluctantly accepted into his family was now a doctor and had given him two grandchildren. Two grandchildren...Julius tried not to think of Georgy, lying so close.

As for Magda, what he had felt instinctively soon after the wedding was only too true. She had never had the slightest fondness for him. She needed a husband and was not going to make the same mistake she had made in marrying Jozef. By opting for a youth who knew nothing about life, she intended to have someone too overwhelmed by the generosity and wealth of his new family to raise his head. Julius was handsome enough that she would not have to be ashamed of him. Had she even thought they would have children? Probably not. It was another lie. She must have feared that, as her first husband had taunted her repeatedly, she could not get pregnant because she had aborted her unborn child. Quite possibly her father was of the same opinion, and that was another reason for him to accept Julius. The other suitors wanted a family, children. They might have decided to divorce a barren wife. But Julius had sworn on the Bible never to leave his wife.

No, Magda had never thought she would be a mother and had resented the two children who had supplanted her in her father's affection and were going to be raised as his heirs. She had never cared for them. The young doctor could almost pity her. Seduced at seventeen, facing a catastrophic pregnancy and the trauma of an abortion; having to forgo an enviable match to settle for a despicable individual; at thirty still totally dependent on a father who had never forgiven her, trapped in another loveless union...

Almost—and yet! She could have attempted to make their marriage work. A few smiles, a little kindness would have done it. He would have paid her back one hundredfold. Who knew? She might have remained with him in Vienna, and their whole life would have taken a different turn. She had not made the effort. Was it because she was afraid her father would tell him the truth? Not only was there little danger of that, but she could have preempted the move by sharing her sad story with a husband who would not have condemned her for what had happened so many years before. Not immediately, perhaps, but maybe after the birth of their first child.

There was only one explanation. She did not care enough. She had no interest in him. She might even have chosen him to spite his sister and her husband who must have been appalled at the news. And that was another thing. Why hadn't they said a word? Manny, he could understand. Difficult to tell your young brother-in-law who is about to marry: "By the way, that old story about how I came to wed your sister? Pure invention. Fact is your wife-to-be was pregnant at the time, and not by me." But Anni, his beloved sister? The answer was obvious, and it was tearing him apart.

At the heart of that sinister plot, like a spider spinning its web, was his aunt Donna. She had known the truth from the very beginning—the whole truth. She had deceived him. Lied to him. How did he know she had not planted the idea of their marriage in Magda's mind? "I did it for you," she would probably try to explain. "You wanted more than anything to be a doctor. You knew exactly the price you had to pay and were more than ready for it."

Which was true. What was no less true was that she had manipulated him. Had Magda, and through her the pharmacist, been manipulated as well? What role had Donna really played in that fateful meeting between Anni and the young banker from Budapest fifteen years earlier? Had she pulled the strings behind the scenes in spite of her denials? What was left of the family history, as Donna had told it to him so many times? Who could he trust now?

There was more. What had Donna said? That Magda could not marry the man who had seduced her, since it was impossible *then*. What did she mean? That it would be possible today, the man having been freed by the death of his wife? When? Julius was not interested out of jealousy. He was remembering that unexpected visit his wife and his father-in-law had paid him in Vienna two years earlier. From what he knew of Magda, she had not been very keen on having a second child so soon. Andreas had been born a little early. Nothing significant, perhaps, except that the boy did not look at all like his brother and did not have the blond hair and blue eyes Gitte had bequeathed to all her descendants, the children of Anni included. Here, again, there was nothing significant, and yet…could it have been that Magda had met her fist love again, now that he was free?

A fresh wave of anguish engulfed Julius. What would he do if his wife told him he had no right to take Andreas, since he was not his father? Bathed in a cold sweat, the realization came to him that people who killed themselves were not necessarily crazy. To go to sleep forever, to never wake up, to never have to think…

Out of nowhere he thought he heard a deep halting voice. The voice of Sandor. "Yuli, stop it. You don't know what you are saying. Get some rest. Tomorrow things will be different. Stop feeling sorry for yourself. You are a doctor; you are respected. We are proud of you. You will find your way."

He sat up, searching the shadows. He saw no one. He was alone.

"Julius, my friend," he told himself, "if you start hearing voices, you really need to sleep." He drew his hand through his thick curls and yawned. Time enough to cross that bridge. If indeed his wife had so shamefully deceived him again, with the help of her father, he would consider himself freed of his vows. He would turn down his mother-in-law's generous offer and leave the city forever. Who knew? He may still have a future in Vienna…

Holding that thought to his heart, he did fall asleep. A dry cough woke him. He opened his eyes to a radiant dawn. A myriad of birds were saluting the new day in song. He stood up, still numb from his stone bed, and did a double take: his father was sitting at the foot of the tomb and observing him somberly. Was Julius hallucinating again? He tried to touch the black-clad illusion and found solid flesh.

"Father?" he asked uncertainly. "What are you doing here? How did you know I was here?"

"So many questions…I shall try to answer them all. Julius, my dear child, I don't know what went on last night—I was so exhausted that I fell asleep almost immediately—but it must have been bad, very bad, since your mother-in-law got scared when you didn't come home. She hoped you had gone back to us but wanted to be sure. So before retiring to her bed, she left a message for us with instructions for the coachman to deliver it as soon as he came to work, unless you had returned during the night. Which the coachman did. By chance I was already up, and I was the one to open the envelope. I say by chance because otherwise Donna would not have told me about it—to 'protect me' is the way she puts it. By the same token, she refused to reveal the subject of your discussion beyond the fact that you were beside yourself. So I asked the coachman to take me to the cemetery."

"But how did you know that was where I was?"

"Through one of these Talmudic exercises you despise so much. You see, my son, when I hurt, when I suffer, I find solace in praying. I go to my synagogue and I ask the Almighty to comfort me. If it doesn't happen, I bow to His will and find some peace nevertheless. But you, my boy, you have turned your back on the One who created you. I don't blame you for it: I bear my share of responsibility, and it is dreadfully heavy. I should never have let Donna raise you with a complete disregard of our religion. Mind you, when I became aware of the situation, it was already too late. Children have to be initiated into the faith of their fathers when they are very young, so they absorb it like their mothers' milk. However, it is too late now. You grew up without believing and now have nowhere to turn when confronted by so much unhappiness. I came to the conclusion that you would come to your mother or your poor little boy to find solace."

"Father, you amaze me. Having guessed where I was, why didn't you send the coachman to fetch me home?"

"You are not the coachman's son. You are my son! I deluded myself into believing I was the one to try to comfort you. I know for you I am a cranky old man who sees nothing beyond his books, but…"

Julius did not let him go on but embraced him warmly, surprised to discover some hitherto unsuspected strength in his wiry old arms.

"What's wrong, son? What happened yesterday evening? I beg of you, don't fob me off. Don't tell me there is no need for me to know. It would cause me unnecessary pain. Nothing you can do or say can hurt me more than what you did the day before yesterday when you left Budapest without saying a word and without taking me with you."

"Father! It was your last day with your eldest grandson, who was about to go abroad, maybe forever! How could I deprive you?"

"Deprive me! Did you stop to think if that was what I wanted? I had just spent a whole week in his company; I had been granted the happiness of watching him performing more than creditably at his bar mitzvah. Such was the image I wanted to keep in my heart. I was ready to say goodbye; in fact, I had already done so. I knew the last hours would be devoted to his friends and to the last preparations for his departure for America—a departure that fascinated and frightened him. Georgy—Georgy was something else. Karoly I hadn't seen much of. The little one I had known since he was born. I had seen him grow up, begin to talk. We used to meet nearly every Shabbat. Don't be so surprised. I knew what Szamuely was up to, knew he was leaving the boy with a servant. After the morning service, I would meet them by the river, and I would sit with him, tell him about the Bible and its heroes, make him recite his first prayers…I was starting to teach him letters, as I used to do in the Talmud Torah, by putting a little honey on the letters so he would know how sweet the holy texts were…"

Julius stared at him. Was the old man losing his mind? Meeting the little boy secretly and never saying a word about it? Impossible!

His father smiled. "It was not so difficult," he said, as if he had been reading his mind. "The servant whose task it was to take care of him was only too happy to leave him with me for one hour, the more so since I gave her a little money from time to time. Keeping her mouth shut was in her own best interest, so I could depend on her silence. And the boy understood it was better to say nothing. He was very intelligent, you know, and, like you when you were his age, he knew better than to mention these encounters when he came home, because his other grandfather would object and put an end to them.

"Don't look so surprised. Do you really believe I was not aware of what was going on when you were children? That I did not see the way you stopped talking when I came in and the sly smiles you exchanged with Donna and Anna? The forbidden foods you hid in the basement? I was weak.

You were three against me, and I did not have the strength to fight. I felt I had lost my rights—to you especially—by having caused the death of your mother. I did manage to make Donna stop taking Anna to the farm when she became a woman, in order not to ruin her chances of making a good match. It was hard, very hard for me to be so alone in the midst of my family. Anni and you, flesh of my flesh, blood of my blood, had become Donna's children, and I...I was the mean old man. Ah, well, all this is in the past. Georgy was the future, the pure light of my days..."

He stopped, drew a deep breath and went on. "The Almighty, who had given me this precious gift, saw fit to take it back, blessed be his name. I only wish I could have been there to say good-bye, to touch his beloved face one last time..."

"It was Shabbat!"

"It was Shabbat? Since when do you care about that? It would have been my problem, not yours. It would have been up to me to decide. And I would have chosen to go with you and do penance later."

"We drove like crazy. You would have been exhausted."

"Was an endless train journey better? No, you did not think, didn't even think of Donna, who adored the child." He sighed. "I know, I know, you thought you were acting for the best. Even on this dreadful occasion, you tried to take everything upon yourself—as usual. You have always been inclined to behave as you saw fit; now that you are a doctor of medicine, you never ask for advice. Even Manny noticed that. Yes, you have studied long and hard to obtain your diploma; what you forget is the Almighty, who endowed you with the gifts that make you a good doctor. You are kind to your patients and offer them warmth—with a touch of condescension."

Before Julius had had time to digest this less than flattering picture of himself, the old man went on. "However, these are not serious flaws; you will grow out of them as you grow older. Now I want to hear exactly what preys on your mind, and let me be the judge of what is good for me."

And so Julius told him the story from the beginning and the hurt he had felt at having been taken for a fool and lied to so many times. His father did not try to interrupt, though it was apparently new to him as well.

"So that's it!" Aaron exclaimed at the end. "To think that for nearly fifteen years I have been blaming my poor daughter, who was blameless!"

"Blameless? What did you think she's done?"

"According to the tale your aunt told me, your sister went several times in secret, on Shabbat, to meet a young man I didn't know, taking you along and making you an accomplice. Such behavior, from a young girl I had thought more respectful of the principles I had taught her, wounded me deeply. We never mentioned it, and I forgave her when I held my first grandchild in my arms, but I wish Donna had told me the truth. I can imagine why she didn't do so. As I explained to you, I had planned another match for Anni. I gave in because I believed her heart had been given to Manny; had I known that in fact my darling daughter had been as surprised by the young man's offer of marriage as I was, I would never have given my consent."

He added, with one of his rare smiles, "This is not what you wanted to hear, right? You expected me to share your indignation. Son, you have every right to be angry, though in fact it is more a matter of wounded pride than anything else. Consider the facts. Fifteen years ago there was no reason whatsoever for Donna to explain why Manny had forsaken Magda for your sister. It was none of your business, and at the time you would not have understood anyway. When the issue of a match between you and Magda was raised seven years later, why should she have mentioned something that was in the past? Be fair. She made what she knew was a monstrous proposal, knowing you would do anything to become a doctor. And you agreed to marry a much older woman, a widow, someone who you didn't care for in the least. Had you known all the facts, would you have behaved differently?"

"I don't know. Probably not, but as you said earlier, the decision was mine to make, and Donna should have told me."

"She'd given her word and she must have pitied Magda."

"Pitied Magda!"

"Do you truly think your wife was so happy with the match? After her first disastrous experience, she was going to find herself, once again, tied to a man she did not love and with whom she had nothing in common. By not telling you why she agreed to marry you, Donna was leaving her a measure of self-respect. There is nothing here to distress you."

"Father! You reserve your sympathy for someone who has behaved abominably and doesn't hide her hostility toward you...and you tell me, your son, that it is only my pride that has been hurt!"

"Your mother-in-law, according to what you reported, is turning a house over to you that will make you free of the pharmacist. After your period of strict mourning, when you resume your service at the hospital, you will once again be Dr. Julius Matthias, a respected member of the staff and a man who knows what he wants from life. As for your wife, what does she want from life? What can she expect from life? To wait for her father's death in order to preside over the wooden counter of the pharmacy? I have no sympathy for her, but that does not prevent me from pitying the woman."

"You don't know the rest!" Julius was indignant. The conversation was not going at all the way he had expected. He went on to mention his doubts about Andreas, the timing of his wife's visit to Vienna, and the curious thing Donna had said about the seducer "not being free then. "

Aaron Matthias took off his glasses and rubbed his eyes. "Georgy took after you and your mother; Andreas takes after his mother's side of the family, though it may be too soon to tell. Regarding the visit, you hadn't been home for months, you were nearing the end of your studies, and Magda's father was beginning to fear that you were not coming back and would stay in Vienna."

"I had given my word!"

"Yes, but maybe the pharmacist and his daughter do not consider oaths to be as binding as you do. Emil probably thought another baby would ensure your return and show the world that all was well in your relationship. Magda was given no choice in the matter: she did what her father told her. Stop making a monster of her. She is more to be pitied. Admit that these revelations, upsetting as they may have been, are not going to change anything in your relationship with your wife and with your father-in-law; they will, however, usher in a better understanding with your mother-in-law. Next week will be a new beginning for you. Try to make the most of it. Enough said. You must come back to the house. You must respect the week of mourning prescribed by our tradition and receive all those who will try to comfort us on the untimely loss of that little soul who so briefly brought us joy and is now at peace with his maker. Give me a few minutes to pray at his grave."

The young doctor hailed a cab to bring his father home. While Julius was taking a quick shower and changing into the spare clothes he kept there, Donna prepared his breakfast. They were alone; Aaron had gone to the synagogue to pray, as he did every morning. He must have talked with his wife before leaving, because Donna, her back to the wall, said softly, "Julius, I was wrong. Please forgive me." Tears were flowing down her face.

Julius ran to embrace her. "Don't cry, dear aunt. It's all in the past. You did what you thought was best. Let's forget about it."

"I must speak about it. You see, I should have told you it was quite possible your future wife could not have children, should have left the decision to you, only I was so afraid you would enlist—"

"You did right. I would have accepted anyway. And she did have children, so it turned out for the best."

"That is generous of you. There is just one more thing. Your father said you were uneasy at the thought that the man who had wronged Magda was now free. Well, it's not true."

"Why did you—"

"Why did I lie? Your wife's mother is an intelligent woman. Magda at seventeen was a very proper girl; there were not that many possibilities. Golda would have realized the truth, and it would have been a disaster for all concerned. That's why I steered her in the wrong direction. She will focus on widowers and not on dead people. Don't ask me more."

"No need. Not on dead people? I believe I know," said her adoptive son, who had a great memory. "It's banker Baumholz, right? He died four or five years ago. Correct me if I'm wrong." Seeing that his aunt was speechless, he continued. "It was not so difficult. Yesterday you explained that Magda, wanting to impress her intended, had met the man several times. The bastard took advantage of her, right? I bet Emil reached the same conclusion. Still silent? I bet also that he made him pay through the nose for the so-called trip to Bucharest. Don't look so shocked. You did well to inform me. It is not that I am jealous, but a man needs to know that the children he is bringing up are indeed his."

"Julius, Julius, how you do go on! You are being unfair to your father-in-law. When he discovered what had happened, he was ready to murder Nathan Baumholz. Only—"

"He was afraid of the scandal?"

"Perhaps, and yet…Nathan—well, he behaved badly. He was already sixty at the time, and he got the impression that Magda…Magda was well aware…I mean, when he discovered that it was her first time, he nearly had a heart attack. He was horrified and wanted to tell Emil. It was Magda who said no, in order not to jeopardize her chances of marrying the Nagy boy."

"You believe that?"

"What I believe is of no importance. Nathan convinced Emil, and it couldn't have been easy. Confronted by his testimony, Magda admitted the facts; she told me so herself. In the end Baumholz made a substantial contribution to the association helping the poor girls of our community."

"Why don't you want Golda to know?"

"The banker's widow is her best friend to this day. I am sure she knows nothing. What would be the point? Julius, it happened many years ago, when you were a mere child. The best we can all do is put the whole thing behind us."

"I have one last question. What really happened at that first meeting? Why did Magda lead Manny to the bench where she knew Anni would be? Was it your idea?"

"My idea? Of course not! You should know your wife better. She wanted to show off the rich and handsome young man she was going to marry to her friend, who was much better looking than she was but penniless. Incredible as it may seem, she believed to the end that she would get rid of the child and marry Manny. When she realized he had discovered her secret, she ran to her parents and complained that he was deserting her for someone else. She never thought he would call her bluff, and she has never forgiven him for what she perceived to be a deliberate insult. She never forgave your sister either for having stolen her intended. She can't bear to see either of them, but she is particularly vindictive toward your sister who is living the life she'd wanted for herself."

"Yet you did not hesitate to suggest that she marry me..."

"I, suggest it? My dear boy, the thought never entered my mind! It was all her idea. Just think about it. How could I have made such a suggestion knowing the hostility, the enmity, of Emil and Golda toward our family? You see, Magda and her father were still living in dread of having the truth emerge. One solution would have been to tell the truth to her future husband, but after the Jozef episode Emil was not ready to risk it. It was Magda who mentioned your name. At first Emil would not hear about it; however, she argued that you would never say a word. I have yet to understand why she did it. In any case Magda came to me with the idea, and I was literally struck dumb. I don't remember what my answer was, but I do know that I did not even mention it to you. It was only later, when it became clear you were seriously considering going into the army, that I began to wonder whether that would not be a better solution. Emil eventually agreed to pay for your medical studies because he had already accepted the idea of that union and understood you would not back down."

"All right. Why does Magda now pretend to hate you, as Emil truly does?"

"I was her confidante for many years; she came to me with her sad stories about Jozef, told me how unhappy she was. When she became a widow, she asked my advice about the men courting her. Today she is married, her father's succession is secured, and she does not need me anymore. She is also well aware of the fact that I will always take your side. So she turned her back on me. The father—he still believes that had I told him the truth then, he would have been able to do something, and he accuses me of not having done so because I wanted Anni to marry Manny. Enough said. You have to go back. The first visitors will be arriving."

7

A DISTANT THUNDER

THE WEEK OF RITUAL MOURNING ended not a moment too soon, given the blatant enmity between the two families. Julius, who now knew the true causes of that enmity, understood better why Magda would not accept her sister-in-law's embrace and refused to shake hands with Manny. He noted bitterly that she showed more emotion on that occasion than at the time of her child's funeral.

Emil Szamuely completely ignored the two visitors who had come all the way from Budapest and did not exchange a single word with them. He professed himself offended by the fact that the Nagys had chosen to stay at the Park Hotel. This former residence of a Hungarian nobleman was famed for its opulence and was considered the most luxurious establishment in the province. For his part, Julius did not talk to his father-in-law and turned his back on him whenever he approached.

His mother-in-law was another matter. She kept her word and turned over the house at number 4 Schools Road, in the newest part of a predominantly Jewish neighborhood, halfway between the hospital and his father's home. Aaron Matthias, though happy for him, was upset that the transaction had been carried out during the shiva. Yet he refrained from commenting when Julius and Magda moved out on Thursday evening, taking with them baby Andreas and Ditta, his nurse.

Magda had tried to object, but she knew it was a closed issue now that her own mother had turned against her, as she put it. Not only had Golda given her daughter's husband the means to escape, she had told Magda that she now knew the truth about what had happened fifteen years ago—and so did Julius. However, though she would not admit it, the young woman was secretly looking forward to her new life. Julius had told her the past was the past and held out his hand to her; for the first time she would be the mistress of her own household, with sufficient funds to make her own decisions. Her father, not wanting to lose face, was making a generous allowance to the couple.

With a smile and a wave, Magda saw her husband off to work before turning contentedly to unpacking. She was assisted by Viola, the cook, a matronly woman of some forty summers who had previously worked for some distant Szamuely; and by Irena, the maid, who was the second cousin of Martha Toth, Sandor's wife. Ditta was busy organizing the nursery. It was a fine day and the young doctor was doing his best not to dwell on the loss of his beloved child but to focus on the resolutions he had made after his encounter with his father at the cemetery. He would make an effort to get on better with his wife. She was bitter because she had suffered; he would try to be patient and understanding. He would also heed his brother-in-law's advice.

"Julius," an incredulous Manny had told him, "what is the matter with you? You have been back a whole year, and you know no one here, absolutely no one! Having an office at the hospital is all very well, but it is with your private patients that you will make your fortune. Don't sneer. Do you want to remain dependent on your in-laws forever? Or worse, on your wife the day she inherits? You must take your place in society as well. I am not talking about the petit bourgeois cronies of your father-in-law or the community leaders you meet at the hospital or through your father. You have here a secular Jewish elite, educated in Vienna just like you were. Professors, architects, engineers, bankers. I am sure you would enjoy their company, and I am convinced they will be happy to welcome you into their circle."

"You are probably right," Julius had replied ruefully, "but it is too late. I can't see myself going to receptions in the coming year of deep mourning."

"Receptions! But who is talking about receptions? This is not about going to cabarets—are there any here, by the way?—or to the theater. There is absolutely no reason you shouldn't have a quiet drink with two or three people or accept a dinner invitation at a private residence. I am acquainted with some of the bankers in the group, and I shall have a word with them."

What Dr. Julius Matthias did not know as he made his way to the hospital on that Sunday, June 28, 1914, his head full of projects, was that on that very same day the state visit of the heir to the double monarchy in Sarajevo, a city hundreds of miles away, was about to plunge the whole of Europe into chaos. Crown prince Franz Ferdinand of Habsburg and his wife, Sophie, targeted by an anarchist

bomb in the morning, miraculously emerged unscathed…
only to die in the afternoon by the bullets from a Serbian
nationalist. The news reached Nagyvarad too late to make
the Monday papers, and Julius left for work in excellent
spirits. He had spent the night with Magda in their conjugal
bed; had taken his breakfast in the ground-floor dining room,
looking through the window at the well-tended garden;
and had encountered Ditta on the stairs, on her way to the
kitchen, with Andreas in her arms. The child had beamed
at his father and had made merry sounds in his direction.

The young doctor was intermittently racked with guilt:
what right did he have to feel so happy when this new situation was brought upon by the tragedy that had befallen his
family? Magda had never been so welcoming and smiled a lot;
he spent many hours with Andreas, who was taking his first
steps. A sunny child, always chortling and babbling with glee,
he was developing a special fondness toward Grandfather
Aaron, who had taken to visiting nearly every day now that
his son lived so close.

The death of the heir to the throne was the main topic
of discussion at the hospital, and indeed everywhere else,
but there was no sense of impending doom. The shock
was all the greater when, on July 28, a month to the day
after the assassination, Austria, having secured the support of German Kaiser Wilhelm II, declared war on Serbia.
Manny, who heard it first, called his brother-in-law on
the telephone installed in the house as a present from the
banker and his wife. Anna had stilled her brother's protests
at the gift by explaining that through the telephone she
would also be able to keep in touch with their father. She
had not gone to Switzerland with the children because of

the political crisis, and she called every Monday to talk to Donna and Aaron, who had begun to come to lunch at the Matthias' on that day. Her husband, who was increasingly worried about the situation, called Julius in the evening at least once a week.

The young doctor did not share his pessimism. Everything was going so well. The future looked bright. He was beginning to enjoy the charms of his bourgeois life. The servants addressed him respectfully as Dr. Matthias and hastened to do his bidding. True to his word, Nagy had recommended him to a few of his business contacts; one of the most influential invited Dr. Matthias to an informal meeting at his mansion. He was introduced to the Austrian Circle, a select group of Jewish notables born or educated in Vienna who held regular meetings in the safety of their homes so as not to attract undue attention. Though by far the youngest, he was welcomed warmly, the medical profession being held in great esteem at the time.

Jewish tradition forbids shaving during the year of ritual mourning, and Julius's beard (trimmed in secret) gave him an aura of maturity. He knew when to keep silent and spoke only when he had something to contribute. Through his new contacts, the number of his private patients was growing. As he explained ruefully to his sister on the telephone, this warlike agitation was decidedly inconvenient. However, it soon worsened. Like a ghastly game of dominoes, greater and smaller states, bound by old and new alliances, tumbled into the fray: Austro-Hungary, Germany, and later Turkey on one side; Serbia, France, Britain, Russia, and later Japan on the other. Romania and Italy chose to sit on the fence and see which way the wind blew.

Though Nagyvarad had thus far remained on the fringe of the fighting, many rushed to enlist. Sandor, who wanted to do so, was persuaded to desist by his wife who told him that since both his brothers were career soldiers, his first duty was to keep the farm going. Julius did not have to ponder the issue: the hospital and its doctors were drafted by the army. Since he could no longer see patients at the hospital, he received the poorer ones twice a week at his father's house and visited the wealthier at their homes.

Yet at first the war had little impact on the young doctor's life. His wife went to the family pharmacy every morning, though what she did there was a mystery; he walked to the hospital as usual. True, the beds were now filled with wounded arriving from the front where the Austro-Hungarian forces were reeling from defeat to defeat. This was a different type of medicine but one he mastered quickly. Days, weeks went by, and summer was about to make way for autumn. Magda had never looked better; her husband's trained eye had revealed the reason to him well before she made up her mind to announce this new pregnancy. She did so a week before the Jewish New Year, which fell on September 21 that year. Julius did not have to feign happiness; he was truly delighted with the news.

Magda seized the occasion and pleaded for him to accept her father's invitation to have the festive Jewish New Year's dinner at his home. The two men had not met since Julius had moved out of the pharmacist's mansion, swearing never to return. Golda visited her grandchild regularly and took him to see his grandfather once a week. Julius's first impulse was to say no; on reflection he suggested a compromise. He would host the dinner, and Aaron and Donna would also be invited. He added, for good measure, three other Jewish guests: a handsome lieutenant from Budapest and the Kahns, an Austrian couple. The first, who had been wounded and evacuated to Nagyvarad but was now on the mend and about to go back to his unit, was barely older than the young doctor, and they had become friends. Theodore Kahn was an architect and a member of the Austrian Circle. Being rather short, the shoes he had specially made to add a few precious inches gave him a mincing gait, leading some people to believe he was effeminate. They could not have been more wrong: Theo was a determined skirt chaser. He was not truly good looking but had a great deal of charm and a sense of humor that made him the life of the party. He came with Isobel, his wife, called ZsaZsa by everyone, who was equally short and fairly stout but full of wit. Her fine dark eyes made her rather indifferent face look beautiful. Fully aware of her husband's straying, she looked on him with an indulgent fondness Julius was hard put to understand.

The evening was a great success. Aaron, sitting at the head of the table, gave the blessings; Isobel flirted in turn with the pharmacist and with the officer while her husband talked about Vienna with an unusually animated Magda. Golda and Donna had lengthy whispered conversations. No one mentioned the war, and no one appeared to notice that the pharmacist and his son-in-law had not exchanged a word. Toward the end of the dinner, Szamuely toasted his daughter and expressed his hope of seeing the family grow before the end of the year. Magda answered, smiling, that he might get his wish before Passover. All joined in congratulating her, and Golda embraced her son-in-law and thanked him for having at long last brought happiness to her beloved child.

Winter came early that year, and abundant snow made the roads impassable. Sledges and their burly coachmen replaced carriages in November. Andreas never tired of watching the flakes falling and turning the garden into a mysterious landscape where white-robed trees assumed fantastic shapes. Not everybody rejoiced with him. Grandfather Aaron, who stubbornly insisted on walking to the synagogue every morning, stumbled and fell one day. Winded, he could not muster the strength to get up; a kind neighbor found him one hour later, shivering and blue. It was two days before his son, worried after not having heard from him, went to see him. By that time pneumonia had set in. Before the war Julius would have taken him to the hospital, but this was no longer possible. Therefore, he had him brought to the house on Schools Road in spite of Aaron's protests—and Magda's.

Donna was in charge of seeing that the room Aaron occupied on the ground floor was locked at all times; little Andreas had an inquisitive nature and, now that he could walk, was all over the house. Aaron mended slowly—so slowly that letting him go home was out of the question. After lengthy consultations with the Nagys, Julius came up with a solution: building a small one-story house for them at the foot of the garden. Money was not going to be a problem, the banker having readily agreed to help; what would be more difficult was finding workers and materials in wartime. The young doctor turned to his friend, Theo, who drew up plans and then directed him to a local builder, explaining with a wry smile that it would be best.

"I could have recommended a colleague, one of ours, who would have done a good job for a good price. However, there would have been talk. You, my dear Julius, live in your ivory tower and don't sense the mood outside it. You would be surprised to discover the number of your fellow citizens who are convinced the Jews precipitated the war and are deriving enormous profits from it. The man I am sending you to will charge you more than he should and will boast of it, which will effectively tone down criticism against you. Furthermore, he is crooked enough to have the right contacts in the municipality and will easily get the permits you need."

Julius thanked him and followed his advice without mentioning that he was well aware of the change in the mood of the country. In the past his contact had been mainly with Jewish medical personnel and Jewish patients; now he was working alongside military doctors who were not Jewish. Some of them made no effort to hide their disdain for their Jewish colleague.

"My dear Matthias," one of them told him patronizingly one day, "this is not your fault. You may be among the best of them, but Jews are an inferior race."

He had been taunted into replying rather more sharply than he would have wished. The other had his answer ready.

"You know, it is the same with pigs: they too do not understand why they are being slaughtered."

Fighting to keep his calm, Julius asked him why his god had chosen a Jewish girl to bear his son. The man nearly had a stroke. As luck would have it, he left the hospital to go back to the front a few days later. Thus forcibly reminded of his brother-in-law's warnings, the young doctor tried to talk it over with his wife who looked at him as though he had suddenly lost his mind. Hungarians, Romanians, Austrians, and Germans hated Jews; that was a fact of life not worth discussing. He should not have been surprised. Magda showed little interest in events in general. Contrary to the stories her mother had told him, he never saw her with a book in hand. She ran the house indifferently, mostly relying on the servants, though she barely spoke to them. She still devoted her time and energy to the pharmacy. Was it to be close to her father? Julius refrained from putting the question to her. No need to rock the fragile equilibrium that made life more pleasant.

On the last day of the year 1914, the temperature was well below freezing and the Matthias family stayed in the warmth of their home. Most of the town's inhabitants stayed in their own homes as well. This was not a time for rejoicing. The war was dragging on, with little success for either side. New rows of tombs in the town cemetery testified to the heavy price paid so far. Dozens of young men who had left so joyously to fight for their country had come home in pine coffins; dozens more had been wounded.

There were rising tensions between the different communities. Romania had yet to enter the war, and there was much bitterness against the large Romanian minority. Yet it was the Jews who suffered most, in spite of their declarations of patriotism and the substantial contributions made by prominent Jews. They were accused of having fomented the war: hadn't the archduke been assassinated by anarchists? True, the man who had fired the fatal shot was not Jewish, but it was a well-known fact that most anarchists and revolutionaries were Jews. As for those who were not political activists, they were bloodsuckers, getting rich at the expense of the people.

All this led to some low-grade incidents: insults hurled at respectable Jewish matrons; harassment of pious Jews on their way to prayers; in one instance an old man's ceremonial fur hat was seized and thrown into the muddy street to be gleefully trampled on. Nothing serious, or so said the community leaders trying to reassure themselves and their flock; all would be forgotten in the euphoria of the victory that was sure to come.

Change was also coming to Schools Road. Magda, who had put on far too much weight, refused to listen to her husband's entreaties to look after herself. She was impatiently expecting the birth of her third child. She was set on having another boy and would not even entertain the thought it might be a daughter this time. Golda had remonstrated her but to no avail.

The small house at the far corner of the garden had been completed in record time, and Aaron and Donna Matthias moved in. They found the new situation perfectly to their liking. They had their own home while being near enough to call for help should Aaron feel unwell; indeed, a bell had been affixed outside the bedroom wall, and trials had shown that it could be heard all over the big house. Irene, the Matthiases' chambermaid, came twice a week to do the heavy cleaning. Best of all, they had unlimited access to their beloved grandchild.

Magda, who had welcomed them grudgingly at first, now passed the running of the household into Donna's capable hands. The only downside of the new arrangement was that Dr. Matthias could no longer see his patients in his father's house. He had to look for a suitable locale and for a trusted female assistant, since his aunt could not leave her husband for long. His newfound friends from the Austrian Circle came up with a solution. Salomon Kalman, one of the architects in the group, had a vacant office suite on the first floor of the Black Vulture Palace, one of the best-known architectural gems in the town, a huge ensemble straddling three streets, with a distinctive glass roof. Built but a scant few years earlier, the place was a great success and was busy night and day. As an added bonus, Amelia Schwartz, a childless widow who worked for Kalman, agreed to act as a secretary for the young doctor who had surgery hours only in the evening. This boosted his fledgling clientele. Indeed, things were moving too fast for him, and he soon found himself busy beyond belief. He no longer had time for leisurely trips to the farm and barely succeeded in being there in time to deliver Martha's second child, a boy, in January. The proud parents called the baby Georgy, a name Julius received with mixed feelings.

That year Purim, the happiest of the Jewish festivals and the children's favorite, fell during the last weekend in February. Aaron declared his intention of taking his little grandson to the Friday evening service, and Julius promised to do his utmost to get home in time to go with them. Andreas was too young to understand, but was full of excitement at the idea of the outing; he was delighted with the brand new clothes bought for the occasion and could not wait for his father to arrive. He kept running to the door at every noise, real or imagined.

Magda, who was home early because she felt unwell, was in a foul mood. Scolding the child for his antics, she yelled that unless he stopped immediately, she would take off his new outfit, put him in pajamas, and send him to bed without dinner. Andreas, terrified, ran screaming to the door; having managed to wrest it open, he made for his grandfather's house. An incensed Magda gave chase. Losing her footing, she fell heavily, hitting her head on the ornamental stone border of the path and lost consciousness. Andreas's cries brought Donna, Ditta, and Irena running.

By chance Julius was just stepping into the drive. Throwing off his heavy coat, he handed it to Donna and told her to take the boy home with her. "Don't argue. I don't want the child here. Leave him with Father and come back. The maids will help me get her inside."

Carrying Magda was not an easy task, so they decided not to take her to her bedroom upstairs and settled her in the small downstairs room. A difficult time ensued. The head wound was minor, but the shock had induced labor a month prematurely. There was no time to fetch the old doctor who had ushered Julius's first two children into the world, and it was left to the young father to deliver a brown-haired baby girl so tiny that his heart missed a beat. Not for long. She started yelling with a strength that brought relieved smiles to the faces of Julius and Donna, who had helped him with quiet competence throughout the birth.

Magda turned her head away with bitter disappointment, refused to take her daughter into her arms, and stated that she did not intend to nurse her. Nothing her mother, hastily summoned, said to cajole her moved her. It seemed the pharmacist was just as disappointed with his daughter; he did not come to see little Elisabeth—a name chosen by Donna and Golda, who, by chance, both had grandmothers by that name.

That very same evening, a wet nurse showed up; it turned out Magda had engaged her a week earlier. Evidently Magda had never intended to nurse the new baby, even had it been a boy. Two months after the birth, she went back to the pharmacy. An indignant Donna took over, spending hours with little Elisabeth, who did not seem to be affected by her mother's indifference. She ate voraciously and gained weight just as she should have. With the coming of spring, she was often taken to the garden, and big brother Andreas came to sit next to the heavy baby carriage, telling her incomprehensible stories that she rewarded with fuzzy smiles.

Julius now started his day with a visit to the baby, and he never went to bed without going to her room to check that everything was as it should be. He had been deeply hurt by his wife's behavior. He knew she did not care much for her children, but this was going too far. Julius and Magda barely exchanged a word these days, and the young doctor moved to the small room downstairs, under the pretext of not waking her up with his comings and goings at irregular hours.

For her part, Magda always made sure to go down to breakfast after he had left for work. This did not mean that the young doctor ate alone. Ditta brought Andreas down, and the two men of the family spent some quality time together. This was fortunate, since most of the time the child was in bed when his father came home. Dr. Matthias had never been so busy. As soon as he finished his shift at the hospital, he went to his clinic where he had so many patients Amelia had to turn some of them away.

Whenever he could he took his little family—Donna, Ditta, the nurse, and the two children, but without Magda, of course—to the farm. Sandor joined him, and they went for long jaunts in the forest, leaving the womenfolk to take care of the small ones. For two or three hours, he could forget all about his problems at home and at work and again become the carefree youngster who had roamed the woods with his best friend. When they returned to the farm, they were met by Martha, who always left everything to greet her husband with a passionate kiss while Julius looked forlornly on.

Donna enjoyed these outings so much that when the young doctor could not leave the hospital, she would hire a coachman to take them to the farm. Martha, who called her Auntie, always welcomed her with a smile, and the two swapped recipes and family stories amid much laughter.

The months went swiftly by. The first anniversary of Georgy's death was getting nearer. The commemoration was to take place according to the Jewish calendar on Wednesday, June 9. It would be marked by the unveiling of the tombstone Aaron Matthias had chosen and paid for, brushing aside his son's protestations.

Donna had waylaid Julius on his way to work. "Yuli," she had said, "let your father do it. He is still upset because he was not at the funeral. By choosing the stone and the text to be engraved there, he feels he is doing something for the child he loved so much. Don't worry. The generosity of you and your brother in law has left us in a position to do so."

A week before the ceremony, Magda came down early and sat down to breakfast with her husband. Barely touching her food, she announced defiantly that she needed a rest and was going away to Bucharest for a month with her mother. Romania was still sitting on the fence and had not yet chosen its side in the conflict, and the country was peaceful.

"When are you leaving?" Was Julius's indifferent response.

"Sunday."

"You mean the Sunday after the ceremony?"

"No, I am leaving this Sunday, upon my doctor's advice. He believes it would be too much of an ordeal for my nerves to attend. Don't look at me like that. You don't care about me. You should worry about my health instead of getting all worked up about a rite that has no meaning for you. You are no more observant than I am. In any case, my mind is made up. My father has agreed, and he is going to accompany my mother and myself in his new automobile. He needs a vacation too. He has not taken one in years."

"I am happy for him and for myself. Believe me, I won't miss him. As for you, my dear, let me tell you that your health and your nerves would be all the better if you lost some weight. A lot of weight."

"How dare you...My doctor..."

Julius was not listening. Throwing his napkin down on the table in a rare show of temper, he strode out without a backward glance.

It had been decided to hold the unveiling early in the morning, so friends could attend before going to work. Two weeks before summer was supposed to start, the sky was overcast, and a bitter wind was blowing. Rabbi Zussman, who was getting on in years, had come to support Aaron. There were many colleagues, and Julius's friends from the Austrian Circle were all there. He barely saw them. It was not tears that blurred his vision. Barely a year had gone by, and he could no longer clearly see the face of his beloved firstborn, and when he tried to remember his voice, he heard Andreas's sunny laugh instead. Yet facing the white stone with the two dates so terribly close, symbolizing the the child's all-too-brief stay in the world, he was crushed by the burden of guilt while his heart broke again. He knew his father was nearby, heard Donna sobbing, but could not find the strength to comfort them. A cold drizzle started falling as the last prayers were said. His friends came to shake his hand and left quickly, but Theo, the architect, lingered to ask for news of Magda, whose absence, and that of her parents, had raised a few eyebrows.

"Is she unwell, or could she not face...?" He asked politely.

"Neither. She was tired and left for Bucharest with her father and her mother."

"Nothing serious, I hope?"

"No, just a vacation."

His friend looked at him strangely and asked when she was coming back.

"I don't know exactly. Three or four weeks, I expect. Why?"

"Nothing. She promised ZsaZsa...but it doesn't matter. Let's talk about it later."

Julius watched him go. What could his wife have promised ZsaZsa? Magda had stopped going to the meetings of the Circle months ago and refused to hold any, citing first her delicate state of health and then her tiredness. When had the two women met? And why? On the other hand, why should Theo lie? It was all very strange, but probably of no consequence.

Setting the matter aside, he turned his attention to work. More than fifty soldiers wounded in battles on the Russian front had arrived that morning; the hospital was so overcrowded that camp beds had to be set up in the corridors. He left later than usual and reached his clinic around six in the evening.

Theo was waiting for him. "I told Amalia it would take only two minutes," he offered by way of explanation. "Let's go into your office." He waited until they were safely inside and out of hearing of the other patients and turned an embarrassed face to his friend. "I want to explain about this morning. I could see you did not quite understand me, and I would not have you think that your wife and I…" Theo, who knew his reputation only too well, raised his hands.

"Don't worry, it did not enter my mind," replied Julius sincerely but with some bitterness.

The architect plunged on. "When you signed the contract for this place, Salomon Kalman noticed your date of birth. He told us—I mean, the friends in the Circle—that you turn twenty-five on June 18. Twenty-five. That's a landmark in a man's life. You must know we are all very fond of you; we thought we would surprise you with a little celebration, which would also mark the end of this long year of mourning. ZsaZsa went to see your wife at the pharmacy, to agree on a suitable date and a gift to go with it. Magda did not seem enthusiastic but promised she would think about it and let us know. She must have forgotten. Now you know. It won't be a surprise, but we all hope you will set a date and be with us. As for the gift, tell us what you want, or take your chance with our choice. No, don't answer, let's talk about it later."

After a moment's hesitation, he covered his friend's hand with his own. "Listen, Julius, since I married early, I could be your father, so allow me to talk to you frankly. Magda and you…it is not working very well. Things like that happen in arranged unions. Nothing dramatic if you know how to behave. Don't let her make you unhappy. Organize your life differently. You adore your children, you have a pleasant home, and you are dedicated to your work. All you need is a nice woman to provide on the side what you are not getting at home. Don't look so shocked. We are not talking about a kept woman. Believe me, in our little world you could easily find someone who has a good situation and is perfectly respectable but would like nothing more than to have a fling with a handsome young man like you."

Julius burst out laughing. "Good idea. I shall think about it when I have time, though as far as I know there is no widow in our circle."

"Who said anything about a widow? Heavens, what an innocent you are, and you, a doctor! See, my boy, after many years even happily married couples enjoy going elsewhere once in a while—even if they still love one another. ZsaZsa and I, we have been married for a quarter of a century, since the year of your birth. We were young and passionately in love. Today she is my best friend, my confidante; my little adventures don't bother her as long as I behave with circumspection. Enough said. I must run before your faithful Amalia kicks me out."

When Dr. Matthias finally made it home that night, all was dark, and the house was silent. He ate quickly, standing in the kitchen and went up to the children's room. Andreas was fast asleep, cradling his teddy bear, a little smile on his face; Elisabeth was not in her crib. He found her in the nurse's room, who had fallen asleep in her bed with the baby at her breast. He lifted the child, who did not wake up, and had to avert his eyes from the woman's swollen breasts, who moved slightly, revealing a rounded belly, and turned around, kicking the sheets in the process and displaying a lush body that made his breath come faster. He felt she was no longer asleep and was showing herself complacently to him, perhaps to signal that she would not mind going further with her master…It took an effort of will to tear himself away and hurry back to the children's room.

The baby, a drop of milk at the corner of her mouth, went on sleeping when he deposited her in her crib, and he walked out on tiptoe. Still troubled by the voluptuous figure of the nurse, he could not sleep. He finally gave up, dressed quickly, and walked through the silent streets to the hospital. Experience had told him that tending to severely wounded patients was a better way of tackling his problem than the cold showers usually prescribed by his colleagues.

8

TRAVELS

THE WHISTLE BLEW ITS MOURNFUL NOTE, and the train stopped again. Wearily Julius checked the time. Three in the afternoon already! Would they ever reach their destination?

Yawning, he sat up straighter. He was alone, his fellow travelers—an army colonel and his aide de camp—having apparently deserted their first-class compartment, perhaps to stretch their legs. Through the open windows he could see the endless Hungarian plain rolling by. A year ago—barely a year ago—he had been racing in the opposite direction through that very same plain, to be there for his son's final journey. Today the ripening wheat was dancing to the tune of the strong western winds scattering the flock of white clouds overhead. The harvest was expected to be exceptionally plentiful, bringing hope to many who wanted to believe this was both a gift from heaven and a good omen. He wished he could share that belief.

Lost in the crowd, he had recently watched a military parade held on the occasion of a local feast. How handsome they were, those young soldiers in their colorful uniforms!

Blue tunics for the lancers, red pantaloons for the hussars, and dragoons in their long coats! How could one not admire the shakos with their jaunty feathers, the boots polished to a mirror shine, the drawn sabers dazzling in the noon sun… But for him it was heart wrenching to see these healthy young men walking so bravely toward the unthinkable. Every day he had to deal with the true reality of the terrible fighting going on beyond the Carpathian Mountains, in Galicia and Bucovina. Broken bodies, youngsters barely out of their teens disfigured, maimed, crippled…He kept remembering the lead soldiers his old Latin teacher had so painstakingly and lovingly restored. Alas, brush and glue would not do the trick here for the men marching so happily to the applause of the crowd.

Lost in thought, he did not notice that the train had resumed its slow journey. This unexpected trip was the result of his nocturnal visit to the hospital. He had found it busier than ever, despite the late hour. Army time is different from civilian time, and the hospital functioned according to the schedules of the trains bringing wounded night and day. A new intake had just come in and was being processed. Men wrapped in blankets were sitting on benches or lying shivering on the floor. Julius went in search of the military commander to get instructions and found him conferring with two officers.

The man looked up and welcomed him warmly, if a little surprised. "Tell me, my friend," he asked jovially, "what are you doing here in the middle of the night? I don't have a choice, but you do. What happened? Your wife kicked you out?" And he laughed heartily.

Julius, who got on well with Commander Mihaly, a man in his early forties with a healthy sense of humor, replied with a smile. "She did nothing of the kind. In fact, she is away. She left with her parents for a short vacation."

"So you are all alone with your small children?"

"Not quite. My mother and their nurse are taking care of them."

"Ah!" said Mihaly happily. "You are just the man I need. Come to my office."

Once seated he offered Julius a cigar, which the young doctor refused, and some French cognac, which he accepted, and explained his predicament. Because of the new arrivals, he needed to send back, sooner than expected, some thirty soldiers who were on the mend; they would be put onboard the train returning to Budapest in the morning, to be transferred to their units or to another hospital. The problem was that there should be a doctor on the train, and Mihaly had none to spare. Would Dr. Matthias volunteer? It would be a quick trip, as another train was expected to bring a new contingent of wounded to Nagyvarad on Friday morning. The army would see to it that he was lodged in a good hotel and driven back to the station on time.

Dr. Matthias volunteered. Why? He was not sure. The need for a break, for getting away, even for a short while? The lurking fear of not being able to withstand temptation and succumbing to the nurse's charms the following night? A wish to see his sister and her family? Whatever the reason, he had gone home for a few hours' rest and in the morning had asked Donna to move to the big house until he came back. He took the opportunity to tell her about the nurse falling asleep with the baby in her bed, something that was expressly forbidden because of the real danger of the child being smothered when she turned in her sleep. Donna had looked at him with her penetrating glance, as if she understood more than what he was saying, and promised to take care of the matter. Only when he was comfortably ensconced in his first-class compartment, with the bag of sandwiches hastily prepared by the cook, did he realize he had forgotten to inform his sister he was coming. Time enough to surprise her with a call from Budapest, he thought.

The afternoon was gone by the time the train stopped at the makeshift station set up southwest of the city, near the town's main hospital, which had been taken over by the army. A small group of medical staff was waiting to take charge of the soldiers. His task completed, Julius strolled to the office to ask the lieutenant on duty about the return trip and to phone his brother-in-law. There was no answer; only then did he remember that his sister had mentioned the family would be going away for a few days. Shrugging philosophically, he turned to the officer who was waiting patiently and explained his predicament.

Fortunately, commander Mihaly had telegraphed instructions, and he was given the choice of three first-class establishments. Knowing none of them, he opted for the Pannonia hotel—for the simple reason that he had seen its splendid façade from Madi's apartment. It was not likely that the boutique would still be open that late in the evening, and he could not risk knocking on her door with her jealous patron quite possibly inside. However, drawn shutters and closed doors were no bar to dreams, and from his hotel room he could fantasize about the lovely redhead sleeping so near.

Thanking the lieutenant profusely, he boarded an army vehicle driven by a bearded corporal who was also going to take him back to the station in the morning in time for the return trip. Situated on the famed Kerepesi Avenue between the National and the Popular Theaters, the Panonnia presented an impressive front to the world. A porter wearing a red and gold uniform opened the car door with a flourish and helped Julius with his suitcase. The army requisition form was met with a disdainful glance and the information that the place was full; however, a gold coin changed hands, and a very good room was found, a high-ranking officer having—allegedly—just cancelled his reservation.

Storing his few belongings did not take long, and Julius picked up the phone to call home and leave the hotel's number. Donna confirmed all was well and put on Andreas who began a long and totally incomprehensible monologue; the fond father listened with a smile and let him go on, though the call was costing a fortune. It was with a lighter heart that he left the room to go in search of sustenance.

A familiar voice made him jump. "I don't believe it! Dr. Mathias? Julius?"

He turned round and found himself face-to-face with Madi who was locking the room next to his. She looked alluring in a demure gray dress, with a daring little hat and a veil shading her green eyes. It would have been hard to decide who was the more surprised of the two. They stood there, not daring to move for fear of breaking the spell.

Pragmatic as always, she took the initiative. "Is your wife with you? Is this your room?"

"Yes. I'm here alone," he replied in a strangled voice. "What are you doing here?"

"Come into my room. I hate discussing my affairs in the middle of the corridor."

In a daze he followed her into a spacious suite, a small drawing room opening onto a larger one, turned golden by the last rays of the setting sun.

"I think we could use a drink," she said. "Come." She took off a pristine tablecloth covering a side table and uncovered a number of appetizing dishes and two bottles of champagne in an ice cooler. In the process of opening the first bottle with a flourish, she followed his glance and smiled. "Food first, right? Men are all the same. Go ahead, we'll talk later."

Julius was indeed ravenous, the morning sandwiches but a distant memory. He fell to with a will under her amused eyes, while she ate sparingly. When he stopped she used her napkin to wipe his mouth slowly, before kissing him and pulling him to his feet. No longer tired, he let himself be drawn toward the four-poster bed. But this was not going to be the hasty embrace of their first meeting. Madi pushed him away with a smile and carefully took off first her hat then the demure gray dress, revealing far from demure lacy underwear.

Later—much later—they returned to the drawing room in search of nourishment. Opening the second bottle of champagne, Madi sank into an armchair with a contented sigh and asked him what he was doing in Budapest, and by what blessed coincidence he had booked into the Pannonia instead of going to his sister's.

"Pure luck. I traveled with a convoy of soldiers returning home and go back in the morning with another convoy, bringing wounded to Nagyvarad. My sister and her family are away, and I chose this hotel because it is closest to where you live—though I could only hope to meet you in my dreams…Why are you here? Why did you leave your flat?"

"What with the war and everything, I have been having problems. Nasty graffiti on the windows, insults hurled at me in the street..."

"Why? What happened?"

"Are you saying nobody is blaming the Jews in Nagyvarad?"

"Yes, but to that extent! You had to close the boutique?"

"No, thank God! I hired a war veteran to watch over the place during the day. I put a chair and a table outside for him and send over my assistant with fresh coffee from time to time, and he happily reads his newspaper. My customers congratulate me for giving work to a true patriot. The problem is that there is no one there at night. There was a lot of yelling, stones thrown at the windows. Neighbors complained..."

"But why? I mean, I haven't heard anything like that. Is that happening all over Budapest?"

"No, no, it's personal. The countess detests me—she has done so for years—and she thinks she can take advantage of the situation to get rid of me once and for all."

"Her husband shares your conviction?"

"He won't say it in so many words, but he knows." She sipped a little champagne and went on. "They have had separate bedrooms since the birth of their third child, a girl who is now twenty. As you can see, it happened well before we met. The countess was only too glad to put an end to something she never cared for. She has a feudal view of life. She would not have minded her noble husband turning to the women of his estate for what she coyly calls his manly needs. That's what my poor Ferencz—the count—did at first; however, as he grew older he discovered he wanted more. Company, a little intelligent conversation...nothing serious, no politics.

I try to give him that. With me he enjoys pleasant evenings, which nowadays do not always end with lovemaking. That is what the countess cannot countenance. However, since the husbands of her best friends all have mistresses, she needed some kind of reason to object. She decided to pick on the fact that I am Jewish. In her circles anti-Semitism is the norm. Ferencz lets her rant but won't give me up. With the war, the situation has gone from bad to worse. He came up with the idea of putting me up in this hotel, which, as you saw, is conveniently close, and booked the suite for the whole year. I come here at the end of the day, faithfully accompanied by my veteran, who picks me up in the morning. I spend my weekends here as well. Whenever Ferencz can, he joins me, taking the adjoining room—where you are today. There is a connecting door, and the key is with me at all times. It does not fool anyone at the hotel, but we maintain the appearance of respectability. I expected him this evening; however, he had to leave for Vienna at a moment's notice. Everything was ready for him…luckily for you…and you can go back to your room—but not yet!—through the connecting door, with no one being any the wiser."

"You told me he was jealous. Aren't you afraid he'll surprise you and show up suddenly?"

"He's not like that, but don't worry. The concierge would call and warn me. Not for the reasons you might imagine. You see, I was faithful to Ferencz until you came along a year ago. Mind you, I have no regrets. That we met again today is nothing short of miraculous, and, as your father was wont to say, miracles are the products of divine intervention. I would like to think the heavens smiled upon us tonight. Who knows if it will ever happen again?"

She paused and went on more slowly, as if talking to herself, "No, I asked the concierge to warn me in order to have a few minutes to check the way I look. Sometimes, when I am all alone here, I feel so unhappy that I try to find solace in a stiff drink or a bottle of champagne. Many years ago one of your colleagues told me it was healthier than taking sleeping pills. You don't agree, I see. You may be right; it may not be such a good idea, but what does it matter? It doesn't happen every day, and anyway, Ferencz will die before I do, and then..."

"He has not provided for you? Made your future safe?"

"My future...He has been more than generous. The boutique and the apartment are now in my name, and there is nothing the countess can do about it, in spite of her influence and her powerful friends. I won't want for anything, if that's what you mean. Beyond that...I have no friends. He is too jealous. We never go out because of his wife. In the past we used to go to Austria sometimes for a few days, but with the war on...I shall be thirty-two this year. Thirty-two, my dear Julius. I would like to live, start anew as they say, maybe even find a man still in his prime, a widower with young children. Get married. Turn respectable. Meet women of my age and discuss school and servants. Become just another good housewife. Grow old in a dignified way. It is not too much to ask, but it is impossible. I know that, and it breaks my heart. Enough. Come back to bed with me..."

The first streaks of dawn were coloring the sky when she fell asleep. Julius, who had gotten up quietly to finish the champagne, looked down on the perfect body of that other Magda, who was the same age as his wife. The firm breasts, the shapely thighs, the softly rounded belly. To be fair, Madi had never borne a child, but still…He too would have enjoyed coming back from work to a welcoming home, a loving wife who would listen to the tale of his day and eagerly follow him to bed. He sighed, and Madi's eyes flew open. He embraced her without passion but with great tenderness. She murmured that he could safely go to sleep, the concierge would ring at seven in the morning. He found it hard to leave her, feeling vaguely guilty for not being able to help. It did not stop him from taking her phone number. After all, why not third time lucky?

The bearded corporal was waiting for him, and the trip to the station took only a few minutes. The train was delayed, and he had to cool his heels for nearly three hours before they got underway. This time he was sharing his first-class compartment with three army doctors; his services not needed, he fell blissfully asleep.

Though there was no loving wife to welcome him, a deliriously happy little boy rushed to embrace him when he reached home. Andreas had been very upset by his absence, reported Donna; he had run to the door at the slightest sound and had not wanted to go to bed. The child now stuck to him like a limpet, and they went upstairs together to see Elisabeth who beamed at the visitors. The nurse was gone.

"I got rid of her," explained Donna. "At first she was defiant and told me she would take her orders only from her mistress. I said if she didn't go immediately, I would have the police throw her out. Your father added that he would denounce her behavior in front of the congregation. That did it. She took the money she was owed and went. Don't look so worried. You can see the baby is doing very well. Ditta is happily coping with both kids. Elisabeth is getting cow's milk and she seems to love it. She is a good baby, always smiling… But here I am, talking, talking, and you must be famished. Come, the cook has made your favorite dish: stuffed peppers in a spicy sauce. I have had my dinner, but I shall keep you company. Oh, Sandor came by yesterday. He had some business in town. They expect us tomorrow—the children and me. One of his cousins will fetch us. Because of Shabbat the carriage will be waiting on the Cluj road—we don't want to offend the neighbors or your father. Sandor hopes you will be able to come too; he hasn't seen you in ages."

As Dr. Matthias settled contentedly in his bed, he counted his blessings. He had his parents, his beloved children, and good friends.

In the morning he got up early and joined his little family for the farm outing. Ditta was coming as well; between the two children and the huge basket prepared by the cook, the three adults had their hands full. The fact that they were all wearing their Shabbat best did not help. They would have to wait until they reached the farm to change.

At the appointed place, they found the carriage, freshly repainted a vivid green and drawn by two sturdy farm horses. Leaving the placid animals unattended, Sandor's cousin, Imre, a lanky young man who appeared to know Donna well, came to help. Terrified at first by the two huge beasts, Andreas let Imre take him by the hand and show him how to caress their satiny flanks. Soon the child was settled on the coachman's knee and helping him to hold the reins.

It was a day Julius would never forget. Summer hadn't begun yet, but it was warm and sunny. Forest flowers were opening their buds, and the first berries had appeared. The farm had a new coat of paint, and Martha's prize roses were in bloom. Leaving the women to sort the children out and get the food ready, Sandor and Julius—who had changed into an old shirt and worn pants—left at a brisk pace. They were not going very far, since they had to be back in time for lunch: a quick trip to the river to try to catch some fat fish and a detour to see whether a hare or two had been caught in the farmer's snares. They were in luck. The water was turning cloudy in the unaccustomed heat, and they caught so many fish they soon called a halt to it. The young doctor would have liked to have tarried along the leafy bank. He found the atmosphere soothing, as if they had the whole forest to themselves. They had encountered only a small group of teenagers shepherded by a sour-faced nun and a youngish priest who limped.

"They come from the Catholic orphanage," spat Sandor. "Romanians, the lot of them."

"You have something against them?"

Sandor, who belonged to the Protestant church of Hungary, shrugged. "I have nothing against the Romanian Orthodox crowd. They have been here for centuries. Most of them speak some Hungarian, and I can make myself understood in Romanian if necessary. But that lot…they behave as though they are better than we are, making a point of not speaking Hungarian and pretending not to understand a word of the language of the country."

"Come on. I may know very little about churches and religious denominations, but I was told the Roman Catholic church on the square across from my clinic was built more than two hundred years ago!"

"You don't get it. The church of Saint Ladislas is Hungarian. Roman Catholic does not mean Romanian Catholic!"

"If you say so. In other words, you don't mind Hungarian Catholics, only Romanians?"

"First of all, most Hungarians are Catholics. I have no idea why our family converted to the Protestant faith or when it happened. It must have been a long time ago. My problem is with the orphanage. Those boys you saw are Gypsies. It's said their parents sold them to the church. They may have become good Catholics, but they still steal whenever they can."

"Now I get it. They visited your farm?"

"They used to. Twice I went to see the director who looked down at me and said sneeringly that if I was looking for thieves, I should start closer to home. So I waited until my brothers came home on leave; we set up an ambush and caught them red-handed, and they got the thrashing of their lives. Attila, who is now a corporal, threatened to forcibly enroll them in the army should they come again."

"Could he do that?"

"How do I know? But it worked as a threat. No more trouble. Come on, time to go."

"Yes, they must all be starving, right? Give me a minute to wash my hands."

Sandor watched him with a smile. Since his return from Vienna, Julius had become a stickler for cleanliness, explaining that a Viennese professor had demonstrated that clean hands prevented a number of illnesses. The farmer was not convinced but indulged his friend. On the way home, he checked his snares and happily picked up three fat hares. Julius asked him why he bothered: didn't his wife keep rabbits behind the farm? Sandor laughingly replied that there was no comparing the taste of farm animals to that of those roaming freely in the wild.

They were almost out of the forest when they heard the orphanage party returning and walked faster to avoid meeting them. Suddenly there was a thud, a cry of pain, and excited voices. Instinctively Julius put down the pail where the fish were still swimming and ran toward the group. The limping priest must have lost his footing; he had fallen and rolled off the path, his haversack by his side. The nun was wringing her hands, and the boys milled about aimlessly.

Kneeling by the wounded man, Julius saw he was breathing normally. He gently checked the priest's head for a wound and found nothing but a harmless lump. The man moved, opening eyes of a deep penetrating blue, and contemplated Julius with curiosity, and no wonder: with his old shirt, faded pants, and wide hat, along with the beard he had not yet shaved off, the young doctor did not cut a very impressive figure. The priest asked a question in Romanian, a language Julius did not speak. According to Sandor these people spoke no Hungarian; conversation would not be easy. Unless... this was a Roman Catholic priest, right? He should be able to understand Latin.

"I am a doctor," Julius tried in that language. This was received with an incredulous smile, followed by a cry of pain. The man was touching his left shoulder; Julius gently removed the hand and checked and then tore the sleeve. There was no open wound, but the shoulder was obviously dislocated.

"I will try to put the bone back into its socket," he said haltingly, the familiar medical terms coming back. "It is going to hurt."

"God's will be done" was the philosophical answer.

"Do not move. Should I ask one of the boys to hold you?"

"It will not be necessary. Just say when."

"Very well. Now!"

He skillfully manipulated the bone and heard it go back with a satisfying crunch. His patient had not uttered a word.

"It's nearly over." Julius smiled. "I need a large piece of cloth."

The priest said something, and one of the youngsters opened the bag lying on the ground and took out a worn but clean towel which he handed over. Julius bandaged the shoulder and helped the priest to stand. The whole episode had lasted barely five minutes. There was a pregnant silence. He looked around and saw the youngsters watching him suspiciously. They must have remembered meeting him earlier with their enemy, Sandor.

"I am Father Octavius," the priest said, still in Latin, "and I thank you."

"I am Dr. Julius Matthias," he replied in the same tongue. "You must now go home and rest at least until tomorrow. In two or three days, you may come to my office to show me your shoulder. I am in the Black Vulture building, across from Saint Ladislas. I am there from five in the afternoon."

"Brother, are you a Hungarian Catholic?" inquired the priest, having noted the reference to Saint Ladislas. "Where did you learn your Latin?"

"In Vienna, where I studied medicine. But I am not a Catholic. I am a Jew."

All must have understood that part of his answer, since there was a collective drawing of breath. The nun took a step backward and crossed herself.

The priest raised his eyebrows but answered in the same tranquil tone, "I thank you, Julius. Go in peace, and I shall come to see you."

Sandor, who had been fidgeting at a distance, greeted Julius's return with relief and asked what had happened. Julius replied, but his friend appeared more worried than ever.

"After all," Sandor remarked, "the man's life was not in danger. There was no need for you to go rushing in to help and even less to tell those people you are Jewish. That was not wise," he added before concluding that what was done was done, and they should make tracks for the farm, which they did, a startled Julius trying to make sense of what Sandor had just said.

They found the trestle tables already set up in the yard and everything ready. Julius hurried to change, since he was to leave with his family immediately after lunch. There was quite a crowd; Toth cousins and several of Martha's relatives had shown up. The women sat at one table and kept an eye on the children, who were running around screaming, and on the babies asleep in the shade. In her big basket, Donna had brought two loaves of white bread and a cold chicken. Aaron had made his son swear he would not let his children eat forbidden food, and Donna faithfully saw to it, going as far as not eating the spicy pork sausages Martha made so well.

The men started drinking and telling off-color jokes while Julius ate sparingly. He could not understand what had happened. His childhood friend had never made the smallest allusion to his religion. Why now? And what was Julius doing here among those peasants and farmers who looked at him askance? What did they know about him? Were they bothered at the thought that they were in the company of a Jew? Why had Donna insisted that he come?

He was to get his answer. Martha, rosily flushed by the wine, stood up and asked for silence. Then she raised both arms like a symphony conductor, and everyone started shout-ing, "Happy birthday, Sandor!" before lustily bellowing a traditional birthday song. Donna took two huge cakes from her basket and put them on the tables. Only then did Julius remember that, born two weeks earlier that himself, Sandor had just turned twenty-five—a fact his cousins made much of in long-winded but good-humored speeches.

Sandor's parents were dead, and it was left to Donna, who had not drunk anything, to tell tales of childhood pranks, which drew laughter. More wine was poured, and then it was Julius's turn; he managed to recount some wild episodes while hinting that he would have said more had Martha not been present. He went on to embrace his friend.

It was already four in the afternoon, and the Matthias party was ready to leave. The problem was that Imre, having lost all his inhibitions with the help of the wine, had disappeared with a strapping brunette. The farmer decided to drive his friend back himself, quashing the pro-tests of his guests by promising to come back quickly and reminding them the party would go on all night; the visi-tors were staying overnight at the farm, the following day being Sunday.

Baby Elisabeth was asleep in Ditta's arms, and Donna was carrying Andreas. The two men sat in the front.

"Is anything wrong, Sandy? You look worried," asked Julius in a low voice.

"I should never have let Martha invite you" came the answer. "This is not your place. You live in another world. Yuli, don't try to deny it. We both know the truth. You are not at ease with my people, and I would not feel at ease with yours. It's a fact."

"Sandy, you and I feel very easy together, and that's what matters. We drank from the same milk at your mother's breast. We are almost brothers. I know I can depend on you, and you know I will always be there for you."

"That is true. It is also true that you can find words I could never find. Anyway, don't bother asking me to your birthday party; I won't come."

"Never fear, there isn't going to be one. My wife has no intention of doing anything, and besides, she probably won't be back. I have a much better idea. I shall come and spend the day with you. We shall grill some fish in the forest the way we used to. Agreed?"

"Agreed," replied his friend with a relieved smile.

"Sandy, since we are talking frankly, I would like you to explain what you meant when you said I shouldn't have answered when the priest asked if I am a Catholic. Should I have kept silent? Lied? Does it bother you to have a Jewish friend?"

Sandor hung his head. "Yuli, I can't explain things the way you do, but I shall try. For me you are Yuli, almost my brother. I know that for other people you are Dr. Julius Matthias, and you are a Jew, but until now it has meant nothing to me. Besides, I know nothing about Jews."

"Come on! You know me, you know your aunt Donna—"

"Aunt Donna, for me, is one of us. She married Uncle Matthias in church, remember? It was a big scandal at the time, his marrying a Jewish woman, even if she was a convert. There are some in the area who say that his death, and the deaths of the children, was divine retribution. Now you— you are also like us. You eat what we eat, and you behave as we do. Your father is a very pious man; we have men like him too. I barely know your in-laws. I don't believe I have ever met real Jews, and so far that has been of no importance."

"So far? And now?"

"Now I am married, a father. I have a farm to run while there is a war going on, and I have many more doings with officials. I have to be careful. I have had nasty remarks. Attila and Zoltan, whenever they come on leave, tell me new tales of Jews making money out of the situation. Even Attila, who knows you well, has advised me to take care in my dealings with you."

"Why didn't you say so? I would not have come today."

"Because for me you are Yuli. I can't say any more. You are more than a brother, more than my own brothers. Martha feels the same—yet we have to be careful. Do you see? You are not angry, are you?"

"No, I am not angry," thought Julius bitterly. Shattered would be more like it. Wordlessly he put his hand on his friend's shoulder. He asked to be dropped with Donna on the outskirts of town; they would walk the rest of the way, in deference to his father. The small children and Ditta would go on with the carriage and get off as close to the house as possible, and Julius would accept the blame. While the farmer's cart trundled on, Julius took his aunt's arm, and they started walking. She immediately wanted to know what had happened.

"You were looking so grim, my boy. You had me worried!"

After a moment's hesitation, he told her the whole story.

"It's all my fault," she said wretchedly. "I should have turned down Martha's invitation."

"Never mind that. You have known them forever. Were you aware of the problem?"

"There was no problem because, as Sandor put it succinctly, for him you are not Jewish. Today he had to face reality. As far as everyone else is concerned—orphanage people, his extended family, neighbors—you are a Jew, and Jews are not very popular these days. What am I saying? They have never been popular."

"You feel it?"

"I barely go out of the Jewish quarter, so…But your father has had some nasty encounters. Don't tell me you have never heard disparaging remarks yourself!"

"I do, but I shrug them off."

"I know, and I know why. You see, dear boy, deep down you don't feel Jewish. Your father has reproached me often enough about it. He is right, and it is my fault. However, you have to be careful and remember at all times that for all the world you are a Jew, even if you are a distinguished and respected doctor. Listen, let's sit down for a minute. Here is a bench."

"Is something wrong?"

"Nothing really, just tired."

"You should have gone on with the carriage."

"No. I'd rather be tired than cause your father pain."

"Well, I shall have you come for a checkup at the office."

"Yuli, Yuli, I am all right. Let me ask you something. Do you know how old I am? No? Well, I am seven years older than your father. I shall soon turn seventy. I have not always had an easy life, and sometimes I feel every one of my years. Not that I am complaining. Thanks to you, thanks to my dear Anni, I have a blessed old age. I live near you, I see my beloved grandchildren every day, your maid cleans my house, the cook makes the most tempting dishes for your father. I have never lived in such comfort or been so happy. I should not be saying that aloud; I don't want to tempt fate. But it will not go on forever. Your father may be younger than I am, but his health is poor. I worry a lot about him. I also worry about myself sometimes. I have always been independent, and I am afraid old age will attack me one day, as it did today. Enough said. Time to go."

As Julius bade her good-bye at her door, he could not help wondering whether his aunt's sudden weakness had not been her way of changing the subject.

9

SHIFTING SANDS

JUNE 1915 DRAGGED ON as Europe turned into one giant battlefield. After their initial successes, the Russians—allied to the French and the British—were retreating from a front one hundred miles wide. The German army was pushing toward Paris. Italy had suddenly joined the fray; forsaking its traditional allies, it turned against Austria-Hungary. In Nagyvarad nobody cared about Italy; all they wanted to know was what neighboring Romania would do now that the old king was dead. He had been a Hohenzollern prince and a former Prussian officer, related to German royalty, who had never forgotten his German roots throughout his fifty-year reign. It was well-known that he had wanted to enter the war alongside Germany but had been held in check by his countrymen's strong pro-French leanings. His nephew, King Ferdinand I, was very much an unknown quantity. Would he maintain Romania's neutral status?

The great powers had all sent emissaries to Bucharest, pressing the new monarch to choose their side. It was not easy. Ferdinand was a Hohenzollern prince too and as such had much sympathy for Germany. On the other hand, by siding with the French and the British against Austria-Hungary and Germany, he might gain back territories with large Romanian populations, such as Transylvania. All the while, the wounded kept arriving at the Jewish hospital which had been taken over by the army; new rows of white crosses appeared in the town's cemetery.

Magda was still away. Szamuely was back; he had come to the house on Schools Road—during the day, so as not to meet his son-in-law—to see his grandchildren and bring them presents: a mechanical wooden dog painted the colors of Romania for Andreas who took to dragging it everywhere with shouts of glee, and a fluffy bear almost as big as she was for Elisabeth. He informed Donna that his daughter would probably arrive sometime in July, together with Golda, who had remained with her. To tell the truth, she was not missed.

Summer arrived and with it sunshine and blue skies. The children practically lived in the garden and had golden tans to show for it. Ditta no longer took them for walks by herself since Andreas was becoming a handful, forever getting into mischief such as running across the road or trying to climb a tree because he had seen a bird he wanted to catch. He was now talking nonstop, and Julius was delighted in his company, though he did not always understand the words tumbling so rapidly from the boy's little mouth.

The two "men" had breakfast together, and the boy waved good-bye as Julius set out on foot for another day's work. At that time of the morning, it was still pleasantly cool, and he enjoyed the walk through this part of the city, where he was well known and the people he encountered greeted him respectfully. Once inside the hospital, he lost himself in the work he loved so much. Never in a hurry, he would patiently explain to a wounded soldier exactly what was wrong with him and what he could do about it. He was popular with the patients and the nurses as well; his colleagues did not resent him, since he was always ready to do more than his share.

Whenever he left the hospital early enough, he would take the tramway to save time and go home to see his children before going out again to see his private patients at his clinic. When he finally went home, he ate his solitary dinner in the kitchen before climbing wearily to his room. He was usually so tired, he fell asleep as soon as his head touched the pillow. This was not a bad thing, because it left no room for soul searching.

"For me you are not a Jew," Sandor had said.

"Deep down you don't feel Jewish," Donna had said.

Yet Julius Matthias knew perfectly well he was a Jew. What he did not know was what it meant. His father had taught him prayers and hymns which he repeated faultlessly in the synagogue, but they had no meaning. He had learned to pray as he had learned history or mathematics. It was something that was expected of him. He found it impossible to believe in an almighty God or in divine providence. He was well aware of the fact that Christians hated and despised Jews but was not quite sure why. So far it had hardly affected him, probably because his fellow students in Vienna had not known he was Jewish.

Here in Nagyvarad he had gone straight to work for the Jewish hospital. It was different, of course, with the military taking over the hospital, and there had been a few incidents but nothing to worry him. His clinic was successful beyond his wildest dreams, and not all his patients were Jewish.

Yet in a few words, Sandor, his friend, almost his brother, had torn down the wall of complacency protecting him. What had he said? That for Sandor he was not a Jew; that of late he had been made aware that having Jewish friends was not a good idea; and lastly that he did not know what to make of his brother's comments about Jews. It was unbearable!

Julius opened his heart to Theo, the architect, who had come to the clinic complaining of some minor ailment. His friend had stared at him with a mix of incredulity and pity.

"My poor little Julius, it is high time you grew up and understood that you are living in a world where, at best, no one likes Jews. So far you have been spared because of the way you look and because you are a doctor. For some unfathomable reason, Jewish doctors enjoy an excellent reputation among non-Jews, some of whom endow them with quasi-magical powers. If you like, it is a different form of anti-Semitism. Throughout history you find such doctors, who reached prestigious positions, close to the rulers of the time. You know the Rambam—"

"I confess the name rings a bell, but as a writer of learned treatises, not as a doctor."

"Shame on you. I may be no more of a believer than you, but at least I have taken pains to know the history of my people."

"And this knowledge helps you fend off anti-Semitic attacks?"

"It helps me. I know who I am, where I come from, and it gives me strength. Obviously if I ever fall foul of a frenzied mob, that is not going to do me much good. However, on a daily basis I find a measure of solace in knowing that those who despise me do so because they know nothing about us." He paused to drink the excellent coffee Amalia had just brought them. "You see, dear boy, it would have been more pleasant to live in a world where Jews were treated like everyone else. However, that is not going to happen. Don't ask me why. So I deal with it while keeping my ears open, waiting for something to happen, as it undoubtedly will. That is why ZsaZsa and I decided not to have children, so as not to offer, so to speak, hostages to fate. You were expecting another answer," he added with a rueful smile. "Think about what I have said. Learn to know who you are and who the enemy is."

"My brother-in-law holds similar views and expects the worst."

"Your brother-in-law is a sound man. Besides, the worst has already happened. Have you forgotten the pogroms of Kishinev and Odessa?"

"Come on. Everyone knows the Russians are barbarians. How can you compare the situation there with what is going on in civilized countries like Austria and Hungary?"

"Similar factors lead to similar effects. Should the war—heaven forbid—turn bad, we shall be asked to pay the price, mark my words. Sorry I can't cheer you up. By the way, have you given some thought to my advice? I have a good friend who finds being a widow lonely yet doesn't wish to marry again, if you follow my drift."

They parted on that note. The young doctor found food for deep thought in the conversation. As luck would have it, the following day, Father Octavius, the man he had treated a few days earlier in the forest, appeared in his office in full ecclesiastical regalia, with a silver cross on his chest, accompanied by an elderly nun whose pinched face and pursed lips showed how much she disliked being there. The Jewish couple in the waiting room rose in fright, the mother clutching the young boy they had brought to see the doctor to her breast. Called by Amelia, Julius hastened to welcome his visitors and led them to his office. The nun sat at the very edge of her chair and opened her prayer book, looking worriedly around.

The priest took his place in the armchair facing the desk. "I didn't want to bother you," he said slowly in Latin, "but I did want to thank you. You do understand me? You really speak Latin? How is it possible?"

"Yes, I understand. I studied that language to help me with my medical studies, and I was lucky enough to find a very good Latin teacher, a Frenchman, in Vienna."

"Then you speak French as well? It would be easier."

"Indeed," replied Julius, happy to abandon a dead language for a live one. "It will be much easier."

"Very well. The doctor I saw told me I was very lucky. It seems that when the shoulder dislocates, it can be set manually but only in the very first minutes. Without your swift intervention, it might have been necessary to operate. At the orphanage they were expecting a substantial bill for services rendered, but since you didn't send one, I have come to pay my debt."

"It's not necessary. I did what I had to do as a doctor, and you owe me nothing. However, I do thank you for your visit."

"Don't be so modest. You did more than your duty. It is not so easy for a Jew to help a Catholic priest. Don't deny it. I saw the way the patients in your waiting room reacted when I came in: you would have thought the devil himself was there. You may speak openly. The good sister here speaks neither Latin nor French and is slightly deaf too."

"You are probably right. Witness the reaction of your good sister who appears terrified to find herself in the lair of a Jew. However, I heard you cry out, I saw you lying on the ground—that was enough. I swore to uphold the oath of Hippocrates. Priest or not, it was my sacred duty to assist you. You see, medicine is my religion."

"That is to your credit. Do accept the letter of thanks the bishop was kind enough to sign upon my recommendation. Who knows? It might come in useful someday." He handed over a very official-looking document to Julius, who was struck dumb, and went on. "I would have loved to get to know you better, my medical friend. Unfortunately, I have to leave your town. I am Italian, and now that my country has entered the war on the wrong side, had I not been a priest, I would already have been thrown in jail. Here is my card; should you ever need my help, it will be my pleasure to offer it."

"Thank you, and I too would have liked to know you better. I'm sure we would have had fascinating discussions. What are you doing so far from Rome?"

"I was doing penance," came the unexpected reply. "To you I can tell the truth, since you are hardly likely to repeat it. Besides, I'm leaving. I let myself be tempted by the devil in a woman's dress—or, should I say, undress—more than once, and I was found out. I was not thrown out of the church—my family is too influential—but I had to go into exile to meditate about the wows of chastity I had taken. The fact is I was never intended to be a priest; however, I am the second son. My older brother will get the title and the lands. I am too lame for the army, so taking holy orders was the only option. Are you shocked?"

"Not in the least. Our rabbis must marry and have children. I have never understood why yours can't: according to the Bible that we share, didn't the Almighty give a female companion to the first man and enjoin them to be fruitful and multiply?"

Father Octavius stood up, laughing. "What a telling argument. Who knows? I might make use of it one day. I have to leave you, my Jewish friend. May heaven protect you and yours!"

"Don't you want to say protect me from your people?"

"That too. Nothing is more dangerous than absolute certainty in religious beliefs, because it turns men into fanatics. By all means make use of the bishop's letter. I had to work hard to get it, but he will keep his word. Farewell, Julius. I dare say you don't know you bear the name of one of the greatest Roman families, gens Julia, the family of Julius Caesar…What a pity I did not meet you earlier. May fate or Providence lead us to another meeting one day." And the young priest embraced the young doctor in front of the nun's scandalized eyes.

That was not the end of the affair. The tale of the mysterious visit became the talk of the community, to the extent that Theodore was back the following day. "I assume yesterday's visitor was the young priest you treated?" he asked even before he had taken a seat, surprising his friend.

"How did you hear about it?"

"He asks me how I heard about it! Julius, that's all they are talking about in the community! A few good people are saying this is your first step toward converting…I nearly got into fisticuffs with them, but—"

"For heaven's sake! He came to thank me and to give me a letter from the bishop. Here, read it."

"Good! Give it to me. I shall have it framed this very evening and bring it back tomorrow. Hang it on the wall next to your diploma. That will shut them up."

"Are you serious?"

"Absolutely. Nothing is more dangerous than rumor, especially these days. It could do you a lot of harm. Don't forget that not everyone among our leaders is your friend. Many are jealous of your success; others resent the fact that you do not grace our synagogues with your presence very often. You wouldn't be the first to convert to avoid problems or to curry favors from the powers that be. You must have seen them in Vienna, these Jews who converted, like Gustav Mahler, who renounced the faith of his ancestors to become director of the opera."

"Please tell everyone I have no wish to be an opera director. I shall duly set up the letter, beautifully framed by you, next to my diploma."

More shaken than he would have liked to admit, Julius made it a point that evening to go see his parents, first humorously recounting the visit of the priest and the nun then that of his friend, Theo, and the tale of the bishop's letter. He added that, suitably framed, it would hang on his wall. His father's relief was evident—proof that the rumors had reached the small house on Schools Road.

"Father, there is something else I want to discuss with you. I believe it is high time I knew more about the history of our people. You could help me with that. I shall try to come to the Friday evening services more often. A man needs to know where he comes from."

"Nothing would give me greater pleasure," said a beaming Aaron. "I am sorry about the painful way this decision was brought about, but better late than never!"

Falling asleep in his solitary bed that night, Julius reflected that in spite of the thick glasses he wore, his father still saw more than he himself would have wished!

The dry and sunny weather held. Already there were talks of an early harvest. Dr. Matthias made an appointment with his tailor, intending to have two or three lighter suits made, which he meant to wear, daringly, without a waistcoat. He discovered at the fitting that during the last year, he had become broader across the shoulders and had put on some weight. The tailor commented with a smile that the honorable doctor had reached a man's estate.

Man's estate? He had indeed turned twenty-five in a world where the life expectancy was less than fifty years for manual workers and peasants. Was it the end of his youth, the end of illusions? Perhaps a time for resignation? Yet this milestone had been marked by a number of events, some of them quite unexpected. It had started with a visit to the cemetery, since Aaron Matthias never forgot that the birth of his son had caused the death of his wife. For him the years had not assuaged the deep feelings of guilt. The pilgrimage took place on the Hebrew date, slightly earlier that year than Julius's official date of birth. Aaron and Donna, holding hands, had cried while Julius stood silent, vainly trying to imagine the mother he had never known and who had been barely five years older than he was now when she died.

The following Friday, on his birthday according to the civil calendar, the Matthias seniors had come to dinner, and the cook had made a chocolate cake for the occasion, to the delight of Andreas. Aaron had a special gift for his son: the recently completed *History of the Jews* in eleven volumes, penned by Heinrich Graetz. There was another celebration a few days later. The Austrian Circle had booked a private room at a forest inn a few miles south of the town. They had chosen the Two Crowns precisely because it was in a secluded spot; in that difficult time of war, celebrations might have been misunderstood.

Fulsome praise had been heaped upon the young doctor in a series of brief speeches; he, in turn, found the right words to thank this group who had adopted him so warmly. The food was superb, the wine flowed freely, and a troupe of dancers performed some risqué numbers to great applause. Julius, who had drunk little, was kept busy fending off the advances of a fetching brunette. It soon became evident that Alix Roth, who managed the Nagyvarad branch of an Austrian sailing and touring company belonging to her late husband's family, was the widow Theo had been so keen for him to meet.

Leaning toward him "the better to be heard," and giving him an unobstructed view of a daring décolletage, she told him the story of her life: the daughter of a Madrilène heiress and a Geneva banker, she had married Heinz Roth while still "very young" and had borne him three sons, all grown up now and living in Vienna. She claimed to be a mere thirty-eight years old and, under the flattering lights of the room, did not look a day older. Though she had arrived barely two years earlier, she spoke Romanian faultlessly, the language being close to her mother tongue. However, she did not speak Hungarian.

They conversed in German, which she spoke very well, with a charming Spanish accent. The main theme of her discourse was the loneliness she felt; the looks she sent him were unequivocal. Somehow he managed not to react. He might be tempted—he was tempted—but there were too many people watching, and he had just seen how fast a rumor could spread.

As he was having a rather late breakfast the following morning, the flustered maid came to tell him he was wanted outside. Andreas ran after him. A chauffeur in uniform stood beside the open door of Szamuely's black car. There was no one inside. The man handed him a sealed envelope. He opened it, drew out the single sheet, and read with increasing incredulity.

"My dear son-in-law"—that from the pharmacist!—"on the occasion of your twenty-fifth birthday, my wife, Golda, and I are giving you this car as a token of our esteem and affection. We shall go on paying the salary of Vadim, the chauffeur, for three months, so you can learn how to drive." It was signed "Emil Szamuely."

A very surprised young man settled in the comfortable leather seat and let Vadim drive him to the hospital. What had prompted his father-in-law to give him such an expensive gift? What did it mean? There was no way out: he would have to thank him in person.

A little after nine that evening, the chauffeur stopped the car in front of the Szamuely mansion on Teleky Street. Julius got out, took a deep breath, and rang the bell. The maid greeted him with stupefaction.

"I wish to see my father-in-law. Will you see if he can receive me?" he said.

"I shall ask him," she replied and led him through the vestibule into the drawing room. He had not set foot there since the end of the shiva for Georgy a year earlier. Nothing had changed. Tears stung his eyes; he wiped them swiftly away, angry at this show of weakness in what he still perceived as the house of the enemy. He looked with loathing at the couch and the chairs and moved restlessly toward the window, though it was dark at such a late hour. A heavy tread announced the arrival of the master of the house. Julius turned around. Emil looked unwell. He had lost weight and new lines marked his haughty face. Their eyes met.

"I have come to thank you for the truly splendid gift you have given me. I never expected—"

"Say no more. Golda and I—we don't need this car. We feel better with our trusty coachman and his horse."

"But should you change your mind…"

"Then we shall buy another car."

"Very well."

As Szamuely was about to add something, Julius raised his hand.

"Wait. I have to tell you…to tell you how sorry I am for some of the things I said when my little boy died. I was so unhappy, so angry, that I said some unpardonable things. I was wrong, and I beg your pardon." He sighed and went on painfully. "It was not your fault that he died. No one could have imagined that the young woman who was in charge would be so negligent of her duties that morning. Whatever caused you to entrust the child to her had nothing to do with the way she behaved. I should have told you these things earlier. Should have told you I know how much you have suffered. You had seen him brought into the world, he grew up under your roof, and you loved him passionately... perhaps as much as I did." He stopped, with a feeling of having done something that needed to be done.

The pharmacist blew his nose to hide his emotion. "Yes. Every day, every hour my thoughts go to him, to his innocent smile, his sweet face, so trusting...And I blame myself. Whatever you say, I blame myself...I thank you from the bottom of my heart. Now, if you have a minute, there is something I have to say to you. I too must apologize. I was mistaken about you, about your character, and I did not treat you fairly. This union with my daughter was repugnant to me because of your sister and aunt's past behavior. It happened a long time ago, and you had nothing to do with it being a mere child at the time. However, ever since you married my daughter you have behaved in an exemplary manner while she was often at fault. Your reputation today brings honor to your wife and to our family. I could not have hoped for a better son-in-law. I suppose it is too late?'

"Too late? Maybe not, if we tackle the issue."

"What do you mean?"

"It is time to look at the facts squarely. Magda lied. She made up the story of an idyll between my sister and Manny in order to make him bear the responsibility of a break— the truth being far different, as you know. Anna had barely exchanged a word with the young man she had met only three times in the presence of your daughter and myself. Manny, being a man of honor, offered to marry her to save her reputation; she was thrown into a state of confusion. She was terrified at the thought of having to leave her family to go far away with a man she barely knew, a man coming from a different world, of education and money."

Magda's father shook his head. "You may be right concerning your sister, but what about your aunt?"

"What about her? She was not there!"

"She knew my daughter's distress. It was her duty to inform me while there was still time."

"Magda had sworn her to secrecy. The idea that you might discover what had happened filled her with dread. She was convinced you would banish her from her home and throw her into the street. Besides, what could you have done? Let's speak frankly. Whatever potions are available do not always work, and some have side effects that can ruin a life forever."

"I would have been beside myself—that much is true. A normal reaction from a father. But I adored my daughter. Your aunt, who is a clever woman, knew which approach to take. So did Magda. It would have been enough to talk to Golda. She would have been the one to tell me. She would have found the right words. Magda was my only child, my only hope of grandchildren. I may have been hard with her, but I would never have abandoned her. Don't take that dubious air. Even if you doubt my affection for my daughter—which was greater then than it is now, I have to say—you know how much I value my good name and the family's reputation. How could I have held my head high if I had driven Magda away? I would have been a laughingstock. My wife and daughter knew me well enough to understand that. Not to mention the fact that Golda would never have let me do it. No. Had I been told in time, I would not have tried the methods you mentioned—I am well aware of their limits—nor would I have called on unsavory women who make a living out of illegal and dangerous practices."

"Isn't that what happened in the end?"

"Yes, but not here, and much later, when there was no other way out. It happened at a reputable and discreet establishment in Bucharest, under medical supervision. Had I known in time, I would have acted differently. A respectable union with a good man, ready to wed a virtuous young girl who had fallen prey to a despicable individual—and whose generous dowry would have made his life easier. He would not have been the first to close his eyes in exchange for a favorable match. The couple would have left immediately for a voyage abroad; the birth would have been announced some nine months later, and my daughter would have been able to come back and start her married life under the best auspices. You will never convince me that Donna did not keep silent because she was making plans for her daughter—or the girl she saw as her daughter—not forgetting the fact that she was betraying a terrified girl who had put her trust in her. By the time all this was made clear to me, it was too late. That dreadful Jozef forced my hand. I had to consent to the marriage to save my child from disgrace and humiliation."

"You are doing Donna a great wrong by accusing her of having done such a black deed. Yes, she loves Anna, but not to the extent of ruining Magda's life. Remember, had Magda not made up that crazy accusation about Manny falling in love with Anna, he would have gone back to Budapest with his family. That is what he intended to do when he discovered the truth. Magda took fright and ran home to present her own version first. He could have told the truth and ruined your daughter. He could have gone home, leaving Anna's reputation in tatters. He did neither."

"Even if that was true, Donna should have told me or Golda."

"Magda forbade her to do so. She wanted to marry Manny and believed until the last minute that she could get rid of the child in time. I am not sure you realize to what extent your daughter can persuade herself that she is right and that she will ultimately get what she wants."

"You don't seem overly fond of her!"

"I tried. I was foolish enough to believe she loved me, had fought for your approval of our union. It didn't last. She never tried. As soon as Georgy was born, it was as if I no longer mattered. You must have seen it. I was her husband, but she forbade me to join her in bed. I made another attempt when we moved into our own house; for a while I deluded myself that something had changed. I was wrong. Let's face it: it is not that she doesn't care for me. She doesn't have the slightest interest in me. I can live with that. What I cannot accept is her utter indifference to our children. You must have seen that as well. She has no patience with them and never shows them any affection. I don't believe she has taken Elisabeth in her arms once since the little girl was born. That said, I have no intention to renege on my vows. Magda is my wife; I shall treat her as such while protecting my children."

"I can't ask for more. I shall also give some thought to what you told me this evening."

"I assume Magda intends to come home soon. Why such a long absence?"

"She will explain. I wish she would hurry, since Golda is with her. She swore she would be back before the end of July." He lowered his head and added quietly, "There is something else I have to say, regarding my relationship with a woman…"

"There is no need for that!"

"Yes, there is. You hold your mother-in-law in high esteem, and what I have to tell you matters to me. After the birth of Magda, my wife had two miscarriages in rapid succession. Dr. Birnbaum explained in no uncertain terms that another pregnancy would be fatal and asked me—ordered me!—to move to another room. I was thirty-three years of age and could not accept enforced celibacy to the end of my days. I thought about a divorce. I could have married again, had other children. I did not. I loved my wife, and I adored my little girl. I have to say too that I would never have been able to pay back Golda's considerable dowry. The solution—you know. Golda did not complain. I was very careful in the beginning, but with the years, more and more people knew about it. Let me tell you it is not the best solution. There is nothing like the warmth of a true home filled with three or four children. One has to make do with the cards one is dealt. There you are. Don't say a word. I just wanted you to understand…"

While being driven home in his luxurious automobile, Julius felt the first stirrings of compassion for the man he had hated for so long. At the same time, he could not help wondering what was keeping Magda and her mother abroad for so long—and what the pharmacist was not telling him.

June ended without bringing an answer but with a few changes. Now that he had a car and a chauffeur, Julius could spend more time with his children when he came back from the hospital, before he had to be in his office. The gleaming machine fascinated his little boy, who listened to Vadim's explanations with him. The chauffeur, a Romanian in his early thirties who spoke Hungarian haltingly, waxed lyrical on the subject of the prestigious makers of the car, Mercedes-Benz. Saloon car, combustion engine, transmission, shifts... It was a whole new world for the young doctor who was eager to learn. Secretly he had dreamed of a car like that ever since his brother-in-law had let him drive one. Had dreamed—but had never really done anything about it. It had been too expensive at first, and when he had been able to afford it, he had come to the conclusion that it would be too ostentatious. And now the pharmacist was making the dream come true...

Julius had begun to study Romanian. Vadim had decided to come clean about his past and had disclosed he was a teacher by training but had been expelled because he had been a little too interested in a precocious student. One of his uncles ran a garage; he had taken pity on the young man who had adapted surprisingly well to mechanics and driving. Vadim and Julius were now conversing only in Romanian. Julius found the language easy enough thanks to his knowledge of French and Latin.

Though he was also beginning to drive competently, he assured Vadim that he intended to keep him on when the three months paid by Szamuely were up. The chauffeur had made himself indispensable, driving Donna and running errands willingly for the household. He had received a stern warning: one wrong move toward the three women who worked for the doctor, and he would be out. He swore he would not dream of mixing work with pleasure. Julius was not so sure, considering his past, but upon reflection concluded that none of the maids would present a powerful enough attraction. Viola the cook, happily married and quite fat, was old enough to be his mother. Ditta, though an excellent nurse for the children, was still unmarried because she was not very pretty. Irena, the maid, was flat where she should have been round and round where she should have been flat.

This little problem solved, Julius abandoned himself to the joys of owning a car. Soon the doctor's black automobile no longer attracted attention, and members of the community took pride in the success of one of their own. By mid-July he could drive alone and indeed would do so on Sundays, Vadim's day of rest. He was thus able to go back to the Two Crowns Inn for lunch, meeting there, by a well-planned "surprise" encounter, Alix Roth. She had taken the initiative elegantly.

"I am going to spend the next weekend at the inn," she had informed him during a chance meeting. "Why don't you have lunch with me? You don't have to answer right away. Come if you can."

He had come. After a very good meal, they drove to the forest for a walk; leaving the main road for a lane winding deeper into the trees, he parked the Mercedes in the shade. The weather was still perfect. They were protected from the sun by the tall trees, birds were twittering happily, and the air was scented by myriad blooms. Having had the forethought to bring a thick blanket, he spread it on the grass and soon discovered with great satisfaction that the charming widow was talented and gifted to a point that reminded him of his French countess in Vienna. Seen at close range, she may have been a little older than the thirty-eight years she owned up to, but this in no way detracted from her enthusiasm. There was an added advantage: it probably explained why she had told him not to worry, that she could no longer have children.

They went back to the inn in time for coffee with slices of the blackberry tart that was the specialty of the house. Dr. Matthias formally kissed the widow's small hand, assuring her it had been a most pleasant day and promising to come back soon. And, appearances thus being saved—neither wanted the affair to be discovered—he had driven home whistling happily to have dinner with his parents.

More than a month had gone by since Magda had left, and she was not missed much. New habits had been formed. Once a week Julius had lunch with his Austrian Circle friends in a private room on the second floor of the new fashionable restaurant recently opened on Theater Square, a bare five minutes' walk from his clinic. The owner, Hans Strauss, had left his Viennese hostelry to follow his wife, a Jewess from Nagyvarad. They called their new establishment the Beautiful Blue Danube in honor of the waltz created half a century earlier by another son of Vienna bearing his name. Well away from curious eyes or ears, the friends would discuss the latest developments and the way the war was going and would comment freely on local news.

Two or three times a month, Julius would have dinner with Theo and ZsaZsa, who had taken him to their hearts and treated him like the son they never had. On Saturday evenings, as soon as Shabbat was over, he went over to his father's, and the two men argued well into the night. They talked about the Bible, about the Graetz book that Julius was reading with great interest, and even about the war. Aaron saw everything through the prism of religion; his son had a liberal, secular approach, and they argued their respective points of view with passion. Donna, knitting silently in her favorite chair, raised her head from time to time to look fondly at her men.

Relations with the pharmacist had greatly improved. He had come for lunch one Sunday, and the weather had been so nice that a table had been set in the garden. Andreas had been allowed to sit with the adults, delighting both grand-fathers. Emil had talked quite civilly to Donna. Seated in the shade, Ditta watched over Elisabeth who was chortling and babbling in her crib. Julius would have called himself a happy man, but the rift with Sandor still hurt. A few times he had almost taken the car to go to the farm but stopped at the last minute, unsure both of his welcome and of his own sentiments.

It was not until Sunday, August 1, that Magda returned to the bosom of her family, arriving with no advance warn-ing just as lunch was ending. There was the noise of a car arriving and of a door being slammed shut. Julius walked out in his shirtsleeves as his wife entered, followed by a chauffeur carrying many suitcases. Magda was ordering the hapless driver about with no regard for her husband who was struck dumb. The mysterious absence was explained: Magda had gone to a discreet establishment to shed her excess weight. She was some thirty pounds slimmer and was wearing a very becoming and costly dress, but her face was almost gaunt, which gave her a hard look.

That was the problem. There had been no inner change. It was the same Magda: arrogant, unhappy with her lot, and angry with the whole world. She crossly rebuffed little Andreas, who had run to embrace the mother he had not seen for so long and had dared to touch her dress. And she did not spare a glance for her baby girl. At night, as husband and wife met in their bedroom, Magda declared haughtily that she had not made such a great effort just to lose everything to another pregnancy; she suggested Julius take over the downstairs room.

That was too much. Pale with anger, he told her it was out of the question. "It is time you understood I am not one of your servants, someone you can dismiss at will. I am your husband, and you owe me respect and obedience. You smile? You are making a mistake. I am warning you. I am ready to take all necessary precautions, but you are my wife and must behave as such. I shall not lead a life of celibacy at twenty-five!"

"What if I refuse?"

"If you refuse I shall consider my oath to your father void, and I shall send you back to him," he said.

"Very well. I shall take the children!" she answered defiantly.

"No, you won't. The children stay here with me. It will not be difficult to find witnesses who will swear that you have been a bad mother. Your absence at the commemoration of the death of Georgy has not been forgotten. Believe me, I shall easily get a divorce and keep the children. Then I won't have any trouble finding a suitable young woman who will gladly share my bed and take care of my children before giving me more."

Magda stood there, hardly believing what he had said, and suddenly burst into tears. It was the first time he had seen her cry. He took her in his arms, and one thing led to another…

Dr. Julius Matthias had won the first battle, but the war was just beginning.

10

UNDERCURRENTS

ELISABETH MATTHIAS CELEBRATED her first birthday on February 18 according to the Jewish date and a little earlier than the actual date on the civil calendar. There was a picture to commemorate the event. The little girl, who had started walking early, was standing and facing the photographer hired by the pharmacist. She was wearing a white fur coat with a matching hat that did not quite cover her vivacious face, and her dark eyes were full of curiosity. Grandfather Emil had bought the coat and the hat over his daughter's protests: they were far too dear for garments that would be too small by next winter.

Andreas, the big brother, already almost three years old, wearing fur-lined boots and a thick woolen coat, stood next to her, a protective hand on her shoulder. They were good friends, these two, and their laughter filled the house with sunshine. Behind them the grandparents, warmly dressed as well since a bitter cold had seized the town. The snow had fallen heavily and only sleds could negotiate the frozen roads.

Emil and Golda were beaming. So were Aaron and Donna. The four had grown closer in the past months. The two men would never be true friends; they had nothing in common bar the two children. Golda and Donna, on the other hand, were now meeting regularly. Together they bought clothes and toys for the little ones or took them on outings to the park. The new situation was not to Magda's liking. Standing to the right of her father, she looked impatiently at the camera seeming anxious to be done. Still as slim as she had been when she'd come back seven months earlier, she was stylishly dressed in a long black mink coat with a fashionable hat.

Dr. Matthias, soberly dressed in a dark suit and heavy winter coat, one hand on his son's shoulder and the other on his aunt's, had a distant look. It had been a difficult time for him. Magda had waged a merciless war, and it had taken a New Year's Eve party where both had drunk too much for her to concede. She had made him pay dearly for that first night's weakness. Not that she overtly refused herself; she simply made abundantly clear the extent to which his unwanted attentions were repugnant to her. Most of the time she feigned sleep when he came to bed. She was angry at him and at the situation, and she did not care if the whole world saw it.

The children knew better than to approach her; she was quick to scold them if they were too noisy. The servants obeyed her wordlessly. Barely a month after her return, she had tried to bribe the chauffeur: she wanted him to spy on her husband and to tell her who the "whore" was that he was sleeping with. Vadim had turned her down and reported the incident to his master. A few days later, the chauffeur had noticed a car following them wherever they went and confronted its driver. It transpired that the younger Mrs. Matthias, convinced that, just like her father, her husband had set up a mistress in an apartment somewhere in town, had turned to a sleazy detective agency to get proof. It was a waste of money.

Julius, extremely prudent as a rule, was even more careful. He did manage to meet Alix several times a month thanks to the tacit help of his friends of the Austrian Circle. In any case it would never have entered his wife's mind that he could be unfaithful with someone who belonged to their milieu and was older than he was to boot. The agency had apparently given up after a few weeks; Magda was still suspicious, still looking for a weapon that would make it possible to leave her husband and take her children with her. She knew well enough that without Andreas and Elisabeth, she would not be welcome in her father's home and would be ostracized by society. However, such a weapon was not easily found.

Julius had made a solid reputation for himself. His waiting room was always full. Of late he had made a point of going to the Friday services at the synagogue with his father, a move that was duly noted and much approved; it was felt he was a credit to his people. Neighbors sang the praises of a doctor who never refused to visit, even when the patient was too poor to pay, though they did not like his wife who was too proud to answer their timid salutations. Not that she minded. She had her own little coterie—four or five ladies with whom she had lunch or coffee once a week, always coming back with a satisfied smile. Strangely enough, her own mother was never invited, which made Julius suspicious: was Magda trying to gather allies for the day when she would make a break for it?

He was right. An agitated Theo came to see him one day as he was about to leave his office and go home.

"Listen," Theo said. "This afternoon I had tea with ZsaZsa at the Two Songbirds—you know, the fashionable new place on the square. Your wife was just leaving but didn't see us. As luck would have it, we were seated next to her table—I mean, her friends were still there. They were talking about you. It seems Magda is feeding them lies. You neglect her; you spend nights away from home; worse, you contribute nothing to the war effort. The last accusation was probably intended for Margit Grosz, who runs a girls' school and whose two sons are in the army." He looked at his friend. "My little Yuli, I don't need to draw a picture, right?"

"Indeed. But what can I do?"

"Think about it, talk to your aunt, but do something!"

"Do something, do something," ruminated the young doctor on his way home. But what? In the end he recounted the problem to his mother-in-law.

Golda listened silently, a pained expression on her face. "I was hoping things were getting better between you two," she said. "You did right to come to me. I know Margit very well, and I shall set the record straight. Next time we meet, I shall make a point of telling her the many hours you spend taking care of the wounded. I shall add that you are a very good father. Coming from me—Magda's mother—it will be enough. Margit is an intelligent woman; she will understand."

The following week an irate Magda came back from her lunch in a foul mood.

Then fate intervened. The year was coming to an end; the Austrian Circle celebrated in their usual room on the first floor of the Blue Danube. There was a lively band, French champagne flowed, and when Julius and Magda got home well after midnight, she turned to him, embracing him with a forgotten passion. Somehow, in the ensuing frenzied love-making, the usual precautions were forgotten. Morning sickness and other symptoms were the result, though she was yet to say a word about it; this child, so eagerly awaited by her parents, was obviously not welcome.

The year 1916 did not usher in great hopes. The war dragged on despite a number of successes. Serbia, the primary cause of the conflict, had been overrun, and its neighbors—Bulgaria, Albania, and Austro-Hungary—were busy contemplating how best to carve it up between themselves. The Italian offensive had been a failure. Turkey was holding England in check on the Bosporus Strait. Russia, whose forces had threatened the dual monarchy, had been no match for the reinforcements Germany dispatched. Abandoning their Polish ally, they were retreating all over and heading for home. However, Germany itself appeared mired in its fight against the French forces.

In his hospital Dr. Matthias and his colleagues were experiencing the terrible price the war was exacting. Russia—the enemy—had been hardest hit: one million dead so far and millions taken prisoner—numbers unparalleled in the history of the Western world. On the winning side, more than seven hundred thousand had been killed or wounded on the Russian front alone. There was now a military section in the Nagyvarad cemetery; in the adjacent Jewish cemetery, the graves with the Star of David were threatening to spill out of the plot they had been allotted. The hospital was proving too small to accommodate the steady influx, and wounded soldiers were lying on makeshift beds in the corridors. Disabled veterans became a common sight in the city's streets; some had taken to begging, and the sight of the haggard faces of these young men, doomed to lives of misery, added to the feeling of hopelessness.

At the same time, a growing number of women were looking for work, the death of husbands or sons having left them destitute. Prices were high, and because of diminishing supplies some goods were fast disappearing from the shelves—some finding their way onto the black market, a new phenomenon. More and more people were blaming the Jews, though there was no evidence they were responsible for the situation or the profiteering. The community was doing all it could for the war effort. They subscribed massively to war bonds issued by the state. Jewish ladies were knitting woolen hats and scarves for the soldiers and visiting the wounded. The promoter of the Black Vulture complex, where Julius had his clinic, founded an orphanage for fatherless children, and once a week Dr. Matthias treated the little patients free of charge.

Of late there had been something else for him to worry about. There had been some developments in Budapest, he believed. Anni denied there was a problem; however, her voice told a different story. Manny pretended not to know what the matter was, though he too sounded stressed. When Julius insisted, he complained about the economic situation and the havoc the war was playing on the European monetary system. It sounded like diversionary tactics. Julius discussed the situation with his aunt who was sitting in the garden with the children one Sunday afternoon; she admitted to having the same feeling.

Magda, who had joined them for some unknown reason, knitted her brows and made a surprising suggestion. "If you are so worried, why don't you go and see her?"

"Go and see her?" Coming from her, that was the last thing he would have expected.

"Why not? You have not seen her in ages!" She gave him a slow, lazy smile. She was looking her best that day, with the special bloom women sometimes have at the beginning of pregnancy. She was yet to put on weight, though her breasts were larger and her face somewhat rounder, softer. She must have known she was pregnant, yet she still said nothing, leading her husband to wonder when she was going to tell him or her parents. "There is no reason you can't take a few days off, is there? Or you could accompany a convoy, like you did last year…" She smiled again, the same lazy smile. "Why don't you take Aunt Donna with you? She would like that, wouldn't she?"

Thus addressed, Donna exchanged a glance with Julius. Magda hated Anni, that was well-known. So why the sudden solicitude? Yet the idea had merits.

Magda was going on: "You don't have to worry about the children. Ditta is taking very good care of them. Besides, I shall stay home to make sure. If you leave on Thursday morning, you could come back on Sunday evening."

"It is very kind of you. I shall think about it."

"Not for long, I hope. She needs you now. You have until Wednesday to settle everything. It should be enough. Tomorrow I shall tell Father; you may phone your sister to tell her about your visit."

"I'd rather wait. You never know. I might not be able to get away—or she might tell me not to come."

His wife shrugged and said no more. The following morning, he went to see Commandant Mihaly who gave his permission on the spot and saw no objection at his staying in Budapest till Sunday.

"Come to think of it, it would be very helpful. There is an important meeting at the War Ministry on Friday; they have to decide what to do in the face of the growing number of wounded. You shall represent us, which will make your trip official, with all attendant perks."

"But I am not a soldier!"

"Perfect! You can say what you want without fear of offending your superior officers."

So happy was Mihaly with this solution to a problem that had been taxing him that he gladly signed all the necessary papers for Donna Matthias to accompany the doctor on that Thursday morning's military convoy. Everything was ready; however, Julius had not said a word to his sister beyond checking that she had no intention of leaving Budapest in the coming days.

Magda was still unnaturally helpful. On Tuesday evening she announced that she would spend the following night at her father's because they had important matters to discuss. "I shall go back with him when we finish work and stay overnight so as not to wake you, but I will be home by mid-morning. By the way, I have bought presents for your sister's children. They are on the low table in the entrance hall."

Once again Julius told himself there was something going on…and then promptly forgot. Taking advantage of his wife's absence, he invited his parents to come for dinner early so Andreas could sit with them. Donna came alone. Aaron had caught a cold. Though not running a fever, he would need to stay home for the next few days. The young doctor was thus not really surprised when his aunt came very early on the morning of the trip to tell him she would not be going.

"I know him too well. He has never been careful of his health. Besides, he hates bothering people, so he wouldn't ask for help if he felt really unwell. I can't leave him alone. He might take it into his head to go to the synagogue on Friday evening. It's a good thing you didn't inform Anni we were both coming, so she won't be disappointed...Me? Of course I am disappointed. I was looking forward to embracing her and her darling children again after nearly two years. But I would never forgive myself if something happened to your father while I was away."

As Julius settled on the train, he could only agree; deep down he much preferred her to stay with his father. Still, he would have liked her presence during the endless voyage.

The first-class compartment he had been assigned had known better days; its curtains were torn, and the leather of the once plush seats was worn. His fellow travelers were two officers rejoining their units on the Russian front; understandably, they were in a foul mood. The train went very slowly and stopped frequently for reasons that were not made clear to the passengers.

In the inadequately heated compartments, the soldiers were shivering in the bitter cold, their heavy coats no match for the wind that invaded the dilapidated wagons. The field kitchen set up on the train could not make hot drinks fast enough. The mood was somber. Those soldiers who had been nursed back to health had no wish to go back into the fray; their disabled brethren were fearful of what civilian life would hold for them. One of them even tried to throw himself into a river as the train rolled over a bridge, only to be thwarted at the last minute by his companions, acting more out of a wish to close the window than to help him.

Called in, Julius found a terrified individual some thirty years old who had lost his right leg and was sobbing hysterically. Julius tried to comfort him and gave him some laudanum to sedate him.

They had left at eight in the morning, but it was not until a few minutes before six in the evening that the train and its weary passengers entered the makeshift station by the hospital. Night had fallen. Dr. Matthias lingered on a platform badly lit by gas lamps. He knew most of the men who were reluctantly leaving the train; he had treated many of them for weeks. Some came to him for some last-minute advice. Others limped by with their parents who wanted updates on their conditions. He was therefore not surprised when a deep voice asked whether he was the train doctor. He turned round with a start and recognized Count Von Thuringen, wearing the uniform of a lieutenant colonel in a Hussar regiment.

"What can I do for you, Count?" Julius asked politely.

"Have we met?" There was no little surprise in the man's tone.

"Indeed. Dr. Julius Matthias, at your service. I am the brother-in-law of Nagy, the banker."

The count nodded and observed him with interest. "Nagy's brother-in-law, yes, I remember. At the opera, right? Before the war... Tonight I am looking for a soldier from my estates. I don't see him."

"He may be still in Nagyvarad. What is his name?"

"Hans. Hans Grunewald."

"The name does not ring a bell. I don't remember meeting him."

The count lowered his head, trying to hide his disappointment. "I understand, thank you." There was real pain in his voice.

"Listen, I could be wrong," said Julius impulsively. "You don't happen to have a photograph?"

"I do, but not here—at my office at the Ministry of War."

"I have to be there tomorrow morning for a meeting. At ten. If you wish I could come to see you before—."

"Could you? That is very kind of you."

The two men made their way slowly toward the hospital where they parted company. The officer on duty was the same Lemberg who had welcomed Julius a year ago. Julius had a moment of irrational fear: was the young man going to mention the Pannonia hotel while the count was still close enough to hear? It didn't happen; Lemberg greeted him civilly and at his request led him to a telephone. Julius was relieved to hear his sister's voice.

"Julius! Is that you? Nice of you to call. Is everything all right?"

"Yes, indeed. What's for dinner?"

"Tonight? It's goulash. Want some?" She laughed at her own joke.

"With pleasure. Hold dinner. I shall be there in half an hour."

"Are you serious? You are in Budapest?"

"I have just arrived. Tell you all about it when I see you."

It was another corporal—beardless this time—who drove him; he was to come back in the morning to take Julius to the Ministry of War. When he was safely ensconced in the best guest room, which bore the signs of recent occupation, Julius passed round the presents so carefully chosen by his wife: for eight-year-old Myriam, a doll in national dress; for Tibor, nearly twelve, an illustrated history of automobiles. The children were delighted; so was Anni with her gift of a lace blouse. There was even a silk scarf for Manny. Once again Julius wondered what his wife was up to.

Later Anni sent the children away, reminding them to write a thank-you note to their aunt right away. Brother and sister remained alone. Anni sat on the bed. She was unusually pale and looked quite upset. Eyes downcast, she seemed in no hurry to speak.

"Who has slept here?" asked Julius, not really interested in the answer.

"Manny."

"Manny?"

"Julius, you have no idea. It is so dreadful!" She burst into tears. He sat next to her and drew her to his chest, but she only sobbed harder. He stroked her hair and murmured soothing words. She dried her eyes and began her story without moving out of the protective circle of his arms.

Two weeks earlier policemen had burst into the house at two in the morning and ordered Manny to go with them, without a word of explanation. He had come back after two days. What he had to say was deeply disturbing. A secretary had gone to the police badly beaten and with her clothes in disarray. She had accused him, her boss, of having assaulted her that very night. By an extraordinary stroke of luck, the banker had been able to prove his innocence: that evening he and several colleagues had been attending an emergency meeting at the Central Bank, which had lasted well into the night. He had then driven one of his colleagues home, dropping him off at one in the morning—exactly the time the woman was claiming she had been attacked.

She had finally admitted that the man who had beaten her was her boyfriend who had discovered she was having an affair with Manny. That was when she had decided to avenge herself on her boss, who, she said, had seduced her and then discarded her contemptuously.

The whole mess had quickly gotten out; the tabloid press had written virulent articles against the "Jewish banker." Stones had been thrown at Manny's car, at the bank, and at the high walls surrounding the house. As the so-called victim was also Jewish, the story had died down. Anni shuddered to think what would have happened had the woman been a Christian. Now she could no longer meet the pitying glances of her friends or the snide remarks of her enemies, and the children were being jeered and taunted at school.

She blew her nose and started crying again.

"What does Manny say?" asked her brother.

"He said it only happened once, and she started it."

"You don't believe him?"

She shrugged wearily. "I don't know. What does it matter? You see, it wouldn't have been the first time. Don't look so surprised. First, men are all alike. Don't tell me you have never been unfaithful; I wouldn't believe you. Now, Manny…When we got married, I knew nothing about…you know. He was very patient with me, never complained that I was too…Anyway, I found out fairly quickly that he was not always faithful. I said nothing. After the birth of our first child, things got much better; he told me I was the wife he had always dreamed of having, and there was no more talk. At least here in Budapest. I supposed that when he was away in Vienna or in Switzerland, he did not always resist temptation. It might shock you, but I did not really mind, as long as it was done discreetly.

"This time—this time it was different. Having an affair with a bank employee, a woman I have met, embarrassing his poor father, putting our children in an intolerable situation, and at this particular time! You should have seen some of the papers. And I am not talking about those two agonizing days when he was in jail, people demonstrating in front of the bank, yelling, 'Death to the Jews'…"

"I understand. Is that why you are making him sleep in this room?"

"You don't think I was right?"

"No."

"No!" She looked at him accusingly. "You are taking his side? Yuli! How can you?"

"I am not taking his side. True, he let himself be tempted, but, as you said yourself, if nobody had heard about it, you would not really have minded. Did you think for one minute about what he went through? About those two days in jail, and in what conditions? At this baseless accusation? You know how proud he is. He had to fight, to hold on, to get it over with, go back to work at the bank, face the nasty remarks and the tasteless jokes, face stones and threats. And he had to do it alone. You, his wife, turned your back on him. You have humiliated him in front of his children by banishing him to this room. In front of his children and in front of the servants as well. Are you so sure they haven't said anything to their colleagues who work for your friends, your acquaintances? Was it wise? Did you give a thought to what will happen tomorrow? To your future? His? That of the children?

"Admit that you haven't been very generous. You might have remembered what happened when Magda tried to blame you for her broken engagement. He chose not to abandon you; he chose to marry a penniless, provincial little nobody.

Yet when he needed you—when he needs you now—you abandon him. That was not well done. You should have stood by him, gone out with him. Looked people squarely in the face. Shown your children that you still loved him, told them not to listen to vicious gossip. The whole thing would have blown over quickly. Believe me, people have other worries these days. I ask you again: did you ever think of your future?"

She pushed him away and ran out of the room. Her brother thought it was a good thing he had come and a better one that he was alone. It might not be too late to help. He took a bath to wash away the journey's grime and went to the library, the room where the family usually met before dinner. Only his brother-in-law was there, but he rushed to embrace him with unwonted warmth.

"My very dear Julius, you have no idea how happy I am to see you. Had I been inclined to religion, I would say providence has sent you. Anni has just left. She hugged me and said as far as she's concerned, that sorry episode is over. I don't know what argument you used to sway her, but I thank you from the bottom of my heart."

"I did what I could because I love you both. That state of affairs was calamitous for the two of you. However, I would never have believed you could be so lacking in common sense."

"I assume there is no point in telling you that you are right, and I have been kicking myself ever since. There is no excuse, though the woman did set me up. She was employed in another department. One evening, as I was working late, she came into my office with some papers that she put down on my desk, and then she allegedly felt faint. I got up to help; she fell into my arms, murmuring she needed air, and started undoing the buttons of her bodice. One thing led to another, though I am not sure I took the first step…It was over very quickly. She came back the following day. This time I wanted none of it, so she tried to blackmail me, threatening to go to my wife. I replied calmly that should she take such an unconsidered step, the bank would have to do without her services. She walked out without a word. As far as I was concerned, that was it. I was having so many other problems…"

"She didn't try to pretend she was pregnant?"

"It wouldn't have worked. Believe me, I had enough good sense to withdraw in time. Anyway, she made me pay very dearly for a few—a very few—moments of pleasure. Mind you it could have been worse: the night she chose to go to the police was the only one in a long time when I had an ironclad alibi. Otherwise…I still wake up at night thinking about it. I spent two days in police custody, not in jail, and was treated well, since I know when to be generous. But Anna…Anna took it badly, and who could blame her?"

"She had a terrible fright. She feared for you, for the children. Anger came later."

"You could be right. Thank God—and you—she is ready to forgive. But here I am, talking away and not even asking what has brought you to Budapest."

"I was worried about Anni. I felt something was wrong, but she would not say anything. As for you, you tried to put me off with lofty talks about the crisis. For some reason the children were never able to come to the phone when I called. Aunt also sensed that something had happened. Well, I have only one sister; she appeared to be in trouble, so I went to the hospital's commandant, who was only too happy to send me here, since he never has enough doctors to accompany convoys—you would not believe the number of wounded coming and leaving on a daily basis."

"What a blessed idea! How long will you be staying?"

"I am returning with the Sunday evening convoy."

"If it were absolutely necessary, could you stay longer? Say a week?"

"Difficult but not impossible. The commandant will not be happy but will do nothing. My secretary will have to reschedule some appointments. What do you have in mind?"

Manny thrust his hand through his hair where more than a few white threads had appeared. "What I am going to ask goes beyond friendship, so listen quietly and think about it. You can give me your answer tomorrow. If you agree, it will take an enormous weight off my chest. If you can't I shall understand, you won't have to explain, and it will never be mentioned again."

"That sounds ominous. You don't happen to have some of that excellent French cognac? Though now that we are at war with France…"

"Please, let's not talk about the war. Pure madness. You know, contrary to what you may have heard, Prime Minister Tisza was very much against it. He had to bow to pressure. We are all paying the price today. However, I have enough French cognac to last the war…and to let you have a bottle to take home." He poured the precious liquid into two crystal goblets, handed one over to Julius, and began.

"The problem I want to discuss is not new, but it is getting worse. It is my considered opinion that we are sitting on a powder keg, the fuse of which has already been lit. It may not explode tomorrow, but explode it will. You see, I do not believe the war will be over quickly. I am privy to confidential reports from our correspondents in all the capital cities of Europe. It looks more and more as if Romania is going to enter the fray on the side of the Allied forces, having been guaranteed all of Transylvania—Nagyvarad included—after the defeat of the central powers. Personally I don't know who will win; nothing has been decided yet, and I am afraid the fighting will go on for a long time, afraid that we are going to see unspeakable horrors. I don't have to tell you the human toll so far.

"Dreadful things are happening. Germany has not been able to advance at Verdun and is now using deadly gas in defiance of all humanitarian principles. The British are using warplanes to bomb their enemies with no regard for civilian populations. Germany is forming its own air force. Austria and Hungary have understood, far too late, that this war is a ruinous folly; many in our government are in favor of a separate peace now that Serbia has fallen. Unfortunately, supporters of Germany in that same government are more numerous and more determined. They are powerful, very powerful. To tell you the truth, I fear them. They hate us; they accuse us openly of making money out of the conflict, of running the black market, and even of collaborating with the enemy. Should the situation get worse, we would be the ideal scapegoat. By 'we' I mean Jews in general and Jewish bankers in particular.

"At the same time, anarchist and revolutionary movements are gaining strength. They don't like us either and target Jewish bankers as symbols of the capitalist system they want to destroy. Never mind that several Jews are to be found in their ranks. Feeding on anti-Jewish sentiments, the wildest rumors are floating around and gaining credence; Jews are accused of growing fat on Hungarian blood, of not taking part in the war effort, of not enlisting in the army. It is true there aren't many Jewish privates, but that is because there are practically no illiterates among us. In fact, ten percent of the officers are Jews—more than double our percentage in the population.

"As you know, I decided more than a year ago to emigrate to the United States. Karol is enjoying himself there and keeps asking us to join him. It will not happen tomorrow since my father adamantly refuses to move. I had to give him my word that we would not leave until he went to join his wife in heaven, as he puts it. However, the situation is so bad that I have been thinking of sending Anna and the children to Switzerland. We have a comfortable house by the lake of Geneva, where we often spend our vacations. The children know the place well and have some friends among the neighbors; if need be they can wait there until the end of the war.

"Today, following that unfortunate episode at the bank, this move has become urgent. Your sister has told you there have been demonstrations outside our home; you can imagine what would happen if there were a sudden crisis. This is where you come in. I cannot leave town now. My father hardly comes to the bank anymore, and I am alone to bear the brunt...Keeping abreast of the ever-changing monetary market is a task that demands every minute of my time. There is more. The government is negotiating a new loan with private bankers to help finance the war effort. It is my honor to have been chosen to represent five establishments belonging to our brethren for these negotiations, which will be difficult. On top of all that, one needs special permits to travel, and I could never get them."

"And you think that I—"

"Yes. I can't send Anni alone with the chauffeur. Not that I don't have absolute trust in him; however, I would feel better with someone like you onboard. You never know what can happen. You will have my car—not the one you knew; I have a roomy Mercedes—and Istvan can make it to Geneva, with suitable breaks for sleeping, in less than four days. If you leave tomorrow, Friday, you should be able to be back in Nagyvarad by the end of next week."

"Probably not. There must be close to a thousand miles to cover, and it will not be easy to find petrol. On the other hand, I shall be able to do my share of the driving. I have a Mercedes myself—a present from my in-laws—and I have been told I am an outstanding driver."

"You mean you agree?"

"Let me think about it."

"That's enough for now. Let me tell you that for organization, you can rely on Istvan. He knows where suitable inns can be found, where one can get petrol, and where repairs can be made if necessary. More important, he is well-known and will have enough gold coins to guarantee prompt and courteous service."

"That is not the question. You have taken me by surprise. I have to think."

Julius took another sip of the cognac he was so fond of—curious, when alcohol in general did not tempt him. To take his sister to Switzerland, to get away from his troubles at home, from the hospital—why not? The idea appealed to him immensely.

"You know," he told his brother-in-law, "if it is possible, I shall do it. Not that I share your pessimism; however, I could be wrong, and I would not want to endanger my sister by doing nothing. As it happens, I may know how to get the necessary permits," he added, thanking the lucky stars that had prompted him to offer his help to the count. "I have a meeting at the Ministry of War tomorrow morning, and I shall see to it. Has Anni agreed? I mean, you have talked it over with her, right?"

"No, but she will agree for the sake of the children. Furthermore, this temporary separation will be welcome. It will give us time to put the recent episode squarely behind us."

"If I obtain the permits, will she be ready to leave immediately? Tomorrow?"

"Absolutely. Don't forget, the house is furnished and fully equipped, and the children always leave toys, books, and clothes there."

"If you are through plotting, dinner is ready." Anna had entered quietly.

"With pleasure," replied Julius. "I am famished. However, I would like to call home to confirm my safe arrival and to check on Father who was not feeling well."

Surprisingly it was Donna who answered the phone. She explained that everything was fine. Aaron was feeling better. However, since Magda was very tired, she had gone to bed early, after asking Donna to await his call.

Brother and sister exchanged startled glances. First the presents and then this solicitude; was Magda changing for the better? However, they had too many things on their minds that evening and promptly forgot about it.

The following morning Dr. Julius Matthias, presenting a fine figure in one of his new outfits, arrived at the Ministry of War. The duty officer checked his name against a list and instructed an underling to take him to Count Von Thuringen who appeared to be held in high esteem. There was no one in the waiting room, but the door to the inner office was open. He entered and stood rooted to the spot.

Standing, the count was pale; facing him, reclining on an armchair, was Madi. There was blood on her hair and on her woolen dress. Her eyes were shut, as if she had fainted. A heavyset woman in her fifties—probably the secretary—was slapping her cheeks, uttering distressed little cries. Julius drew a deep breath, pushed the woman aside, and bent over Madi, throwing a questioning glance at the count.

"My relative, Mrs. Corvin, was struck by a stone while she was on her way to work. She refused to go to the hospital and came directly here," was the brief explanation.

Julius winced. This was what Madi had been afraid of… He took off his jacket, rolled up his sleeves, and delicately probed her head with his fingers. Then he asked for hot water and a towel, which the secretary promptly brought, and he carefully cleaned the wound.

Madi opened her eyes and jerked her head in surprise. "Dr. Matthias!"

"You are acquainted?" The count was looking from the one to the other.

"Madame was at school with my sister," replied the doctor without stopping.

"And have you kept in touch?"

"I am afraid not. I had the pleasure of meeting her again a year or two ago when I came in to buy lace handkerchiefs for my wife." His examination complete, he stood up with a smile. "All that blood comes from a rather shallow wound.

Nothing to worry about but the shock. Give her a hot drink and let her rest for an hour. I will check again when my meeting is over, but there is no cause for alarm. She never lost consciousness, did she?"

It was the count who replied. "I don't think so." Turning toward the young woman, he asked: "You didn't faint, did you? How do you feel now?"

"No, I didn't faint. I was far too frightened to do so. There was a hackney carriage going by, and I ran toward it. The chauffeur was reluctant to let me enter because of the blood, but I gave him a gold coin…Now I have a headache, though I do feel better. I must call the boutique and ask the girl to bring me clothes, a hat, and my makeup. I must look a fright."

The two men exchanged smiles. If she was worried about her looks, she must indeed have been feeling better.

"I am sorry. No hat for the moment. I have to put on a bandage," said Julius.

"I have to wash my hair! I can't stay with all that blood.'

"Let your assistant do it for you. Now go and lie down, please. You have had a shock. You must rest.'

"I am indebted to you," said the count after the secretary had led Madi to the small salon attached to the suite of rooms. "Please be seated."

"Don't mention it. I had heard the streets here are not safe, but to that extent! Fortunately, it was a bad fright, no more. You wanted to show me some pictures?"

He looked long and hard at the picture of a young man who had more than a passing resemblance to the count. The son of a tryst with a woman of his estates?

Julius shook his head slowly. "Sorry, that soldier was never in my hospital."

"I was afraid of that. There is another possibility; however, I am loath to further impose upon your goodwill."

Julius decided the moment had come. "As it happens, I have a favor to ask of you…"

"Excellent. If it is in my power, it shall be granted" was the courteous reply.

"Because of the situation, my brother-in-law and I would like to see Madame Nagy and her two children safely settled in a property the family owns in Geneva. Nagy himself cannot leave Budapest now, as you can imagine. On the other hand, I might be able to take a few days off. By driving twenty-four hours a day—with the help of the family chauffeur—this could be accomplished in a week. The problem is that one needs a number of permits to travel in times of war…"

The count smiled at him benignly. "My dear young man, it seems providence has led you here…Go to your meeting. We shall discuss this further when you come back."

11

BETWEEN WORLDS

BARELY IN ITS FIRST QUARTER, the moon's feeble rays were no
match for the heavy cloud formations above. The empty
road, in a sleeping countryside where nothing moved, was
bathed in yellow by the car's headlamps. Cattle had been
rounded up to take shelter for the night, and field creatures
were snug in their burrows.

Though the temperature had not dropped below freezing, the wind was brutal, and it was bitterly cold. The car
windows were tightly shut, yet sudden gusts of glacial air
somehow managed to make their way in. Happily, everything possible had been done to ensure the passengers would
keep warm. Blankets would not have done the trick; heavy
furs, of the kind used for sleigh rides, covered them almost
from head to toe. Only the tops of their fur hats were visible.
Thick carpets had been laid on the floor. The three copper
braziers down there still exuded residual warmth; briquettes
heated almost to a breaking point had been put inside in place
of the usual hot coals.

Well wrapped in furs with only his cap emerging, the chauffeur was fast asleep. Both his hands on the steering wheel of the powerful car, Julius felt himself floating between two worlds. Behind him was Hungary, his familiar universe; in front of him stretched the unknown. He did not feel the cold in his bearskin jacket, his thick fleece-lined pants, and his fur boots; a fur hat with earflaps protected his head. He drove carefully, fighting the urge to go faster on a road he was travelling for the first time. Some unknown obstacle might spring up at any time: a tree trunk uprooted by last night's storm, branches torn by the wind, the carcass of some stray animal hit by a car. He had even been startled by a magnificent stag appearing from nowhere, bounding across the road. His worst fear was encountering a patch of ice.

There would be time for speed later, though there was no longer any need to hurry. A surprised but unconcerned Mihaly had readily agreed to Lieutenant Colonel Von Thuringen's request to extend Julius's absence "on a mission vital to the interests of the country, which would have to remain secret." Calling home to inform his wife, Julius had again found himself talking to Donna. In too much of a hurry to ask for explanations, he had informed her that he would be away for a week or longer and asked her to warn Amalia.

There was a lighter patch ahead, and he slowed down. But no, this was no ice patch, only a stray moonbeam that had broken free of the clouds. He accelerated again. He would not have admitted it for the world, but he was feeling better than he had in a long time. A series of coincidences was setting him on the path to a welcome jaunt under the best possible conditions. Manny had given him a startlingly large sum of money, and the count had entrusted him with an impressive document bearing a number of seals and signatures, ordering all subjects of the dual monarchy to render him every possible assistance. Official travel permits had been issued for each of his passengers.

His passengers...He risked a backward glance. They were all asleep after a hectic day. It had happened so fast. The meeting at the ministry had been over quickly in spite of the number of participants—some thirty people, the colorful military attire of the officers contrasting with the severe black dress of the civil servants. They were united in the same dismal conclusion: less than two years after the beginning of hostilities, hospitals all over the country, flooded with record numbers of wounded, were on the brink of collapse. Not enough beds, not enough equipment, not enough medical supplies, not enough nurses and doctors. Representatives of the relevant ministries, while not disputing the seriousness of the situation, had nothing to offer. There was no money left in the state's coffers and warehouses were empty.

To tell the truth, Julius had not followed the discussion closely in spite of a few choice remarks about the profits individuals of the Hebrew persuasion were making out of the misfortunes of their country. He had said nothing. What would have been the point? He was haunted by the memory of Madi, her head all bloody. Today she had escaped with a minor injury; however, with such an implacable enemy as the countess—who doubtless felt she could act with impunity under cover of the rising tide of anti-Jewish feeling—she might not be so lucky next time.

When Julius went back to the count's office, he had found Madi gone. It seemed she had insisted so much that the count had sent her home in his car, together with her assistant.

"I am sure there will be no new attack today. I have dispatched two veterans from my regiment, and they will stand guard," the count noted. He cleared his throat and went on. "You are a man of the world, so I shan't hesitate to tell you this person has been living under my protection for some ten years. You may have been aware of that fact through your family. I am sure I can depend on your discretion. I have let it be known that she is a distant relative I am helping as best I can."

Julius nodded his assent as an orderly bearing a tray with two cups of steaming coffee entered, putting a momentary end to the conversation. The flaky pastries also on the tray were very welcome since he had barely eaten at breakfast. When the man left, the count resumed. "Let us go back to your problem. You worry about your family; that is perfectly normal. I shall be happy to provide the necessary authorizations this very morning. I shall also supply you with sufficient vouchers to procure enough petrol for the trip, this commodity being severely rationed, as you know. However, I fear this will not be enough in these troubled times. Your automobile, or that of your brother-in-law, might be requisitioned by an overly zealous or corrupt officer at a chance roadblock. Therefore, I intend to put my own limousine, with the family coat of arms, at your disposal as well as a trustworthy corporal from my troop as chauffeur. This will ensure that you reach your destination safely."

He beamed with satisfaction at the young doctor who was looking at him speechlessly, trying to make sense of what he had just heard. The count took a sip of his coffee and added, "No, don't thank me yet. The fact is I have a favor to ask, and it is a big one. I am deeply worried about the fate of Private Hans Grunewald, who is a kinsman of mine. Therefore, after having seen your sister safely installed in Geneva, it is my hope that you will stop in Vienna on your way back. There are rumors that Hans was seen there, in one of the hospitals. I have been told you know the city well, having studied there. I would be very grateful if you could devote some hours—a day at the most—looking for him. You may not find him; it is quite possible the rumors are unfounded, and the poor boy was killed during the recent bout of fighting on the Russian front. However, my conscience will not let me rest until I have done everything in my power to ascertain what has happened to him."

The young doctor expressed his thanks, assuring the count he would do all he could to find the wounded soldier. To which his host said, in a slightly embarrassed manner, that he hoped Madame Nagy would not object to Madame Corvin's joining them on the trip to Geneva.

"Madame Corvin wishes to go to Geneva?" came the startled reply.

"To tell the truth, she does not know it yet, since I have not broached the subject with her. I thought about it just now, listening to you. However, there is no doubt she will immediately understand how necessary this trip is for her safety. Your sister, who is under the protection of her husband, does not feel safe because of her origins. Madame Corvin is in a far worse situation. You saw what happened this morning. A superficial wound, that's what you called it. What if the stone had been heavier, sharper? If it had struck an eye? If there had been more than one man throwing stones, or if he had thrown more than one stone? If a carriage had not so conveniently arrived? I am not always in town;

should I be away there would be no one to assist her. This cannot go on any longer, and I shall not have a moment's peace while she is so vulnerable. I was at my wits' end when you came in this morning; listening to you; it was clear that providence had sent you. Once in Geneva, she will be safe. She will have all necessary funds to await the end of the war."

He paused, searching for the right words. "I hope you will be able to explain the situation to your brother-in-law. I am sure he will realize how much safer it will be for his family to travel under the protection of a high-ranking nobleman and will persuade his wife…" The count looked questioningly at Julius who had been thinking furiously.

"Since you have done me the honor of talking frankly, let me answer in the same vein. Society has rules and shows no mercy to one who has left the fold, no matter how worthy that person may be. However, we are not living in normal times. I believe it will be possible to convince my sister by stressing that, thanks to your generous assistance, she will find sanctuary for herself and her children in Geneva after a safe journey. As for my brother-in-law, he too is a man of the world and will not hesitate for a minute."

"Very well. Let's get practical."

Warned by a hasty phone call, Manny arrived home as Julius was getting out of the army car, telling the driver not to wait for him. The two men settled in the library.

"What's the matter?" asked the younger man. "You look somber. Have you changed your mind? Anni doesn't want to go?"

"No, she does not refuse, far from it. She is extremely worried by the situation but hasn't discussed it with me, because…well, you know. Otherwise, she says, she would have been the one to suggest she go with the children to Switzerland. She looks forward to getting away from vicious gossip and false friends. Also, like me, she hopes a few weeks or months of separation will be good for us. She is already busy packing and getting the children ready."

"So what's the problem?"

"I am the one who is getting cold feet at the thought of such a long journey through countries at war. You have no weapon; neither has Istvan. What if you encounter bandits? It happened to one of our clients, and he was lucky to get out alive."

"Well, I can lay your fears to rest." As Julius recounted the count's generous proposal—and the attached condition, but not the special mission he had been entrusted with—Julius had the satisfaction to see his usually unflappable brother-in-law rendered speechless.

"Let's have a drink of the French cognac you are so fond of. I must say this takes my breath away."

"As it did mine, as it did mine. However, you must admit it is the perfect answer to all our problems. We shall sail through all checkpoints and never lack petrol. Furthermore, Anton, the count's corporal, has a weapon and knows how to use it."

"Petrol vouchers won't get you far without some gold coins to go with them. Yes, the proposal is not without merits. Only…"

"You are afraid of your wife's reaction."

"Yes. And I am not exactly in a good position to…"

"After all, they were good friends once."

"That's all in the past. The fact is you are talking about a kept woman, someone rejected by society. Your sister is convinced that today her peers are divided between those who pity her and those who despise her. She is bound to think travelling with this person would only start tongues wagging more furiously and make it impossible for our daughter to find a good match."

"Tongues wagging…Who will know? What do you think?'

"I think it's nonsense. I think the only thing that could threaten Myriam's chances would be for our bank to go bust. But I am afraid Anni will not agree. To tell the truth, I fear your sister is going to make a scene."

"Let me take care of her. After all, I am blameless, right? Listen, there is no time to lose. The car will be here at six, though we probably shan't leave the house before seven. Anton will drive until midnight, and then it will be my turn."

"I will get things ready. You deal with your sister."

"Deal with me? What do you mean?" Anni came in; she had been listening with mounting incredulity. "Yuli, are you out of your mind? Do you think I will agree to travel with a loose woman? That I will let her near my children? It's absolutely out of the question. Find another solution. Let her go in her paramour's car; we shall leave with Istvan."

"Too late. I have given my word. If you refuse I will have to go with her. Make up your mind quickly, because if you aren't coming, she will take her maid."

Her eyes filled with tears. "You would abandon your family, let us go alone, for a woman like that? Besides, why does she want to go? What is there in Switzerland that she can't find here? Silk for her hats?"

Julius, who was quite aware of the enormity of what he was asking, and who knew had he not been acquainted with the lovely redhead, he would not have agreed so readily, had prepared his argument carefully. "You forget that for the man in the street, she is as Jewish as you are. Since the war started, she has been insulted, spat upon, harassed. This morning she was attacked by a yelling mob; stones were thrown at her. She was lucky and escaped with minor injuries. Next time she might not be so lucky."

"Are you serious?" Anni had gone white.

"Perfectly serious. When I arrived in the count's offices this morning, I found her unconscious and covered in blood. Fortunately, the wound was not serious. Needless to say, she was terrified, and her friend was deeply worried. That's why he has agreed not only to procure us all necessary travel documents but also to let us have his car and a driver. Dearest, before you became a society lady, you were Madi's friend for many years. You must know she probably didn't have much choice when she agreed to live under his protection. He tells me they have been together for ten years. That does not make her a woman of ill repute. There is more. If you refuse, the count will be deeply offended. Can you, your husband, your family, afford to make such a powerful enemy? Look at Manny. He knows only too well how dangerous the man could be, especially these days, if he turns against you. Believe me, it would be far, far wiser to put him in your debt. You never know when you may need his help."

"But what will I tell the children?" she wept.

Manny, who had been holding his breath, released it with a relieved sigh. The worst was over.

"You can tell them she's an old school friend who has asked for your help. They are too young to ask questions. Come on, dry your tears and get moving. You leave at six!"

"You haven't had lunch yet."

"I am sure the servants will find something to give us. Go."

In the end the meeting between the two former friends went without a hitch. The sight of Madi, still very white, her head wrapped in a huge bandage, looking at Anni with a terrified expression, was all it took. Anni rushed to embrace her. The two women burst into tears under the satisfied glances of Manny and Julius, who then left them alone and went to make plans with Anton, who was wearing his uniform with all his decorations. He appeared to be in his late forties. The beginning of a paunch gave him a benign expression, belied by hard eyes in an impassive face. With great attention, he observed the way the two women met and would no doubt report it to his master.

Together they finalized the last details. The car, a luxurious Mercedes sedan less than a year old, was roomy enough to accommodate two people in front and three in the back—the two women and the two children would travel in comfort. Anton proudly pointed out the outstanding characteristics of the car to the banker, who did not try to hide his enthusiasm. A six-cylinder engine with ninety-five horsepower that could, under optimal conditions, reach eighty miles per hour. Anton admitted that he had never tried, adding that he hoped to achieve an average of thirty miles an hour—taking into account the state of the roads and the necessary stops.

Then it was time to get ready. Luggage—only what was strictly necessary—was stored together with two great hampers of food; there was still room enough in the vast trunk for two jerry cans of petrol in case of emergencies. Farewells were kept to a minimum since Anni was close to tears and the children uneasy, torn between the fun of the sudden trip and the fear of being separated from their little world.

Manny, trying hard not to show how anxious he was, shut the doors on both sides, and Anton drove carefully out of the yard. He navigated the narrow streets with unhurried skill; Julius lay back in his seat and immediately fell asleep. At midnight the chauffeur woke him up; the car had stopped at an army petrol depot. They were already on Austrian soil, having crossed the border without having had to stop. The driver's uniform and the count's coat of arms on the car, well-known in these parts, had been enough for the guards.

The women and children had not woken up. The two men traded places, and the powerful car resumed its journey with Julius driving. Anton watched him for a few minutes; apparently satisfied, he wrapped himself in the fur and went to sleep. They stopped again a little before six in the morning, at an inn not far from the Austrian town of Liezen. They had not taken the most direct route, which went through Germany, having deemed it more prudent to stay on Austrian territory, where the count had vast estates and his family was well-known, until they reached Switzerland. There was another advantage: they would be avoiding the main roads where most of the military traffic passed.

The *Stag and Hare* was a reputed hunters' inn, with the added bonus of a resident mechanic hired to see to the needs of a newly motorized clientele. One of the count's assistants had phoned ahead, and they were expected despite the early hour. Rooms had been held in readiness so they could refresh themselves and enjoy the hearty breakfast ordered in advance.

The children were still fast asleep. Julius picked up Tibor while Anni carried Myriam. Trailed by Madi, still pale and with dark rings under her eyes, they made their way to an upstairs suite while Anton together with the mechanic took care of the car. Two hours later they were on their way again. Though the clouds were mostly gone, it was bitterly cold. Fortunately, during the halt the briquettes had been warmed again until they were white hot. The passengers mainly complained of boredom after being cooped up for so long in the car.

Short stops were made every two hours, so Anton and Julius could switch sides. They were neither bored nor tired. Very much on the defensive in the beginning, the corporal was visibly thawing. Tibor pelted him with questions about the car, to which he replied good-humoredly. Having been told that Madi was an old friend of her mother's who had been hurt in an accident, Myriam had taken her under her wing, asking every few minutes whether she was feeling better. At the inn she had come to take Madi's hand when Julius had changed the dressing. Both adults had been relieved by her presence. On the one hand, they hadn't had a moment alone and had many things to say; on the other it was essential not to raise Anton's suspicions—which he would certainly have shared with his master—or those of Anni, who would have been deeply wounded by this new evidence of the duplicity of men.

Madi, without makeup, with little crow's feet around her eyes, awoke conflicting emotions in Julius—tenderness and lust together. He wanted to take her in his arms, cover her face with kisses, and then carry her to bed. She must have felt it, since she looked at him longingly. He hastened to finish the dressing and moved away, telling her the wound was healing nicely, and she would be able to do away with the dressing at journey's end.

At one o'clock the children started clamoring for their lunch, and the car stopped near a convenient meadow. Hampers were taken out, a blanket spread on the grass; Anton was persuaded to sit down as well, and they all ate happily. The sun was still high in the sky, the wind had died down, and the cold was bearable thanks to the heavy coats they all wore. All constraint gone, Anni and Madi were talking a mile a minute, recalling long-forgotten events and friends and turning from time to time to ask a bemused Julius whether he remembered a particular incident.

Then it was the road again. Tibor had brought a pack of playing cards, and soon laughter could be heard from the back seat. The two men were talking quietly. As Julius had surmised, the corporal had been born on the count's estates, to whom he owed everything, including the small grocery shop his wife was running in his absence. It was evident that he had known very few Jews and had never been in the company of so many—an experience he appeared to find disconcerting.

By late afternoon the passengers were becoming restless; even the women wanted to stretch their legs. However, there was no time for unscheduled stops, and during the short halts for refueling, the children were not allowed to get out. Twice they encountered army patrols. The count's coat of arms worked its magic, and the soldiers saluted as they went by. There was no dinner stop; sandwiches were passed round in the car. Not until two in the morning did the Mercedes finally reach the inn where they were to spend the rest of the night. Once again they were expected; once again the children were fast asleep and had to be carried to their rooms—at which point they woke up.

There was a suite for the ladies, another for the men. Tibor roomed proudly with his uncle while Anton declared his intention of sleeping on the ground floor, where a window overlooked the parking lot, the better to watch over the car. Well rested and well fed, they embarked on the last leg of the journey. Julius, who had paid the staggering bill with the money his brother-in-law had given him, thought they were lucky to be traveling under such good conditions.

At noon that Sunday, they reached the Swiss border. Thanks to the impressive sedan and the official documents, formalities were kept to a minimum, and they were soon on the Geneva road. It had been decided in Budapest that the chauffeur would leave the Nagys in their house by the lake and would then take Madame Corvin to the city where she would look for a suitable hotel. However, after the intimacy of the trip, Anni would have none of it. She declared in a tone brooking no argument that she was not about to let her friend go alone into a town where she knew no one. She would spend her first night with the Nagys.

There was a room for the driver as well. Anton demurred at first but let himself be persuaded when told that banker Nagy was well-known at a nearby garage, and he would get excellent service for his car before the long drive home. It was a strangely subdued group who sat down to dinner in the Nagy family's summer home. There was nothing wrong with the food; having been warned by Manny, the caretaker had managed to track down the cook and the maid they usually employed, who were free since it was the off-season. The weary travelers had found a well-heated house, bedrooms readied, and a hearty meal awaiting them. What they did not find was answers to the questions that plagued them. The children wanted to know how long they would be staying and what school they would be attending; their mother simply did not know.

The adults were happy that the long journey was over; nevertheless, the days looming ahead were full of uncertainties. Later, the children safely in bed and fast asleep, Julius and the two women sat in the pleasant drawing room. Logs were burning brightly in the chimney while in a corner a stout stove was doing the real job of keeping the place warm.

Anna looked downcast. During the trip she had worked hard at presenting a smiling face to the children so as not to frighten them; tonight she was facing the consequences of their hurried departure. Twisting a small lace handkerchief in her hands, she expressed her fears aloud. What if the war went on and on as her husband feared? When would she see him again? When would she be able to go home? How was she to manage here? She had never spent more than short vacations in Switzerland, always in the company of Manny, who took care of everything. She knew no one; she did not even speak French, and her school German was rusty from never being used. There was so much to do! Finding a school was her first priority; how to go about it? How would the kids manage in French? Who would prepare Tibor for his bar mitzvah the following year? Where would they hold the ceremony?

Madi nodded in agreement, saying nothing. Her friend stopped suddenly, reddening. "Here I am, talking, talking about my small problems while you—what are you going to do, dear Madi, alone and with no one to help?"

Madi shrugged. That evening she had dressed her hair artfully to hide the wound. Her color was better, perhaps due to some subtle makeup. She was wearing a becoming dress; altogether she was looking as respectable as her hostess who was as charming as usual in a gown of fine wool, a gold necklace glinting at her modest décolletage.

The redhead smiled at her with affection. "You are very kind to worry about me, and I thank you. Let me reassure you; I am used to being alone. I have no family left. Thank God I am far from being penniless; by a stroke of luck, I was able to sell my boutique and the apartment on Friday afternoon before leaving. You see, a Hungarian milliner who had a thriving business in Moscow had to return home because of the war between the two countries. She wanted to go into partnership with me, and I was trying to make up my mind. She was delighted by the opportunity to buy the place outright. I didn't get the best possible price, of course, yet combined with—with my savings, I have enough to live quietly for many years."

Julius noted her hesitation. She was probably about to say *combined with the money the Count had given her*.

Madi went on. "My problem is the same as yours: if I knew how long this horrible war will go on, what condition our country will be in when it ends, if there will be anyone waiting for me...then I could decide what course to take. I have been thinking of nothing else these last three days. I'm not afraid of work. In theory I could set up a shop here. In theory only since I don't speak French, and I know no one. On top of everything, I am not sure Hungarian fashions would suit the ladies of Geneva who are generally considered staider, if not stuffier. I will sleep on it tonight, and tomorrow I shall see my way more clearly. Let me just tell you how much I appreciate your kindness, your generous hospitality. You knew about my situation, yet you took me in your arms. During these three blessed days, I have felt like the carefree girl of yesteryear; even more, I was made to feel like a member of your family. I shall never forget it.

Now I am going to leave you alone with your brother. I'm sure you have a lot to discuss before a separation that may be lengthy."

As Madi stood up, Anni raised her hand to stop her. "Not so fast. Madi, there is something I want to tell you. As I was listening, I thought you were right: we are indeed facing the same problems. Don't look at me like that, just listen." She stopped, took a long breath, and went on. "Why don't you stay with me for a while? You will be able to get to know the town, the country, and you can learn French with me."

Madi studied her for a long minute. There were tears in her eyes. "Anni, you are too kind. You don't know what you are saying. This is impossible. You forget who I am—what I am."

"You are Maria Corvin, a dear childhood friend. I talk to you like a sister. My children adore you. If you stay it will be a tremendous help. Believe me, I am afraid of being alone here. With you it will be better. Listen, we are in Geneva, not in Budapest. Nobody knows you here. Nobody has heard of you."

"Your husband…"

"My husband is in Budapest. He has nothing to say."

"Dr. Matthias, tell your sister this idea is not possible!"

Julius looked from the one to the other, his brows knitted in concentration. At first glance his sister's generous proposal was unreasonable. There was an abyss between the respectable wife of banker Nagy and Count Von Thuringen's kept woman. Yet the idea had merit. Life would be hard for Anna in this foreign city. It might be easier with her old friend by her side. The question was, would Madi's past come to light?

He decided to take the plunge. "Before the war I would undoubtedly have said it is impossible. Today…today the world is changing. I don't know how it's going to end, when and how the war will be over. Your presence would bring comfort to my sister. It's worth a try. It will require some ingenuity."

"What do you mean, little brother?" asked Anni.

"You will present your friend as a respectable widow whose husband died in battle on the Russian front. It will be up to you to decide how long she needs to wear black."

"Yuli, you are a genius! The perfect solution. Don't you think so, Madi?"

"I want so badly to accept that I don't know what to think. What if someone recognizes me?"

Julius coughed. "Forgive me, but aren't you exaggerating your own notoriety? I am convinced that for the majority of your clientele, you are a respectable milliner. As for those who might have heard rumors, they won't say anything when they see you living under the protection of the respectable wife of the reputable banker Nagy."

His sister grimaced. "Reputable banker, you said?"

"Believe me, when the war is over people will be so busy picking up the pieces, trying to resume normal lives, there will be no one to mention old scandals of little importance."

Anna looked at him with affection. "My little brother the philosopher…You may be right. Anyway, you have convinced me. Madi, there is nothing more to be said. You have no idea how happy it makes me to know I will have you with me."

There was so much sincerity in her voice that Madi had no answer. She wiped her eyes, embraced her friend, and retired to bed.

Brother and sister were left alone. He went to sit next to her and put his arm around her shoulders. "I am proud of you, you know. You have been very brave. I fear that the next few weeks or months won't be easy."

She nodded, lost in thought. "Maybe. Yuli, I am so afraid... For Manny, for you, for Father, for Aunt Donna. For your children. If Romania joins the fray, what will happen to us?"

He shrugged resignedly. Suddenly he laughed. "Don't you remember? Father used to teach us that some medieval sage had said that since the destruction of the Jerusalem temple, the gift of prophecy was given only to fools and to young children. Well, I am no longer a child, and I hope I am not a fool. Therefore, I shall not hazard a guess. I am not as pessimistic as your husband, though I bow to his better understanding of the international situation. In any case I would bet anything he will find a way to come and visit you much sooner than you think. For myself...I have never been interested in politics. Should Nagyvarad fall under Romanian rule, I don't think it would change much. I already speak the language fluently."

"But when shall I see you again? What about Father, Donna?"

"You know I shall keep taking good care of them. For the rest...Who can tell? We shall find a way to communicate: telegram, telephone, letters...The war will not go on forever. You and your children are safe, that's the main thing. Stop worrying. It's late. Let's go to bed."

"You are right. Little brother, I haven't thanked you. No, don't stop me. You have accomplished miracles in less than three days. You have made peace between my husband and me for which I shall be eternally grateful. You have left everything—your family, your patients—to come to our rescue. You have been on the road for hours and hours, and tomorrow you will do it again. Yuli, you are the best of brothers, and it breaks my heart to see you go. Thank you, thank you from the bottom of my heart."

"And you are my beloved big sister who helped our aunt raise me and never complained. Enough, otherwise we shall both drown in a flood of tears!"

12

HOMECOMING

THEY HAD BEEN TRAVELING FOR HOURS. There was no question of stopping for the night at a welcoming inn; they would keep going until they reached Vienna. Anton and Julius traded seats at refueling stops. They barely exchanged a word: everything had already been said. Lighter by four passengers and their luggage, the car was running faster, going up to fifty miles an hour on good stretches. However, both drivers were tired to the bone, and there was no longer any satisfaction in driving such a powerful machine.

Julius's mind was in turmoil. Parting had been painful. Anni had done her best not to cry; the children had clung to him, Tibor manfully conquering his tears, Myriam sobbing desperately. In the end Madi had taken Myriam in her arms, and she had quietened down.

Madi.

They finally had been able to talk, though it had taken some contriving on her part. That Monday morning, he had told his sister he needed to go to his bank before setting off on the return journey. Madi had asked whether she could accompany him, having, she said, an account at the same bank. Anni had to go downtown, to introduce herself to her husband's agent. A plan was worked out. Anton would drive Julius and Madi to their bank then double back to fetch Anni and the children, who would wait at a lakeside coffee-house for the other two to finish their transactions and join them. Julius would then make his farewells; Anna, leaving the children with her friend, would walk to her bank, which was practically next door.

At nine Anton deposited Julius and Madi in front of the majestic bank entrance on the Rue du Rhone, near the lake. Left alone, they hesitated for a minute. She looked vulnerable in her long black fur pelisse, with a tiny matching hat that hid her wound. Her light makeup gave her an unusually serious expression.

She smiled at him. "Julius, my dear, I have a confession to make. This is not my bank. Not yet. I have never had an account in a Swiss bank or dreamt of having one. Today I have to make a start. It occurred to me that it would be easier if I showed up together with a respectable physician who already has an account. Forgive me."

He smiled too, captivated by her looks and her well-re-membered scent of violet, while telling himself he was falling in love, and it was madness. The long journey had revealed another Madi. One who never complained, who listened patiently to the children and played with them. One who had kept a smiling face despite being desperately worried about her future. In short, the kind of woman he would have wanted for his wife.

The bank officer dealing with his account welcomed his "cousin" readily enough. Julius moved out of earshot when she murmured the amount she intended to deposit, but the alacrity with which the banker took her to a small salon to fill in the necessary papers told him it must have been respectable. Having finished his own business, Julius was surprised to be called to the room: Madame Corvin wished to give him power of attorney for her account and the safe she would be renting.

"Being a widow," she explained charmingly to the beaming older man, "it is important for me to have a reliable relative to help."

He nodded and patted her small hand paternally.

Emerging into the feeble sunlight, Julius and Madi made their way slowly toward the coffeehouse. There was a hint of spring in the air, which carried a hopeful note. Nature was awakening after a harsh winter; maybe the war would end as well? It was so pleasant to see people strolling by, enjoying the fair weather in a city that had remained neutral and where one did not have to see maimed young men with haunted eyes begging on every corner..

"Do you know this is the very first time we have walked quietly together?" Julius remarked. "Openly, without having to hide, as if it were the most natural thing in the world."

She stood still for a minute and let out a sigh. "Yuli, Yuli, you are hopelessly romantic. This is the first time—though I fear it will be the last."

"Don't say that. Fate has brought us together for the third time. Why should it stop now? The more I see of you, the more I am convinced I should have married a woman like you."

"Yuli," she replied with great tenderness, "no one has ever told me such a flattering thing…and something that is so palpably false. You see, my dear doctor, when I was still a respectable young girl looking for a husband, I would have been over the moon with a man like you. However, life has taken me in another direction. Suddenly we met again, and you have become very dear to me. No, no, wait, let me finish. Had we been on the stage in one of these Franz Lehar operettas so popular in Budapest, our story would have turned into a fairy tale. This is, unfortunately, far from being the case. You have to face reality. When we were young in Nagyvarad, the six-year gap between us was too large to be bridged, not to mention the fact that we were both as poor as church mice. Now, even if we were both free, such a match would deal a death blow to your medical career. Nagyvarad is not Geneva; in our provincial hometown, people have long memories. Be reasonable. We have been very lucky. It is over. I shall dream of you during my solitary nights. Please, say no more; this is painful enough for me as it is. Let us change the subject. Let us talk about young Grunewald."

"You know about that?"

"Ferencz—the count—trusts me. Until you came along, his trust was perfectly justified. Anyway, Hans is his son. The way it happened was that one of the count's men was badly wounded during training maneuvers. It took Armin Grunewald two years to die; for most of them he was unconscious. The count came to visit more than once. Grunewald's wife was comely. You can imagine the rest. Ferencz behaved with his usual generosity, and the husband's family accepted the boy who was lucky enough to be born barely five months after his 'father's death. Needless to say, the countess knows nothing."

"The countess, the countess—I fail to understand. Your count appears to be an intelligent man, well respected. Yet he lets his wife terrorize him! Can't he make her behave?"

She laughed bitterly. "Make her behave? The daughter of a Russian princess, who is first cousin to the czar and related to the Prussian royal family? Her brother is a general in the Austrian army. Madame is welcome—or was—in all the royal courts of Europe. She is almost as rich as he is, not counting the jewels she got from the imperial family in Russia. Their daughter is married to a Prussian duke. Both sons have married well but always side with their mother against their father. They are officers; were they to learn of Hans's existence, an illegitimate younger brother serving in the army would not be long for this world. This is why my poor Ferencz has to act with the greatest discretion and why he called upon you."

"You know this Hans? He doesn't resent you for taking his mother's place?"

"The connection died with Armin. The widow married again two years later. In order to explain why the boy looked so much like the count who was taking such an interest in him, the new husband was told his wife was the illegitimate daughter of the count's brother, dead thirty years. You have no idea how proud Ferencz is of that son who was in his second year of medical school when war broke out. By the way Anton knows all this. Come, we must not make your sister wait. We had a long talk yesterday before she went to her room. I told her everything—why I had to leave home and what happened next—except for you. Julius, I wish this walk would never end, but it is time. Let me tell you that I owe you an immense debt of gratitude. Our first meetings and what happened this week were nothing short of miraculous. I was desperate; I was saved and found new hope. Maybe Geneva will give me the new beginning I have hoped for. Please, do not answer. Do not look at me. I must not start sobbing in front of your sister and Anton. Here they come."

He said nothing and wasn't even able to kiss her good-bye.

Traffic became heavier as they approached Vienna; roadblocks stopped them time and time again. After a brief discussion, Julius agreed to sit in the back and let Anton, who was still wearing his uniform and his medals, drive for the last leg. It worked admirably, and they made excellent time, reaching, toward noon on Wednesday, the Hotel de France, a first-class establishment close to the university. Their billets were accepted reluctantly; Julius added a crisp twenty-crown note, a princely sum, and suddenly a very good room was found for Herr Doktor and a second smaller one for Herr Korporal, and their luggage was taken up.

A little later a hackney carriage was called for Herr Doktor—no point in drawing attention by using the limousine with the count's coat of arms—who went first to the hospital where he used to work. Professor Steiner was away; a former colleague escorted Julius from room to room. Hans Grunewald was not there. Six hours and five hospitals later, Julius was ready to call it a day.

"Tomorrow," he told himself, "I will check smaller places on the outskirts of town. That's it. I cannot allow myself to be away any longer."

Back at the hotel, he felt restless, so in spite of his fatigue he went for a walk carrying his medical bag with all his travel documents since he was uneasy about leaving them in the room. Night had fallen. Without conscious volition he turned toward the university and was surprised not to encounter a single student. Were studies suspended during the conflict?

He did not know, and it did not matter. He almost went by without stopping; in the end he could not resist the wish to see the place where he had spent so many happy hours. He crossed the yard and entered. Instead of the familiar porter, there was a guard in uniform who, seeing the bag, asked him, surprisingly, whether he was a doctor. Having answered in the affirmative, he was instructed to take the first corridor to the right.

He did so, more out of curiosity than anything else. The view that met him stopped him in his tracks. The vast corridor, with its high ceiling that he had taken so often to go to classes, had been turned into a hospital. Dozens of beds lined the walls; only a narrow passage was left. He started walking, shocked beyond belief at hearing a confused medley of sounds he knew only too well: hacking coughs, moans, groans, and sobs. It appeared that in the very heart of the old imperial capital, the situation was no better than in neighboring Hungary: the flood of wounded had compelled the authorities to requisition the buildings of the lofty seat of learning that was the town's pride and joy!

He walked on, unbelieving. Everywhere he saw the same dazed, downcast faces, the same hopeless despair, and felt the permeating odor of disinfectant ineffectually trying to cover other unpleasant smells.

And then he saw him. A young soldier with a huge dressing on his head and another on his right arm, gazing at nothing. A soldier who looked very much like the photograph the count had given him. He told himself he must be wrong; still, he went closer.

"Hans?" he asked.

The wounded boy turned, searching for a familiar face, hope in his eyes, and then sighed in frustration at the sight of a stranger.

"Hans Grunewald?" repeated Julius.

"That's me" came the indifferent answer.

Dr. Matthias's quest was over just as he had been about to give up. He sat down at the edge of the bed and explained who he was and why he was there. The young man crossed himself and closed his eyes, murmuring a quick prayer of thanks. The two men talked. Hans had suffered a saber cut to the head on the Russian front; he had had time to block another cut with his arm, which would have been deadly, before passing out. He regained consciousness in a field hospital and lost count of the days. He did not know why he had been sent to Vienna or how long he was supposed to stay. The cut on his arm was not healing properly, and he lived in dread of being sent back to the front.

Dr. Matthias nodded, went to wash his hands, and found the head nurse. Coming back with her, he undid Hans's dressing and carefully cleaned the wound. He then informed the nurse that her patient man would be evacuated to Budapest in the morning, and she should have him ready early. She wrote the orders down with deference, assuring him it would be done. Leaving the young man torn between gratitude, incredulity, and hope, Julius went back to the hotel, whistling happily.

At six the following morning, Anton, still in his uniform, a little the worse for wear by then but still impressive, went to fetch Hans Grunewald. He helped the soldier walk to the car where Julius was waiting. They took the road to Budapest under sunny skies and made good time, the traffic being relatively light. From then on things moved very fast.

They brought Hans to the military hospital by the train station; there they said their good-byes. The young soldier tearfully embraced his savior before Anton led him inside.

Julius went to see the duty officer to check on the nearest convoy to Nagyvarad. He was in luck; the train was already there, and the wounded were being taken aboard. Departure was scheduled in two hours. This gave him time to call Manny and ask him to phone his home to warn Magda of his arrival and to have his driver waiting. His brother-in-law insisted on coming to say good-bye. They met outside the hospital and settled on a bench in the courtyard. The weather was still remarkably sunny and warm that early afternoon.

"You look tired," said a surprised Julius, provoking a laugh.

"I look tired? Anxious, maybe. But have you looked at yourself in a mirror? My poor Julius, you must have driven like a madman—and accomplished miracles."

"Miracles, miracles! How you do go on. We were very lucky. Not a single flat tire, no mechanical problems, and, thanks to your money and the vouchers the count provided, petrol and food in abundance."

"Don't be so modest. I managed to telephone your sister the day before yesterday, and she could not stop singing your praises."

"You are not angry at me for not talking her out of bringing along her friend?"

"Don't try to change the subject. Let me thank you from the bottom of my heart. You have taken an enormous weight off my chest. No matter what happens here, what happens to me, my wife and my children are safe in a neutral country eager to extend its benevolent hospitality to those rich enough to settle there. Anni will never want for anything, I made sure of that. Believe me, I am beginning to sleep better at night. As for being angry at you—what for? I know your sister far too well: once she has set her mind on something, nothing will make her budge. I don't really care. I had never met that woman before; her banker, who is a friend—and who knows exactly how she is situated—tells me she is a good and fair businesswoman. I have no reason to fear she will exert a bad influence on my wife or on the children who apparently adore her. If by being with Anni she can help her through the difficult times ahead, so much the better. I have enough worries right now without this minor issue."

"Has something happened? I haven't seen a newspaper in a week."

"The Russians have managed to defeat the Germans who are still stuck in Verdun. That is not a decisive blow, but I have it on good authority that King Ferdinand of Romania, who was vacillating, is now ready to throw in his lot with the Allies, believing that Germany and Austria-Hungary are losing the war."

"Is that what you believe?"

"About losing the war? I don't really know. I can see only the problems we are having, not those of our enemies. About Romania entering the war against us—yes, unfortunately. They have been promised Transylvania, and that is too good to refuse. I assume they will wait a few more weeks to see which way the wind blows. My considered opinion is that at the latest, they will declare war when the harvest is in. Which brings me to another point. As a banker I like to think ahead. Should the Allies win the war, should Nagyvarad, together with the whole of Transylvania come under Romanian rule, communications between us might become difficult. That's why I am thinking of acquiring some property that would bring in enough income to cover our part of the expenses for your father and Donna. Please don't tell me you can take care of everything alone; that's out of the question. Now, the property should be registered in your name to simplify things. I thought about an elegant apartment on Teleky Street, unless you have a better idea?"

Julius thought quickly. "Listen, instead of buying an apartment, why don't you buy the suite of offices in the Black Vulture complex where I receive my patients? The rent I pay would cover your part of their upkeep nicely."

"Very good idea. Why is the owner willing to part with such a valuable asset?"

"The owner is an Austrian architect. He spent a year in Bucharest and is forever complaining about the hatred of Jews there. Should the town become Romanian, he will leave."

"And that does not bother you? You don't think…never mind. You know where he banks, this man?"

"Indeed. Banque du Commerce."

"Very well. Discuss it with him. If he is interested, have his banker contact me. Good. I shall now go in search of my Istvan, who should have gotten our stuff from Anton's car, but first I shall accompany you to your train compartment. I will call your home as soon as I get back to work."

On their way they saw the count conversing with a high-ranking military doctor. Leaving his companion, he came swiftly toward them.

"Dr. Matthias, I am happy to have this opportunity to tell you how deeply grateful I am. You have accomplished all I had wished for and more. I hope one day I can repay you. This gentleman is your brother-in-law, I believe?"

Julius introduced the two men who shook hands.

"Mister Nagy," said the count, "let me tell you candidly that I am in your debt. You and your wife have behaved with great generosity to…I won't say more. However, rest assured that should you ever need help, you can count on me. Here is my card."

He clicked his heels and left Julius and his brother-in-law rooted to the spot.

"My God! Does that mean I have to thank you again?" exclaimed the banker. "Never in a million years would I have thought…You have no idea how precious his support could be if things really turn ugly."

Fairly satisfied, Julius settled into his seat. It was difficult not to be flattered by the compliments heaped upon him. True, he had been very lucky, but as his erstwhile Latin teacher had loved to say, being lucky was the first thing the French emperor Napoleon demanded of his generals.

After an uneventful trip, Julius reached Nagyvarad at one in the morning. He was gratified to be met by Commandant Mihaly in person. "My dear Matthias, I have no words to thank you," said the man. "Apparently your behavior brought credit to our unit; furthermore, Lieutenant Colonel Von Thuringen offered to make up for your absence in any way he could, and will earmark an extra allotment of medical supplies for us. Enough said for now. Your chauffeur is waiting to reunite you with your family. Take the day off tomorrow—you well deserve it."

Julius walked out with a smile. Vadim had the car waiting, with the door open. Julius thanked him for coming so late to fetch him and asked whether everything was all right at home.

"I believe so," replied the man in a colorless voice. "A hot meal awaits you in the kitchen."

A hot meal at one in the morning! How pleasant to know that his wife had taken the trouble to stay up, to welcome him. Maybe the tiny new life she was carrying would give them a new beginning…

His hopes were quickly dashed. Magda was not in the kitchen; in her stead an old lady was dozing in her chair. She opened her eyes when he came in, and he recognized his aunt with a start. When had she grown old? Had it taken this short absence for him to see a change that must have occurred over a period of months, if not years? He embraced her while scolding her gently, telling her she shouldn't have waited, that he was more than capable of warming his food alone.

Her answer struck terror in his heart: "I didn't want you to come home to an empty house."

"What! Magda has gone and taken the children with her?'

"No, no, the little ones are sleeping upstairs. She went with her mother to a convalescent home in Băile Felix, half an hour from here."

"My god! She has lost the baby!"

Donna nodded and went to the stove where a heavy saucepan was simmering and poured him some soup. He started eating, all the while telling himself it was not so bad after all, that they had two beautiful children and would have more, yet feeling an unreasonable pain at the loss. "I shouldn't have left," he said after a few minutes. "Had I been here…"

"It would not have made any difference."

"Really? Have you discussed it with her parents? She must have told them it was all my fault, that I abandoned her to go and see my sister, right?"

"That's what she had intended. Fortunately, very fortunately, because of your father I had not left with you, and I was right here when she came back on the morning of your departure, white as a sheet and leaning on Vadim. When she saw me she became whiter still and nearly fainted. I understood immediately. She did not say a word, did not ask why I had not gone. She went straight to bed."

He shook his head. "She got rid of the baby?" he asked in a strangled voice.

Donna nodded mutely.

"Now I understand her strange behavior. Her sudden solicitude for my sister, whom she hates with a passion; the way she encouraged us to go; the presents she bought...You know, I had a feeling she didn't want that child. I wondered why she hadn't yet told me she was pregnant. I kept telling myself to be patient, that she would see reason. After all these years, I still don't know her. She must have planned well ahead. If you hadn't remained here, I would never have known the truth, would have believed it to be a spontaneous miscarriage, and I would have felt guilty and blamed myself for leaving her alone."

She sighed wearily. "That's about it. Providence kept me here. Dear boy, I am ashamed to confess that when I understood what she had done, my first thought was not for that poor little life snuffed out. It was for you. I had to protect you, not let that woman do you the harm she had intended, perhaps use what happened as an excuse to go back to her parents with the children. I took my coat, went out, and started questioning Vadim. He would not answer at first, but I was beside myself with rage, and finally he told me everything. How the previous evening he had taken her to an address he didn't know, and how he had returned at nine in the morning. She'd come down with a dour-faced woman in a white uniform.

"I did not hesitate and instructed him to take me straight to the pharmacy. When Emil saw me, he believed his own version of what had happened; purple with rage, he led me to his office and started ranting that you were a murderer, that you had left your wife who was feeling extremely unwell to go and see your sister. Apparently she had left the pharmacy early, complaining of pains and crying that you were leaving her alone. What a diabolical woman! Had I been away, it would have worked. Everyone would have believed her. The servants would have said nothing.

"I stopped Emil and told him what had really happened. He did not believe me at first, so I told him to go and talk to Vadim, who used to work for him, as you know. When he came back he was incandescent with rage. He wanted to go and see her immediately; however, I said we should also bring Golda. They both went up to Magda's room. You should have heard Emil screaming. He yelled that she was a monster, a murderer, and that he would never let her back into the pharmacy, that he never wanted to see her again. Ditta came running down with the children who were scared to death, and I sent them to your father.

"Emil kept on and on. I almost took pity on his daughter; she must have been in pain and needed peace and quiet. I don't know how Golda managed to get him out of the room. He came down to the kitchen shaking so violently I was afraid he would have a heart attack. I told Viola to make him some very hot tea with plenty of sugar and, while it was brewing, gave him some of your good French cognac.

He was fighting his tears. After a while he calmed down, got up slowly, told me he had to go back to work, and left."

"What happened next?"

"Golda remained to take care of her daughter. Needless to say, Magda was furious at me since her plot was foiled *because of me*, as she put it. She wanted me to leave the house, but I refused to go until you came back. The children needed me. The two women thought you were coming back on Sunday; they deemed it more prudent not to be here when you arrived and went to Băile Felix. I assume they intend to wait there to see your reaction. That's all, and that's enough for tonight. Go to bed; tomorrow you must tell me all about your trip. Manny sounded very mysterious on the phone."

"Wait. The children—how are they?"

"They are anxious. They are not sleeping well. Their mother is gone, their father is not back, grandfather Emil yelled a lot and no longer comes to see them. I did my best to reassure them. I even made a promise you will have to keep."

This drew a reluctant smile from Julius. "What exactly am I supposed to have promised?"

"I said you would get them a black puppy with white spots. You should have seen how happy they were."

"What!"

"Don't worry, it will stay in the garden. We already bought a small kennel for it."

"Bravo! And where am I supposed to find the black puppy with white spots?"

"At the farm. Sandor is keeping it for them."

"Sandor? You went to see Sandor?"

"No, he came here. He had heard there was something wrong—Irena the maid is a relative, remember?—and he came three days ago, asking to speak to me. Since Magda was not here, I let him in. He brought three dozen nice farm eggs and two live chickens—he knows that your father won't eat them if they are not properly slaughtered. We had a long talk. He told me how unhappy he was because of the rift between you two, that he had drunk too much on his birthday, that he had many business worries and had said things he should not have, and he had not meant them. He said he wished you would forgive him. He is a very good man, you know, and has always been a faithful friend. You should forget the whole thing."

"Wait, wait. How did you get to the black puppy with white spots?"

"We talked about the children, and I said that what they needed was a pet to keep them busy..." She was trying to look innocent but did not quite succeed.

"And it just happened that he had the right pet? When is he bringing us the dog?"

"He is not bringing it! You must see it first. The children too. Besides, it is still too young, not weaned yet. The best thing would be for you to go to the farm with the children."

He began laughing in spite of himself. "Darling aunt, in other times you would have been burned at the stake. Enough for now. I shall walk you through the garden. It would not do for you to fall in the dark."

"I am not going anywhere. I am sleeping in the downstairs bedroom with your father." She shook her head. "Aaron was very upset. He did not like your wife before, and you can imagine how he feels now. He wanted us to leave our small house right away. I can't. It would break my heart to leave the children. I hope you can talk him out of it."

Alone in the great conjugal bed, Dr. Julius Matthias was fighting tears. After the elation of his escapade, reality was staring him in the face. It was not his wife's duplicity so much as the sheer cruelty of what she had done. She must have planned it for days, for weeks. And it had almost worked. Had Donna not been there…

So what should he do now? Go on as if nothing had happened, keep the oath he had given? Or try to regain his freedom, get rid of a woman who did not care for him, or their children? A woman ready to go to any lengths to achieve her goal? He shook his head wearily in the dark. The oath he had taken when he was a callow youth of eighteen had been tacitly renewed two years earlier when his wife's mother had given him the house where they now lived. In light of recent events, Emil and Golda might understand a separation but never a divorce, let alone his remarrying. Besides, it was too late for a new start. He had left his heart by Lake Geneva.

He finally fell asleep. But not for long. Through the door, which he had not shut properly, he could hear Andreas crying. Andreas, who never woke up at night. Yes, the boy was crying and had woken his little sister, who was crying too. Julius jumped out of bed, put on his dressing gown, and walked barefoot up to their room. A light was on. Ditta, in a modest nightgown, was trying to hush the children. When they saw him, they stopped crying and started yelling together, "Daddy, Daddy!" Andreas got out of bed and rushed to him while Elisabeth held her little arms to him through the bars of her crib. He picked up the boy in one hand and lifted the little girl with the other and drew them to his chest. He met Ditta's glance; she looked tired and anxious.

"They aren't sleeping well," she said defensively. "They don't understand what's going on and are afraid to sleep alone. I told them you would be back when they woke up, so they have been waking every few hours and calling for you."

"Very well. I shall take them with me, and they will finish the night in my bed. What do you say, children?"

They approved wholeheartedly. Ditta accompanied them to help Julius push the heavy double bed against the wall so Elisabeth would not risk falling out accidentally.

"They will probably wake up early. Bring them to me," said Ditta, and she left, smiling.

Lying on his back, a child under each arm, Julius felt a strange peace. His little girl still had her baby smell which filled him with tenderness. She fell asleep almost immediately. Andreas drew as close to his father as he could and was holding on to his pajamas as if afraid he would disappear in the middle of the night.

After a few minutes, Andreas whispered, "You are no longer angry with us? You aren't leaving?"

"I have never been angry with you, and I am staying."

"And mother is not angry? She is coming back soon?"

"Your mother is not angry, and she is coming back."

"Grandfather Emil will not yell at her anymore?"

"No."

"Why did she leave us?"

"She was tired. She went to get some rest with Grandmother Golda."

"David's mother, who plays with me in the park, went to get some rest and never came back. David says they put her in a big black hole with lots of earth on top of her. Will they put mummy in a big black hole?"

"No. She is coming back soon."

"You swear?"

"I swear."

That was all the child needed; he fell asleep immediately, and his regular breathing mingled with his sister's.

Sleep eluded Julius for a long time. It was clear to him that everything had changed. There was no more room for doubt. The little ones needed stability. Calm. They also needed the mother who took so little care of them. Try to understand a child's heart…Maybe they felt she loved them in her way. He did not know. What he did know was it was up to him to protect them at all costs. A burden he would probably be the only one to bear.

There was no use complaining. He would have to reorganize his life, call a truce with Magda, have the first floor rearranged so they could each have their own quarters. She would no longer have to suffer his unwanted attentions. And though he was not ready to take a mistress, he would feel free to take advantage of the lovely ladies who were more than ready to sleep with him. His father-in-law would understand; as for his mother-in-law, well, he would have a heart-to-heart talk with her. Yes, that was what he would do. Not an ideal solution, but such was life. He would soon turn twenty-six. His situation was enviable. He had a comfortable home, two lovely children, the profession he had always wanted, and good friends too. He had come a long way and should not complain. Besides, he could always dream. When the war was over, he might be able to take a vacation—in Geneva, for instance…

PART TWO

13

ORADEA

AFTER PROTRACTED NEGOTIATIONS between Golda and Julius, Magda returned, moving grudgingly into the bedroom prepared for her. She had also been made to accept the continuing presence of Donna and Aaron in their house at the end of the garden. That was a bitter pill indeed, since in Donna she saw the cause of her misfortune: for wasn't it thanks to the older woman that her carefully laid plans had come to ruin and that her own father had banished her from his home and the pharmacy?

Golda advised her daughter to be patient but to no avail. Magda found fault with everything and everyone, constantly reprimanding the servants and scolding the children who did their best to avoid her. Happily, they were distracted by Azor, the puppy, who had taken up residence in the kennel. The day after Julius returned, he had driven with the children to the farm, and they had been in rapture over the little dog and quite disappointed that they could not take it home right then; the puppy was not completely weaned and was too young to be left to the tender mercies of two small children.

The meeting between Sandor and Julius had gone surprisingly well. The two exchanged sheepish glances without saying a word and fell back into the easy camaraderie that had been theirs from infancy. Sandor's wife gave Julius a timid peck on the cheek and said she was glad he was back. The young doctor was glad too, very glad; the separation and its cause had been hard on him.

After that he tried to get to the farm as often as he could, which was not that often, as his days were busier than ever. Once a month he lunched with his friends from the Austrian Circle. In the evenings he often dropped in unexpectedly at Theo and ZsaZsa, where he was always welcomed with open arms. Then there was Alix. He now "treated" her at home for some unspecified ailment, without fearing gossip: she had engaged a companion who kept discreetly to her room during his visits. He had not forgotten Madi, but Madi was far away…

On Sundays he would meet Alix for lunch in one of the many inns dotting the forest beyond the city. They had taken to speaking French when alone; Julius had made great strides in that language and was even trying to read the novels Alix recommended. She particularly enjoyed the novels of a scandalous French woman called Colette; he was hard put to share her enthusiasm. Theirs was an easygoing liaison. They were both aware it could not last but made the most of it while it did.

Every Friday Julius went with his father to the synagogue; Saturdays were devoted to the children. Sunday mornings he drove them to the Szamuely house, and Golda brought them back in the afternoon. Not a bad life, or so he kept telling himself.

Manny had been right. King Ferdinand, having hesitated for many months, declared war on the Central Powers on August 27, 1916—as soon as the harvest was in. His army immediately marched north to Transylvania, encountering very little resistance and getting dangerously close to Nagyvarad. Tensions flared between ethnic Romanians and Hungarians. It was said that Romanians were deserting the Hungarian army in the hope of making a triumphal entrance with their advancing brothers. This hope was swiftly dashed. German reinforcements pushed the invaders all the way back to Bucharest and beyond, occupying the Romanian capital in November. The king and his court fled. There was great rejoicing among the Hungarians of Nagyvarad while the Romanians adopted a low profile.

Less than two weeks later, the sudden death of the Austrian emperor put an end to the euphoria. Franz Josef had reigned for nearly seventy years, having ascended to the throne in 1848. He was the living symbol of the union of Austria and Hungary. His only son, Rudolph, had died tragically at Mayerling; his son's beloved wife, Elisabeth—Sissy—had been assassinated by an Italian anarchist. The murder of his nephew and heir, Archduke Franz Ferdinand, at Sarajevo had triggered the war. These tragedies had endeared the old man to his people. His great-nephew, Charles, unpopular and lacking in experience, succeeded him at a critical time for the dual monarchy. The Germans had not been able to break the French at Verdun, and the two armies were engaged in bloody trench warfare. Italy had blocked the advance of the Austro-Hungarian army, and on the Eastern front Russia was going from victory to victory.

Weeks and months went by. The year 1917 began with no decisive victory for either side; there was an uneasy truce between the communities in Nagyvarad, each making preparations for a victory parade—and for alternative solutions, should their side lose. As usual they vented their frustrations on an all-too-familiar target: the Jews.

During Easter week finger pointing at the "Christ killers" reached fever pitch. That year the vagaries of the calendar had the Jews celebrating Passover on the eve of Good Friday. In the morning Theo Kahn, that most secular and freethinking Jew but nevertheless faithful to the tradition of his forefathers, walked by the Hungarian Catholic church carrying a box of unleavened bread. Blood libels about Jews killing Christian children and using their blood to make Passover bread were common at the time; the sight of the box enraged the worshippers streaming out of the church. They set upon the hapless architect with a vengeance. Somehow, despite two broken ribs and numerous contusions, he managed to break free and sought sanctuary in the Black Vulture complex nearby. The following day Julius found him better, though his face was still swollen with one eye partly shut. For once completely serious, Theo told his friend he was leaving.

"You are going somewhere for your convalescence? Not a bad idea."

"Who is talking about convalescence? ZsaZsa and I are getting out. We aren't staying here." Seeing the look of incomprehension on Julius's face, he added, "My dear boy, I have been living in Nagyvarad almost twenty years. I have worked on I don't know how many buildings and private homes. My wife and I contribute generously to dozens of benevolent societies, Jewish and Christian alike. We have never hurt anyone. My little transgressions are carried out with the utmost discretion and never outside our own community. In a word we are model citizens. I was foolish enough to believe this would keep me safe from what is called, euphemistically among my non-Jewish friends, *a deplorable incident.* Julius, I truly thought my last hour had come. There were people I knew in that clamoring crowd—people who had welcomed me into their homes in the past, people who had dinner here in this very house. Yet at that moment, everything had been wiped out of their minds, and I was nothing but an accursed Jew. It is said that fear gives wings: it must be true, because I can't begin to understand how I found the strength to run so fast. Had I not been able to do so, I'm afraid they would have killed me. I shudder to think of it."

"Kill you? Come on!"

"You weren't there. Let me tell you, I never want to find myself in that situation again. And do me the favor of not telling me it was all my fault for passing in front of the church at the wrong time."

"Of course I won't. After all, the same thing happened to my sister's friends a couple of observant Jews who were walking in the street with my little niece, Myriam, who has our blond hair and blue eyes. The crowd was ready to murder them, believing they had kidnapped a Christian child for their evil ends…My question is, do you honestly believe you will be safer in Budapest? In Vienna, even?"

"In Budapest, of course not. In Vienna, before the war maybe. Today…"

"Don't tell me you are taking ZsaZsa to Palestine!"

"Don't be silly. We are too old for that."

"What then? America?"

"Even less. No, what we shall do at first is go to Geneva. They are no fonder of Jews there, but they welcome our money. We shall await the end of the war in comfort. Time enough after to make a decision. Who knows what shape our poor old Europe will be in by then? Listen, Julius, there is something I have to say. We are not going alone. Alix is coming with us. She too has felt the ugly wind rising. In fact, she is the one who suggested Switzerland. Her father comes from Geneva, and she still has family and friends there."

He sighed and put his hand on the younger man's shoulder. "I shall miss you, my boy, and I shall worry about you. I know you don't want to leave, and I won't try to change your mind. However, you have some serious thinking to do. Today we are leaving; tomorrow or the day after, other members of our Circle will follow. Mark my words: that accursed war will see the end of the Austrian Circle."

Julius went home in a daze. Was his friend right? He himself did not think things were as bad as all that, but what did he know? What he was sure of was that losing these two dear friends would be bad; the fact that Alix was leaving with them made it even worse. He liked the situation as it was and was not at all keen to find himself alone again, so to speak.

Nevertheless, that is exactly what happened. A scant ten days later, the Kahns departed the town together with the widow. She promised to write—a promise she and Julius both knew they would not keep. Once again Julius found himself bereft of female companionship.

In a matter of months, Theo's prediction came true, as the Austrians left one after the other. The Circle ceased to exist, as did the monthly lunches and the friendly encounters. The news dispatches from Budapest were few and far between. Manny rarely phoned; when he did, he was extremely cautious, doubtless suspecting the phone lines were being monitored.

He did say his wife and children were adjusting well and had celebrated Tibor's bar mitzvah without him. There was never a word about Madi in these short conversations.

Dr. Matthias, who turned twenty-seven in June, felt lonely. So lonely that he began to see more of his father-in-law, who was lonely as well. Emil refused to go to Schools Road; he had not seen his daughter for over a year. Julius brought him the children every Sunday morning. With Alix gone, he sometimes went to fetch them home as well. One day he arrived to find that Golda had already taken them back because she intended to have lunch with her daughter, and they were too much of a handful to be left alone with Grandfather Emil. The older man invited him to share his meal; Julius did not refuse. After some desultory talk, his host told him he was sorry to hear that his friend had left for Switzerland.

"Which friend is that?"

"The lady from the travel agency," Emil replied. "Don't look so worried. I have no intention of mentioning her to Magda. I know how things are between the two of you. You are too young to remain celibate. You behaved with commendable discretion. However, Nagyvarad is not Vienna: here, secrets are hard to keep. What I can't possibly understand is my daughter. She has been fortunate in finding a young and handsome husband, yet instead of thanking providence and filling her home with children, she is doing her best to get rid of you!"

There was nothing to say to that, so Julius simply nodded.

"I would like to tell you a story," continued the pharmacist, who appeared lost in thought. "A story that begins like a fairy tale. It is about a young man who is madly in love with a girl who has the happiest laugh in the world. In one of those youthful love letters that one cannot read later without cringing, he compares her laugh to the twittering of birds. She loves him as well; they are planning to wed and have many children. Then the young man's father dies, and he discovers that the family business is heavily in debt. His love has a very small dowry; there can be no wedding. For five long years, the young man works hard to get out of debt but to no avail. The creditors lose patience. The girl he loves marries another man. He is in utter despair. Suddenly he is offered a way out: marriage to an heiress. She is neither young nor beautiful, but she has had a good education and comes from a respectable family. Without too much hesitation he accepts; ruin is staring him in the face."

He sighed and drank from a glass of wine. Julius, who was beginning to understand the point of the story, listened, spellbound.

"His new bride accepted her wifely duties, albeit without enthusiasm. A year after the wedding, a little girl was born. The birth was difficult. Two years later a little boy, born prematurely, did not survive. Another attempt brought a similar result. The family doctor reluctantly informed the young couple that the next pregnancy might be fatal for the mother. That very day she left the conjugal bed forever and moved to another room. There was no question of divorce: through the marriage contract, she had become the real owner of the family business. She was nothing if not fair-minded, letting her husband know that since she was no longer capable of assuming her duties, she considered him free of the oath of fidelity made at the time of the wedding." He sighed heavily. "Life is not a fairy tale. They did not live happily ever after and did not have many children."

He stood up and walked to the window. With his back to the room, he added painfully, "Fate gave me a single daughter. For many years I adored her—too much, perhaps. I could see her faults, her unpleasant temper, her arrogance even, but was always ready to find excuses. Until the tragedy that ended with the loss of what should have been the first of my many grandchildren. I told you: had she put her trust in me, that child would have been born. It was a boy; he would be fifteen today. I was a long time forgiving her. I think of him often. He has a place in my heart alongside Georgy."

He blew his nose noisily. "And then she goes and does it again. She has a good husband, she wants for nothing, she can have all the help she needs. It has wounded me to the core. Golda keeps urging me to forgive once more. I can't. Not yet. I will probably do so at some point, for the sake of the children—they don't understand why I no longer come to their home—but I need more time. Enough. I have talked too much. It was kind of you to listen."

Spontaneously Julius went over to embrace the older man—for the first time in his life.

There were other lunches. An unlikely friendship emerged between the two who had been at loggerheads for so long. Emil has showed another side of himself, one Julius had not known existed, with intellectual curiosity, a broad culture, and dry humor. They took to meeting every other week to discuss the way the war was going.

Sometimes Golda joined them. One day she took her son-in-law aside and begged him to give Magda another chance. Having seen the error of her ways, Magda was ready to go back to the conjugal bed, perhaps to have another child. Weeks had gone by since Alix had left, and Dr. Matthias had still to find a substitute. He let himself be persuaded. In September the whole family celebrated the Jewish New Year under the pharmacist's roof, to mark the reconciliation between father and daughter. The children were over the moon; Julius remained skeptical. He was convinced that his wife's change of heart was purely tactical and that she would revert to her old ways sooner or later.

At the hospital, wounded soldiers kept arriving. The war went on still undecided. The United States had thrown in its lot with the Allies, though its contribution had yet to be felt. The Russian Empire, in the throes of a popular revolution, withdrew from the conflict and, in December, signed a separate peace with Germany. Romania, three-quarters of whose territory was now occupied, was asking for an armistice. The Italian armies were retreating. Nagyvarad welcomed the New Year—1918—with high hopes of a prompt victory by the Central Powers.

In the Matthias household an uneasy peace reigned. A pregnant Magda had not yet been allowed back to the pharmacy, her father having ruled that she would have to wait for the birth so as not to endanger the baby. Indeed, she was not feeling well; a difficult pregnancy was followed by a protracted delivery, culminating in the birth of a baby girl—a fact the mother kept bemoaning until her husband put an end to it by coldly reminding her that the child she had gotten rid of might very well have been the boy she had hoped for.

As for Emil, he was delighted with little Gabriella who had Georgy's blond hair, blue eyes, and lovely smile. So was Aaron who saw in her the image of his late wife, while Donna was reminded of her beloved younger sister. Andreas and Elisabeth were fascinated with this new addition to the family. Magda declared herself too weak to nurse, and a wet nurse was hired, to the satisfaction of Ditta, who now had her hands full.

Spring also ushered in the massive arrival of American troops in Europe, turning the tide in favor of the Allies and dashing the hopes of the Central Powers, which had been so close to victory. Defeat was a mortal blow for the old Austro-Hungarian Empire. Large chunks of territories were given to the victors. In Hungary, revolutionary movements, born of the people's frustration, led to anarchy. Soldiers mutinied and murdered Prime Minister Tisza, who was considered responsible for the disaster. Emperor Charles of Austria was forced to abdicate Hungary's crown, where a transient republic took over, soon to be swept away by the bloody Soviet Republic of Hungary, until the entrance of the "victorious" Romanian army put an end to that red terror.

Three months later, Romania had to evacuate the town in accordance with the peace treaties; a reorganized Hungarian army made a triumphal entry. After the red terror came the white terror, targeting the former revolutionary leaders. Since there were many Jews among them, the community was subjected to terrible repression. Hundreds of Jews were hanged without trial; thousands saw their properties stolen or confiscated. In banker Nagy's house, no one answered the phone, and the Matthiases lived in dread for weeks until a terse telegram informed them that Manny and his father had managed to escape Budapest and were in Geneva with Anna.

In Nagyvarad things went more quietly: a few demonstrations, some Jewish activists thrown in jail, but nothing approached the scope of events in the Hungarian capital. Calm was restored with the formal surrender of the town to Traian Moşoiu. The Romanian general made a triumphant entrance in April 1919, welcomed solemnly by local authorities who presented him with bread and salt, according to tradition.

The Treaty of Versailles had spelled disaster for Hungary, amputating two-thirds of its territory. King Ferdinand had indeed made the right choice, and Romania was rewarded with Transylvania. Ethnic Romanians rejoiced while Hungarians were hard put to accept the new situation which turned them into Romanian subjects and forced them to use Romanian in all their dealings with local authorities and have their children learn the language at school too.

Many Hungarian civil servants left to return to Hungary. Attila and Zoltan, Sandor's elder brothers, decided not to come back to Oradea—the town's new official name—but to pursue their military careers in the Hungarian army. Romanian civil servants, teachers, and businessmen were arriving in droves. The city underwent a profound change; Hungarian street names gave way to Romanian names. The last wounded soldiers were evacuated, and the Jewish hospital once again devoted itself to the community.

Dr. Julius Matthias viewed these changes with equanimity, never having involved himself in politics and speaking the new official language fluently. His waiting room was full to capacity every evening. He was making new friends, including a merry Romanian woman—forty-years-old, the new director of an elementary school. Vivi—the lady's nickname—was not Jewish, so he waited prudently for her to make the first move and succumbed only after it had been made clear that she knew who and what he was. Nevertheless, they conducted their liaison with the utmost secrecy, so as not to compromise their respective situations. Julius was beginning to think that, contrary to the dire predictions of his friends from the defunct Circle, he would not suffer at all from the new state of affairs.

The Greater Romania, born out of the peace treaties, was twice the size and double the population of the old kingdom. The regime was working hard to find enough civil servants. In Oradea, situated nearly five hundred miles from Bucharest, the new functionaries, hastily trained and lacking in experience, did not appear threatening. During the first few years, the king implemented a number of reforms—part of the demands made by the great powers in the negotiations leading up to the Treaty of Versailles. All citizens were granted the right to vote; an agrarian reform brought real change in the peasants' conditions. In 1923 a new constitution granted equal rights to all, regardless of ethnic origin.

These measures—especially the last—were well received by the Jewish community. Transylvanian Jews still felt closer to Hungary than to Romania and still resented the need to speak Romanian—while deep down adjusting very well to the new regime. The country as a whole was undergoing a period of exceptional economic prosperity; Oradea got its share. Factories were dotting its landscape and trade was booming.

Dr. Matthias was doing well too. He now spent only three days at the hospital and devoted more and more time to his private patients. True, the memory of Madi sometimes intruded on his trysts with Vivi, but he kept hoping travel would soon be possible. At home his prediction had been right. Magda went back to her room after the birth of Gabriella, and he knew he would not be welcome there. She was once again spending her days at the pharmacy and showed no interest in her children, while he could not see enough of them.

Andreas was excelling at school; despite his youth he had a passionate interest in all things mechanical. For his eighth birthday, Grandfather Emil ordered, all the way from Berlin, the newest construction toy, something called Meccano. Elisabeth was devoted to her dolls, which she treated for imaginary ailments "like Daddy." Gabriella observed her brother and sister gravely. In spite of their mother's neglect, they were happy children. The elder Matthias could not give them costly presents, but Grandfather Aaron was always there to help with lessons, and they ran to Grandmother Donna whenever they fell or needed a cuddle.

Magda, who hated her in-laws with a vengeance, found a new ploy to get rid of them: she began telling her father wistfully that she would like to move, to be closer to him. He liked the idea and proposed his help in buying a suitable house. The pharmacist, who turned seventy-two in 1922, no longer went to work regularly; he had hired a man in his fifties to run the pharmacy with Magda. Julius understood the situation, though he was not keen to leave his home. The children were happy there; more to the point, what would happen to his parents? Aaron was often unwell; a simple cold sent him to bed for a month. Aunt Donna, who was older than Emil by three years, had trouble walking. To separate them from the three children they had practically raised from birth would be the death of them.

The issue was still unresolved when, in the beginning of the summer of 1923, Emil Szamuely died suddenly in his sleep. Far from mourning her father, Magda rejoiced at the thought that henceforth she would be the owner of the pharmacy; she went as far as to tell her mother, during the week of ritual morning, that she intended to move immediately into the Szamuely mansion, believing she had inherited that as well. Golda, who had always been her daughter's most loyal supporter, was deeply wounded.

Magda was to pay dearly for her attitude. When she discovered her mother owned the pharmacy and the mansion, she had a terrible shock. Hysterical with rage, she ranted and raved while Ditta and the children ran once more to the safety of Aaron's house. Julius hoped they had not heard their mother screaming that she had been tricked into having another child. When the dust settled, Magda nevertheless had the satisfaction of running the pharmacy; few people knew the accountant presented the books to her mother every month.

Now a widow, Golda was more than ever desirous of having her grandchildren close by. Julius having agreed to the move and to put their old house on the market, allowed Golda to buy a spacious apartment close to her own on the other side of the street. Magda was delighted; not only would she be getting rid of Donna and Aaron, she would also leave behind Azor, the black puppy with white dots who had grown since coming from the farm—and whom she hated, for some reason. What she did not know was that her mother, well aware of Julius's uneasiness at leaving his parents behind, had told the old couple they would be more than welcome in her home where they would keep her company. This proved to be the perfect solution. Golda and Donna got on like a house on fire, and the widow was never lonely. The children spent more time at what they called the Grandparents' House than in their own apartment, especially since Azor's kennel took pride of place in the inner courtyard.

Magda was quietly seething, but there was nothing she could do. She had her own quarters in the new apartment, as did Julius. They hardly shared a meal and barely spoke. Often Julius took a short break to have lunch with his parents; Golda welcomed him with open arms—in fact she had become fonder of her son-in-law than of her own daughter. The children went there after school and did their homework with Aaron who still enjoyed teaching. In the evening, when Julius was not too tired, he took Azor for long walks along the river. Coming back, he was sure to find his father peering over some learned text or chatting with Donna and Golda who rarely went to bed before midnight. Thus he never felt alone.

The long years had not lessened Julius's longing for Madi. He wondered what had happened to her. Had she found a good husband, become respectable? He always arrived at the same dreary conclusion: what did it matter? She was forever lost.

Yet she kept troubling his dreams…

14

FAMILY REUNION

ANDREAS MATTHIAS CELEBRATED his bar mitzvah in April 1926. Long separated by the war and its aftermath, the descendants of Aaron and Gitte were finally reunited for the occasion. Anna and her husband had not been back to Nagyvarad—now Oradea—since the death of Georgy; Julius had not seen either of them since taking his sister to Geneva ten years earlier. Even after the war was over, there had been only a sporadic exchange of cautiously worded letters, as envelopes were routinely opened by censors.

Julius had made doubly sure the invitation would reach the Nagy family by not only sending a letter but enlisting the help of his new friends, Isidor and Adolphus Weinberger, Romanian bankers who happened to be Jewish—and who had excellent contacts abroad. He had had no real hope of a positive answer, so his sister's letter came as a complete surprise. Not only was she coming with her husband, wrote Anna; her whole family was coming, and that included their four children as well as the wife of Karoly, the eldest, who had left for the United States so many years ago. Rooms should be booked for all of them in a nearby hotel, she added.

To this last request Golda strongly objected. The Nagys would stay with her; the house was big enough, and wasn't Manny her relative? Early in the morning of April 23—a Friday and the eve of the celebration—Dr. Matthias was waiting eagerly on the platform as the train entered the bustling station. In the joyous hubbub of the meeting, he heard, to his dismay, that the Nagys had come to say there farewells; Manny's father had passed away two years earlier, and the banker was about to fulfill his long-cherished dream of going to America.

Two of his sons were already living there. They had come back for one last nostalgic visit. Karoly had graduated from the Chicago law school and worked for the family bank. He brought along his wife, Katherina—Katy—the daughter of Jews from Odessa who had crossed the Atlantic in search of a better life at the turn of the century. A year older than her husband, she was already a pediatrician in a major hospital. A tall, blond woman whose modern dress scandalized the congregation (her skirt did not cover her ankles! Her lipstick was so red!), she was busy snapping pictures during the ceremony on Shabbat. Aaron, the patriarch, seventy years old, did not reprimand her. How could he when she had given him a baby who had the eyes of Gitte and the smile of Georgy? He wept with happiness when he held his first great-grandson in his arms though he had no way of communicating with the mother who spoke neither Hungarian nor German and barely knew a few words of Yiddish.

It was difficult too to get used to his eldest grandchild's new name. Karol Nagy had become Charles Newman. A new name for a new country, he explained with the engaging smile he had inherited from his mother, and *Charles* was the English equivalent of *Karol*. But the baby was named Isaac, a good traditional name. Tibor, sent to join his brother when he was eighteen, had adopted his new name with enthusiasm; there being no equivalent for Tibor, he became Tony, which he found modern. About to graduate from college at the end of the year, he was waiting for his parents' arrival in order to marry the daughter of a Hungarian businessman.

Manny said he had not quite made up his mind, but according to his wife it was only a matter of time before he too changed the family name while keeping his first name. In his late forties, the banker had put on a little weight, but his face was unlined and his hair was as black as ever—probably with the help of his hairdresser, thought Julius unkindly. At forty-two, his sister had kept her youthful silhouette in spite of having borne four children and was still serenely beautiful. What Julius did not know that day—she would tell him later—was that she had nearly cried when she saw him. Not yet thirty-six, still slim and handsome, he cast upon the world a weary and aloof gaze; it was only when he smiled at her or at the children that she saw in him the happy boy she had grown up with.

The ceremony was held in the great Neolog synagogue of Oradea. Erected in 1878 on the left bank of the Cris River, the synagogue's white dome was reflected in the swiftly running water. This was an imposing building—the greatest of its kind in Europe. The Neolog stream of Judaism claimed to be strictly orthodox but with a more modern and open view which suited Julius better. Besides, it was only five minutes' walk from his office and ten from his apartment.

Aaron Mathias had followed him there reluctantly after the death of his old friend, Rabbi Zussman. Father and son would go together to Friday services nearly every week. Not that Julius had discovered religion; he was just making a statement. As they had done for Karol's bar mitzvah in that distant month of June 1914, they all posed for the traditional photograph. Vadim, now married and a father of three but still on the job, took the picture with Katy's camera. She had given him precise instructions—nobody having told her he spoke no English.

Andreas stood very straight in the middle of the photo, as was his privilege, for this was his day. He had not finished growing yet and would probably be taller than his father; his hazel eyes reflected a lively mind. Aaron Matthias was on his right with Donna, now three years shy of her eightieth birthday. She was a very old lady; she could barely walk alone, and without the robust arm of Tibor—she couldn't bring herself to call him Tony—around her shoulders, she would not have been able to stand long enough for the photograph.

On the other side of the boy Grandmother Golda, dignified in her widow's black but spry enough though she was nearing seventy, leaned on Elisabeth, a sturdy girl of eleven with a pleasant open face. Behind Andreas were his parents. Magda had put on a lot of weight, and her expensive satin outfit did nothing for her silhouette. She had on her usual peevish expression.

Anna and Manny were next to Julius. Myriam Nagy stood beyond Magda. At eighteen she was as lovely as her mother, though one could see she had ten times Anna's vivacity. The three younger members of the family were sitting on the ground in front of Andreas. There was Gabriella, already a great beauty at nine years old; Julia Nagy, six, a happy little girl born of the reunion between Manny and his wife after the war, who looked startlingly like her father, was holding baby Isaac, who had a broad smile for the camera.

On Friday evening Golda Szamuely hosted a festive Shabbat dinner. Extensions had to be added to the massive oak table to accommodate the fifteen people gathered for that extraordinary family reunion which would probably be their last. While Aaron Matthias pronounced the ritual blessings, his son had to work hard to hide his sadness. His beloved sister was leaving Europe, and he was not sure he would ever see her again; his nephews had turned into cheerful strangers; there was no common language. Karol—Charles—had not forgotten his native tongue but felt easier speaking English; Myriam, who had spent the last ten years in Switzerland, was speaking French with her little sister, Julia, born in Geneva, but addressed her brothers in school English. Both girls had trouble speaking Hungarian with their grandparents and their Oradea cousins.

Elisabeth, already determined to be a doctor like her father, looked at Katy with adoration but was unable to exchange a word with her. Her father would have loved to talk to his young colleague but could not, though he spoke four languages—Hungarian, German, Romanian, and French—and she two: English and Russian. He had more success talking with his nieces, who wondered how it was that he spoke French with a Geneva accent, just as they did. The result of his long conversations with Alix, no doubt... He shrugged off the question without answering.

Aaron and Donna were looking at their children and grandchildren with grateful wonder. To a tearful Anni, feeling guilty at leaving them and going so far away, her father had replied gently, "My dear child, because of the war we haven't seen you for more than ten years. Now who knows whether in a year, in two years, we shall still be here, Donna and I? Don't worry. Your coming to see us with all your family has given us so much happiness that it will warm our hearts until we draw our last breaths. Go in peace." Which, of course, made her cry even harder.

One person was not enjoying herself. Magda hardly said a word and did not try to hide her impatience for the meal to be over so she could leave. Which she did, to no one's surprise, as soon as her father-in-law had recited the last blessing. Andreas, who wanted to study his text one last time for the morning ceremony, followed her regretfully together with his two sisters. Leaving the younger Nagys in possession of the drawing room with their grandparents, Julius, Anna, and her husband escaped to what used to be the pharmacist's office, but was now rarely used. Taking with them the bottle of French cognac Manny had thoughtfully brought for his brother-in-law, they settled down for a long chat. Glasses in hand, they reviewed the events of the past years. Manny spoke of the terrible days that followed the end of the war in Budapest and of the crowds yelling, "Death to the Jews." Julius interrupted him to say he had not realized the situation had been that bad.

"That bad? If not for you, I would have been killed and Father as well," came the startling answer.

"If not for me? What do you mean? I was not there!"

"True, you weren't there, but you are forgetting our last meeting and our encounter with Von Thuringen. I don't know what it was that you did for him, but it must have been something quite out of the ordinary, for he came in person to take us to safety. An ugly mob had set fire to our home and was nearing the bank where I had taken refuge with Father and Istvan who steadfastly refused to abandon us and who brandished his old army pistol. We were going to lock ourselves in the bank's vault, which was empty, as you can imagine—I had managed to transfer everything out of the country—in the hope that the armor-plated doors would resist long enough for the mob to lose patience and leave. Not that I believed they would do so, but what choice did I have?

Suddenly the doorbell rang. It was so unexpected that I went to open the door. The count was there with that great black Mercedes of his, bearing his coat of arms. He told me I had to leave immediately, that he would see me out of the city safely. I thanked him, but when I explained I could not abandon my father, who refused to budge, he raised his eyebrows and asked to talk to him."

Manny smiled at the memory. "You should have been there to see that scene. My father, all in black, a book of psalms in hand, completely oblivious to what was going on; the count, resplendent in his army uniform, calling him a murderer and explaining that unless we left without delay, we would be killed. 'Let the Almighty's will be done; I am not afraid of death' was my father's answer. 'You are to be congratulated,' replied the count tersely, 'but do you not understand that your stubbornness will condemn your son to death and bring ruin to the family bank and, through it, to your children and to your grandchildren?'"

"He said that?" Julius could not believe his ears.

"Indeed. Father looked at him, drew a deep breath, and turned to me, saying: 'The man is right. I beg your pardon.

Let us go.' You should have heard Istvan sigh with relief. We all ran out of the bank and were barely seated in the car when the first demonstrators appeared. Had the count arrived ten minutes later, it would have been too late."

He took a sip of the cognac and resumed his tale. "As you can imagine, I was wondering how the count would get us out of the city since Father, having yielded on the main issue, was not ready to yield on minor ones, such as changing into garments slightly less conspicuous. The man thought of everything. He made us embark on a barge going upriver to Vienna on the Danube. The sailors were working for him. What an adventure it was! The journey took nearly a week, Istvan and I disguised as bargemen and Father coming on deck only at night."

He stopped, and Anna took up the tale. "They were in such a hurry to reach Geneva that once in Vienna, they boarded the night train, unshaven, with dirty clothes and no luggage. I still wonder how the Swiss authorities let them in. They looked like vagrants. You know, Yuli, I hadn't heard any news for days and days and was already fearing the worst—"

"Your sister was wrong, as you can see. Anyway, by that time it had become obvious that for me, for my family, Budapest, Hungary—that was over. My father also understood. I stayed in Geneva until I made the necessary arrangements—"

"And provided a little sister for Myriam." Anni was smiling.

"That too. Then I deserted my poor wife and the new baby once more to sail for America with Tibor. I found a house, hired servants, gathered information on local schools and colleges; it took time. I had planned on coming back earlier to fetch my wife and children, but Karol made me stay for his wedding, saying he had waited long enough. I had missed Tibor's bar mitzvah; I was not about to miss the wedding of my firstborn. I came back to Geneva and made a quick trip to Budapest, where life was more or less back to normal, to liquidate what assets I had left there. Istvan, who accompanied me faithfully through thick and thin—and who did not like America at all—decided to remain in Hungary. With some of the money I gave him, he bought a cab. He writes that he is making a good living."

"Your father remained in Geneva all that time?"

"He refused to live with us. We were lucky to find a retirement home run by the local Jewish community where a dozen Hungarian Jews resided, including four men he knew. There, he spent his last years. The children took turns visiting him; once a month Anni went to fetch him for Shabbat, and he stayed overnight. He passed away the week following my return from America, happy to have seen the photos of his eldest grandchild's wedding. Anni and I decided to wait another year—until Myriam's graduation—before leaving for good. It has turned out very well since it gave us a chance to be here tonight." He stopped with a smile. "Here I am talking away, and I know nothing of what happened to you."

"Nothing much. There was some revolutionary agitation, demonstrations, tracts on the walls. A few anti-Semitic incidents. With the arrival of the Romanians, it all quieted down. There has been no major change for me. Streets have new names—so what? The Jewish hospital is independent again, and I am one of the directors. My private practice is growing by leaps and bounds. So far the new regime has been liberal enough. Which doesn't mean there are no problems.

The children have had to learn Romanian. Magda can't get used to that language. Worst of all is the more virulent strain of anti-Semitism now appearing. So far it's only a matter of speeches and newspaper articles. Hopefully it won't go any further."

"You still won't consider leaving?"

Julius knit his brow. "Consider it? I did. I do. So what? Listen, Manny, try to think like a banker. In America your bank awaits you, you have bought a house, there are servants to welcome you. Your eldest son is working; the younger is about to start as well. One of your daughters is going to college, and the little one will be at home with her mother who does not work. Now I—I am a doctor. A good one, if you will. I do not speak English, but let us say that being gifted at languages, I could learn it fairly quickly. I would also have to acquaint myself with American medical procedures and medicine. Again, not an impossible task.

"I have enough resources to buy a decent house and wait until I can start earning decent money. *Decent* being the operative word. Magda will not be able to work. I have three children to feed and educate. Then there are Father, Aunt, and Golda. Are you still counting? Anyway it is a waste of time. They would not go. Didn't you have to wait until your father was dead? Magda would never agree. Here…here my parents are aging peacefully, in their own little world. My children are getting good educations. Emigration may be on the cards for them in due time—but not for me.

"I admit I would gladly get out of here; I have never liked the town. Not to go to America, a place I know little about and that doesn't tempt me; I am thinking of France instead. Don't laugh. I toyed with the idea of going to that new

Jewish colony in Palestine where thousands of Romanian Jews have already settled. I dropped it quickly. Had I been alone, I would've been tempted. There is something great, awe-inspiring even, in this return to the country where our ancestors once lived free. Going with elderly people, with children, is out of the question. Believe me, there is nothing more to be said. We have a lot to do tomorrow, and I still have to take the dog for a walk—I promised Golda I would."

"Let me come with you." Anni stood up without waiting for an answer.

"Aren't you tired? You travelled all night…"

"I'm not tired, and I want to walk with you one last time. I shan't be back. I can feel it."

Tactfully, Manny did not propose to go with them. With Azor frisking about ahead, brother and sister strolled to the river swollen by the winter's heavy rains. The full moon was only three days away, and it was a starry night; there was no wind, and it was not very cold. That late, they met no one.

They went by the great synagogue and kept walking hand in hand, each lost in thoughts and half-forgotten memories. Wordlessly they sat on a bench, perhaps the very bench where they used to sit on those faraway Shabbat mornings, the bench where Anna had met Manny for the first time. Julius picked up a few pebbles and threw them into the water, trying to skim the waves, and discovered he had lost the knack. He turned to his sister. She was looking straight ahead, very close to tears. He gathered her into his arms.

"You don't want to go?" he hazarded softly.

"It breaks my heart to leave Father and Aunt Donna. They have aged so much! And you have to take care of them alone."

"Come on, you know your husband has always paid his share, with great generosity."

"Who is talking of money? You make them happy. You gave them grandchildren they can see every day. My children—they don't know them. I am far away. That is not my fault, yet the thought that I shan't be here to close their eyes, to accompany them to their last resting place…it breaks my heart. Swear you will send me a telegram so I can mourn them properly, have my family sit shiva in our new home. Swear."

"I shall, if you promise to stop crying."

She blew her nose. "I promise. Tell me little brother, things are not any better with Magda? Auntie hinted that she lost the baby she was carrying when you drove us to Switzerland. I assume she's still angry at you and me?"

"She didn't lose the baby. She got rid of it."

"No! You can't mean it! Why…wait, is that why she encouraged you to go? I remember we were both puzzled by her sudden change of heart."

Briefly he told her what had happened in that long-ago month of March.

"My poor Yuli! What a dreadful woman."

"It's over and done with. Still…you were her friend. How do *you* explain her behavior?"

"Her friend, her friend! She didn't have friends. She resented the fact that she was not pretty and found comfort in the fact that she had everything we did not have, the two other Magdas and I. She basked in our admiration. I'm ashamed to say I used to admire her, or rather envy her. Yet when I think about it, she wasn't happy. Her father was forever talking of the many grandchildren she would give him. She didn't want them to usurp her place. That may be why she agreed to marry a distant relative of her mother's who lived in Budapest. It would have been a way of depriving her father of those future children whom she was already jealous of. Aunt still refuses to tell me what exactly happened with her and Manny. One thing is sure: Magda never recovered from that tragedy. On top of it, by marrying so well, I now enjoy a status equal if not superior to hers. So…she hates the whole world, refusing to admit it's all her fault. There is nothing you can do about it. Still, it distresses me to see you shackled to a bitter woman who hates you."

"Don't. She can't do me any harm, and I lead my own life. Let's talk about you. Are you afraid?"

"I am not sure I shall be strong enough to cope. I am not like you; I never wanted an adventurous life. I got married at seventeen, remember? Well, leaving home, leaving my family, my friends, was difficult. Budapest was hard at first. My in-laws were nice to me, but they were still complete strangers. I didn't know anyone. When I became pregnant, I was sure I would die giving birth, like our mother." She sighed. "I had nightmares and had no one to talk to about them. You were a mere boy, and Auntie couldn't have left Father alone to come and help me. I was ashamed to be so unhappy. I had everything I had always dreamed of. The Nagys were sending money to my parents. Of course in the end it turned out all right.

"Then the war started; there was that horrid episode at the bank; I had to leave for Switzerland with no advance warning. All of a sudden, I had to learn a new language, make new friends—in a word, build an entirely new world for myself. Every morning I woke up terrified that something had happened to Manny, that he had died before we could truly make up. Eventually he came. We decided to have another child. Life was good. Now, after ten years in Switzerland, I have to start all over again. A new language I can barely speak, a country I know nothing about.

"Manny has made a wise decision for us, for our children; I am aware of that. I didn't object. But yes, I am frightened. You see, as soon as we get there, my husband will start going to his bank every day; I shall be left alone. The children are grown. Karol has turned into a near stranger. His wife has nothing to say to me and doesn't understand when I try to speak English with her. Mind you, I don't understand her either. Tibor is marrying a girl I have never met. Not that I am complaining: at least she speaks Hungarian. Myriam will go to college next autumn. I will remain at home with my little Julia—yes, I gave her the name of my darling brother, whom I hadn't seen for so long. Little Julia who nearly killed me coming into the world. I can barely cope with her, she is so lively! If only Madi were still with me…"

He hugged her closer and at last uttered the question he had been dying to ask. "Why isn't she going with you? Did you abandon her by the lake?"

"Madi?" She straightened up. "She didn't write?"

"Madi? Write to me? Between the day she left Nagyvarad and the day we departed for Switzerland, I met her only twice."

"You mean you don't know?"

"What don't I know? All I knew about your life in Geneva was what you wrote about, and I don't remember you ever mentioning her."

"I thought you would show my letters to Auntie and to Father who would surely have asked questions. Besides, I was not sure your Magda knew she was with me. She did not,

right? She did not even know you had driven us to Geneva."
Shaking her head, she went on. "Back to Madi. One evening,
well after the war, Anton—the count's driver, you remember—knocked on the door and handed her a letter from his
boss, asking permission to visit us the following day. We were
no longer living in the house by the lake; I had taken a large
apartment by the river, much closer to the city center and to
the children's schools. Madi had found a smaller apartment next
door—a stroke of luck, that!—and we spent our days together
even after Manny arrived, since he was always working as usual.

"You know, without Madi I don't think I would have
managed for the first two years. She was always smiling,
always cheerful, making me forget how unhappy I was.
We had become inseparable, and the children adored her.
Anyway, that evening we had a long conversation. Obviously
if the count had come to Geneva, it was to try to talk her
into going back with him. She didn't want to leave me, to
leave the children; on the other hand, she realized it would
have to happen sooner or later. She was wise enough to know
there would be no room for her in our new life in America.

"I told her going back would be madness. She had become
respectable and was being courted by several worthy men,
two or three of them quite suitable. All she had to do was
make her choice. In fact, I couldn't understand why she
hadn't done so. Let's face it: she is a little older than me, and
time was slipping by. Anyway, to go back, become a kept
woman again, living in the shadows and having to fear the
countess? Why? She replied that she owed everything to the
man who had taken her under his protection when she was
young and alone, with no money, no family, and a poorly
paid job. It seemed to me that there was more—that there

was someone in Hungary she was very fond of. She never said a word, and yet…In fact I thought at one time it might have been you. She had a way of saying your name…Of course that was impossible. You had been a mere child when she'd left, and I don't see how the two of you could have met in Budapest without my knowing about it."

Julius gave a start in the darkness. Anna went on without noticing. "The following day the count came. Fortunately, he was not aware of the fact that Madi had her own apartment. I must say he cut a good figure in spite of his years. He was extremely polite, and we made small talk about our respective families. His children had emerged unscathed from the war; his countess had not. She had had a bad fall from a horse and had died a few weeks later. He was now a widower. I could see Madi perking up at the news.

"I left them alone for quite a while. When I returned, I could see she was half inclined to go back with him. I had made plans; I suggested the count escort us to the opera that evening. He was a little surprised, but he agreed. After he left, Madi admitted the death of her archenemy changed everything. Also, she found her friend much older and needing her. Still, she asked for a day or two to make up her mind. I said nothing.

In the evening, at the opera, I took a stall. Madi and I were wearing the latest Paris fashions—ably copied by a seamstress under her direction. She had one of those fantastic little hats she loves so much and that she still made for her personal use. During the intermission we were mobbed. Madi was behaving like a society lady to the manner born. From time to time, I could see the count watching her. He knew very well what I was doing.

"I had booked a table in the best restaurant in town for after the show. Once again several people came to greet us. When dessert had been served, I turned to the count. 'I know what my friend owes you,' I told him. 'Yet if you truly care for her, how can you take her away from a town where she is admired and respected—and make her an object of scorn again?' At that point Madi turned brick red. The count didn't flinch. Looking at me squarely, he said he cared for her very much, that he had even considered marrying her—you should have seen her face, she almost fainted—but had backed down because he knew his family would not tolerate the match. He could not cut himself off from his children and grandchildren. In any case, society would side with the children and turn a cold shoulder on his new wife.

"'Are you telling me that should your family accept her, you would be ready to marry my friend?' I asked.

"'Absolutely,'" he replied. By then Madi had tears in her eyes and looked at him adoringly.

"'Very well,' I said. 'I believe I know how you can get them to accept her. Are you willing to listen?' At this point, he surprised me by saying that he wished for nothing more.

"'When you go back to Budapest,' I told him, 'gather your sons and your daughters-in-law. Tell them you cannot live alone, that you had first considered marrying an old and dear friend but, being aware of the fact that they wouldn't welcome her, you regretfully gave up the plan that was so dear to your heart. Therefore, you were thinking of settling for a union with a highborn widow who would bring honor to the family.'

"Yuli, you should have seen them: they were listening as if I were some kind of magician. I went on, 'You will tell them next that although she is very much younger than you, she would be ready, you believe, to marry you in order to be able to raise her three children who were orphaned when their father died on the battlefield, leaving them practically penniless. You will then conclude by saying you feel sure your daughters-in-law would welcome her and treat her with the respect due to the wife of the head of the family.'"

She laughed in the dark. "Madi looked at me as if I had gone mad, but he shook his head and said if the army had had strategists as good as me, it would have won the war. He went back to Budapest and decided to put my theory to the test. You see, since the death of the countess, the wife of his eldest son had more or less taken over the running of the mansion. On no account would she want a younger woman of noble birth to usurp her place and perhaps give him another child or two.

"Of course that was not quite the end of the affair; his children wanted to make sure their rights were protected if he married Madi. Three months later, the count came to Geneva with his eldest son and the family lawyer who had drafted a stringent contract. I showed it to our bank's lawyer who introduced a few changes. Two days later my little redheaded friend became the new Countess Von Thuringen in a simple ceremony at a local church. Turned out she never told me she had converted to Christianity when she changed her name to Maria Corvin, when he had bought her the boutique and the apartment. After a modest reception and a wedding night at the town's most prestigious hotel, the happy couple departed for Budapest. Isn't that amazing?"

"Amazing. Her gain is your loss. Let's go home."

They walked back silently. He did not sleep well that night. Madi, his Madi, making a triumphant return to Budapest. He should have been glad for her. Yet, with this unwelcome union, she was now forever out of his reach. No more dreaming…

In the morning, Dr. Matthias was the perfect host. The ceremony went without a hitch; Andreas behaved with aplomb, reciting the blessings without hesitation and singing his portion of the Pentateuch exactly as he should, easily reciting a difficult text. Julius happily accepted the congratulations of the congregation while replying modestly that all credit was due to his father who had prepared the youngster for the ceremony. In the evening, he received friends and acquaintances in the great ballroom of the Blue Danube Inn.

A number of photographs commemorated the brilliant evening, which was the talk of the community and indeed of the town for many days. One of them showed Julius, handsomer than ever in a made-to-measure suit, dancing with his sister, stunning in a form-fitting pale-blue dress from the best French couturier. They were both smiling.

Dr. Julius Matthias was heartbroken, but that was no reason to spoil the festivities.

15

THE TWO TELEGRAMS

AUNT DONNA TOOK TO HER BED a few days after the departure of her beloved Anna. She would not eat and only drank a little water. There was no medical condition that Julius could see. The old lady had simply lost her will to live. Often, she seemed lost in some other world, talking to herself; she appeared terrified—not of death itself but of meeting her sister.

"You understand," she would say, looking at some unseen person, "I have stolen her husband, her children, her grandchildren, and even that little great-grandchild of hers…Aaron thinks of her from time to time, but for the others she doesn't exist. Anni's children don't even know her name. It's all my fault, and now Gitte will be reproaching me forever…"

Her husband, standing by her bed with his book of psalms, tried vainly to reassure her, telling her in her more lucid moments that she had done nothing wrong; that her sister would thank her; that without her, baby Julius would not have survived; that he himself would not have known how to raise their daughter.

She would have none of it. "I should have come earlier that day. I stopped on my way. Had I been in time, she wouldn't have died. It's all my fault."

"Aunt Donna, you never attempted to take her place," repeated Julius. "You never let me call you Mother, though you were the only mother I knew."

She refused to listen and kept on picking aimlessly at the bedcover. On the last evening, when it had been made clear that the end was near, she opened her eyes and looked at the two men beseechingly.

"I don't want to be buried next to her. Please swear you won't put me next to her!"

"Do you want to be next to Georgy?" suggested Julius, whose heart was breaking.

She turned to him with a relieved smile. "Please! Next to my little angel, I shall rest in peace."

A few minutes later, she fell into an uneasy sleep. Julius persuaded his father to get some rest and took his place in the darkened room. Two candles on the dresser threw their soft light on the dying woman who seemed to have shrunk in a matter of days. Julius contemplated her with tears in his eyes. Who would have known she had been carrying such a burden of guilt for so long? She had never said a word. Should he have guessed, seen her suffering?

Too late now. She, who had always been there for him, who had given him all the love and tenderness he had craved as a child, was now beyond help. In the silent house, Dr. Matthias put his head in his hands and sobbed unashamedly. He had had to see his beloved sister go; had learned Madi was lost to him; and now the only mother he had ever known was dying. Toward dawn he sensed she was awake. He blew his nose and stood up. Her eyes were wide open and searching for something—or someone.

"I am here," he said softly, taking her hand.

She pushed him away impatiently. "Lotsi! Miklosh! Don't look at me like that!"

"Auntie, there is no one here. Calm down."

"Quiet! I see them. They're waiting for me. They look at me with anger."

"What are you talking about?"

"My children. My own children, who died in the fire that engulfed our house. Had I been there…"

"You would have died with them. Please, dear aunt, calm down."

"You don't understand. I abandoned them! From the day I married your father, I have never been back to their tombs. Your father made me swear on the Bible that I would never again go to a Christian cemetery, never again pray in front of the crosses on the tombs. I was weak. I turned my back on my two boys, flesh of my flesh. I banished them from my life, and now I will have to face them!"

"They are together with their father. They forgave you a long time ago."

"No! Julius, do you want me to go in peace?"

"There is nothing I want more."

"Then go see Sandor, and ask him to put flowers on their graves. Now. Please, go!"

"I cannot leave you alone, and I don't want to wake Father."

"Go. I promise I won't die before you come back," she said with a semblance of her old self.

But Aaron was already awake and sat beside her without asking where Julius was going so early in the morning.

Julius found Sandor having breakfast with his wife in the big kitchen. The farmer got up to welcome him, listened gravely to his request, and then walked with him to the back garden where Martha had planted a profusion of roses that were now in full bloom. The two men chose the best ones and put them in the back of the car. It was a short drive to the cemetery. The gate was not fastened; there was nothing there to steal.

Sandor showed him the way to a white tombstone; under a tall cross, two little eaglets were sheltering under the wings of a marble eagle. This was the last resting place of Donna's first husband and her two children: Ladislas—Lotsi—the eldest, born in 1868, the second in 1869. They died in 1882. Lotsi was almost fourteen at the time. Strange that he had never given a thought to these two, who had been his first cousins. Donna must have thought about them often, especially when Georgy died. She had never said a word, and he—he had never asked. For him, for his sister, this part of their beloved aunt's life had never existed. She had borne her sorrow alone.

Sandor reverently laid the fragrant flowers on the grave and crossed himself. "May I come to see her, to say good-bye?" he asked awkwardly.

"Get into the car. Let's go."

"I am not dressed for visiting," protested the farmer.

"Never mind that. Come as you are. Vadim will take you home."

They found Golda and Aaron with Donna. When Sandor moved forward, they exchanged looks, and moved by some instinct, he left to give him a few moments with his aunt.

It was a clear spring day; a golden light was filtering through the half-opened shutters.

The farmer came to the head of the bed and began talking of the freshly cut flowers laid on the grave and the mass he had had said every year on the anniversary of the deaths of his uncle and cousins. He added—with an apologetic look directed at Julius—that he would say a special mass for Donna and would ask the good Lord to welcome her into his heaven.

Donna's sigh of relief was clearly audible; she even managed a smile. She grasped his hand feebly and thanked him. He bent to kiss her cheek one last time and silently walked away.

She died an hour later. Her last words had been for Julius: "Thank you for the roses, my dear boy. Thank you for everything." Aaron was at her side, but it was Julius who closed her eyes, vainly trying to reconcile what he knew of his aunt with the terrified old woman pursued by imaginary demons and looking for solace in a religion she had allegedly abjured. He resolved to forget about those last few hours and only remember the seemingly indomitable Donna who had nurtured him and lavished so much love on a motherless baby.

Then he sent Vadim to the post office with a telegram. "My dear little sister," he wrote, "our beloved aunt died peacefully in her bed." There was no need for Anni to know more.

In the meantime, the rituals of death were underway. Golda threw the men out, and together with Ditta—she had hired the woman when Magda had sacked her before the move, saying the children were old enough to do without her—proceeded to prepare the body. Donna Matthias was laid to rest at four in the afternoon on Monday, May 24—a month to the day after the bar mitzvah ceremony. Spring was in the air, and the cemetery trees were in full bloom. Aaron Matthias moved like an automaton, supported on one side by his son and on the other by his grandson. He recited the Kaddish with utter despair and added, "Donna, I can't wait to join you."

Indeed, during the weeklong shiva he appeared absent. Even his grandchildren were unable to draw him out. Fortunately, he was unaware of the altercation between his daughter-in-law and her mother. As soon as she heard that Donna was dead, Magda had rushed to the house, and before the body had been taken away, told her mother imperviously that an old-age home should be found immediately for Aaron Matthias, since it would be unseemly for him to continue living under her roof now that he was a widower. An angry Golda told her not to talk nonsense, adding that the old man would be welcome in her house as long as she lived.

"But what will people say? Don't you care for your grand-daughters who will soon be of marrying age?"

"Don't be ridiculous. We are both over seventy years old!"

"Nobody will believe that a man and a woman living in the same house do not sleep together."

Golda looked at her daughter and answered witheringly, "Why not? That's what is happening under your own roof, and you and your husband are thirty years younger!"

Magda turned brick red and left with a furious glance at Julius who stood aghast at the scene. She then refused to go to the cemetery, saying Jewish tradition did not deem it compulsory for a wife to go to her husband's aunt's funeral.

When Julius tried to thank his mother-in-law, she raised her hand to stop him. "I gave my word to Donna when we were talking of them moving in with me. She knew she would be the first to go. However, it was for you that I agreed, that I gave my word your father would have a home here as long as he lived. I know you will do the same for my daughter. We understand each other, don't we?"

He nodded wordlessly. His mother-in-law drove a hard bargain, but she was fair.

Somehow, as always, the week of ritual mourning helped. So many people came that at times the big Szamuely drawing room overflowed. Julius's colleagues at the hospital, community leaders, patients…but also, to his surprise, former neighbors from number 4 Schools Road who had not forgotten the mother of "our good doctor."

Magda, when she made one of her rare appearances, would sneer at the humble folks bringing modest gifts—homemade cake, fruit or vegetables from their gardens—but Julius was deeply moved. Happily, he had made new friends after the Austrian's departure, and they came daily to sit with him. Among them were the Weinberger brothers, both bankers; factory owner Mozes Wollner, whom Julius had first met as a patient and immediately bonded with; and Jeno Halasz, a stocky man of some thirty years with his trademark bright-red hair who wrote for the Hungarian Jewish daily. Interestingly, the paper's circulation had not gone down in spite of the regime change. They were in the habit of lunching together once a month at the Blue Danube Inn, to which Julius had remained faithful.

On Sunday, as the week of mourning was drawing to its close, Sandor and Martha came in their best finery. Martha spoke eloquently of the aunt who had been always ready to help and advise her when she had been a newly married woman and later a frightened young mother. The following week Julius attended the mass Sandor was having in memory of his aunt, as he had promised. It was not Julius's first visit to a church; in Vienna he had attended a funeral service for one of his professors. He knew how outraged his father would have been were he to know, but saw nothing shocking in the simple ceremony attended by half a dozen Toth family members.

Life went on. He worked harder than ever. He often told himself he was not unhappy. His children were growing up, and he enjoyed being with them. Andreas was an even-tempered youngster who didn't show the slightest interest in medical or pharmaceutical studies. He was a born mechanic and already knew more about the motor of his father's Mercedes than the chauffeur did. More and more often, Vadim turned to him when there was a problem. Andreas had no doubt about what he wanted to do: first study engineering and then build cars.

Elisabeth was an outstanding student with a sunny disposition. She had been the one to inherit her grandfather's shortsightedness. She had not lost her fascination for her father's work; however, it was too early to know whether it was serious or just the reflection of a girl's natural admiration for her father.

Gabriella, the youngest, was by far the quietest. She had a disconcerting way of looking at her father with Anna's eyes. She was not very interested in school and often cajoled her brother or sister into helping her with her homework.

Magda had begun to show an interest in her daughters, taking them to the seamstress and to the hairdresser and accompanying them to piano lessons. Slightly apprehensive at first, since their mother had been rather indifferent in the past, the girls let themselves be wooed. When summer vacation began, the impossible happened: Magda deserted her counter at the pharmacy to go out with her children. It was as if she no longer cared for the pharmacy which had for so long been the center of her world. At the same time, she was making a conscious effort to mend fences with her own mother.

Was this the dawn of a new era? Julius was far from certain. He wondered whether this sudden change of heart was not inspired by Magda's fear that her mother would leave a substantial part of her estate to Julius or to her grandchildren directly, bypassing her own daughter. Whatever the case, the older woman basked in her daughter's renewed affection and was delighted by her sudden devotion to her children. She mentioned it to Julius who had come to see his father who was unwell and had remained for lunch.

"Have you noticed that Gabriella is her favorite and that she shows it a little too much?" Golda wanted to know.

"I have indeed. Since discussing it with her would get me nowhere, I let it go."

"Things are no better between the two of you?"

"You could say there is less hostility in the air. We manage to exchange small talk without quarreling. It's not much, but…Anyway, it doesn't go any further. She stays in her room and I in mine, if that's what you mean."

She looked him over, knitting her brow. She was getting old too, he told himself with surprise. Her hair was completely white, and she had lost weight…Of course she was exactly the same age as Aaron, even though she had always looked younger and still did.

"I had hoped…What a pity. She doesn't understand that marrying you was an extraordinary piece of luck for her. She could have stayed young, as your sister did. Seeing them side by side nearly broke my heart. Still, there's nothing to be done about it now. Let's go back to the subject of the children. When I talked to her, she immediately admitted I was right and that she did favor Gabriella. You will never guess why."

"Isn't it because she is the youngest?"

"Not at all. She says she reminds her of your sister."

"What? But she hates Anna!"

"You don't get it. When she sees her daughter, she tells me, she sees your sister as she was thirty years ago when they first met. Those were the best years of her life, she says. They called her Magda the Great, remember? Daughter of the pharmacist. She had the world at her feet. She wasn't the most beautiful, but she had it all: the best dresses, boots that came straight from Paris…She could pity her friends, the two other Magdas and your sister; they were more beautiful, but each had only one coat and wore the same shoes all year round. She was sure she would make a brilliant marriage while they would have to do with far less and would keep on envying her. My poor child…"

He patted her hand and left her without replying. Poor child indeed! A spoilt child, an arrogant young girl who thought she deserved everything because she was rich when her friends were not…A young girl who, confronted with a catastrophic pregnancy, refused to acknowledge what was happening and believed to the last minute that she would be able to fool the rich young man her parents wanted her to marry…A young woman who had treated Julius as if he were some inferior hireling, who had not thought twice before getting rid of another baby that did not fit into her plans. He was happy at her change of heart regarding the two girls, but he would still be on his guard. And pay special attention to his son, who had not been included in the new magic circle. Andreas might not appear to mind, but his father did, and therefore did his best to take him along whenever he could—for instance when he went to the farm, where over the years he had delivered Matthias, Thereza, and Eva, Martha's last three children, and resumed his easy camaraderie with Sandor.

A new school year started; the children went back to their studies and Magda to her pharmacy. Julius kept on working, dividing his days between the hospital and his surgery. He also visited private patients at home, which had the added benefit of being a convenient way to hide short-term liaisons. Vivi had gone back to Bucharest; however, he met enough young women who wanted nothing more than brief flings with the good-looking doctor. He was always very careful, first making sure they knew what they were getting themselves into and behaving with the utmost discretion.

Once a month he met his friends at the Blue Danube. They talked about the world situation, the new Europe; they discussed the Nazi Party emerging in Germany and the rising wave of anti-Semitism in Romania. Some political parties had actually adopted it on their political platforms. Should Julius and his friends be worried?

There was the National-Christian Defense League, established in 1923 by A. C. Cuza, a professor at the University of Iași. The man proclaimed that Jews were battling Christians to gain control over Romania and was agitating for the abrogation of the new constitution granting equal rights to all citizens. His rallying cry, "Romania to Romanians," was making headway in Transylvania. There, ethnic Romanians, still a minority who were fighting to gain the upper hand over the Hungarian majority, accused the Jews, who tended to speak Hungarian and to look to Budapest, of not being patriotic enough. Romanians Jews, for their part, had seen the writing on the wall and were emigrating to Palestine by the thousands. The question was duly thrashed out in the Oradea lunches—after which talk turned to more interesting subjects, such as the latest scandalous gossip. The mood was generally upbeat, and the friends would part smiling. Julius usually went on to visit one of his favorite female "patients."

No, he was not really unhappy, even though sometimes the sight of a daring little hat perched on an alluring silhouette made his heart beat faster…

He was by now considered one of the leading physicians of the town. His Christian colleagues consulted him on difficult cases. One day he was called to attend the bishop. The man's own doctors had not been able to determine what was causing his pain; with the situation deteriorating, someone had had the bright idea of calling in the Jewish doctor who would make a readymade scapegoat should the prelate die. A point that Julius had grasped immediately while knowing he could not refuse. He was lucky in making the right diagnosis on the spot. It was acute appendicitis in an atypical form. The two other doctors ridiculed his idea, but the patient overruled them. Operated upon immediately, he made a good recovery and started singing the praises of the Jewish doctor who had saved his life—something that said doctor could have done without because it angered his Christian colleagues unnecessarily.

These and other worries were wiped out of his mind one bright morning when, arriving in his opulent office at the hospital—now that he was a director, he had even his own secretary—he found on the table a large black-rimmed envelope with Hungarian stamps. He opened it absentmindedly, wondering which of his former patients had died. When he read the name, he had to sit down.

Count Ferencz Von Thuringen had been gathered to his forefathers.

The following day, Dr. Julius Matthias took the earliest morning train to Budapest. He would have left earlier, but he had to reschedule meetings and appointments and find a reasonable excuse for this sudden journey. Eventually he told his staff he had decided to accept the long-standing invitation of Mihaly, the former military commander of the hospital, who had left the army and was now the director of a private medical establishment.

This was the first trip Julius had taken since 1916. The circumstances were vastly different. The first-class compartment lived up to its title; the dining room was luxurious; however, there was now a border to cross, with sour-faced officers on either side. He was travelling on a Romanian passport, having obtained one as things had calmed down, in preparation for a visit to Switzerland that had never taken place. However, nothing on the document indicated his religion, and, being a doctor, the passport gave him a measure of respect; formalities were kept to a minimum.

He did not pay much attention: his mind was elsewhere. He had barely slept the previous night yet could not close his eyes throughout the journey. Madi herself had sent the letter, of that he was absolutely sure. Any other person would have written to his home address or to his clinic. Therefore, she wanted him to know—and to come. He did not dare go any further. Indeed, he had a return ticket for that evening, though he hoped he would have to change it.

A hope that was to be dashed. Nevertheless, Julius was whistling happily when he settled down in his leather seat for the return journey later that day.

At four-thirty in the afternoon, he had presented his visiting card at the imposing town house, situated in the best part of the city, where the dowager Countess Von Thuringen was in residence. She had been expecting him, as he had phoned earlier while touring the exclusive medical facility run by his erstwhile commandant who had treated him to an excellent lunch and offered him a very good position at an impressive salary. Julius had hedged; not that he had any intention of accepting, but he wanted to leave a door open in case he needed another excuse to come to Budapest.

There was a mood of deep mourning in the house where a vague smell of incense floated. In the vestibule, a portrait of the count in parade uniform, saber in hand, was draped in black crepe. The servants—he counted three on his way—were all in black; so was Madi. Her tawny hair was the sole note of color in the somber black covering her from head to toe. Had she changed? He could not have said. He saw only her feline eyes looking at him hungrily. There was a dour female hovering by, some relative of the late count, pressed into service as chaperone by the family.

Julius bent to kiss Madi's little hand, wondering how he would manage to talk to the widow under her guardian's beady eye. He reckoned without the Madi's wit, who, having listened gravely to his words of condolence, asked him graciously to sit down and sent her companion to order some refreshments. The woman slunk out to show her disapproval and came back a mere two minutes later to find the countess, seated at a respectable distance, having an animated discussion with her guest—in French, a language she did not understand. She was clearly not happy about the situation, but they did not pay her any attention.

Madi, eyes demurely downcast, the very picture of respectability, was explaining that the count's will had turned her into a virtual prisoner, shackled by golden chains. The house was hers as long as she lived—unless she remarried; the considerable allowance she was to receive would cease should she leave her home. The other heirs would watch her like hawks, ready to pounce should she fail to observe the rules. Dabbing her eyes with a delicate lace handkerchief, she threw a roguish glance at him and murmured that she had nevertheless managed to get them to agree to let her go to Switzerland in the spring for a few days' rest, since she was exhausted, having nursed her husband through his long illness. Now, if Julius could manage to be there at the same time...

He found the idea marvelous. She had thought of everything, named places, dates...He listened with fascination, nodding his head, drinking in the well-remembered subtle violet fragrance. They agreed on a May morning at the terrace of the very café that had witnessed their good-byes ten years earlier. She rose gracefully, indicating their meeting was over. He kissed her hand again, kissed the companion's hand as well for good measure, and walked out, trying hard not to show his elation.

As the year 1927 started, Julius would have been very happy in anticipation of that longed-for reunion had it not been for his worry about his father. Aaron Matthias's mind had taken to wandering. He spent hours at the synagogue, usually coming back in time for meals as if by instinct. However, he had been known to roam aimlessly through the streets for hours. Julius found a good man to look after him. A nurse by profession, Jacob Farkas had worked in the Jewish hospital before the war and then enlisted. Badly wounded, he had lost one eye and had been disfigured by an ugly scar running from the corner of his mouth to his ear. His fiancée had turned her back on him and married another. The only place that would employ him was the insane asylum, as the inmates were not in a position to complain about his appearance.

Julius, who valued the calm and the competence of the tall, brawny nurse, had not deserted him, recommending him to people wanting someone to watch over loved ones who, having lost consciousness and living their last hours, were not likely to be frightened by his twisted features. Aaron Matthias, reluctant at first to accept a minder, had let himself be persuaded, since Jacob, though not very observant, never seemed to resent the many hours spent in the synagogue. Farkas was soon a welcome addition to the Szamuely household, always ready to lend a helping hand and not above taking Azor, sadly neglected by the children during the school year, for an evening walk.

Time passed quickly. Winter was drawing to an end and spring was in the air, and with it the long-anticipated journey to Geneva. Neither Julius's wife nor his mother-in-law had questioned his need for the trip. His father was doing well and appeared happy with his new companion. It was thus with a relatively clear conscience that Julius left for Switzerland.

He arrived far too early at the meeting point but found Madi already there, lovelier than ever. She was wearing a dark-gray dress, almost black, as befitting her widowed status, and a marvelous little hat with a veil, and he wanted to make love to her there and then. She had thought of everything; she had booked a room at a pleasant inn situated in an isolated part of the country where they were not likely to run into people they knew. Mr. and Mrs. Matthias arrived in the late morning and immediately went to their room "to rest."

A considerable time later, Madi turned languorously toward him. "Tell me, is it better with a countess?" she asked with a satisfied smile. "Did you notice a difference?"

"I'm afraid I didn't give it a thought," he replied, laughing. "Besides, you are not the first countess I have slept with…"

She sat up, surprised and a little piqued. "Are you serious? Who is she? Is she a real countess?"

"It happened ages ago, when I was a student, and she was not nobly born. Just like you, she became a countess when she married a count. To tell you the truth, I had forgotten all about her. Anyway, why are we wasting our time talking?"

It was an enchanted week. They were together every minute of the day, going for long walks in the countryside, where spring was running riot, stopping for lunch at some little restaurant over a babbling brook before returning at a leisurely pace to their inn. In the evening, they dined in the inn's snug dining room and went to bed early in the great four-poster.

They never spoke of the past or the future. They were living for the present and its daily joys. Breakfast in their room, the window wide open to a sunny landscape, where birdsong joined with the tinkling bells of the cattle in the fields. Then it was back to bed for a protracted lie in and bouts of renewed lovemaking. Julius never tired of watching a half-naked Madi brushing her long hair and twisting it into an elaborate coiffure. The countess was plumper than the milliner had been, but he was not complaining. On their last day, she clung to him with something akin to desperation, and they left their room only to go down to dinner.

In the morning they returned to Geneva, where they parted company—Julius to go back to Oradea, and Madi to return to the establishment where she had allegedly spent the week. They made plans to come back in the spring of the following year, and before that, hopefully to meet in Budapest where the countess intended to part company with her companion at the end of the year of her official mourning. They both knew these projects might not come to fruition yet wanted to believe that fate, having taken such a benevolent interest so far, would keep on doing so.

On Teleky Street nothing had changed in Julius's absence, and only Azor barked happily and jumped with joy when he saw him. Routine set in once again.

Toward the end of June, Juno Halasz, the reporter, brought two visitors from the city of Iași, capital of the province of Moldova, to the monthly lunch. One was a doctor, the other the son-in-law of the president of the Jewish community. They told of recent events that they found deeply disturbing. A disciple of A. C. Cuza, one Corneliu Codreanu had just launched a new movement, the Legion of Archangel Michael, which was even more extremist than the National-Christian Defense League. The man was dangerous because he was so well connected; he had spent a ridiculously short time behind bars for the murder of the town's chief of police—in the courthouse!

The others listened to their story politely with the appropriate murmurs of sympathy, but with no great concern. Iași was nearly five hundred miles away. Oradea was going through an unprecedented phase of prosperity; Jewish industrialists and storekeepers were doing well. The community had its own school network. There were very few anti-Semitic incidents. Later—much later—Julius would come to the conclusion that even if he had taken the warning more seriously, there was nothing he or the others could have done.

The summer vacation ushered in a new era. Suddenly the children were no longer children. Andreas disappeared all day with two or three boys his own age; having brought them home once and been roundly berated by his mother, he now took them to Golda who beamed and always had a piece of her famous cheesecake for each of them. Elisabeth had gone through a spurt of growth, making her almost as tall as her brother, which Magda saw as a problem; she complained no man would want a woman taller than himself, and one who wore spectacles to boot. Golda told her favorite granddaughter not to mind, and her father told her she would break hearts one day. The girl, who had her own coterie, took criticism and praise with equanimity.

Gabriella was another story. She was so beautiful that heads turned when she walked down the street. She spent hours preening herself in front of her mirror, encouraged by her mother, who was never cross with her. Yet there was something in those extraordinary blue eyes that her father found disconcerting. As if she looked down on people—just like Magda.

The summer ended, and suddenly the dire warnings of the visitors from Iași took on another dimension. Throughout the country students were demonstrating, calling for the immediate implementation of a numerus clausus—a disposition limiting the number of Jews admitted to the university—and agitating for a full ban later. The far right elements were adding fuel to the fire in what they called the fight against the nefarious Jewish influence. The Students' League intended to hold its annual meeting in the town of Arad, some sixty miles west of Oradea. However, fearing incidents similar to those of the previous year in Iași, the mayor of Arad refused to host the event. Student leaders then turned to Oradea, backed by the minister of the interior, who pledged he would see to it that law and order prevailed.

Some five thousand students arrived on December 4th, welcomed by the army band before marching through the streets where the town monuments were decked with national flags. They then divided into two groups to attend a solemn Te Deum service in the two Romanian Catholic cathedrals of the town. Later they gathered in the theater and started their deliberations. By late afternoon, having left the theater, they went on a rampage, attacking Jewish shops. The army was called in to restore order; faced with thousands of young men belting out the national anthem with fervor, they retreated without intervening.

Then the mob turned toward the six main synagogues, breaking everything inside and defacing holy symbols. Aaron Matthias was sitting in the Neolog synagogue when some thirty students broke in yelling and ran to the velvet curtains protecting the Torah scrolls. While the few Jews present fled, the old man walked to the vandals and commanded them to stop. He was thrown aside contemptuously and kicked by a number of booted feet as he lay on the ground. Jacob, who rushed to his assistance, was hit with a chair and fainted.

When he regained consciousness, the students were gone, leaving a ravaged hall and the lifeless body of Aaron Matthias. Jacob kneeled by his master and started crying, not wanting to leave him alone and not knowing what to do. Outside, the shouting was dying down, and two congregants walked in cautiously to check the damage. Jacob made them swear to stay by the body and ran to the hospital where Dr. Matthias was on duty.

Having heard that something was happening, Julius called home and learned his wife and children were safely indoors, and Vadim was on his way to fetch him. He stared uncomprehendingly when Jacob burst into his office, chalk white and his head bloody, and told him his father had been beaten to death in the synagogue. At first Julius thought there must have been a mistake, that the man's brain must have been addled by the blow. Still, having attended to the wound in spite of Jacob's entreaties to hurry, he went with him to the car where Vadim was already waiting. On the way, Julius saw the devastation: the vandalized storefronts, their contents thrown into the street, where the frightened owners were speedily picking up, fearing a return of the students. Was this what a pogrom looked like? Pogroms happened in Poland, in Russia, not here! Romania was a civilized country. Students were not Cossacks.

The car stopped in front of the synagogue. Julius made his way through the little group standing there who parted to let him through. One massive wooden door bore the mark of repeated blows; it was hanging on one hinge. Inside, an acrid smoke rose from the velvet curtains. A few women were busy sweeping up the debris; in a corner, men were lamenting loudly, prayer books in hand.

His father had not been moved and lay where he had fallen. A rabbi Julius did not recognize was reciting psalms. Julius knelt down in the dust and took a hand already cold, looking for a pulse he knew was not there. He contemplated the wide-open eyes in the waxen face, the hat fallen on the ground, the tufts of white hair, the dusty clothes. On the left shoulder, he could clearly see the imprint of a muddy boot.

A terrible pain tore through him. He closed his father's eyes, straightened his hair, and covered it with the hat. "For dust you are, and to dust you shall return" ran the biblical words, he thought. But why like that? Why...He knew he should get up, set in motion the ancient ritual of death, but he could not. The rabbi said something, but he did not hear. He wanted to scream, to call, "Father! Father!" to one who could no longer hear him. Then strong arms picked him up and stood him upright: Vadim and Jacob. Men were coming with a stretcher. He recognized members of the hevra kadisha, the community funeral organization.

He heard himself ask a question: "Shouldn't we wait for the police?" People looked away uneasily.

A familiar voice, that of Jeno the journalist, answered. "Julius my friend, why bother? They will make a great show of listening and then do nothing. Come on. Where do you want to take him? Did he live with you?"

He thought quickly. He did not want the children to see their grandfather like that. He told Vadim to drive ahead and warn Golda. Then he took the head of the little group who were taking Aaron Matthias back to the Szamuely house.

Later he sent Vadim to the post office with another telegram.

"My darling little sister, Father has left us too."

16

DECISION TIME

AARON MATTHIAS WAS BURIED THAT NIGHT. The city was still in turmoil. All the shops were closed, their shutters heavily padlocked. Rampaging students, some quite drunk, were roaming the streets, stopping anyone who had the misfortune to be in their way and demanding to see his papers. Woe to the unfortunate Jew caught! Jeered at, beaten, he was lucky to escape with his life.

Consequently, it was a very small group of courageous people who accompanied the patriarch on his last journey. His friends were too old and too frightened to leave the safety of their homes; as for his son's colleagues, few risked the streets and their dangers. Julius's closest friends were there, as was the rabbi of the synagogue with two assistants. Bringing up the rear was Jacob Farkas, who had flatly refused to stay in bed, as he had been told. He was in pain; there was a huge dressing on his head; however, he proudly wore his old army uniform and had fastened his regulation gun to his belt.

"Had I taken it with me today, I could have saved Aaron," he lamented, adding, "I want to make sure he is buried in a dignified manner. Don't worry, I shan't have to kill any-one. I know the type—good at yelling but no stomach for a fight. A warning shot and they will scatter like the miserable cowards they are."

It was perhaps fortunate that they encountered no stu-dents. The gravediggers had already finished their work and waited, shovels in hand, for the short ceremony to be over.

That night sleep eluded Dr. Julius Matthias. It was not sorrow that kept him awake. Aaron Matthias had said his fare-wells a long time ago and was more than ready to relinquish his grasp on life. It was the manner of his death—beaten and trampled by a heartless bunch of students who felt no remorse over killing a helpless old man. His son was filled with impotent fury. Unbidden, the attack on his friend, Theo, came into his mind. Had he not fled, would the mob have killed him? This led to another, more painful question. Shouldn't he have listened to his brother-in-law? Taken his family away, made them go into exile? Aaron would still be alive, would not have been murdered...Julius was still tor-turing himself with these many questions when dawn came.

The children were told of their grandfather's death in the morning. Their father took them to the seldom-used drawing room and made them sit down. While they looked apprehensively to him, he simply said the old man had passed away. Elisabeth burst into sobs; Gabriella ran to her room, slamming the door behind her; Andreas was the only one to ask for details. Of the three, he had been closest to the old man. Julius opted for the truth. The boy would hear it sooner or later from his school friends or even from the servants.

"It is not right, Father," said Andreas quietly, with a look of anguish.

"No, son, it is not right," he had replied. And then, surprisingly, Andreas embraced him.

It was in that same drawing room that the shiva was held. Magda had strenuously objected, arguing it would upset the children. Julius replied coldly that Aaron had been the head of the family, and it was in the family home that the week of mourning would be held. Upon which she had declared her intention of moving into her mother's house for the duration, taking the children with her. The girls went willingly enough; their brother flatly refused. Having attained his religious majority the year before, he was determined to stay and receive condolences together with his father.

The Jewish schools had not reopened, as bands of students were still roaming the streets. The Sunday events had profoundly embarrassed local authorities; there were wide swaths of white in the town's papers, the censors having worked hard at trying to prevent the news from spreading. Community leaders were no less embarrassed. To admit that what had happened was, for all intents and purposes, a pogrom would have been to admit a reality they did not want to acknowledge.

Julius was told over and over again that one should not see in one tragic incident a manifestation of anti-Semitism; regrettably, some unsavory elements, probably out-of-work war veterans, had taken advantage of the student's presence. After all, it was argued, very few students had misbehaved, and those who had were drunk. There had been instances of vandalism, yes, but the government had solemnly promised full compensation. Duca, the minister of the interior, had sent a telegram to the governor, asking him to convey the apologies of the government to the people of Oradea and to the chief rabbi of the town. The rector of the University of Bucharest pledged to have troublemakers expelled from all the universities of the country—as soon as they had been identified, of course. None of this convinced Julius, who suspected his visitors were as skeptical as he was. The Christians were too ashamed to admit the truth; the Jews were afraid of voicing their darkest fears. He therefore listened politely, nodding from time to time when friends and acquaintances repeated the official version, well aware of the fact that by protesting he would lose the tremendous amount of goodwill he was getting. For the sake of his family, for his own sake, even for the sake of the community, it was better to keep silent. And so he did—feeling bitterly ashamed.

Only once did he allow himself to vent his true feelings. The bishop, whose life he had saved, paid him a highly political visit in order to offer his condolences—and to insist that one should not blame anti-Semitism for the despicable actions of a few black sheep.

"Let me ask you a question," said Dr. Matthias softly, so as not to be overheard. "During the two days of rioting, was one Christian shopkeeper molested?"

Having gotten a sigh and a helpless shrug for an answer, he thanked the man profusely and personally walked him to his car. He felt like the lead actor in some sinister play. At times he had to resist the urge to stand up and shout, "My father has been murdered! Kicked to death in a house of prayer! A house of prayer desecrated and vandalized because it is a Jewish place of worship. The murderers walk around free; there is no ongoing investigation to find them. You speak of an incident, yet there are some who are saying, more or less directly, that if my poor father had not *provoked* the mob, he would still be alive!" Somehow he controlled himself, but at a price. He could not eat, and he slept poorly.

Two days before the end of the week of mourning, an unexpected visitor brought some comfort. It was relatively late, and Julius was alone; Andreas, who had a test the following day, had gone to bed. The entrance door was still unlocked according to tradition, and Julius was considering turning the key to signify he was no longer receiving visitors that day. He was very surprised to see a well-remembered figure entering the drawing room.

"Father Octavius!" he exclaimed.

"My enemies call me Monsignor these days, but you may call me what you like, my friend. Allow me to say how profoundly sorry I am that we are meeting under such sad circumstances, and accept my heartfelt condolences."

Indeed, though the man had not changed much, the rich ecclesiastical robes he wore attested to his new status. He had spoken in French, and it was in that language that Julius answered.

"I thank you. Please sit down. I am happy to see you again. So you are Monsignor now? What happened? The church has forgiven you?"

"Forgiveness is a part of our tradition. Besides, I have been lucky. My father was kind enough to make a generous donation, and my superiors discovered I have some talents in the field of diplomacy. Which, by the way, is the reason I am here."

"I fail to see what interest has led your church to send such a distinguished diplomat!"

"As a result of what I shall call recent events, our Romanian Orthodox brethren have seen fit to take over a number of properties belonging to Hungarian Catholic institutions. Naturally the church is anxious to have the properties returned."

"It can't be easy."

"That is where you are wrong. The government of Bucharest is thinking of world public opinion—today more than ever. I have been able to make local authorities see the light, and matters have been settled quietly. Julius, my friend, I have not come to talk about property. I have come to apologize, indeed to beg for your forgiveness. The church I represent bears some responsibility for the death of your father. When I heard what had happened, our parting words came back to haunt me: 'May the heavens protect you and yours' is what I said, and you replied, 'Don't you mean protect us from yours?' To you I can admit how worried I am. Not only because of your father's tragic demise. An ill wind is blowing over Europe."

"Will your church see the danger, do something?"

Monsignor Octavius sighed wearily. "I wish I could answer in the affirmative. I can't. Part of the hatred that is rising like some loathsome lava was born within us. Few will admit it, fewer still measure the danger." He stood up. "I leave tomorrow. May you and your family know no more tragedy. Friend, I don't know why providence united us briefly or why I feel such a bond of sympathy. Were I a believer, I would say I shall pray for you. Here is my visiting card. If you ever need it, contact me. I shall do my utmost for you. And if the kind fates ever send you to Rome, know you have a friend there."

As the two men embraced, quick steps were heard, and Gabriella ran into the room. She stopped at the sight of a stranger.

"But she is ravishing!" exclaimed the priest. "A true Madonna! What is your name, child?"

"She does not speak French," replied Julius, smiling for the first time that week. "Try Romanian."

Monsignor Octavius exchanged a few words with the child who appeared awed by the elegant visitor and departed after shaking her hand gravely.

"Is he a prince?" she wanted to know when he had gone.

"A prince of his church…"

"May I have his card?"

"What for? I might need it."

"I will take very good care of it. I shall put it in the leather box Grandmother Golda gave me for my birthday."

"Very well. But what are you doing here so late?"

"Mother sent me to fetch a letter she forgot on her table."

"You came alone?"

"Of course not. Jacob is waiting downstairs with Azor. He will see me home and then take the dog for a walk."

On the last day of that week, Golda, who had come daily to comfort him, asked Julius to accompany her home. In front of the ornate door of the Szamuely mansion, she suddenly suggested they go for a little stroll. It had not snowed recently; the sidewalk was dry and the cold quite bearable. When they reached the corner of the street, she stopped and, facing him squarely, told him Magda wanted her to move in with them.

"Dear Golda, you are most welcome, and the children will be delighted."

"Of course I would have to sell my house…"

There wasn't anything he could contribute on that subject, so he kept silent.

"I have given much thought to her proposal," she went on. "It is true I don't want to be all alone. Too many phantoms come to trouble me at night. Yet this is my home. I have lived here for twenty years. So I have a better idea. Why don't you come and live with me? There is plenty of room—in fact more than where you live. I would be staying in my own home. I take comfort in the thought that I shall one day forever close my eyes in my own bed. You can sell your own apartment. Magda has been talking of expanding and renovating the pharmacy; this would give her enough money. The house will be yours when I am gone…"

"Have you talked it over with Magda?"

"She claims you will never agree to move into what you still call the pharmacist's house."

"She is wrong. I made my peace with Emil long before his death. Anyway, we don't have a choice, do we? What would happen to Azor if you were to sell?"

She smiled happily. "That's settled, then. Good. Don't worry, I shall take care of everything. There is just another thing I have to tell you. It's about a wedding."

"Who is getting married?"

"Jacob and Ditta."

"Are you serious?"

"He was going to tell you last week…"

"I understand. When are they having the ceremony?"

She laughed. "As soon as possible."

"Do you mean…"

"Why not? They were both very lonely, they are not so young anymore, and they want to have children while they still can. I promised Ditta a dowry; she has been a good and faithful servant, first to our poor little Georgy and then… Anyway they want you to give her away."

"I shall do so with pleasure."

"I will tell them tonight. They were afraid you would be angry at Jacob for not having protected your father."

"Angry at him! If he had not lost consciousness when he did, they might have killed him as well. I will talk to him tomorrow."

"Now I am at peace. Thank you, dear boy. Let us go back. Listen, I have a feeling you blame yourself for your father's death. You are sorry you didn't listen to Manny, didn't leave as he did."

"How do you know about that?"

"Do you really think your sister didn't discuss it with Donna? With her father? With me too? The three of us told her exactly the same thing. One does not uproot an old tree at the end of its life. Donna ended her days in the city where she had been born and where she had lived all her life. Your father…your father would not have been able to adjust to a different existence. I have thought about all this a lot since his death. Since she left him, he was tired of living. He would often tell me so. He was conscious of losing part of his mind every day and was terrified of becoming senile. I am not sure he had time to think about it, but I believe he welcomed a death that would set him free. He died for something."

"For something! How can you suggest such a thing?"

"He rose to defend something that was dear to him. He confronted a dozen brutes. He has shown the community and the town that an old Jew can be more courageous than the good Christians who saw the rampaging students go by, looked the other way, and went home. Many people came to tell me that."

"I wish I could believe you but I cannot. I am sure they will soon have forgotten—and that there will be other attacks."

"Julius!"

"Golda, it is time to face up to what's staring us in the face. Forget the speeches you have been hearing. It was not a bunch of illiterate peasants who did this, nor was it some embittered war veterans. Students did this—students! The future of the country. In twenty years, maybe less, they will be everywhere: government, administration, universities. Believe me, the worst is yet to come."

"Are you saying you have changed your mind and want to leave?"

"Have no fear. Yes, had I been single, with no family, I would have left long ago. That is not the case. You want to die in your own bed, and I can understand that. Your daughter will never agree to go. I cannot abandon either of you. For me it is too late. What we must do is see to the future of the children. They will have to leave. When they graduate from high school, I shall send them abroad to study. It won't be easy, it will be expensive, but it is the only solution. Now I beg of you not to say a word to Magda who will never agree. We have plenty of time. Andreas is only fourteen, and his sisters are younger still."

"You are so sure it will get worse?"

"I can't afford to risk it. If I am right, I will have saved their lives. If I am wrong—it won't matter. They can always come home with their diplomas."

They had returned to the house. She put her hand on his shoulder to kiss him good-bye. There were tears in her eyes. "You may be right. I don't recognize the world we live in anymore. I won't say a word to my daughter, and you stop torturing yourself. You did everything in your power to protect your father. Let him now rest in peace."

January 1928 saw the Matthias family settled in their new home. Magda demanded—and received—the room that had been her father's and derived immense satisfaction from that fact. Julius slept alone in the room set aside for the young couple when he had returned from Vienna but from which he had been banned. Each of the Matthias children had his or her very own room on the second floor. A delighted Azor kept running up and down the stairs and was petted indulgently.

An uneasy calm now engulfed the city, where all traces of what the foreign press had dubbed "the Oradea Pogrom" had been swept away. Yet the most virulent papers continued their attacks on the Jews, and the trial of the handful of rioters who had been arrested was a mockery of justice. Professor Cuza himself had defended them, with the assistance of some of the best lawyers of the time. Only one student was found guilty and sentenced to a mere six months in jail. The events, duly reported abroad, intensified international protests. The Romanian government was being pressed to do something.

Manny, who must have received reports from his correspondents, managed to place a costly transatlantic call to ask for details about the death of his father-in-law. Mindful of the ever-vigilant censors listening in on all foreign calls—it was well-known that they would immediately cut off the line should the conversation take a so-called improper turn—Julius explained that his father had died in the great synagogue, the count not having arrived on time. A shocked silence on the other end told him Manny had understood the reference to what his fate would have been had Von Thuringen not arrived just in time to save him from a hanging mob.

"Tell me, my dear Julius, how are you doing?" asked the banker.

"As you can imagine. On no account repeat this to Anni or to the children. No point in making them unhappy."

"Regarding Anni, don't worry. However, the boys are old enough. They need to know. Tell me, have you changed your mind about coming for a visit?"

"Not yet." And, changing the subject, Julius asked about the younger Newmans. They were doing well. Charles and Katy had a little girl, a sister to Isaac. Tibor—Tony—was expecting his first child. Myriam was engaged to be married, and Anna declared herself delighted with her new life.

The news that his sister and her family were safe and happy was the only consolation for Julius in those dark days. No one talked about the events anymore, not even his friends. At their monthly lunches, their main concern was the increasing instability of the financial and monetary markets and whether one should buy or sell. Was he the only one more worried about what was to come than about the stock exchange?

All was not black. The children were back at school, seemingly untouched by the tragedy. Magda, caught up in the extensive renovation of her beloved pharmacy, was unusually pleasant. Far from complaining about the continuous hubbub at home, Golda Szamuely was thriving and looked ten years younger. Julius often wondered bitterly if he was the only one to mourn his father.

He was to get his answer on a cold March night. It was about three in the morning. There was a brutal wind blowing; a window that had not been properly shut was repeatedly crashing in a downstairs room. The noise woke him up.

Going downstairs to investigate, he found Golda battling the heavy wooden shutters. He pushed them into place, fastened the window, and was about to go back to his room when she surprised him by suggesting he have a cup of tea with her. He protested that it was far too late—or too early—and that she should go back to sleep.

"I was not asleep. I have trouble sleeping when there is a storm. When I was little, a maid once told me the souls of the damned who had managed to escape from hell for a few hours made that infernal noise. I was frightened to death. Of course I no longer believe that nonsense, yet I still feel ill at ease. I twist and turn in my bed and think of all my dead. Especially of Emil. He gives me no peace."

"Emil? What does he want from you?"

"I think he wants me to do something for Andreas. Have you noticed that the more that boy grows, the more he looks like Emil?"

"I can't say I have."

"Of course, you didn't know him when he was young." While she was talking, she busied herself with making tea and absentmindedly cutting slices of the cake she had made the day before. "Well, not very young. He was already thirty years old when we met. I was twenty-five. Did he tell you the story?"

"Broadly."

"Meaning? Come on, nothing can hurt me now."

"He explained it was an arranged match. He needed money to save his pharmacy, and you…" Embarrassed, he stopped, searching for the right word.

"And I was an old maid, not very pretty and desperately looking for a husband? Don't worry, it is not so far from the truth. Not so far, and yet…Do sit down."

She brought the tea and the cake to the table and sat down next to him. "I was not a great beauty, but I was not ugly. I could have been married much earlier. I had my share of proposals. Money will do that. I turned them down. I was an only child; my mother was ailing, and I was running the household for all intents and purposes. It suited me. My father, a university professor, let me attend his lectures. Not as a student—it would not have been proper at the time—but as a kind of secretary. I sat in the front row and took notes. I loved it.

"Suddenly my mother died. She was only forty-two years old; my father was forty-five at the time. A year later he announced his intention of getting married again, of having more children, perhaps boys. He had found a girl from a poor family, the eldest of ten children, who had accepted him. She was a year younger than I was! I was devastated. Father wanted me married, and married quickly, so he could start his new life. He had heard of Emil, knew of his strained circumstances.

At first I wanted none of it. Why go so far away, trade Budapest and its lively intellectual world for a provincial backwater, which was what Nagyvarad was fifty years ago? I had a dreadful quarrel with my father. He would not listen, told me I was not being reasonable; I should see how embarrassing it would be for all concerned if his new wife and his daughter happened to be pregnant at the same time and in the same city. Needless to say, that argument only infuriated me more...I came to Nagyvarad with the firm intention of finding fault with the suitor my father had chosen for me. I came, I saw Emil—and I fell in love. Just like that. Not that he was that handsome, just a nice man with an open face and a lovely smile. Anyway, I said yes. A month later we were married."

She smiled to herself and sipped some of her tea. "The wedding was held in Nagyvarad since Emil could not leave—he had no assistant at the time. During the reception that followed, a woman approached me. Had she not been pregnant, I would not have believed she was married: she looked so young! So young—and so pretty. She had a high, sweet voice, like a bird. I see that you understand. He told you about her, right? About his lost love? I knew nothing, of course. There I was in my wedding dress, deliriously happy… She came close, very close, and told me Emil did not love me, that he would never love me because he loved her; that the only reason he was marrying an ugly old maid like me was to save his pharmacy, that that night he would close his eyes and think of her…"

"My poor Golda!"

"I was dying on my feet, my heart was breaking, and I had to keep smiling…Needless to say, our wedding night was not a resounding success. You know the rest." She laughed bitterly. "I should have repeated her words to him, brought everything out into the open. Later, much too late, I heard he had not said a word to her since she had gotten married. By that time my coldness had discouraged Emil. He found solace elsewhere. Had we had more children, the son he wanted, we might have had another chance. It didn't happen. Then we had Magda's tragedy. He never really forgave her. And he stopped smiling."

She took another sip and shook her head. "I don't know why I am telling you all this. Yes, of course, it is because of Andreas. I would not want him to have to make the choice his grandfather and you, his father, had to make. He must not have to marry a rich wife…Don't interrupt. You want to send your three children abroad to study. It will be costly: you are looking at three or four years at the very least. Magda won't help. She will do her best to prevent their departure. By the time they finish their studies, you won't have enough money to help them. It will not matter for the girls. Elisabeth wants to be a doctor; if she doesn't change her mind, she will be able to earn an honorable living. Gabriella—Gabriella is so beautiful, she will always find a man ready to give her the moon.

Now, Andreas, being a man, will be expected to support his wife and children. It won't be easy at first. That's why I want to help. I still have property in Hungary, property my father left me in his will, though we were estranged for many years. Anni's husband had been managing that property, with commendable discretion. When he left he recommended a most excellent agent. I have instructed that agent to sell everything, which he has. I want you to go and see him in Budapest, take the money and deposit it in a Swiss bank. From something your sister said, I assume you have an account there. Don't worry, I haven't breathed a word, least of all to my daughter. Are you ready do this for me—for your son?"

"Nothing would give me greater pleasure. Do you intend to tell Andreas?"

"Certainly not. He is too young to keep a secret. Besides, it would be unseemly for him not to tell his mother. There will be time enough to inform him when he departs for his studies. If I am still here, it will make me very happy to do so. If I am gone, please tell him this money comes to him from his grandmother and his grandfather. It would please me to know he will call one of his sons Emil…" She smiled at the thought. "Dear Julius, isn't it fortunate that the storm has afforded us such a perfect occasion for a quiet talk? One last thing. I have been told there was a great deal of secrecy surrounding Swiss bank accounts. Do make sure that should anything happen to you—God forbid!—the money will not lie forever in the coffers of a banker who will know neither of your death nor the names of your heirs."

"You are perfectly right. I believe the best thing would be for me to let Manny know—Manny and his son. I shall send them a detailed letter from Switzerland."

Settling back in the big four-poster, Julius thanked the fate that was presenting him with such a golden opportunity to travel to Budapest and visit Madi. He had heard nothing from her since his return, but that was only to be expected. She had to be very prudent.

He left one rainy March morning. Magda had not commented on his departure; Amelia, his long-suffering secretary, her hair now completely gray, had wished him bon voyage, adding that she hoped he would remember to inform her should he be delayed. The question that occupied his mind during the long journey—the train was still prone to unscheduled stops—was not how Madi would receive him. Having decided to send his children to study abroad, he had yet to determine where they would go. It did not have to be where they would find the best universities; what they needed most was a safe country, a place where they might one day settle and live in peace. Budapest and Hungary, Vienna and Austria were enticingly close, but anti-Semitism was rampant there.

There was Palestine where so many Romanian Jews were living already and where a Jewish university had been established some two or three years earlier. However, the surrounding Arabs were hostile, and there had been murderous attacks against the newcomers. Not to mention that ridiculous notion of resuscitating Hebrew, the language of the Bible. What did the pioneers think they were going to do with a language nobody understood?

America seemed the logical choice. Julius's sister and her family were already there. However, he did not want his children to go there. It was too big. They would study in different universities in the four corners of the country and would not be able to keep in touch. It was too far away as well. England would be a possible compromise—except that he knew nothing about the country.

Julius linked his arms behind his head, stretched his long legs, and smiled. Who was he trying to fool? He had made his decision a long time ago. He would send his children to fulfill his old dream. They would study in Paris; they would settle in France. There might be some anti-Semitism there as well, but it was vigorously opposed—not by the Jews alone but by a vast majority. It had been clearly demonstrated in the affair of the Jewish officer wrongly accused of spying. Hundreds of thousands of Frenchmen, mostly Catholics, had rallied to his defense and had managed, after a protracted struggle, to have him set free and cleared of all wrongdoing. Yes, in France his children would be happy; hopefully he could visit them.

In spite of Golda's misgivings, paying for their studies and upkeep for a number of years—at least five for medical school—would not be such an insurmountable issue. Dr.

Matthias was highly successful. He owned his suite of offices (his brother-in-law had bought it and put it in his name back in 1916); he and his family were living in the pharmacist's house, and Golda would not let him contribute toward the expenses. Soon after the international situation had stabilized after the war, he had resumed his regular transfers of money to Switzerland through the Weinberger brothers.

During his forthcoming trip to Geneva, he intended to convert all he had into gold pieces—a decision he had made after listening carefully to his friends who were extremely pessimistic regarding the recovery of financial markets in the coming months. He would undoubtedly lose the revenues he would have received from his investments, a loss offset by the safety gold would provide. Long-term planning would be needed.

Andreas would have to wait until Elisabeth graduated from high school before departing for France; it would be easier for both to go together. Gabriella would join them later. The two eldest would, in all probability, not start out before autumn 1933. Which gave Julius plenty of time to begin what his old French and Latin teacher, who considered himself a military expert, had called preliminary maneuvering: to ask the advice of his friend, Theo Kahn, who had not liked Switzerland and was now happily settled in Paris, from whence he sent enthusiastic letters. To try to reestablish contact with Marie Christine, his former fellow student and lover, who was also in Paris, a fact he had discovered while idly fingering a medical review. A discreet advertisement recommended an establishment promising beauty treatments and esthetic surgery; there was a picture of the director, "Madame the Doctor Marie Christine Gilles, a graduate of the peerless School of Medicine of Vienna." She had not changed much. He wondered what had happened to her noble husband and what circumstances had returned her to her native France. He would write to her as well, see if she remembered him. Of course she might not reply…

He had taken a room at the Grand Imperial Hotel on the vast Andrassy Avenue, near the splendid park nestled in the heart of the Hungarian capital. The agent who was taking care of Madame Szamuely's affairs met him there. Having exchanged Golda's letter of authorization for the draft in his name, drawn on a Swiss bank, Julius immediately deposited it in the huge hotel safe. The amount far surpassed his expectations. Andreas was a lucky youngster.

Then the father of the lucky youngster walked to the mansion of the dowager Countess Von Thuringen and presented his card to the porter who ushered him into a small salon and politely asked him to wait. Declining to sit down, he observed his surroundings. The portrait of the late count had been taken down and with it all outward trappings of mourning. A few minutes later, a maid curtsied and gave him a sealed letter. "Five o'clock at the Lake Grand Café," read the message, heavily underlined and unsigned, though there was a distinctive scent of violet. He knew the place; it was in the center of the park. He thanked the maid, gave a coin to the porter, and walked out with a smile.

The weather was cool but fair. He strolled through the palaces and monuments of which the town was so proud before having a late lunch at a very elegant restaurant commanding a stunning view of the lower city. Then he went back to the hotel, changed into less formal attire, and turned toward the park, whistling happily. The sun was about to go down and the wind was rising, but it was not yet cold.

As soon as he entered the coffeehouse, he heard her laugh, a throaty sound he knew and loved so well. Seated by the vast picture window, she was saying good-bye to a prissy gentleman some twenty years older than she was. She saw Julius and extended her hands in welcome.

"Professor Matthias! But what a pleasant surprise. The baron was just leaving. You may keep me company until my driver arrives."

He greeted the baron who looked him up and down curiously before walking mincingly away and sat down facing her. She had discarded her widow's blacks and wore an elegant velvet dress in a subtle old rose color, which somehow complimented her tawny hair, artfully gathered under the inevitable little hat. Today it was a nest upon which a tiny redbreast preened itself. It was extravagant and charming at the same time. An expensive mink coat had been thrown over the chair next to her.

She looked at him with unusual gravity, and he shivered, suddenly apprehensive. When the waiter brought the coffee he ordered, she spoke.

"My dear Julius, I shall not mince words. The time has come for us to part. Wait, let me speak. I could tell you it is for your own good, that our romance has no future, that I have just turned forty-five, and that the years between us will soon become too many to bridge—all of which is true. However, that is not the point. I tell you frankly: nothing, but nothing will tempt me to risk the position I have now achieved. When the count was alive, we rarely went out; age had slowed him down, and he was not sure how I would be received. All that has changed. I have been very careful, behaving with the utmost propriety throughout the year of deep mourning, a year that was so painful I had to go to Switzerland to get some rest. People felt for me. But then we were lucky, so lucky. I learned that a scant two days after our departure from the inn, a couple I know arrived there for a week. I still wake up at night in a panic when I think how close I was to disaster. I never want to find myself in the same predicament again. You see, today I am the dowager Countess Von Thuringen, a respectable widow who is welcomed everywhere. I go out almost every night—to the theater, to the opera, to private parties. I have a number of admirers who are not very young and who are happy to escort a lovely woman without demanding anything in return beyond a chaste kiss on the cheek when we part.

"I attend Mass every Sunday, sitting in the family pew in the front row. The two sons of the count find me charming; the wife of the youngest tells me everything and blindly follows my advice on clothes and hats. Her two daughters adore me and call me Grandmother Maria. Oh, I do not delude myself. The count has left me some splendid pieces of jewelry and a number of precious objects, which his children hope to inherit one day. The family lawyer is forever asking me—quite civilly—to make a will. I am in no hurry; in the meantime, the sons and the daughters-in-law are incredibly nice to me…"

She paused, seemingly lost in the contemplation of a street vendor. Perched on a gaily painted cart drawn by a white donkey with ribbons at its neck, he was selling cheap trinkets to well-dressed children accompanied by their governesses.

"She is indeed getting old," he told himself, noting the fine lines on her lovely face, "but I don't care. I find her as alluring, as desirable as when we first met, and I would give anything for us not to be having this conversation."

Madi sighed and went on without looking at him. "I won't lie: a part of me rebels at the thought of never seeing you again, never again knowing our nights of passion… The other part tells me it is time to turn the page. Please do not torture yourself at the thought that, had you decided to leave your wife for me, it would have changed my decision. To be brutally frank, even if you were free today to ask me to marry you, I would not accept. In Oradea I would again be the girl who had had to leave town, the woman who had led a dubious life in Budapest. People would be just civil enough not to offend the good doctor Matthias. Here… here I am living a dream—no, never in my wildest dreams could I have imagined what I have now. Julius, I know what I owe you. I know that without you—and especially without your sister—I would not be where I am today. But I am there now. Please, not a word. My mind is made up. Let us part as friends."

She stood up, and so did he; wordlessly he helped her into her opulent cloak and went with her to the door. He followed her with his eyes as she walked away with small elegant steps in her small, chic Italian leather boots, with heels far too high for comfort. An old gentleman with a carnation in his lapel stopped as he saw her, and they had a short conversation. On the other side of the lane, a chauffeur—hers, probably—was opening the door of a car. Julius remained rooted to the spot, fighting tears. He gazed hopelessly at the woman who had enthralled him for so long.

Over. It was over.

The wind had died, and the setting sun was bathing the scene in a golden light filtered by the tall trees. To the patter of the street vendor hawking his wares was added the song of the park birds, which were beginning to converge on the treetops as night approached. A postcard picture for the end of a marvelous tale. A tale that had brought him so much happiness and, above all, so much hope.

He could not bring himself to blame her. The frightened girl driven out of her hometown, the kept woman—Madi had left them forever behind. She was rich, respected. She was happy. There was nothing more to be said or done. Another few minutes and it would really be over. She would walk to her car with that inimitable time-defying, alluring walk...

There. The conversation was ending. The man raised his hat and bent to kiss the little hand that was proffered. The dowager Countess Von Thuringen settled in her car, and the door was firmly shut.

17

LEAVING THE NEST

GOLDA SZAMUELY HAD HER WISH. It was in her own bed, in the house that had been her home for a quarter of a century, that she died peacefully in her sleep. It happened on April 12, 1933, just one day after the Seder night, the traditional dinner ushering in the week of Passover. Family and friends had gathered under her roof, for this was a special occasion: there would be no more family reunions for many years. Andreas and Elisabeth were about to depart for Paris.

Julius had had to work hard to achieve his goal. Magda had bitterly opposed the move. Caught between their father and their mother, and slightly apprehensive about going so far away alone, the youngsters had not been too keen at first. While the battle was raging, Golda had remained neutral and refused to speak her mind, fearing to antagonize her daughter. In the end, Elisabeth had won the day for him. She had not wavered in her decision to be a doctor, and when it had been made clear to her that with the de facto numerus clausus that drastically limited the number of Jewish students admitted to Romanian universities the odds of her being accepted were practically nil, she had brought her brother round to the idea.

This first hurdle safely behind him, Dr. Matthias turned his mind to other weightier problems. In the new Europe born of the war, one needed passports and visas to cross borders. Even more difficult, to be able to study in France one had to be accepted by an academic institution. True, France and Romania enjoyed excellent relations and had recently concluded an agreement mutually recognizing high school and university diplomas which made the process far easier. Still, being accepted was not an easy task.

Julius had therefore turned to his two friends in Paris. Theo Kahn was now a French citizen, as was his wife. He had also ditched his Jewish name for something slightly more ambiguous: he called himself Theodore Castan.

"See, my little Julius," he had explained in one of the numerous letters they had exchanged, "it is my wish to end my days in France, a truly lovely and pleasant country. As you know I have, like you, a natural gift for languages, and I speak French like a native. With my new name, I hope to be spared the need for explanations whenever I meet new people who ask me where I come from and other tricky questions. Dear ZsaZsa, who has not been able to get rid of her atrocious accent, passes herself off as a Hungarian noblewoman. It works wonders."

Kahn or Castan, he had worked hard on behalf of Andreas, and the boy had been accepted by a private engineering school established in 1905. The director was a friend of the old architect. Marie Christine, who had replied cordially to Julius's first letter in which he congratulated her on having achieved her dream, had since kept up the correspondence.

Nothing had been said of the reasons that had led her to leave Austria and go back to her native France, and he had not asked. She good-naturedly promised to facilitate Elisabeth's registration and even to keep an eye on the young girl. So that was settled.

As for Gabriella, she was still undecided. It had not prevented her from demanding to attend the French lessons her brother and sister were taking to prepare them for their new life. Like most scions of well-to-do Jewish families whose parents spoke Hungarian at home, the Matthias children spoke three languages: Hungarian and German as well as Romanian, which had become compulsory. They were happy to discover that knowing that language made learning French easier. From time to time, Julius went to sit through the lessons; he loved listening to the lilting voice of Irina, a young widow left nearly destitute when her husband died from a heart attack at barely forty. She now taught French to supplement her meager resources and came four times a week to the Matthias household. She was very pretty despite the ample black dress she wore in order to pacify the wives and discourage the husbands.

One evening, the lesson having ended later than usual, Julius took Irina home through the badly lit alleys of the Jewish quarter, deserted at that late hour. He went with her up the narrow wooden steps leading to her apartment in an old building. He knew the place well, having gone there a few times to treat her husband. As she put the key in the door, he gave her a chaste peck on the cheek. She turned back and embraced him feverishly before drawing him inside. He did not have the heart to push her away and gave her what solace he could in the sagging double bed where her husband had breathed his last. He did feel embarrassed when she murmured her thanks as he was leaving. It did not stop him from walking home whistling happily. Magda was still up and looked at him suspiciously but said nothing.

It did not happen again, and a few months later Irina married a widower older by some twenty years but very well off who took her to live in Bucharest. Magda found another teacher—an elderly man whose mother had been French. For Julius no woman had come close to filling the void left by Madi. From time to time, he reminded himself ruefully that they had barely spent a total of two weeks together over the years; yet often at night he dreamed of her laugh, smelled her perfume, and woke up reaching for her on the empty side of the bed.

Once again he found refuge in his work. War and its aftermath had left millions wounded throughout Europe, spurring medical research and new discoveries. He was keen to keep abreast of the new developments and was avidly reading the expanding medical press and subscribing to French papers. French scientists had just discovered a vaccine against the dreaded tuberculosis; there were so many innovations coming from across the Atlantic that he was seriously considering learning English to access the information more quickly.

Julius divided his time between the Jewish hospital; the orphanage set up after the war, where he volunteered to treat the children, and his private patients, whose numbers were growing. He had never earned so much money. He had also been very lucky. The storm raging throughout the financial world since 1929 had left him largely unscathed. He had converted his Swiss holdings into gold in 1928; back home he had taken to investing his savings in real estate, which incidentally brought him additional revenue. Nonetheless, he was careful not to flaunt his wealth. It was not just that he was saving for his children's forthcoming voyage to France; there was no point in presenting a tempting target to the growing anti-Semitic circles daily denouncing the "international Jewry" they accused of having caused the monetary crisis. Like most of the Jews of the city, Dr. Matthias had become more cautious since the events of 1927.

He turned forty on June 18, 1930. A milestone. The first step on the wrong side of life's curve. Time to forget youth's dreams and passions. Time to settle into staid middle age. Yet in the morning, his mirrored wardrobe still reflected the same handsome figure and the same blond hair untouched by gray, and he never lacked female companionship.

This significant birthday was largely ignored at home. Neither the children nor Golda even knew the date, and Magda didn't seem to care. It was therefore a pleasant surprise to be greeted by a chorus of "Happy Birthday" and the sound of a champagne cork popping when he arrived for his monthly lunch at the Blue Danube. There was even a fancy package on the table.

"Don't thank us," joked Isidor, the elder Weinberger brother. "You are getting good wishes and champagne from us, but the present is from your brother-in-law in Chicago. He wrote that he is sending you the very latest American contribution to the pursuit of happiness. We are all dying to know what's in the box."

Loud guffaws followed the opening of the mysterious box. Nestled in tissue paper were three smaller packages each holding ten condoms made of sheer latex—a vast improvement. The friends laughed louder still when Isidor read the detailed explanations enclosed in each package. Julius, who was laughing as well, solemnly presented each of his (married) friends with two preservatives, which they accepted gratefully while carefully copying the address with views to ordering many more themselves.

The following Sunday Julius went to see Sandor who had not forgotten his birthday and who gave him a hunting knife. Julius had deliberately missed the big party Martha had organized for her husband's birthday with the couple's five children, their three grandchildren, and their myriad of cousins but had sent Vadim with a solid Swiss watch. The two friends spent the day in the forest. Though he was as strong and energetic as ever, Sandor looked his age and more, his pleasant face lined by too many hours in the sun; there was a lot of white in his erstwhile black hair. As usual they barely spoke during the long day. As usual Julius felt at peace with his old friend.

He tried to convince himself that life was not so bad… and failed. He had not changed his mind about the importance of sending his children abroad to study, but he was discovering how much he would miss them now that they were turning into adults. Andreas was now taller than Julius— not by much, but still! —and broader in the shoulders. Golda had been right: the boy looked more and more like his maternal grandfather. He was showing a decided interest in the opposite sex, and the reputation of France in that respect was, for him, an added attraction. Elisabeth also took after the Szamuely side of the family, though her open countenance and sunny disposition were vastly different from her mother's usually peevish expression. She was tall but not overly so, slim and graceful. In spite of the spectacles that gave her a serious appearance, she never lacked suitors. Julius doted on her, enjoying her sense of humor and ready smile.

Gabriella was something else. She had his eyes, but they seemed larger, more luminous, and the blond hair bequeathed by Gitte to some of her descendants; the oval of her face was perfect. The face of a Madonna, Monsignor Octavius had said. Magda was inordinately proud of Gabriella's beauty and was already dreaming of a splendid match for her. Julius often wondered what went on behind those brilliant blue eyes. The child—for she was still a child—was forever watching, yet spoke very little.

He had his moments of doubt. Europe, still reeling from the impact of the economic crisis that had thrown millions into the streets, was now grappling with new threats. Nazism and Fascism—new names for old evils—were on the rise. Was a new war brewing? He always reached the same conclusion. If it did it would engulf the whole continent. Hungary would risk everything to get back the territories lost under the Versailles Treaty. Oradea, now a border town, would find itself at the heart of the fighting. And the Jews would once again be blamed—by both sides. Therefore, sending the children away was still a sound decision.

Andreas turned eighteen in April 1931; two months later he graduated with distinction from his high school, as his father had done nearly a quarter of a century before. Elisabeth still had two years to go before graduation. Having weighed enrolling in a local college during that time, the boy chose to acquire some practical experience instead. Mozes Wollner, the industrialist who was a friend of his father, let him be apprenticed to a master mechanic; eighteen months later, having shown himself an apt pupil, Andreas left to work in the printing press of the paper where Jeno Halasz was by then the star writer. Jeno later told Julius in confidence that a not-so-young lady in the accounting department had given the youngster lessons on a quite different subject.

Preparations for the departure accelerated in 1933 on the background of a worsening situation in Europe. Adolf Hitler became the ruler of Germany; in Italy, Mussolini's Fascist regime was getting stronger; there were dictatorships in Austria and in Portugal. More than ever, France appeared an island of peace and tranquility.

At home Andreas was struggling through technical books in French; his sister often went to her father's office to pore over medical reviews and familiarize herself with French medical jargon. Together she and Julius read treatises on anatomy and pathology in preparation for her first year at the school of medicine, which was reputedly the most difficult.

Magda was no longer talking about the departure, of which she disapproved. Gabriella, soon to turn sixteen, still would not say what she wanted to study. One person openly lamented the move: Vadim, now portly and pushing fifty, was wondering how, without Andreas, he would manage to take care of the family Mercedes, which had left the factory some twenty years before. He too went to the clinic one evening to have a word. He had learned that a colleague's master, beset by money problems, was trying to sell the car he had recently bought for less than half of its value. Julius agreed to buy it on the spot—a decision his son bemoaned: why get rid of their beloved car which was good for thousands of more miles, as he put it?

"Thousands of miles indeed! Be serious," laughed his father.

"Don't laugh. I know what I am talking about. The engine runs as sweetly as ever, the tires are new, and if Vadim was not so lazy, he would not have any problem."

"Is that so? I just had a thought. Do you believe we could drive all the way to Paris with that car?"

Andreas beamed. "What a fantastic idea. Of course we could. The three of us could take turns driving…"

"The three of us? Since when does your sister drive?"

"Since I taught her. I often take her out of town when you let me have the car on weekends. She is a very good driver, careful and has excellent reflexes. She has also managed to grasp something about how the car runs and how to fix minor problems."

"Neither of you saw fit to mention it to me, right? Never mind. The more I think about it, the more I like the idea. I'm ready to try. And if we do get to Paris without trouble, I shall leave you the car and take the train home."

Andreas jumped for joy and embraced him; so did his sister. Suddenly the journey was turning into an adventure. They pored over maps—it was deemed wise to avoid German territory and go the long way around, so as not to risk the attacks against Jews that were getting more and more frequent. They made plans; computed miles, oil, and petrol; and discussed the merits of various places to stop. Their enthusiasm infected Golda, who had taken it upon herself to equip them from head to foot. Clearly enjoying herself, she went with Elisabeth to the seamstress and with Andreas to the tailor.

Her sudden death cast a pall over all that happy activity. She was nearly seventy-seven but had never known a day's illness. Magda reacted with a hysterical show of grief. When her mother was laid to rest alongside Emil, her heart-wrenching sobs almost drowned the voice of Andreas, who was saying Kaddish for his grandmother. When Julius tried to comfort her, she violently pushed him away.

Later Elisabeth asked him the question that puzzled all three children. "Why is Mother so sad? She was forever quarrelling with Grandma. And why did she push you away?"

"Maybe your mother is reproaching herself because she hadn't always been nice to her mother. Also suddenly she finds herself bereft, having lost the last link with her happy childhood. As for me…You know how it is between us. I was very fond of Golda, and Golda was very fond of me. Magda did not like it. She complained I was stealing her mother away from her."

Two days after the week of ritual mourning, Andreas and Elisabeth marched into their father's office. They were upset. Elisabeth perched herself on the massive desk while her brother remained standing. It was he who spoke.

"I went with Mother to the family lawyer this afternoon. What he told her made her very angry. Now she is accusing you of having stolen the money her mother had in Hungary and of using that money to send us to study in France against her will. She also had terrible words about Grandmother Donna and Aunt Anna. She says you married her for her fortune by taking advantage of her lack of experience. I repeated all this to Elisabeth, and we decided to talk to you. If the money doesn't belong to you but to her, we can't use it to go to Paris when she doesn't want us to go."

An outraged Julius stared at his children, unable to believe what he was hearing. Then he took a deep breath, stood up, and went to the sturdy safe hidden in what appeared to be a book cabinet. Closing his eyes to recall the combination, he opened it, withdrew the envelope Golda had given him, and handed it over to his son who took it uncertainly.

"Read it," Julius said. "This letter is for you."

The youngster took a letter opener from the desk, carefully opened the envelope, and drew out two papers. He started reading, summing it up aloud for the benefit of his sister.

"Grandmother entrusted Father with the money from the sale of her Hungarian properties. That money is for me. It is intended to help me set up my own establishment one day and marry the woman I love. She didn't say a word to Mother because she knew she would be very angry. On no account am I to give her back the money. She has already received enough and will get more; she inherits the pharmacy and the house, which belonged to Grandmother." He set down the first letter on the desk and started reading the second. "It is from Uncle Manny. He acknowledges receipt of a letter in which Father informs him of the money deposited in my name and gives him all the details concerning the bank. He also says he will do as Father asked and write to inform me when I turn twenty-one."

"See?" Elisabeth was clapping happily. "I knew Father would never have done the dreadful things Mother accused him of. We can go to Paris after all!"

"True," replied Andreas with pessimism, "but there can't be much left of the money after the crash."

"That's where you are wrong, son," said Julius. "I converted almost everything into gold coins, which today are worth much more."

"Father, you are a genius."

"Thanks. Now, children, I want you to listen very carefully since I shall now answer your questions afterward. I married Magda in 1908. She was born in 1883 and I in 1890."

"You were only eighteen when you got married? Two years younger than I am today? Impossible!"

"You want to see our wedding certificate? Remember, your brother, Georgy, was born one year later."

"Mother was still unmarried at twenty-five?" Elisabeth found it hard to believe.

"She was a widow. Her first husband died a year earlier. If you like I can show you his grave in the cemetery. It says 'Jozef Fried, beloved husband of Magda.'"

"So why did you marry her? Were you in love, or was it her fortune?" Andreas was still trying to understand.

"You know, we never discussed money. It was an arranged marriage, of course. The Szamuelys wanted a young and healthy husband who would give her children, her first husband having been unable to do so. And I accepted because they were going to put me through medical school."

"And a generous dowry?"

"No, my boy, Magda did not bring a dowry. In fact, we had to live with her parents at first."

"But that's monstrous," exclaimed his daughter. "How could Grandfather Aaron and Aunt Donna have let you do that?"

"I didn't have many options. We were very poor. My dream was to be a doctor, but there was no way. I was ready to enlist in the army. Marriage with Magda was a better choice... My parents thought they were acting for my own good, and they were right. I have no regrets. I have the best profession in the world and the best children in the world. Unfortunately, I haven't been able to make your mother happy..."

Both children hugged him wordlessly, and there was no more talk on the subject.

Whatever transpired between the children and their mother could not have been pleasant for Magda; she was furious, spending most of her time at the pharmacy or with her lawyer and absolutely refusing to discuss the forthcoming journey. Elisabeth graduated at the top of her class in June, and the departure date was set for mid-August. They would have to travel over some twelve hundred miles of roads ranging from very good to very bad, with a car that had known better days. They would also need time to stop in Geneva on the way.

The family, being in deep mourning for Golda, held no joyous farewell party. Mozes Wollner, who had become fond of Andreas, came to give him a state-of-the-art Agfa camera. Dozens of photographs kept in Julius's desk testified to the progress of the aspiring photographer. There was the pharmacist's house, taken from every possible angle; Azor, now seventeen and nearly blind, his muzzle completely white, died two days before they left; Vadim with his chauffeur's cap, drawing his imposing belly in as far as he could, proudly standing in front of the new car; and Gabriella, impossibly lovely. There was a picture of Magda wearing black and looking down her nose, but she tore it up.

One last picture immortalized the day of departure. Wollner, coming to say good-bye with a bottle of champagne and a box of cigars, took it. Andreas, wearing flannel trousers and a checkered shirt, had his arm round Elisabeth's shoulders, who wore a flower-print dress. Both were smiling. Julius, behind them, looked barely older than his son. Magda was not there, having left the day before with Gabriella to visit an elderly relative in Budapest "so the poor child does not suffer too much at being abandoned by her brother and sister."

Andreas never sent home the many pictures taken during that long leisurely journey through the old Europe that was not aware of the chasm about to open. Pictures of a happy trio enjoying to the fullest extent a succession of perfect days under a benign sun. Local roads encumbered by heavily laden carts, since this was harvest season. Friendly inns where, after hours of driving, one could relax over a hearty supper, talk of the day's adventures, and discuss the itinerary for the next day. Country breakfasts before setting out again. Sandwiches munched on under the shade of trees as noon brought the countryside to a standstill. Unscheduled detours to admire an ancient fortress and a romantic castle.

For the children who had never left Oradea before, each new day was an enchantment; their father rejoiced in their happiness while remembering another journey so many years before when he was taking his sister—and Madi—to safety. He also knew he had to make the most of these precious moments, the prelude to a painful and probably lengthy separation.

The three of them took turns driving; Elisabeth showed herself to be calm and competent. Andreas saw to it that the car was kept in perfect condition. Indeed, though bad roads led occasionally to flat tires, the old Mercedes behaved admirably.

They stopped in Geneva for two days. Leaving behind Elisabeth, who had announced her intention to go to a hairdresser, Julius decided to give power of attorney to his son. True, the boy was not yet twenty-one, but at his age, Julius had been married and was a father. With that precious document, Andreas would be able to quickly and discreetly access the money earmarked for him by his grandmother. Having filled out all the relevant papers, Andreas went down with his father to the imposing room that housed the safes. Though awed by the pile of gold coins that was his inheritance, he seemed more interested by the safe's mechanism and the armor-plated outer doors and their locks.

They reached Paris in late August. For Julius, this was the beginning of an extraordinary week. First there was the emotional meeting with Theo and ZsaZsa in their impressive Paris apartment, situated on Passy Street, a prestigious address. They stayed there for the first few days. ZsaZsa had not changed; still plump and homely, she fussed over the children and cosseted them to death, clucking over Elisabeth's provincial dresses and promising to buy her much nicer things. The architect looked much older—he must have been close to seventy; Julius, who was forty-three, remembered his friend telling him that he was twenty-five years older— but had lost none of his energy.

They did not get much sleep the first night, too busy catching up and discussing the political situation. Theo was intensely pessimistic. Germany would go to war sooner or later, he argued, and France would not be able to stay out of the fight. This did not stop him from begging his friend to leave Romania immediately. The circumstances of the death of Aaron Matthias, whom Theo had known well, had profoundly affected him.

"You understand, my boy"—this made Julius smile; no one called him *my boy* anymore—"I am not saying the French are not anti-Semitic. I am afraid that today there is anti-Semitism everywhere, with the possible exception of some as yet undiscovered tribe in the wilds of Africa.

Nonetheless, here it is different, a form of snobbery, a way of feeling superior. There is no hatred. Indeed, it is in the upper classes that you find it, not among the workers. At the head of the Socialist Party, which is very powerful, stands a man called Leon Blum. Here a pogrom would be inconceivable; in Nagyvarad it has already happened."

"You know very well that I can't go. Getting the children out was a major effort. My wife will never leave, and I... Please, drop it."

"As you wish. Just remember that should you ever change your mind, ZsaZsa and I will be only too happy to help you."

He heard the same argument and the same promises—for different reasons—from Marie Christine. The private medical establishment she owned and managed was situated on a quiet street a stone's throw from the fabled Eiffel Tower he had heard so much about. Having made an appointment by telephone, he arrived there one morning together with his daughter. They were ushered into an elegant salon that did not look at all like a waiting room. Marie Christine came in hurriedly; pushing away the hand Julius extended, she soundly kissed him on both cheeks.

"So this is your daughter? She is charming!"

Elisabeth observed her with surprised admiration. "Father told me you studied together in Vienna, but you look far younger than he is!" She could not have found a better way to find favor with Marie Christine. If truth be told, Marie Christine certainly appeared younger than the forty-three years she must have been—at least. She was still alluringly slim in a dark-green suit, an expensive cut, that emphasized the right curves. The ministrations of her colleagues at the clinic might have had something to do with her unlined face, but if so it had been so well done that there was no trace of any intervention.

"Marianne, please ask Mr. Metzger to come in and remind my secretary we are implementing program B today," she told the young woman who had entered the room with her. Then, turning to her guests with a smile, she added, "Benjamin Metzger is a fifth—and last—year student. He is already working for me doing night watches. I have instructed him to accompany your daughter to the school of medicine and help her with the last necessary formalities. He will also take her on a tour of the buildings and then drive her home in his car."

Ten minutes later the two doctors found themselves alone, each observing the other as if trying to find traces of the lost years.

"Program B," mused Julius. "Dare I ask what program A was?"

"I had to be ready for all eventualities…After all, I was not sure it was my handsome fellow student with his sea-blue eyes who would arrive. He could have been transformed into a distinguished physician, portly and bald!" She was laughing.

"Which would have launched program A? You would have told me regretfully that there was a very important customer in your other waiting room?"

She sighed theatrically. "Life is so full of surprises, most of them unpleasant…You have to admit that most of our contemporaries don't take the same care of themselves."

"You are so right. Let me tell you that you are even more beautiful than when we met in Vienna! I am happy to see that you have achieved your ambition. Congratulations! What happened to your count?"

"My count died a hero's death on the battlefield. No, don't be embarrassed. I was fond of him, but things were coming to a head between us. You see, he had gotten his two boys one after the other—that was a piece of luck for me—and I thought that, having fulfilled my part of the bargain, I would be able to start practicing medicine. Turned out he would have none of it, repeating that a mother's role was to take care of her children. His own mother and his unmarried elder sister, who both lived in the castle, were whining that having his wife in intimate contact with perfect strangers would be a blot on the escutcheon! Can you believe it? Mind you, when he died they were only too happy to see the last of me—especially since I was leaving the better part of my dowry behind. They were also delighted to have the opportunity to raise the heirs in a fitting manner."

"It must have been hard to part from the children."

"It was. The hardest thing I have had to do in my life. They were cute, my two little darlings. But I had no choice. Staying would have meant being buried alive. I knew I was leaving them in good hands. I have never regretted it. Today my sons are cheerful young brutes—one is nineteen, the other eighteen—and quite aware of their aristocratic lineage. They dream of military careers while vigorously pursuing the fair sex. I send them money, and I see them twice a year. That's more than enough. Here, I do what I always wanted to do. Already, in Vienna I was dreaming about this type of medicine."

"I must say I know practically nothing about aesthetic surgery. It was barely mentioned in our studies."

"True. Sad to say it took that terrible war and the thousands and thousands of soldiers wounded and mutilated, sometimes turned into frightening monsters by burns, for that branch to be taken seriously. Today I am reaping the benefit of the enormous strides made in the field on both sides of the Atlantic and putting them—at an extortionate price—at the service of society ladies wanting to maintain the illusion that they are still young and alluring. My establishment is prospering; I am reasonably happy. Reasonably. Come on. Enough said. Let's have lunch at my place. We can walk there. Don't look at your watch. We shall find something to do until it's time to eat…You have no idea how often I have thought of you since that lovely June morning in Vienna when we went our separate ways…Now it will be your task to show me that today's reality is as good as yesterday's memories."

Both had changed quite a lot in the past twenty years, yet the fire was still there, which they discovered as they once again met with passion and curiosity.

"I was right to hope," said Dr. Gilles, stretching languorously while lighting a cigarette. "You are more experienced—and have lost none of your qualities."

"You should have let me speak first, my dear colleague. It was better than ever. I don't want to sound too satisfied with myself, but what are those qualities?"

She laughed. "You must have been told more than once. You are extraordinarily patient, letting your partner be in tune…I had found it quite unusual back then. Most of our fellow students were more of the 'good morning, good-bye' type."

"Haven't you ever wanted to marry again?" he asked her much later, as they were lunching on the terrace of her luxury apartment.

"Marry again? Why on earth should I? I have all the money I need, and I did not want more children. As it is I have the best of both worlds. I am independent...And let us admit, I have the title. I may not use it, but people know, and it opens many doors. I never lack for male companionship, if that's what you meant. But I intend to see as much of you as I can during this too brief stay of yours."

As it was, they managed to meet only three times for lunches where they discussed everything from medicine to life to the future of the Old Continent. She too believed war was coming—a war that would pit her two boys against French soldiers. Dr. Gilles was different from all the women he had known. Intelligent, knowledgeable, and clear sighted...until they found themselves in her vast bed for extended siestas that left them exhausted but at peace. Never did he stay the night, for she was careful of her reputation.

She took him for a tour of her medical establishment, where patients were pampered beyond belief, and took his breath away by offering him the post of medical director. He shook his head and explained he would give anything to be able to accept but was honor bound to go back to his wife and his younger daughter. Marie Christine did not try to make him change his mind and simply said there would be a job for him as long as she was in charge.

"You mean as long as I do not turn into a portly, bald man?" He answered to lighten the mood.

"Exactly."

In the evenings he discovered the charms of Paris by night with Theo and his wife. They even took him to the Folies Bergère with Andreas and Elisabeth who admired the show with all the wonder of the little provincials they were.

The week was over far too soon. Julius left with a clear conscience. Theo had taken Andreas under his wing; he and his wife had promised to keep an eye on the boy and his sister. Marie Christine would follow Elisabeth's progress and find her part-time work in her clinic as soon as the girl was qualified. A suitable apartment had been found on the fourth floor of a bourgeois building on the corner of a street called Rue des Écoles—Schools Road—which the children thought a good omen. It was close to the school of medicine, and Elisabeth could walk there easily. Andreas, who had found a convenient garage for the Mercedes, intended to travel to classes by the metropolitan railway, a mode of public transportation Julius found admirable.

Nothing in the world would have led Dr. Matthias to admit how much he had been tempted to stay, to start anew in this fascinating city. To go back to Oradea, to a woman who made no effort to hide her lack of feeling for him, was not going to be easy. Such, however, was the price he had agreed to pay; those were the shackles he had so willingly assumed. He hoped Gabriella would fill the void left by the elder children's leaving.

He was not looking forward to the long and solitary journey home; he would have to change trains many times and cross several borders. Border and customs officials were not as pleasant to railway travelers as they were to passengers in luxury automobiles…In the end he let himself be tempted by an extraordinary suggestion put forward by Theo and bought an exorbitantly expensive plane ticket. Elisabeth and Andreas went with him to the offices of CIDNA, the French-Romanian Company for Air Transport, situated on Rue des Pyramides. There, a company bus was to drive him to Le Bourget Airport.

It was a painful moment. In spite of the years of preparation, the actual separation was fraught with emotion. Elisabeth was in tears, and the two men were doing their best not to cry. After a last embrace, Julius climbed aboard, watching, from the open window, the tall silhouette of his son and the slighter one of his daughter until he could no longer see them.

When he saw the fragile aircraft he was to board, he was seized by doubts. Was this the famed *Oriental Arrow* linking the French capital to faraway Constantinople through Strasbourg, Vienna, Budapest, and Bucharest? How puny was the plane that was to brave the skies with its fifteen passengers and three crew members!

Yet the journey was a revelation. Julius could see Europe at his feet in ever-changing patterns—tiny roads and villages, the long ribbons of mighty rivers, dark forests, fields, and great cities...The last leg of the journey was accomplished at night. He landed in Budapest less than twenty-four hours later feeling like a hardy pioneer and took the new express train to Oradea.

Once again his euphoria did not last. When the taxi he had taken at the station deposited him in front of the house, he found a team of porters busy at work. His wife, who was directing them, seemed unpleasantly surprised by his turning up ahead of time. She welcomed him with a false smile.

"Julius! You are back, and we haven't completed the move yet. But your room is ready, never fear. Come, Viola will give you lunch."

He followed her. Not very far, only to the end of the street. In his absence she had sold the house—hers now that Golda was dead—and bought a handsome apartment overlooking the river. Without consulting him, of course. He later learned she had purchased the place before his departure and that work had begun there in July. Needless to say, the new apartment was in her name alone.

That was not the only surprise she had in store for him. She had also—far worse—left Gabriella in Budapest. She delivered the news with a vengeful smile. The young girl, she said, had not wanted to remain alone after the departure of her brother and sister. She had heard about a distinguished establishment for girls in the Hungarian capital where the daughters of the best families were to be found. Preening herself, Magda added that she had managed to enroll her daughter in a boarding school run by French nuns.

"How did you do that?" Julius asked.

"Thanks to you."

"To me?" He was nonplussed.

"Yes. We wrote in your name to your friend in Rome— the very important priest who came to see you when your father died. Gabriella met him then and kept his card. She sent him a very nice letter in French to ask for his help. He was only too happy to do so and sent you his best wishes." She preened herself again with a satisfied air.

"I see." Julius was making a supreme effort not to show how hurt he was. "Are there many other Jewish girls there?"

"Of course not!"

"You mean she will be the only one?"

"No! Nobody is to know she is Jewish. It's all arranged."

"Are you saying she will be passing herself off as a Christian? Going to church?"

"So what? Are you so religious yourself? Do you believe that in Paris your children will go to the synagogue regularly?

Gabriella will have the best possible education. She will then decide what to do next. Should she want to join the others, she will speak perfect French. But she won't. She will make a great match here, mark my word."

"When is she coming home?"

"Nothing is decided yet. I shall go and see her at some point. Anyway, I have already paid for her two years of schooling before she graduates."

"It never occurred to you to ask my opinion?"

While they were talking, they had reached the drawing room, and they sat down.

"Ask for your opinion? As you asked for mine before tearing my children from me and sending them away?" She sneered.

He contemplated her. She wore a shapeless black dress; her black hair, peppered with gray, was badly cut, and she looked older than her fifty years. It was for this, for an empty home and a bitter and unpleasant woman who did not even try to take care of herself, that he had refused the proposals of his friends in Paris!

He managed to keep calm and to reply politely. "I understand. You wanted revenge and did not hesitate to send a lonely child who is not yet sixteen to a foreign country where she knows no one. Should she be unhappy among those society girls, she will have no one to turn to. What an admirable mother! Tell me, Magda, if you hate me so much, now that the children are no longer living with us, don't you think the time has come for us to part company? You will live in your beautiful new apartment, work in your beloved pharmacy, keep on doing whatever you want—and I shall go back to France to live with the children. What do you say?"

She went white. "You can't do that. You gave your word!"

"I know very well what I promised. What I do not understand is why you are so keen for us to stay together. You don't love me. You don't even like me. Sometimes days pass without us exchanging a word. When you see me, you look away. Your mother has left you more than well off. Why do you need me to stay?"

"You have no right—"

"Forget about right. I am asking a simple question. Why do you want me to stay? For us to keep on torturing each other? Wouldn't you be happier without me?"

"You cannot leave me. You swore! You would turn me into a laughingstock, the woman her husband has abandoned. If you leave, I shall throw myself into the river, but first I shall leave a letter for the children, telling them it is all your fault!" Suddenly she burst into loud ugly sobs.

"Of course," he thought. "What would people say? "That's all that matters to her. Nothing else."

"Very well. I shall stay," he said coldly. "If you care so much about what people are saying about you, at least try to take better care of your appearance. Now, if you don't mind, I am going to lunch with friends."

18

A PACT WITH THE DEVIL II

THE NEW APARTMENT TOOK ON the impersonal character of a temporary dwelling. Like strangers sharing a roof, husband and wife lived their lives side by side but apart. Yet Magda had taken her husband's threat seriously. She went to the hairdresser regularly, visited the beauty parlor every month, and had new dresses made—all of them black, since she would mourn her mother to the end of her days. She even agreed to host his friends two or three times a year.

A tenuous truce had been accomplished: Magda clinging with desperation to a husband she did not like, fearing she would be an object of pity and ridicule should he leave; Julius having come to the bitter conclusion that the devil, having fulfilled his obligations under the bargain, had found the time ripe for presenting his bill.

Husband and wife did share a common worry: Gabriella did not write. She telephoned once a month but always briefly. She knew her parents' routine and took great care to call when her mother was home. Magda never let Julius speak with his daughter. In late November the girl phoned her father at his clinic.

"Listen, Father," she said in a rush, as if afraid of being overheard. "Do not be angry with me. I needed Mother on my side to come here. It was obvious to me that had I discussed it with you, you would have vetoed the move. I am sure you understand that she helped me because she wanted to get even with you rather than because she loves me. Father, had I stayed at home after Andreas and Elisabeth left, I would have turned into a punching bag between you and Mother. I love you both; it would have been hell for me.

"Please forgive me for using your friend. I had heard of this wonderful school in Budapest and desperately wanted to be admitted. It did not seem possible at first—until I remembered your priest. It took all my courage to write to him, and I was afraid he would not even answer. He could not have been nicer and supervised the whole thing from start to finish. Imagine, he even asked in a roundabout way if we wanted the tuition to come from what he called his 'special scholarship fund'! I said no, without even asking Mother. We were corresponding in French, you understand. He still keeps in touch; the nuns have to send him quarterly reports on my progress. Apparently he is very important. Mother Superior is very impressed. It is a big help."

She laughed, a joyous, girlish laugh Julius had not heard in a long time. "The girls and teachers at the school are convinced I am here under an assumed name and that in fact I come from a very important family. When they ask me, I get mysterious and change the subject."

"It can't be that easy! Don't you feel lonely? So far from your family, your friends, your people?"

"It was awful at first. I was so scared! Scared of being found out, scared of being alone in a foreign country. It didn't last. Everyone has been fantastically kind—thanks to Monsignor Octavius. I am doing well in my studies, better than at home. I have made friends. Mother surprised me by giving me quite a lot of spending money. Listen, Father, there is something I need to tell you—but on no account tell Mother." She took a deep breath. "I am never coming back to Oradea. As soon as I graduate, I shall join Elisabeth and Andreas in Paris. Please understand. I can't—I won't die like Grandfather Aaron. I have to go now. I love you."

A stunned Julius remained rooted to his spot. She had been barely ten at the time! He, who was so attuned to the feelings of the two elder children, had not seen her distress. He had thought her indifferent. How wrong he had been! He marveled at the inner strength that had led her to seek—and find—a way out for herself. He did not, of course, discuss any of this with his wife.

In December, as Magda was happily preparing for a trip to Budapest, Gabriella phoned to tell her not to come: she had been invited by a friend for the Christmas vacation. A resentful Magda tried hard to hide her pain and started planning for Easter. That did not work out either due to another invitation. It seemed their girl was so popular, her friends fought for the honor of entertaining her.

Worse was yet to come. Gabriella announced she would spend the whole of the summer vacation in the vast estates of her best friend's father—a duke, no less! Torn between pride at her daughter's success and her own disappointment, Magda waited for school to start again and went to Budapest in October 1934. She barely said a word upon her return;

when Julius insisted, she explained that she had seen the girl briefly one Sunday afternoon. There was no more talk of Gabriella returning home for the Easter vacation or the end of the year. Her mother told herself the girl would have to leave Budapest after graduation. Indeed, she was planning to travel to bring her back—until, at the end of June 1935, a letter dashed her expectations.

Gabriella had decided to join her siblings in Paris. She was going there directly, taking advantage of the fact that several nuns were going home for their summer vacation and would chaperone her on the train. Magda took the news very hard. She had been so sure her favorite daughter would be back and was so looking forward to parading her beautiful and talented child among envious society matrons! She hinted at a match she had been trying to make with a man she would not name.

After the first storm of grief had passed, Magda turned on her husband, blaming him for putting foolish ideas into the child's head. This degenerated into a full-blown scene, leading him to ask again whether she wanted him gone. This time she became so hysterical, he had to sedate her. The following morning, pale and trembling, she went to ask for his forgiveness for the first time in their twenty-seven-year union. She told him tearfully that she was afraid of being left all alone and begged him to stay.

Dr. Matthias stayed; there would be no more talk of leaving. It was not only the weight of the shackles so willingly assumed so long ago but the word he had given to the pharmacist and the promise made to Golda when she gave him his first home on Schools Street, renewed after the death of Donna, when Golda refused to turn Aaron away, as her daughter had requested. "I gave my word your father would have a home here as long as he lived," she had told him. "I know you will do the same for my daughter."

Quite simply, he could not abandon his wife and join his children in Paris. They would not understand; they would blame him. He had also come to the reluctant conclusion that Magda needed him. The defection of her favorite daughter had broken her. She was desperately unhappy. Every so often he would suggest that they leave, go together to France, be with the children. There was nothing to keep them in Oradea; by selling their properties they would have enough money to live in comfort. She would look at him piteously and burst into sobs. She was clinging blindly to her pharmacy. Behind its wooden counter, she was someone else: the owner, a woman of substance. Without it she would be nothing. Each time a defeated Julius would shrug hopelessly and turn to his work, his friends, the farm.

Sandor was always delighted to see him. The patriarch now tended to the accounts, and Martha still ran the place. Their sons were adults, and they shouldered most of the work, together with their wives. Julius spent many Sundays there, roaming the woods and trying to tell himself life was good. These outings sometimes served as cover for less innocent meetings; Julius would drive to the Two Crowns Inn, where a charming woman was waiting for a pleasant interlude that never developed into anything else.

These little episodes were getting rarer. He wanted more. Someone he could talk with. The quiet happiness of falling asleep in the arms of the one he loved and who loved him, and waking up in the morning to find her still there. A happiness he had seldom known.

Coming home during the week after a long day at work, he would eat a solitary dinner. Viola, gray haired and a grandmother several times over, worked only part-time; a cleaning woman came twice a week. He took to visiting his next-door neighbor, a retired Hungarian physician who lived alone, his wife having died years before. After a chance encounter on the stairs, the two men had become friends. Lazlo Kadar, a Protestant, had embraced his younger Jewish colleague and taught him to play chess; they would often spend hours playing while listening to Hungarian music, drinking tea, and feasting on the mouthwatering cakes prepared by the old man's housekeeper. Their taste brought back fond memories of similar delicacies Julius had eaten in Vienna when he was a hopeful medical student. Soon Lazlo became Lotsi and Julius Yuli. This new presence assuaged some of the deep loneliness in Dr. Matthias.

There was very little news from America. Twice a year Anni sent chatty letters replete with details that held no interest for him. The family bank had weathered the crisis and was no longer in the red. Karol—Charles—had three children. Surprisingly Tibor—Tony—had abandoned a promising banking career to take flying lessons; he was now a pilot in the air force. Myriam taught history; she was married and had a little girl. Julia was in college.

It was all very far away. Julius filled page after page with tidbits about life in Oradea, which had as little meaning for his sister, and never mentioned the issues that troubled him. He assumed she was doing the same on her side of the Atlantic.

From Paris, which was far closer, there was a curious dearth of information. Elisabeth and Andreas took turns penning a monthly letter that kept getting shorter and shorter.

Andreas was in his third and last year at the engineering college and intended to pursue his studies at a higher teaching establishment. He had found a part-time job. The young man always reported that he was managing the family money carefully and that all three children had enough for their needs.

Elisabeth, also finishing her third year, would go on to the fourth—the penultimate—year of medical studies. Marie Christine—whom she formally called Dr. Gilles—was keeping her word; not only was she supervising Elisabeth, but she was already letting her take up night shifts in the clinic.

Puzzling out what was said and not said in these monthly offerings, Julius felt that his daughter was no longer living with her brother. Had she moved in with a man? A fellow student, perhaps? Was she afraid of telling her parents? There was no point in asking Andreas, brother and sister having early on assumed the habit of covering each other's back.

No less puzzling was Gabriella. She never wrote letters; from time to time, there was a hurried scrawl from her. Since her arrival in the French capital, she had been living in a convent school, teaching languages there in exchange for board and lodging—though she did not need to work, there was enough money for her too—and studying humanities at the Sorbonne. All three sounded happy enough.

There was no information to be had from Theo and ZsaZsa. They still saw Andreas, but Elisabeth had stopped going. As for Gabriella, they had not seen her since they left Oradea. A third puzzling factor was the reluctance of the children to come home to see their parents. They were always too busy or working too hard. Julius was dying to go to Paris yet afraid his wife would misunderstand and, believing he was leaving forever, try to kill herself.

In June 1936 Leon Blum became France's first Jewish prime minister. Dr. Matthias was excited. He had been right! He had made the best possible decision for his children. However, at home the situation was going from bad to worse. The moderate prime minister, who had tried to curb the Iron Guard, a Fascist and anti-Semitic movement, had been brutally assassinated. The far right was gathering strength. In Bucharest students led more demonstrations against the Jews.

King Carol II paid a state visit to Adolf Hitler, who had embarked on a terrifying policy of repression and degradation against the Jews. The German ruler was openly laying claim to neighboring territories and preparing for war. Once again Europe was turning into a powder keg. Romanian Jews were fleeing to Palestine by the thousands, establishing new cities. Jacob and Ditta Farkas had gone there, settling in a communal village they called a kibbutz. There they were happily raising their four children—having started late, they had seen no reason to tarry. In a blurred photograph they sent him, Julius could see the two of them on an endless beach, surrounded by four small children, all blinking under the strong sun. He kept the picture on his desk; for some reason it comforted him greatly.

The overall restlessness had not spared Oradea, although it affected Romanian and Hungarian Jews in different ways. The latter were making a great show of unconcern. Never had the city been so prosperous; it had easily weathered the 1929 crisis. The Jewish community was doing well, and the Jewish press counted no less than nine periodicals showcasing the works of poets and writers in Hungarian. An impressive network of schools catered to the needs of a growing number of children. Dr. Matthias, now considered one of the town's leading physicians, often had to stay late into the night to see all his patients. His faithful secretary, professing herself too old for the long hours, intended to retire as soon as he found someone to replace her.

Romanian Jews, however, were beginning to panic. Many of them—those who could—were preparing to leave. At the same time, the Weinberger brothers, acutely attuned to what was going on, were discreetly liquidating their assets in preparation for their departure for America. Mozes Wollner had not quite made up his mind to follow them, but he was in the process of selling his factories and transferring the money to Switzerland. The less affluent members of the community were worried but did not have the money to be accepted by the country of their choice and make a living there.

Events started moving at breakneck speed. Hitler sent troops to the Ruhr area in violation of the peace treaty, then occupied Austria, forcing that country in 1938 to accept a union with Germany. Austrian Jews were submitted to the harsh decrees enacted in Germany. Thirty thousand Viennese Jews were deported to newly created concentration camps. History was repeating itself: courted by both sides, Romania was vacillating between its fear of the German might and that of the Soviet troops massing at its borders.

A letter arrived from Paris announcing there was a new doctor in the family. Elisabeth had graduated brilliantly and was going to specialize in gynecology while working full time at Dr. Gilles' establishment. She asked her parents to direct their letters there. A scant two months later came the startling news that Elisabeth had married a colleague—whose name she did not mention. For once Magda and Julius were in unison in concluding that the man was not Jewish and that their daughter—foolishly—thought they would be upset.

They sent back a reply wishing the young couple long life and prosperity while stressing that they were sure, whatever his origins, the man she had chosen would make her happy. They also asked for news of Gabriella, who had not written in months. Elisabeth thanked them for their good wishes without giving more details about her husband; she did say she would bring him for a visit "as soon as possible," adding that through her marriage she had become a French citizen.

As for her sister, she added, Gabriella had chosen a path that was sure to delight her mother and was doing very well. Andreas was working as an engineer for a world-renowned company and would surely write. She also gently chided her parents for worrying he was not yet married at twenty-six.

Six long years had passed since Julius had said farewell to France. Far too long. Taking a deep breath, he knocked on his wife's door and told her it was time to go and see the children. Miraculously, she agreed. He began to hope: maybe once they got there, she would change her mind, agree to stay to be near the children and—perhaps one day soon—the grandchildren. It was decided they would travel in June 1940, so Julius could celebrate his fiftieth birthday with all his family around him.

However, the long-hoped-for journey never happened. The storm that had been brewing for so long suddenly arrived. War broke out in September 1939. Travel was no longer possible. There was no happy birthday celebration. By June 1940, France had been overrun.

"It's all your fault!" sobbed Magda. "You sent our children to their deaths with your stupid schemes!"

He had no answer.

After many sleepless nights, a letter arrived from the Clinique de Chirurgie Esthetique. Dr. Gilles was informing her esteemed colleague of the successful operation carried out on "the patient he had recommended"—a clear reference to Elisabeth. She added that said patient had gone to the south of France to convalesce near her brother and sister who were already there. Dr. Gilles would, of course, keep Dr. Matthias informed of further developments.

Dr. Matthias sent a formal reply and slept better at night. Not that the situation at home was good. Romania had hesitated too long: by the time it threw in its lot with Germany, Russian troops were already occupying Bassarabia and North Bucovina. In 1941, Hungary officially got back North Transylvania and its one hundred sixty thousand Jews. Its army had not waited for the official announcement and had entered Oradea—now Nagyvarad again—by early autumn 1940. Those Romanians who had settled there after World War I fled; so did the Weinberger brothers. Hungarian Jews rejoiced and welcomed the troops, waving little flags.

A few weeks earlier, King Carol II had issued a series of decrees closely copying the Nuremberg racial laws: Jews could no longer be civil servants, join the army, or sit on the boards of large companies. They were forbidden to marry non-Jews. Hungary had passed similar measures and immediately extended them to Transylvania. In Nagyvarad, Jewish places of business were ordered to vacate the main street and the theatre square. Jewish papers were banned. Nearly all Jewish lawyers were disbarred. Heavy taxation on Jewish businesses and factories forced many owners into bankruptcy. Others put their trust in straw men who were not always reliable and often ended up taking over their businesses. Soon Hungarian businesspeople of dubious ethics flocked into the city, usurping Jewish property with the tacit approval of the authorities.

The medical profession had not been targeted, and Dr. Matthias was still seeing his patients—Jews and non-Jews. He did not encounter major problems, though he took great care not to have anything to do with the new civil servants who had replaced the Romanians and were treating Jews with undisguised contempt. With so many businesses closed or taken over and so many breadwinners out of work, the community started feeling the pinch. The few Jewish organizations still allowed to work were doing their best, handing out a little money to those who needed it most. Julius was no longer charging some patients for his services; he was discreetly helping some of his father's old friends and former neighbors. He was still getting rent from the buildings he owned, but for how long?

It was time to do something about it. He therefore signed his properties over to Sandor, whom he trusted with his life. The farmer, an ethnic Hungarian, was content with the new order and was delighted to meet his brother, Zoltan, now a staff sergeant. The farm was prospering, and he kept on illegally—and at great personal risk—supplying eggs, cheese, and poultry to his friend, who, however, insisted on paying the full black market price.

Julius also "sold" his suite of offices in the Black Vulture complex to his neighbor, Lazlo Kadar. The old man immediately drafted a will leaving Julius said offices should he die before his younger colleague. The Mercedes he gave away to Vadim, who, married to an ethnic Hungarian, had not left the town and was able to get a permit to become a taxi driver—though he went on driving Magda to work and back. These were palliative steps at best. The future had never appeared so bleak. The news brought no relief. In Bucharest a pogrom had turned violent; dozens of bodies lined the streets, among them that of soft-voiced Irina, who had taught the Matthias children so many years ago. In the city of Iași and the provinces of Transnistria, Bucovina, and Bassarabia, Jews were being murdered by the tens of thousands. Terrible tales of the fate of Polish Jewry were filtering in, though people preferred not to believe them.

Dr. Matthias found solace in letters from the Paris clinic, which still got through. Under the guise of business communications, Marie Christine was giving him news of Elisabeth. In early 1943 he was delighted to learn that his daughter had had a baby boy whom she called Emil. Dr. Gilles took advantage of that occasion to suggest that her esteemed colleague attend a medical symposium in Geneva. A very official invitation from a well-known Geneva institute was included. Julius had a grateful thought for his faithful friend and tried to talk his wife into fleeing while they still could, thinking that the birth of her first grandson would mellow her. He was once again proved wrong.

"If she named him Emil to please me, she was wide off the mark. My father never got over his disappointment at having only a girl. In vain did I try to make him proud of me. It was as if I did not exist except as a means to give him grandchildren—boys, preferably. He had no more affection for me than I for him. As for fleeing, not for me, thanks.

It is far too dangerous. We shall stay safely at home until things get better."

Julius had to give up the plan he had so carefully prepared. As a first step, they would have taken the train to Budapest, ostensibly to visit his sister, Anna. She was no longer there, but the authorities did not know that. From Budapest they would have gone on, with fake documents and medical certificates, to Switzerland, remaining there to wait for the end of the war. The plan would entail the cooperation of a few go-betweens, for which Julius would pay hefty fees. It was their only chance of escape, or so he believed.

Magda did not. She remained adamant in her refusal and did not perceive the danger until it was too late. By the time she understood—after two supercilious civil servants came into her pharmacy with their eyes on taking over the Jewish-owned property—it was too late. Jews were forbidden to ride trains. Julius and Magda were far too well known to travel under false identities. Escape was no longer possible. They tried to go on with their lives in a steadily deteriorating reality, hoping against hope that, the worst having already happened, they would survive until things got better.

The year 1944 began hopefully. The Americans, who had entered the war on the side of the Allies in 1941, were now putting their formidable resources to work. German troops were driven out of North Africa; Anglo-Canadian forces landed in Italy. There was talk of an Allied landing on the coast of Normandy.

On March 2 a fantastic rumor shook the city: Russian troops were now a mere sixty miles away! It was well-known that Horthy, the Hungarian ruler, was ready to make a deal with Stalin to avoid a humiliating capitulation. Hope faded quickly. Hitler had felt the threat, and his troops occupied Hungary, still nominally his ally. They brought with them one Adolf Eichmann, a name that struck terror into the hearts of all Hungarian Jews, Transylvania's included. All knew this was the man who was in charge of deporting European Jews to concentration camps. Soon German officers were seen strutting in the streets of Nagyvarad, looking down at the Jews and losing no time in implementing drastic rules.

On March 29 Jews were expelled from the few places where they could still work. The Jewish hospital was requisitioned, its patients sent home. A team of doctors came from Hungary to take over. Dr. Matthias, vacating his office for the last time, felt a hand on his shoulder. Turning round he came face-to-face with a man in his forties who looked vaguely familiar.

"I am Dr. Grunewald. Hans Grunewald," he said. "We met in Vienna in 1916. A word, if you please."

They had a short, half-whispered conversation, with the other doctors watching curiously.

"I am devastated by what is happening," said Grunewald. "The Germans are making us do it. Let me know where I can find you, and I shall try to help. The count thought highly of you, and I have never forgotten what you did for me."

Julius looked at him, desperately wanting to ask what had happened to the dowager countess. Was Madi safe under the protection of her illustrious husband's family? Had they thrown her to the wolves to take back possession of what they surely considered their property? No; even asking could endanger her. He nodded and left without saying a word.

Every day brought another blow. Jewish property was being evaluated prior to being confiscated. Jews six years old and over had to wear yellow stars prominently on their clothing. Dr. Matthias seethed at this new indignity. Patients he had treated for years were now crossing to the other side of the street to avoid him. His only comfort was the sure knowledge that his children were spared this humiliation, that he had been right to send them away.

Suddenly people were being arrested. Jeno Halasz had been assaulted in the street and taken away bleeding to an unknown location. Nothing more had been heard. A sustained press campaign, orchestrated by the new rulers, portrayed the Jews as a fifth column sabotaging the war efforts and transmitting vital intelligence to the enemy. New measures followed. Jewish assets in banks were blocked; Jews were forbidden to have more than a fixed amount of cash at home. Once again Dr. Kadar proved a true friend, letting Julius hide, in his bedroom wardrobe, the small safe where he kept the rather respectable pile of gold coins he had managed to buy when it was still possible.

There was nothing of value left in the Matthias apartment except the state-of-the-art Phillips radio receiver Mozes Wollner had left Julius when he fled. Mozes had been lucky. Having waited almost too long, he had been warned at the last minute that the police were looking for him. He escaped hidden in the trunk of the car of a notorious smuggler who knew whose palms to grease. Wollner had the good sense to give him only one-third of the agreed upon sum, the balance to be paid when he reached Switzerland. A postcard sent from Geneva told Julius his friend had made it.

Late at night he would carefully close all the doors, draw all the blinds, and switch on the set, trying to tune in to Radio Luxembourg or the BBC news in French or German. This link to the outside world brought him a measure of relief. Having a radio was strictly forbidden and indeed punishable by death, so he did not say a word to his wife.

Toward the end of April 1944, though Germany had suffered many setbacks, there was still no discernible relief in view. The Jews of Nagyvarad, deprived of their livelihoods, hungry and cold, cowered in their homes and tried to convince themselves that because Hungary had not deported its Jews since the war had started four years ago, it would not do so now that Allied forces were getting the upper hand. They were forgetting the determination of the Germans.

Late on April 30, 1944, Dr. Grunewald paid a surprise visit to the offices where Julius still saw his Jewish patients. Glancing nervously from side to side and speaking in a low voice as if afraid of being overheard, he warned Julius of a new and terrifying measure: Jews would have to leave their homes and go into "temporary camps." He professed not to know why or for how long, but vehemently urged his colleague to flee without delay—while flight was still possible.

On his way out he hesitated. "Dr. Matthias," he said wretchedly, "I am ashamed. Ashamed of what is going to happen. Ashamed for my country. Ashamed because I dare not do anything. There are no longer men of the count's stature. I am not hero material. I have a wife, children. Here, take my identity card and my security pass. I shall wait as long as I can before reporting them lost. Should you be arrested, please say they fell from my pocket when we met at the hospital and you picked them up." He left without waiting for an answer.

Grunewald had told the truth. Jews were ordered to assemble at a number of points, to be taken to designated areas where they would have to stay with no possibility of getting out. No one was using the word *ghetto*, but it was obvious to all. Julius was perhaps one of the few to be convinced this was the prelude to deportation to the dreaded Nazi extermination camps, the existence of which was no longer a secret. However, nobody shared his conviction. Hungry, frightened, people still clung to hope. The Allied forces would get there in time. Russian troops, stationed so close, would intervene.

Magda still refused to flee. "Julius," she said, "be reasonable. Hungary took over the city four years ago and has already taken all we have. Isn't that enough for them? Besides, they let us go on working, you and me. You will see. It will be the same in the new place. After all, if they want to send us to camps, why not do it straightaway? Why should they want to kill us? How could we escape even if we wanted to? We are not allowed to use the tramways, let alone the train. Can you see me, at my age, running through the countryside? Hiding in the forest? Here we are known, respected. The war will not go on forever. Bucharest has already been bombed by the Allied forces; Russian troops are progressing, and, according to the broadcasts from London that you listen to every night without a thought for the risk to you and me—yes, I know about the radio; I just did not say anything so as not to anger you—the Normandy landing is due to start at any time. Be patient. Everything will be back to normal soon. In fact, I would not be surprised if, when we tell them who we are, we are allowed to stay home and not to go to the assembly place."

He could not believe his ears. He knew there was nothing more to say. She would not budge. There was no point in mentioning the foolproof plan he had so carefully made when escape had still been possible. Fleetingly he thought of running away alone that very night. Wouldn't it be better than to be herded like animals, waiting to be taken to slaughter? Only fleetingly. He could not do it. Not because he had given his word; not because of Golda. He just could not leave his wife. Magda was over sixty; she looked and acted like an old woman. Her hair had turned white, and she had lost so much weight that she was now as thin as a rail. It had been a long time since their last quarrel. She was acquiescing to all he said—except when it came to leaving. Alone she would never be able to survive the horror and the humiliations that awaited. Besides, should he manage to escape, he would never be able to explain to the children how he had gone like a thief in the night to save his own skin, leaving their mother behind.

On the eve of the fateful day, while Magda was busy preparing the single suitcase they were allowed to take with them, he thought to himself that he was soon going to be fifty-four; they had been married for thirty-six years. He had never been a model husband. Well, he would do his best now.

That night—their last in the apartment, which had never become a home—his wife came timidly to his bedroom and looked at him beseechingly. Wordlessly he made room for her, and she lay by his side for the first time, shaking like a leaf. He embraced her.

"Julius," she whispered, "I am so afraid. Please forgive me. I should have listened to you."

Vainly he tried to comfort her as she sobbed her heart out. They fell asleep chastely embracing.

They woke early on the morning of May 3, 1944. That day it would begin. They sat down in their kitchen for their last breakfast there. The coffee tasted bitter—it was not real coffee, which was no longer to be found—and Julius had to make an effort to eat a slice of stale bread with what was left of the goat cheese. Faithful to the end, Sandor was still sending them some food.

A gray dawn filtered from the open window; they could hear the voices of a little group of Jews who were assembling in the street opposite their building. Magda washed the dishes, dried them, and put them away. She dressed with unusual care and put a hat on her white hair. Julius felt his heart breaking. The poor woman still believed that appearances mattered.

They toured the apartment one last time and locked the door as they left. Hand in hand they went down to the street, carrying their single suitcase. Dr. Kedar was keeping Magda's jewelry and the family documents "until they returned." Only when they got downstairs did Julius remember that he had not given the address of the Paris clinic to his neighbor—an address that would be necessary if his children had to be notified of...of what, he did not know.

Depositing the suitcase at his wife's feet, he ran up the stairs and knocked on the door. He was in the act of putting the paper where he had inscribed the relevant details in an envelope when terrified screams came from the street. He rushed to the open window with Lotsi. A group of soldiers had started herding the fifty or so assembled Jews. A very young blond girl was struggling in the arms of a leering officer. She had a lovely face and soft blue eyes, a little like Gabriella's. The officer tried to kiss her, and she screamed again.

Completely oblivious to the situation and to the danger, Magda tried to help the girl free herself. A soldier struck her in the head with the butt of his gun. She fell heavily to the ground. A low murmur rose from the crowd. A man standing nearby, a neighbor they knew by sight, protested indignantly. The soldier shot him point-blank. He fell; for good measure, and probably to serve as a warning to the others, the soldier emptied his magazine into the two bodies lying on the ground.

The whole episode lasted less than a minute. No one said a word. Julius started running for the door, but his friend held him in a strong grip.

"Yuli, don't. Stay. There is nothing you can do for her or for him. Stay; hope they leave without you, and try to save yourself. Think of the children!"

"Who will close her eyes?"

"I shall do so. Stay."

Kadar went down and kneeled painfully by the two bodies. After checking that they were indeed dead, he closed their eyes. The officer asked to see his papers; he produced them wordlessly. Soldiers had gotten hold of the two suitcases and were busy sharing their contents while making loud jokes. None of the terrified people spoke; no one mentioned that Dr. Matthias was missing.

Lazlo came back. Together with his friend hidden behind the graceful white drapes of the window, he watched the unfolding drama below. The two bodies were thrown into a horse-driven cart; prodded and pushed by the soldiers, the little group, haggard and white faced, were marched away. Julius could not tear his eyes from them. He knew most of them and had treated many. There was a notary; two lawyers; an old rabbi, almost blind, leaning on his son's arm; the fifty-year-old erstwhile owner of a fashion store expropriated several months earlier. There were also a host of poor people from the ancient tenements at the other end of the street. He knew he would never see them again and felt his tears flowing.

Kadar led him to a chair and gave him a glass of cognac, which he refused at first, but Kadar made him drink. Time passed. By nine in the morning, the street was once again empty and unusually silent. Blood had dried on the pavement. The street's inhabitants who were not Jewish had remained in their homes. Were they ashamed of having done nothing to help neighbors and old friends? Or were they afraid of being abused by the soldiers? It was as if the whole city was holding its breath.

Then the sun broke through the clouds, and the first passersby appeared. Traffic started flowing. Shopkeepers opened their wooden shutters and began arranging their wares. Nagyvarad was beginning an ordinary day—as if nothing had happened. Of course the Jews had been marginalized for so long that their absence was barely felt.

A shocked Julius tried to come to terms with the new situation. Death had severed the shackles and ended the pact signed with the devil. Through an extraordinary display of selflessness, Magda had given him a second chance. However, there was no time to lose. The Germans had lists; his absence would soon be noted. Best to leave right away.

Lazlo tried to convince him to take a sedative and wait for nightfall. He shook his head. At night, patrolling soldiers would stop anyone caught walking around. Better to go brazenly in daylight. The old man, still shaken by what he had seen, finally agreed.

Julius went back to his own apartment to change the suit he was wearing for another, which did not sport the yellow

star, and put the documents Hans Grunewald had so generously given him in his pocket. They might fool anyone who
did not know him. He embraced his friend one last time, put
on an old fedora and the heavy tortoiseshell glasses Lotsi gave
him, and grasped his grandfather's a wooden stick. Not the
best disguise in the world, but it would have to do. His own
papers and the gold coins were hidden in his medical bag.

The two men embraced, and Julius left a little before
noon, having written a short note that his friend promised to
send to Paris. "The mother of your Oradea patient has succumbed to the scourge that had taken her husband's father.
Said husband is going to Switzerland to convalesce and will
contact you when he gets there."

It took all his courage to go out into the street. He made
himself walk slowly, head lowered, trying to hide his height
and grasping the staff heavily. He avoided looking at the
dark stain of dried blood. His shoulders were twitching;
he expected to hear a voice at any moment, commanding
him to stop. Only when he had gone the length of Teleky
Street without being recognized and left the Black Vulture
behind did he begin to breathe more easily. He lengthened
his stride and straightened up.

He had chosen a roundabout itinerary, avoiding the
predominantly Jewish areas. Twice he saw small groups of
people from afar; no one challenged him. He ran across a
Christian shopkeeper he knew, but the man turned his head.
There was no roadblock, and he got out of the city without
being stopped.

He never knew how he made it to the farm. He suddenly
found himself in the yard, barely standing. The dogs were
barking furiously—he had not come for so long that they

did not know him anymore—and Sandor came out to investigate. Checking anxiously that there was no one around, he drew Julius inside. Everyone was working in the fields, and they were alone with Martha.

Julius told his tale briefly, and when a shaken Sandor offered to hide him, he refused. His presence could not be kept secret and would endanger not only the friend who was so generously trying to help but his whole family. He did not stay long. Martha, who had not joined her husband in offering to hide Julius, hastily prepared a sack of food. Sandor advised him to leave by a little-used dirt track at the back of the farm. They embraced, knowing well that this meeting would be their last, though the farmer swore to return all his friend's properties when he came back.

"There is only one thing I want you to do," said Julius. "Not now, not right away; when it is safe. Find where they have taken Magda and have a marker put on her grave. Something simple, with her name and the date of her death. I want to believe that one day, the children will be able to come and pray at her tomb."

He walked away without turning back, followed by the sobs his oldest and dearest friend could not stifle.

EPILOGUE

THE SPRING OF 1944 turned into summer; the war refused to end, and its death throes were still being felt throughout Europe. Julius Matthias walked on, emerging unscathed from danger after danger, as if fate, tired of tormenting him, had turned to other victims. He still had some of the food Martha had given him when he met a band of Gypsies hiding in the forest. He was not one of them but was welcomed because he was a doctor, and they had a badly wounded man. Three weeks later, as they were nearing the Yugoslav border, he parted company with them and found a boatman who took him across the Danube River. He encountered three wounded partisans and treated them, and together they kept travelling for many miles before joining a bigger group. Dr. Matthias fought with them for two months, putting down his gun from time to time to tend to a comrade who had been hit.

He had left the past behind; not knowing what the future held, he lived for the day. He lost weight and was burned by the sun yet felt more alive than he had in a long time. The nights were difficult. Georgy in his sailor suit, lips blue by death; Aunt Donna, terrified on her deathbed; the body of Aaron on the floor of the synagogue; Magda, dying with her black hat still firmly on her head. They all came back to torment him, though sometimes it was Madi and her bird's nest of a hat who came to visit. He had not forgotten his main objective, which was to reach Switzerland. Therefore, he left the partisans toward the end of August, having met two Italian deserters who were going home now that their country had switched sides and joined the Allied forces. Knowing the region well, they crossed easily into Italy. Then it was each man for himself.

Julius went on alone. Nobody challenged the fiftyish man with graying hair walking purposefully, medical bag in hand. For someone who spoke Romanian and French and had studied Latin, managing in Italian was easy enough. At night he looked for an isolated house and asked for shelter. He was rarely turned down. He even remained on a farm for a whole week, helping the farmer's wife with the harvest—her men were all dead or prisoners. At night he slept in her bed; she urged him to stay, but he was eager to reach his goal.

The news was good: Allied forces were progressing in France; Rome and Florence had been liberated. In Northern Italy underground fighters had driven the Germans away from several key points. Julius bought an old car which was still running smoothly. Four months after his departure from Nagyvarad, his stock of coins was severely depleted, but the Swiss border was not far. In a Torino synagogue, he welcomed the Jewish New Year on September 18, 1944. For this unbeliever, it proved to be an extraordinarily moving occasion, and he found himself crying like a child. There was a small reception after the ceremony; there he met an Italian doctor who gave him a bed for the night.

Three days later, freshly shaved and groomed, wearing a well-cut suit and carrying his trusty medical bag, Dr. Julius

Matthias, who had had the foresight to sell his old car and hire a chauffeur-driven limousine to take him to Geneva, presented his passport to a bored guard at the border and entered his own promised land.

CONTENTS

ABOUT THE AUTHOR

Michelle Mazel was born in France. A graduate of the Law School and the Institute for Political Science of Paris, she was a Fullbright scholar to the United States. She married an Israeli diplomat and for forty years she went with him from one interesting country to another. She took to writing, becoming a frequent contributor to "The Jerusalem Post" and to "Israel Scene" magazine.

She has taken part in a number of collective works such as the "Macmillan Illustrated Dictionary" and "Concordance of the Bible and the Grolier Holocaust Encyclopedia". She is a regular contributor to the Jewish Political Study Review.

In 1993 she published her first thriller, "Stone Moon", originally published in Hebrew, then in French. It was followed by "Sirens over Jerusalem" as well as published in Hebrew and in French. In 2003 she wrote in Hebrew "Wife to the Ambassador", a memoir of the eight years she spent with her husband in Egypt. "La Maison du Pacha" an updated version of that book, was published in France. In 2014 she published in Israel "Dancing with the Ambassador" a nostalgic and humorous memoir of her 40 years on the diplomatic circuit. Another thriller, "The Sheikh from Hebron" was published in French in November 2015.

"A nostalgic tale, sometimes to the slow rhythm of a staid Waltz, sometimes to that of a dizzy and wild tango".

Shimon Peres